CHAIN
REACTION

CHAIN REACTION

A Dez Limerick Thriller

JAMES BYRNE

MINOTAUR
BOOKS
NEW YORK

First published in the United States by Minotaur Books, an imprint of St. Martin's Publishing Group

CHAIN REACTION. Copyright © 2024 by James Byrne. All rights reserved. Printed in the United States of America. For information, address St. Martin's Publishing Group, 120 Broadway, New York, NY 10271.

www.minotaurbooks.com

Designed by Omar Chapa

Library of Congress Cataloging-in-Publication Data

Names: Byrne, James (Suspense fiction writer) author.
Title: Chain reaction : A Dez Limerick Thriller / James Byrne.
Description: First edition. | New York : Minotaur Books, 2025. |
    Series: A Dez Limerick novel ; 3
Identifiers: LCCN 2024030666 | ISBN 9781250319784
    (hardcover) | ISBN 9781250319791 (ebook)
Subjects: LCGFT: Thrillers (Fiction) | Novels.
Classification: LCC PS3558.A84875 C43 2025 | DDC 813/.54—
    dc23/eng/20240808
LC record available at https://lccn.loc.gov/2024030666

Our books may be purchased in bulk for promotional, educational, or business use. Please contact your local bookseller or the Macmillan Corporate and Premium Sales Department at 800-221-7945, extension 5442, or by email at MacmillanSpecialMarkets@macmillan.com.

First Edition: 2025

10 9 8 7 6 5 4 3 2 1

The great people at Minotaur Books have been there for Dez's journey from the start: I'm so grateful to Keith Kahla, Grace Gay, Kelley Ragland, Hector DeJean, Stephen Erickson, Ryan Jenkins, David Rotstein, Omar Chapa, Ervin Serrano, Alisa Trager, Ginny Perrin, Diane Dilluvio, and Paul Hochman. My literary agent, Janet Reid, deserves kudos for working her magic to make this series a reality.

And of course to Katy King.
I would not wish any companion in the world but you.

—THE TEMPEST

CHAIN REACTION

PROLOGUE

EIGHTEEN MONTHS AGO, OUTSIDE OF MADRID, SPAIN

The innocuous-looking car approaches the research campus at five minutes before eleven at night. The driver's name is Dez. He's wearing civilian clothes today, which is unusual for him. Seated next to him is a fellow Englishman whose name is most decidedly not Jamison, even though his newly forged passport identifies him thusly.

The research campus is dark. There should be no one here except security and janitorial crew. And one fairly prickly biologist. Dez is idling the car just outside the gate, studying the sprawling, three-acre campus.

Jamison is smoking, his window cracked open, blowing the smoke out. He eyes his driver. Dez is wearing an olive sweater and khakis and lace-up boots. He isn't tall but he's beefy, with wide shoulders, a fifty-inch chest, powerfully cut forearms.

"Damn good of you to do this. And on short notice," Jamison says.

Dez grins in the dark. "I'm a soldier, me. Go where I'm ordered."

"How did you draw the short straw for babysitting duty?"

"I've a skill set. My commander thought I might be useful."

Jamison nods. "Let's do this."

Dez puts the Land Rover into gear. They roll up to the armored fence and gate and a guard steps out of his shack. Dez lowers his window. "I've a Mister Jamison here t'see Professor Eduardo Castillo," Dez says in fluent Spanish.

The guard consults a clipboard. He shines a penlight into the car, focusing on Jamison, then on Dez. The guard is not armed.

"Very good. Building seventeen."

Dez puts it in first as the heavy gate rolls open.

"See what you mean about skill sets," Jamison says. "Glad you speak the lingo."

"No worries, mate."

They roll into the quiet campus.

"Is Dez short for anything?"

"Desmond Aloysius Limerick."

Jamison smiles. "Vengeful parents?"

"It's quite a nice name." Dez sounds a little hurt. "Distinguished, if you was to ask me."

"Yes. Very."

They find building number seventeen, and Dez parks. Dez clips a holster to the belt of his khakis. The holster holds a PAMAS G1, nine millimeter, with a fifteen-round mag and a bullet preloaded in the pipe. Jamison eyes it, and Dez notices.

"You spy types learn t'carry your own weapons, you wouldn't need a soldier like me watchin' your back, squire."

Jamison throws away the stub of his cigarette. "Who said anything about spies?"

"Right, right."

Another guard is waiting for them, wearing the same sand-colored uniform as the man at the gate. Dez speaks to him briefly in Spanish. This guard looks nervous. He uses a magnetic ID card on a lanyard to open building number seventeen. He escorts them in, then into an elevator. The same magnetic ID gets the elevator car moving to the top floor.

The corridor is sterile, bland, the walls and ceiling white, the floor polished. Both newcomers wince at the glare.

"Lights are set on 'migraine,'" Dez observes.

The guard takes them to room 804 and uses his ID card on a monitor set into the wall. The door clacks open.

Room 804 is a biology lab. Spectacularly well outfitted, from the looks of it. No expense spared.

They are met by a smallish man in an old tweed jacket and an enormous mustache. He wears round, wire-rim spectacles. He's perhaps in his midseventies. With him is a young woman wearing a plain skirt, orthopedic shoes, a simple blouse, and a white lab coat. Dez thinks she's quite lovely despite her unattractive eyeglasses, ill-fitted outfit, and no makeup that he can spot.

She steps forward and offers a hand. "Mr. Jamison?"

The guard stays out in the corridor. Dez stands back by the door, out of the way.

Jamison takes her hand. "Hallo. You must be Miss Gomez. Dr. Castillo's assistant."

She adjusts her glasses. "Yes. The doctor speaks no English, I'm afraid. You don't mind my translating?"

"Please."

Professor Castillo rolls out a standing, vertical flat-screen monitor on twin stands, upon which the image of a complex biological formula has been sketched. Lots of hexagons and letters. Dez reads the monitor: $C8H10N4O2$

Professor Castillo nods to it. "Do you know what this is, Mr. Jamison?"

Miss Gomez translates into English.

"I'm hoping it's the formula you've been working on, sir. The formula that would make synthetic opioids nonaddictive."

She translates.

The old man nods. "Yes, yes. This is the work that has driven the last seven years of my life for king and country, sir."

Dez has noted a security monitor on a table. He strolls that way. It shows a high-res, black-and-white image of the guard who led them up, and the exterior of the door he just been leaning on. The guard checks his watch and, a beat later, checks it again.

"This bit of formula?" The professor finds a remote control. The hexagons shrink and are revealed to be part of a much, much larger chemical structure. "It works. It can eliminate the addictive qualities of synthetic opioids."

"This would . . . change many things," Jamison says, and the assistant translates. He gestures around to include the whole lab. "This is a government-owned facility. The formula is owned by you, and not the Spanish government, sir?"

Miss Gomez translates.

"It is mine. Wholly mine."

"Then Great Britain is prepared to meet your price, Professor. But know that it is our intention to share this with every other nation on—"

Everyone starts at the distant sound of automatic gunfire.

Jamison turns to Dez, eyebrows raised.

Dez sits at the security monitor and begins typing on the keyboard.

Miss Gomez spots him. "I . . . I believe they said the security monitors can only be accessed by campus personnel, Mister . . . ?"

"Dez," he says, keys clacking away. "Dez Limerick. And aye, likely. I've some small training with computers. Might be able to . . ."

The screen changes, first to six separate images of the campus. Then twelve, then twenty-four. All from closed-circuit security cameras.

Jamison hurries over, hovering over Dez in his chair. Dez targets the camera monitoring the main gate.

The gate is open. The guard who let them in lies on the ground, bleeding from a bullet wound.

Dez shifts to another camera: Two large SUVs are moving through the campus, lights off.

"Heading our way," Jamison says. He draws his phone and checks. "I've no signal."

"Aye. Professor? Who else did you tell about your fantastic discovery?"

The woman says, *"Profesor, con quien—"*

"That's not necessary, love. Your mate here's no more Spanish than I am. He speaks Spanish with the accent of one who learned it in the Southwest United States. An' the question stands: Who else knows about the formula?"

Jamison turns to the professor and his assistant. "Well?"

She says, "There were other bidders, but . . ."

Dez changes to the camera that is right outside the lab.

Their guard is gone. So he's in on . . . whatever this is. Paid off, probably, Dez thinks.

On the security monitor, they see the two SUVs have arrived at building seventeen. Side doors slam open, and a dozen heavily armed men with balaclavas and Kevlar begin jumping out. They carry HK417s. They also have a magnetic card to bypass security.

"It strikes me," Dez drawls, "that there might be some what don't want nobody messin' with the addictive qualities of opioids. Yeah?"

Jamison sighs. "Quite."

Dez spots a tool kit under one of the tables, kneels, draws a screwdriver, and moves to the door. He begins tearing apart the wall-mounted security monitor by the door.

Jamison says, "What are you doing?"

"Buying us time, squire. Here."

Dez draws his nine-millimeter pistol and hands it, butt-first, to the British agent, then goes back to fiddling with the innards of the security system.

"The professor speaks English?" Jamison asks.

"He does." Dez addresses the wiring he's now exposing. "An' his magical formula for opioids? The good professor was showing you a compound consistin' of, ah, eight carbon atoms, ten hydrogen, four nitrogen, an' two oxygen atoms, if I've done me sums right. Yeah? 'Less I miss my guess, they was showin' you the atomic structure of caffeine."

Miss Gomez says, "How did . . ." Then catches herself.

Jamison says, "Jesus."

A puff of smoke roils up from the security device. "Should do. Get me that acetylene torch over there, will ye?"

Jamison sees it, moves swiftly toward it.

Dez grins at Miss Gomez as he takes the torch from Jamison. He quickly whisks up his left sleeve and shows her a tattoo of a two-faced Roman god.

"Janus. God of beginnings an' gates, transitions an' time, duality an' doors, passages an' endings. I'm what's called a gatekeeper, yeah? Can open any door. Can keep it open as long as is necessary. Can control who does—and who don't—get through. Means I've studied me chemistry, miss."

Jamison brings him a sparker, too. Dez fires up the acetylene torch.

He winks at Jamison. "Them's the skill sets my commander was thinkin' of when I drew the short straw."

Ten of the assault squad crowd into the elevator; two stay in the lobby. The elevator quickly rises to their floor.

He turns to Miss Gomez. "This lot's not with you, I assume?"

"Oh, hell no!"

"Then we all need t'get out of here, pronto."

Dez holds the torch to the doorknob on the inner side of the door. He speaks over the hiss of the flame. "Dr. Castillo and Miss Gomez, I'm guessin', are thieves. Was hopin' to take the British government for several million pounds sterling. An' if they're any good at what they do, they've an exit strategy. In case this caper went pear-shaped on 'em."

The assault squad is on their floor now. One man draws a magnetic key card and attempts to open the door. It's not working, because Dez bollixed it from the inside.

Dez continues to hold the torch to the doorknob.

"We . . . we do have a way out," Miss Gomez says.

The alleged Professor Castillo spins on her. "Cat! Shut the fuck up!" He speaks English. They both sound like Americans.

She ignores him, checks her watch. "If you can keep them out for eight minutes, we can get gone."

Dez says, "Well, love, your way out just became everyone's way out. Ta."

The woman—Cat—whisks off her glasses and throws them in a trash bin. "The building AC is set to go off in just over seven minutes. When it does, small packets of explosives will blow the air filter mesh in a maintenance tunnel, back this way." She points deeper into the lab. "The AC will mask the vibration of the explosion. We can crawl out to the roof. There's a ladder down to the parking lot on the north side. The explosives are on a timer, so we can't blow it early."

"Cat, for fuck sake—" her accomplice growls.

Outside, the assault unit has given up hoping their stolen magnetic card will get them through the door and into the lab. One of them does what people always do in these situations: He grabs the doorknob and rattles it, to see if, miraculously, it's unlocked.

The man screams in pain, smoke roiling from his charred hand.

"Door's got a steel core," Dez tells the room, turning off the torch. "Same with the wall around it. Spotted it as we entered. Watch what happens when they try t'shoot their way in. Which they will."

On the monitor, one of the men unslings his HK and fires a burst at the door.

His own ricochet nearly cuts him in two.

The oppo is down to nine on this floor, and one of those nine has third-degree burns on one palm, so he won't be using his HK. There are still two more in the lobby.

"Them lot's not getting in that way. Unless they brought explosives," Dez says. "Hang on a bit."

He moves around the lab, opening cabinet doors, searching behind desks.

"Aw! This is nice." He produces a canister of liquid nitrogen. "Ah, Cat, was it? Call out the time, love."

Two of the assault squad are kneeling and opening their backpacks. Jamison watches the monitor. "C4, Limerick. You called it."

"Aye. Tried the magnetic lock. Tried rattlin' the door to force it open. Tried shootin' through. Now they'll try blasting through." Dez shakes his head sadly. "It's how every tosser an' their cousin tries to get through a door. Feckin' amateurs. Cat?"

The American woman says, "Four minutes."

Dez holds the canister under one arm, a hose in his other hand, and begins spraying the door hinges with liquid nitrogen.

"Right lovely ball peen hammer in that cabinet yonder, squire. Fetch it smart-like, will ye?"

The inside of the door is turning white around first the upper hinge, then the lower one. Dez switches back and forth. Ice from the liquid nitrogen coats the metal, whisps of smoke curling off it.

Dez keeps pouring the nitrogen on the door. The icy buildup continues.

Jamison returns with the hammer. He and Cat are watching the monitor. He says, "They're attaching explosive packets near the hinges. Just as you said."

Cat glances at her watch. "Three minutes."

"Right, then." Dez sets the empty canister down. He picks up the hammer. "You lot head back toward the maintenance tunnel. Right behind ye."

Jamison says, "I'll stay, all the same."

"No. Go. Right behind ye."

Jamison hesitates, then sprints after the two American thieves.

Dez is a gifted cricket player. A very good batsman, yes, but also a top-line bowler. He takes fifteen steps back, then winds up and hurls the ball peen hammer, overhand, at the supercooled metal door.

He doesn't wait to see if he hit it. He turns and sprints after Jamison and the others.

In the corridor, two of the assault squad are kneeling, applying C4 explosives, gingerly attaching wires to blasting caps. The others are getting ready to back off.

Just as the supercooled hinges of the door shatter.

Triggering their explosives early.

Of the nine men they brought, two are disintegrated by the explosion. Four more die as shrapnel and the high-pressure energy wave radiates down the corridor. Three survive, back by the elevator, but all three are on their asses, stunned by the explosion.

Three still alive on this floor. Two in the lobby. The odds are better but still bad.

Two minutes later, Dez, Jamison, and the thieves watch as a heavy, wire-mesh grille over a maintenance tunnel sizzles and falls away from the tunnel entrance. The ersatz professor has doffed his mustache, glasses, and wig. Dez guesses his true age at midfifties.

The con artists lead, then Jamison, then Dez.

It's a winding, circuitous route, and they do it on their hands and knees. Thirty feet in, they find a metal ladder, leading upward. Cat takes the lead. She's quick and sure-footed. The non-professor goes next.

Jamison pauses to slide Dez's gun into his belt, freeing his hand, then he climbs as well. Dez on his six. Jamison's jacket catches on a rung at one point, costing them about five seconds.

By the time Jamison and Dez get to the roof, the two thieves are long gone.

Jamison checks his phone. "I've a signal." He starts dialing. "We're assuming the welcoming committee represents an organization making its piles pushing opioids in Europe?"

"Seems likely, aye," Dez says. He walks to the edge of the building near the metal ladder and peers over. No sign of the thieves. "Appears organized crime bought the cock-an'-bull story about the professor's ingenious discovery."

Jamison presses a series of buttons on his phone. "SOS. We'll have backup here within minutes." He looks up, smiling ruefully. "His majesty's government bought the cock-and-bull story, too, Dez. We're as gullible as the bad guys."

Dez glances down behind an air-conditioning unit and spots Cat. She's seated, legs drawn up against her chest, arms wrapped around her knees. She looks up into his eyes.

Jamison sighs. "Our thieves will be far away before the cavalry arrives, I assume."

"Oh, aye," Dez says, and winks at Cat. She blinks in surprise. Dez puts a vertical finger to his lips, turns, and saunters back toward Jamison. "They got away with naught, though. Not much point in pursuin' them."

"Agreed. Besides which, there are still two gentlemen in the lobby with HKs."

"I'm betting a few survived in the corridor, too. Best to stay up here. Wait for the cavalry."

Jamison finds a cigarette pack and a lighter. "You saved my life, Mr. Limerick."

"Which means you're buyin' the first round, squire."

"Quite. You were very calm back there. Methodical. Do you do this a lot? Tangle with armed gangs?"

"Me?" Dez laughs. "'Course not! I'm the peaceable type. I never go lookin' for trouble."

EIGHTEEN MONTHS LATER.
TODAY. NEW YORK CITY.

Catalina Valdivia has made herself a scalding hot café con leche and is carefully poring over every bit of information she can garner about the new Liberty Convention Center. Every exhibitor, performer, contractor, staffer, and all of the administrative crew. She examines the upcoming schedule the way a forensic surgeon studies a CT scan. She keeps notes and cross-references them.

Three cups of coffee on, she spots a band that will be performing that weekend at The Liberty, as an opening act for a much more famous performer. She gasps, her mahogany eyes go wide.

Mouth agape, she reaches for her phone.

"Hey. It's Cat. . . . You will never guess who I found. . . . Remember me telling you about a Dez Limerick?"

CHAPTER 1

YESTERDAY

Dez is breaking fast at a little diner in Portland, Oregon, when a text lights up his phone.

> Disaster! Big big big show Tuesday! In Newark. Bassist has covid. BEGGING for your help. KJack

Dez grins around a mouthful of bangers and scrambled eggs. It's Monday, and he's a continent away from New Jersey.

He's only been retired and living in the States since the start of the year and spent some of that time in Los Angeles, picking up musical gigs where he could as a bass player and pianist. He did a couple three shows backing up vocalist Jack O'Herlihy and his band, Kansas Jack and the Blacktop. The band—bigger than most, with keyboards, strings, percussion, and a horn section—covers a lot of classic rock 'n' roll from the fifties and sixties, focusing on rockabilly standards. The band is fun and the sound is a bit outside

Dez's wheelhouse, especially when he's asked to provide background vocals. It makes for a decent challenge. He quite enjoyed those gigs.

He also has nothing else on his schedule. He gulps down some coffee and responds.

Set me up with place to stay, I'm in.

By the time Dez is paying the bill, his phone chirps again.

Could kiss you!

Dez types back:

Please don't.

Dez, at thirty-five, owns few things. He travels with a Vietnam-era army surplus duffel bag for his clothes, which includes a lot of black T-shirts he has to buy online to get them big enough for his chest, neck, and pecs; a black jacket; black jeans; underwear; and lace-up boots. He also has a Gibson Ripper bass guitar; plus a tablet computer that's a bit larger and bulkier than most, and a mobile phone that is the same.

Dez designed some of the aftermarket additions to the tablet and phone.

He checks his luggage—there are two knives buried in the bottom of the duffel. He carries on only a banged-up leather messenger bag. He buys a paperback to read on the plane. He gets to talking to the retired middle school teacher seated next to him and they're fast friends before the plane leaves the Rockies in its wake.

En route, Dez checks Jack O'Herlihy's website. Kansas Jack and the Blacktop are performing on Tuesday at some big, new convention center adjacent to Newark Liberty International Airport. And he's already updated his promotional site by adding Dez to the band lineup. That was quick.

This week appears to be one enormous grand opening of the center, which includes a flash new hotel, and a spacious convention space, and restaurants, and play areas for the kiddies, and whatnot. Dez gets the desperation in his mate's text now. This could be a really big event for a band that occasionally turns a profit, mostly via its merch, but more often than not just breaks even.

Jack's band is opening for . . .

Dez's jaw drops.

Unbelievable. They're one of four opening acts for Calvin Willow. A rock legend from the 1980s and '90s and, as some would have you believe, one of the three or four best guitarists in the history of rock.

Dez has owned nearly every album Calvin Willow ever recorded, either as the headliner for his band or his solo works. Dez has memorized and covered a wide array of his hits. In the military, if a Calvin Willow song came on Spotify, well over half the men in Dez's unit could sing the lyrics.

The man's a right legend.

As his plane lands, Dez texts Jack and they agree to meet for dinner in Newark, and to go over the playlist.

Got you a room at The Liberty Suites, Jack texts.

In the Newark airport's domestic terminal, Dez spots signage for the light-rail to the brand-new, spiffy Liberty Convention Center. Known simply as The Liberty. And below the fancy logo, he reads A FLAG FAMILY EXPERIENCE!

He buys a ticket and hops on the light-rail train that looks like Santa has set under the tree and some good boys and girls have just opened the box. It doesn't even feature any graffiti yet, and the car floor is as clean as Sister Yolanda's secondary level classroom.

The train stops at a fancy new terminal inside The Liberty. The place feels like the set of a science fiction movie. Everything is glass and steel and very vertical. It's all under one way-high glass roof. It offers 2.2 million square feet of exhibition space with a ten-acre footprint. Dez's brain isn't wired to understand the vastness of this convention center. He thought it contained a hotel. Nope. It contains three of them. Five-star, three-star, and a no-frills knockoff brand. That's the one Dez is staying at, naturally.

He has a bit of ready cash. He gets to The Liberty Suites and its new but low-key lobby and changes the credit card from Jack's to his own. Only fair, despite their deal. Jack O'Herlihy will go without food to help out a bandmate. Dez has seen him do it.

He scopes out his room. Nice enough. Small but clean. A double bed. Well, Dez is only five-eight, so a longer bed seems like a waste of linen. The view is of the inside of the conference center.

He leaves his duffel and guitar in the room, throws his tablet computer and his folding Raptor knife, with its nylon sheath, in his messenger bag, and goes walking. He'd like to check out the venue for Tuesday's show, if he can get in.

There are little, amoeba-shaped parks with sculpted trees, randomly placed. The pathways are brick and gold in tone, à la Oz, and none of the paths travel in a straight line. He sees a big exhibition space, next to a really big exhibition space, next to a gargantuan exhibition space. He spots restaurants, including Asian cuisine, Latin American cuisine, French and Italian cuisine, and an O'Malley Burgers, those near-ubiquitous fast-food restaurants all up and down the Eastern Seaboard. It's laid out cheek by jowl next to a grand restaurant owned by a famed chef with a constellation of Michelin stars.

There must be well over a thousand people bobbing about, Dez thinks. There's a comic book convention in one of the spaces, and he spots several kids and families in cosplay. Many people are wearing business attire, so obviously professional associations are gathering here already, although the place has barely opened.

Dez also has spotted two men with a military mien and no smiles, and he quickly takes a knee, his back to them, tying his boots.

His hackles have just risen. Dez was so preoccupied playing tourist, he's only now aware that the pair he just passed aren't the first soldier types he's seen.

They're the third pair.

He wants to smack himself for missing the obvious.

The men aren't wearing uniforms, and someone who hasn't done what Dez has done for most of his adult life wouldn't recognize them for what they are. They wear dark trousers of stiff, tough canvas and lace-up boots like Dez's. They wear dark, thick sweaters under long coats. That alone should have set Dez's alarms blaring.

Such sweaters are ideal for disguising ballistic vests. And ballistic vests tend to bind under the arms and across the chest. Men wearing them sometimes subconsciously grab the tops of their vests and pull downward to relieve the binding sensation. Dez spots a guy do precisely that.

Those long coats also would hide belt holsters and guns just fine.

They're well-built guys. All men, so far. Caucasian.

Equally important, the men are as serious as a snakebite. Glowering looks. Hard eyes taking in their surroundings. Moving with intent and with purpose.

Two more such men pass Dez and, kneeling, he casually glances at their hands.

They have the same calluses on the web between their thumbs and forefingers that Dez has. You can only get those calluses after hours upon hours on firing ranges.

Could be these are the good guys. Could be there was a security threat, and the New Jersey National Guard or whatever is out in force to keep the peace. This could all be a heaping great bowl of nothing.

But it just doesn't feel that way.

Dez was making his way to the Delphi Insurance Center, the venue for Tuesday's concert. He takes a seat on a bench under a manicured oak tree in a postage-stamp garden. He picked up a convention center brochure with a map in the hotel lobby and pretends to read it.

He spots another duo of soldier-types. That makes ten guys so far. Ten guys heading every which way; not toward any one destination.

He checks the center's website on his phone. There are no military-style events planned at any of the exhibition halls.

"As I live and breathe."

Dez hears the voice and glances up. A stunner of a woman smiles down at him. She's his age, Latina, with night-black hair cascading to the middle of her back. She's wearing a cropped white tank under a red leather bomber. That and matchstick jeans do a most admirable job of showing off her curves. She's playing the ensemble high-low by pairing it with diamond stud earrings, plus Keds.

Dez has other things on his mind, but knockouts don't just chat up a lad every day of the week. Dez puts away his brochure. "Help ye?"

She smiles. And waits.

Dez smiles and also waits.

She squints at him, turns her head a bit. She has a cleft chin. Dez is a little bit nuts about girls with cleft chins. She has high cheekbones and deep brown eyes that suggest a sense of humor and a sense of her own beauty.

The waiting goes on.

Dez rises.

"Dez. Pleased. Have we met?"

"We have." She slow-rolls it, the knowing smile in place.

"Then I'm an absolute idiot for not recognizin' you, ma'am. I'm also losing me mind in me old age, clearly, and need t'be put down for my own good. An' you are . . . ?"

"What I'm *not* is a translator helping a kindly old professor to sell the formula for café con leche to the British government for three-point-are-you-fucking-kidding-me pounds." She bats her eyes. "Sterling."

"Cat!"

Now the smile grows.

"Jay-sus, but I didn't recognize you out of that meek librarian getup you was wearing! What's it been? Year an' a half?"

"Close enough," she says. "And it was a meek lab assistant getup. I worked hard on that. I tried on thirty glasses before I found exactly the least attractive pair."

Dez offers his hand. She ignores it.

"C'mon. I'm buying you a drink. I have some questions to ask you."

Dez spots two more of the soldier-types. "Now wouldn't be the worst of times to get a drink, I'm thinking. And sharpish, if ye've a mind."

CHAPTER 2

They find a martini bar with some chef's famous name on the door and about seven trillion variations of booze. Dez spots some vodka flavors that one normally finds only in a box of kiddies' cereal, and his stomach roils a bit.

The woman he knows only as Cat picks a table far from everyone else and the waiter lands on them as if he'd been dropped from a helicopter. There's a benefit to getting a drink with a lustrous bird like this one, Dez thinks.

They order drinks. "I have, like, a million questions for you," she says.

He extends his hand. "Desmond Limerick."

She studies him a moment. She chews her lower lip when she's contemplating. Finally, she reaches across and shakes.

"Catalina Valdivia. And that's the third time I've said my full name aloud to anyone in a decade."

"Hence *Cat*."

"That's right."

"Pleased. I've a question of me own, but you should go first."

Their drinks arrive: an old-fashioned for her, a Rob Roy for him.

She leans in over their small, round table, to keep her voice down. "You could have had me arrested that night."

"In Madrid? An' what unholy powers d'you reckon I have, I can make arrests in Spain?"

"You could have told the Englishman you spotted me."

"An' have him arrest you for failed larceny? That's a crime now, is it?"

She smiles and sips her drink. She gives him a quick glower, and he realizes her eyes are the color of hot cocoa laced with cinnamon, and that they're capable of Gatling-gun emotional switch-ups. "*Failed,* because of you. Don't think I've forgotten that. We didn't expect Jamison to have a chemist with him."

"Not a chemist. Just a quick learner."

"Uh-huh. You hacked the security monitors so you could watch all the CC camera feeds. I'd been inside their security system for days. It would have taken me an hour to do what you did in twenty seconds."

Dez shrugs.

"You screwed up the electronic locking mechanism on the door, the exact same way I would have. And I'm a professional thief. But in my very, very best moment, I wouldn't have thought to make the doorknob too hot to touch, or used liquid nitrogen to screw up their explosives."

"Some days you get the bear, an' some days the bear gets you."

She squints at him. It's a look designed to intimidate and it's clearly been honed to a scalpel-like sharpness. "Killing those men, and apparently not being emotionally affected by that. Knowing the atomic structure of caffeine. Knowing our Spanish accents were American . . ."

"Where is the good professor these days?"

"See?" she says. "You don't talk about yourself, you deflect." She makes a sudden wave of several fingers, which, Dez thinks, is a very Iberian gesture. "And we parted company that same week. He had a tendency to tell me to shut the fuck up. Do I look like a girl who shuts the fuck up?"

"Not in the least."

"You said something about being a gatekeeper."

"I meant goalkeeper. Played some football, me."

Again with the knowing squint. "And you just did it again. You deflect. Who are you?"

"A bloke. Can I ask you a question?"

"You only get one," Cat Valdivia says. "But you need to answer one question from me, first. And I'm a mutant. My mutant power is: I can detect all lies. Ready?"

Dez leans her way, too, suddenly enjoying himself more than he should.

"How is it you can do the things you do, Desmond Limerick?"

Their faces are close together. He says, "I served in a military unit overseas and I learned how to control egresses. It involved a wide array of scientific skills, including, but not limited to, computers, chemistry, an' engineering. I'll not tell you more than that, because it's none of your feckin' business. Please excuse me language."

A beat. Then she smiles.

"My mutant power tells me you speak the truth."

"Do. Aye."

"Your turn: one question."

"Just the one?"

She says, "Yup."

Dez inhales deeply. "So this here convention center's brand spanking new and it's filled with a couple thousand civilians, at a guess, all smack-bang against one of the busiest airports on the Eastern Seaboard of these, the United States of America, an' right now I can't help but notice that there are upwards of a dozen men roaming about who appear to be wearing body armor and who might or might not be armed, though I'm leanin' toward *armed*. And they move as if they've a purpose, and my own mutant powers—humbled, of course, next to your own powers of divination—tell me they are up to no good, an' I was wondering if an itinerant thief an' lovely lass such as yourself has noticed them as well, or if she's, heaven forfend, connected to 'em in some dark and mendacious way. Ma'am."

They lean toward each other like that a bit.

Cat Valdivia's smile evaporates. Her eyes lose their bon vivant luster.

"*¡Dios mío!* You're serious."

Dez says, "Am."

"Do . . . do you think they're planning to rob the place?"

"Dunno."

She studies him, and her eyes shuffle quickly, focusing on his left eye, his right, his left.

Cat drops her voice even lower. "Are you thinking terrorists?"

"Dunno. Could be."

She sits bolt upright. "Then why in the name of almighty fuck are we having a drink?"

"Because you're stunning an' funny an' obviously smart, and you have a nontraditional lifestyle." Dez finishes his drink. "An' I'm a lad what believes in priorities."

Cat starts to reply. That's when they hear the first explosion.

Dez shrugs. "Not that my priorities couldn't do with a tweak."

CHAPTER 3

A series of three explosions rock the martini bar. They're far enough away that no one here is injured, but glasses dance on tabletops and a chandelier over the bar shimmies. Absolutely everyone hears the muffled *booms*.

Dez and Cat Valdivia stare at each other. Her eyes are wide.

"Those men . . . ?"

"Started the party without us, aye."

Cat says, *"Us?"*

Then a speaker in the bar chitters and crackles. It's a PA system, though Dez can't spot it.

"Attention, attendees of The Liberty Convention Center." It's a male voice with a Slavic accent. *"This broadcast is going out to the assembly halls, the hotels, the restaurants and shops, and to the public address system in the open spaces between buildings. Remain where you are. If you are inside an establishment, stay there. If you are out on the paths between establishments, stand still until armed men escort you into one of the establishments. This*

facility has been occupied by a professional, armed militia. The explosions you heard were the first three guests who attempted to leave The Liberty. Remain where you are and no one else needs to die."

The voice stops. Nobody moves, nobody speaks.

Then everyone freaks out.

Everyone but Dez and Cat.

"This is so very not good," she says, fear rising in her voice.

"Fair analysis, that."

A man in cowboy boots, who'd been drinking a beer at the next bistro table over from them, bolts to his feet and sprints toward the door. Dez rises, but the guy's got a good lead on him. He hits the double doors of the bar and bursts out into the glass-covered, exterior area of the mall.

Dez moves to a window to watch. Several patrons and the waitstaff do, too.

The man in the cowboy boots makes it about fifteen steps at a dead sprint before a sniper cuts him down.

In the martini bar, people scream.

The dead man had been moving at a good clip, Dez thinks. Whoever they are, their marksman is no joke. And in a bloody big campus like this one, that rooftop shooter won't be the only one.

Dez turns back to Cat. He gestures and leads her to a corner where they can talk.

"Are you the kind of thief what's good at picking pockets?"

She says, "What?"

"Thief. Pockets. Picked."

"I . . . I'm the best you ever met. But—"

"Good. Need t'get me hands on one of their guns. Know what they're carryin,' and I'll know more about the oppo. I'll get a distraction going, you nab a gun, we'll learn what we can of these bastards."

Cat Valdivia stares at him.

"Cat?"

"Are you out of your fucking mind?!" Several heads turn their way. Some people are crying. Others are holding each other. Dez notes a couple attempting to get a signal on their phones; from their faces, no Wi-Fi is getting through. He checks his own. No bars.

"You want me to, quote, 'nab a gun'?" She jams her fists onto her hips, eyes ablaze.

"Yeah. It'll be a laugh. You'll see."

"A gun?"

Dez thinks a moment. "You're right. They'll have comms units, too. Need t'know how they're communicating. Could just deck the first bastard I spot, but they'll have good unit cohesion—must, t'try a hostage caper in ten acres of glass-walled buildings. Which means regular comms checks, yeah? Have t'be a bit more crafty than normal. Thank God I've got you."

Cat runs her palms through her lush, wavy hair. "Out . . . of your . . . mind!"

"Ye can do it, can't ye? Pick a pocket?"

"Oh, for Christ's sake." Cat suddenly steps in and hugs him. "This is so scary!"

"I know, love."

She steps back, reaches to the inside pocket of her bomber, and produces Dez's wallet.

"My God!" He takes it back. "That's bloody amazing! How'd you—"

She reaches into the jacket again and hands him his watch. It was secured, tight, around his left wrist.

"You're a bloody marvel, you!" He grins, re-buckles his aging watch strap. "What say? Want to help?"

Cat steps into his space and speaks as if to someone who doesn't understand English, miming with her hands as she does. "Bad guys, outside. Booze, inside. Inside, better."

"Have t'do what I can. You stay here. Stay safe. I'll take a mosey an' see what's what."

"There's a man out there in cowboy boots and an extra sphincter who took a mosey!"

"I'm more cunning than that, love. Worry not."

She scrapes her hands through her hair again. "Aaargh! Why? Why do you have to *do what I can*?"

Dez thinks a moment. "If there was somebody better trained, I'd want them t'do it. But there isn't."

"There might be two thousand people in The Liberty! You don't know that!"

He smiles kindly. "A couple thousand souls, trapped in here. Know what that requires, yeah?"

She waits.

Dez grips her upper arms with both hands. "Someone who can tend to doors."

CHAPTER 4

"Breaking news, and we're getting this live. . . . Is it? . . . Okay. Breaking news: a group of heavily armed men have taken over the ten-acre, glass-encased facility known as The Liberty Convention Center in Newark. Stunning scenes of civilians being shot were posted on Facebook and Instagram before they were taken down. We have heard reports of an explosion in the underground light-rail tunnel linking the convention center at Newark International Airport. And now we're being told that, ah, yes, all cell phone service is being blocked there. The . . . I'm seeing now that The Liberty has 2.2 million square feet of convention space, three hotels, and more than two dozen shops, bars, and restaurants. We don't yet know how many people are inside, but men with assault rifles and masks have been spotted. Newark Police and New Jersey State Police have cordoned off the area, and the National Guard is on standby. All flights in and out of Newark International have been delayed or canceled. There have not been, so we're told, any demands. So far."

★ ★ ★

Dez moves into the kitchen of the martini bar through double-hinged, saloon-style doors. He checks the place out.

One of three cooks says, "You know what's going on, man?"

"Don't. Borrow this?" He picks up a six-inch paring knife, raises his pant leg, and slides it into his boot. "Ta, mate. Give us a hand here, will ye?"

Dez hops up on a metal table and begins fiddling with a large aluminum hood over the kitchen's four stoves. Everything in here is shiny and spotless; a month from now, and this smoke hood will be too greasy to touch. Dez puts his shoulders into it, shoving, twisting, and the hood pops free.

"Here."

He hands it down to two cooks. Both reach for it and fall on their asses, unprepared for the weight of it.

He peers up at the ventilation system that was hidden by the hood and uses the heel of one hand to punch straight up. A mesh screen pops free. He hands it down to the cooks.

"Going to go find some help. You lot, get the patrons and front-of-house staff in here, yeah? Then move them big butcher-block workstations. Blockade the door."

The kitchen staff stares up at him.

"Move with some alacrity, people. Hop to."

They begin hopping to.

Dez starts climbing up into a vertical ventilation shaft.

The designers of this building doubled the ventilation shaft with a maintenance shaft, then hid them above the mesh screen and the smoke hood. It's easy enough climbing.

It's a two-story building with, he guesses, administration, storage, and staff spaces above the bar. Dez is nearing the roof when he hears noise beneath him.

He looks down.

"Cat?" he whispers.

Cat Valdivia is climbing up after him. She's tied her hair back in a quick ponytail. She looks up at him. "You saved my ass in Spain. I hate owing anyone anything. Especially men."

"Shh. Could be a sniper on this roof." He beams down at her. "You're a gem, y'know that? So glad we met again."

She says, "To be clear, I'd like to stick a bridge girder up your ass. But yeah. I'm helping."

"Splendid. Slower, this next bit, kindly."

There's a tiny aluminum structure at the top of the shaft, shaped like a doghouse, with air vents on all four sides. Dez sticks his head up into it and looks west, then north, then east, then south. He uses the rebar ladder to drop gingerly back toward Cat.

"Yeah. Armed guard, long gun, to the west. Over the entrance t'the bar. He's the one shot the cowboy boots fella. Can tell from the angle. This arsehole has his back's to us, but it's a gravel roof. Bit noisy. You ready?"

"I've met you twice," she whispers. "Once in Spain and once here. And both times, men with guns showed up. I'm superstitious. Right now, I think you're a bad luck magnet."

"Me?" He starts climbing again. "I'm the luckiest bloke on God's green, love."

Dez returns to the little doghouse-like structure. It's easy enough to unscrew three loosely done bolts and free the doghouse from the roof.

His head and shoulders rise up to the roof level. It's the roof of the martini bar; not the glass roof of the ten-acre convention center. That's still well above him.

The man on the roof isn't lying on his belly, supported by his elbows, like they do on TV and in movies. That posture's hard to hold for any amount of time, no matter how much yoga one does. This guy is sitting cross-legged, a long rifle with a bipod stand for the barrel rests on a foot-high barrier that circles the roof. He's got binoculars and he's wearing a brimmed baseball cap, his eyes shaded.

He's looking for more panicked or fleeing civilians to shoot.

The man's long coat and sweater are off. Dez can see his Kevlar vest and the belt-clip holster snug against his spine.

The trick now will be to get Cat up here and to lift the man's handgun without him knowing it. If Dez can see what they're carrying, he'll have a sense of who outfitted them. Know that, and he'll be a step closer to knowing who they are.

He peers down the shaft and gestures to her: *Come up.*

She looks un-thrilled. But she ascends anyway. Dez had climbed up quickly and quietly. Cat Valdivia does it faster and quieter. Tricks of the trade, he imagines.

She gets to the roof and spots the shooter.

She rubs her sweaty palms over her denim thighs, but nods. Taut with a cocktail of adrenaline and fear, she begins inching forward over the crushed rock that lines the roof.

Dez can't hear her at all. He's impressed.

She gets within four feet of the shooter and the man stiffens. Cat freezes. The shooter has the binoculars to his eyes, looking down and to his left. He sets down the glasses, lifts the long gun, sights up.

Dez grabs a rock the size of a racquetball, throws it hard. It pings off the back of the man's head.

He grunts and slumps forward.

Ignoring the noise, Dez sprints over the crushed rock, past Cat, gets the stunned man in a sleeper hold, and drags him back, away from the roof and his rifle.

He struggles but, stunned by the blow to his head, and against Dez's superior strength, it's no contest.

The shooter's out cold.

Cat hisses a whisper. "That wasn't the plan!"

"He was about t'shoot a civilian, love. The plan was well and truly fecked. Pardon me language."

Dez gingerly peers over the edge of the roof and spots a woman, maybe forty, and a girl, maybe fourteen, hiding behind some shrubbery in one of the micro parks. The sniper apparently had spotted them.

Pulling back, he draws the man's handgun and studies it.

Interesting.

He hands it up toward Cat, who backs off, palms forward. "I don't touch those things. Bad luck."

"Good policy, that." Dez pats the guy down. No more guns, no knives. No ID, naturally. He's wearing an earjack and Dez reaches for the power source on the man's belt. It's got a four-digit lock-out.

"Worthless," he whispers. "I'd listen in on them confabbin', if I could. They accounted for that, the bastards."

Crouched, he scans the area in three hundred and sixty degrees. He sees lots of shiny new buildings and, beyond them, the glass walls of The Liberty. But he can't spot any other bad guys. Not from here.

He rises but bent low at the waist and gingerly creeps to the northern edge of the roof. He spots two men, armed to the teeth, one directly below, one forty paces out.

He turns and walks to the southern edge of the roof, peers down.

Nobody.

He creeps back. He touches Cat on the upper arm. "Important question: Are ye squeamish?"

"Yes. Why?"

"Because if the lad comes to, he'll raise a racket and the leaders of this here mob'll descend on the people in the bar, demandin' answers. That means I've got to kill him, an' make it look like he slipped an' fell. Will you be okay with that?"

The color drains from her face. "No!"

"He was about to shoot a woman and a wee girl down there. If we tie him up, or whatever, we'll be drawing wrath on the civilians in the kitchen. I am sorry about this. I won't resort to violence if and when I can help it. But needs must when the devil drives."

"Okay, well . . ." She wipes sweat off her upper lip. "I have no idea what that means but . . . okay."

Dez duckwalks to the southern edge of the roof again. Nobody in sight.

He walks back to the unconscious man. Dez slings the rifle over his own shoulder, then picks the man up, the fingers of his left hand snug under the back of the man's ballistic vest. He uses his right hand to grab the man's belt and hefts him, straight up. The man hangs there, horizontal.

Dez walks him to the southern edge of the roof and chucks him over.

He watches the fall, which breaks the unconscious man's neck.

Dez checks that the safety of the man's handgun is on, then tosses that over. Then rests the long rifle on the raised edge of the roof, where it will be visible from the ground. He uses the side of his boot to ruck up some of the crushed rock. With a wee bit of luck, it'll look like the man was walking the rounds, stumbled, and fell to his death.

Okay, that might require slightly more than a wee bit of luck.

He returns to Cat, whispering, "There's a fire ladder down that side. No one's watchin', so far. You can go back t'the kitchen and wait for help. I'll understand."

She thinks about it a second. He realizes that her hands are shaking.

"This is a hostage situation."

"It is, aye."

"And hostage situations don't get taken for their full seriousness until hostages start dying."

Dez says, "Like as not."

"Then I'm safer with you."

CHAPTER 5

The tension lies thick in conference room G, on the seventh and top floor of the smallest of the three assembly halls within The Liberty. The annual meeting of the board of trustees of a York, Pennsylvania, liberal arts college began that morning. Close to forty people are in attendance of the annual retreat, including trustees, the college president and her staff, members of her cabinet, deans included, and the day's roster of presenters. The morning agenda had included "Anti-Semitism vs. Free Speech on Campus" and "New Federal Guidelines for accepting NIH Grants, Explained."

The group has just broken for lunch when they hear explosions, followed by gunfire, followed by the PA announcement that the entire convention center had been taken over by *"a professional, armed militia."*

No one dares leave conference room G. Including the caterers who'd just delivered the boxed lunches.

Ray Harker is there, wearing a nice suit, shiny shoes. He wears the lapel pin of a staff member of The Liberty, and has told people he'd dropped by to see if the trustees and guests needed anything. He's a handsome man, well built at six-two, and blond.

He checks his expensive, highly precise chronometer. It's been counting down, and when it hits zero, Ray begins moving toward one of the members of the board of trustees. He times it so the trustee is alone, then clears his throat.

"You're Peter Garvey?"

The man turns. "Hmm?"

Ray keeps his voice down, keeps a neutral expression on his face. "I'm Tom. I went to school with your daughter, Jenna. At NYU. We dated."

Garvey, like everyone else, looks keyed up and a little strung out. "Ah. Okay. Nice to, ah, meet you. Tom? She . . . mentioned you."

That's a lie but a polite one.

Ray keeps his voice soft. "Sir, I work for The Liberty. Please listen carefully. There is a panic room in this building. It's not big enough for everyone. We can fit two people in there. I couldn't ever look Jenna in the eye again if I didn't do everything possible to save her dad. Sir, are you willing to come with me? It has to be you and you alone."

Peter Garvey stares up into Ray's eyes. His face is sweat-sheened. He whispers, "Seriously? You can . . . ?"

Ray nods.

Garvey lays a hand on his forearm, squeezes. He tries to look unexcited, forcing his face to relax. "Thank you," Garvey whispers. "Thank you."

"Okay, I'm heading out to the balcony. Wait a minute, then—"

"It's not safe out there!" Garvey hisses, glancing around to make sure no one has noticed.

"I've been out there. No snipers spotted me. I can get you to the safe room, but only by going that way. Do you want in?"

Garvey draws a handkerchief and dabs at his neck and forehead, but his handkerchief became sweat-soaked thirty minutes earlier, when this all began.

"Sir?" Ray presses.

Garvey makes up his mind. He nods.

"Okay. Give me sixty seconds. Come alone. I can't take more than you and me."

Ray Harker separates from the man. He walks to the folding tables set up for the boxed lunches, grabs a bottled water, cracks it, sips. No one's looking his way, so he sidles out onto the conference room G balcony, facing the north side's massive glass wall and, beyond, a hint of the Manhattan skyline.

He checks his watch.

Peter Garvey steps out onto the balcony.

"Nobody saw you?"

"No!" Garvey shudders a little. "You're sure it's safe out here."

Ray says, "'Safe' is a relative word," and jabs the knuckles of his left hand into Peter Garvey's windpipe.

The man's eyes bulge. He opens his mouth but his lungs are locked up. No sound emerges.

Ray checks the balcony's sliding glass door, peers in at an obtuse angle. Nobody is looking his way.

He grabs Peter Harvey by both lapels and throws him off the seventh-floor balcony. The silenced man falls, arms pinwheeling.

Ray presses two studs on the side of his watch, simultaneously, and holds them for two seconds. Sending a burst transmission to his partner.

Then he buttons the middle button of his suit coat, picks up his bottled water, takes another swig, and steps back into conference room G.

He spots the college president, talking sotto voce to her cabinet members. He heads her way.

"Ma'am? I'm going to check the lobby. There might be more people out there. If so, I need to get them inside."

The president gives him a fatigued smile. "Thank you. We know this isn't The Liberty's fault. You're really holding up well."

Ray Harker smiles. "Doing my best."

Olivia Gelman steps into the men's bathroom, adjacent to the ground-floor restaurant of the largest of three hotels in The Liberty. The Aviator serves classic American dishes and includes an all-day brunch.

Adam Levkowitz, a physician from Westchester, New York, is washing his hands at the sink. He looks up into the mirror, down at his hands, then does a double take.

Odd enough for a woman to waltz into the men's bathroom. But Liv—as her friends call her—is gorgeous. She has wavy, pitch-black hair, vivid eyes, and a quick, mischievous smile. She is well proportioned, wearing a tight dress scooped low enough in front to catch his attention.

"Hallo," she says, and waggles her fingers at him.

Well, a woman in the men's room wouldn't be the weirdest thing to happen today. "Hi. Crazy out there," he whispers.

Liv laughs. She has an infectious laugh, but it makes Levkowitz frown. Nobody in the Aviator restaurant has been laughing for the last thirty minutes, and he suspects that's true of the entire hotel, and the entire convention center.

"Adam Levkowitz?" she says.

"Ah. Yes. Do I . . . ?"

"I've been dying to meet you!"

She has an interesting accent, and he can't place it. European, but with something else.

"Well. I wish it were under better circumstances."

"It is under the best of all possible circumstances," Liv says, and feels her watch vibrate. Ray Harker has just sent her a burst transmission from conference room G. His part of this is going to plan. "At the end of this corridor, you will find a door that leads out to a dumpster. 'Dumpster'? That is the word in English? Big, wheeled garbage bins?"

Levkowitz says, "What? I mean: yes. That's the word. But—"

"Most excellent. Now, I wish for you to go to that door. It is normally locked but not at this moment, because I have some small skills with doors and locks. When you step outside, you will spot a shed, thirty meters to your left. It contains snow- and ice-clearing equipment used by The Liberty's grounds crew. Head directly to that shed, Dr. Levkowitz."

He says, "Are you nuts? I can't—"

"Move quickly. The shed also is locked at normal times, but again, I have my way with locks and keys and such, yes? Step into the shed. Close the door after you. There is an overhead light. Turn it on. You will then spot a trapdoor, which leads to a maintenance tunnel, which extends beyond the glass walls of The Liberty. A car is waiting for you on the other side. Do you understand?"

"You're insane!" Levkowitz says, his voice rising. "I go out there, I'll get shot!"

"I have been out there, and I am not shot," she says. "It is a secluded area. The villains, they don't think to watch out back. You will be fine. But timing is critical."

"Why are you doing this?"

She ratchets up her smile. "Your father-in-law is U.S. Representative Frank Goldman, yes? He sits on the Commerce Committee. My agency . . . occasionally testifies before him. He reached out and asked for the tiniest of favors."

Adam Levkowitz feels his heart trip-hammer. He takes a step in her direction. "Frank? Frank's doing this for me?"

"The congressman is doing this for his daughter and his grand-daughters, Adam. May I call you Adam? I think I should. We are the besties now, yes? The congressman wishes that his granddaughters do not grow up without a father. He wishes his daughter happiness. So yes: He is doing this thing. Not *for* you, per se."

Levkowitz thinks about all this. His father-in-law doesn't much like him; he's known this for two decades. But the man dotes on his daughter and grandkids.

"How do I know I can trust you? How do I know that shed is unlocked?"

Liv turns and lowers the right strap of her dress, showing him her tattoo. She readjusts her strap and turns back.

"Do you know who that is?"

"The two-headed god. The god of doors. Ah . . ."

She beams at him. "Yes! Very good! Janus. He watches my back—quite literally, you see—and because of him, doors always do as I tell them to. Always."

Liv Gelman winks at him. "Trust me."

Four minutes later, Adam Levkowitz opens the unlocked, rear door of the hotel and quickly ducks behind a dumpster. His heart threatens to burst out of his chest and he's aware that he's hyperventilating. He wills his lungs to slow down, then stands tall and races toward the shed, which is exactly where the mysterious beauty had said it would be.

Levkowitz is only five paces away when he spots the padlock on the door. The padlock is, well, locked. As normally it should be.

But that woman! She'd promised—

Blood from an exit wound in Adam Levkowitz's chest paints the door and the padlock of the shed, even before he realizes he's been shot in the back.

He's dead before his body ricochets off the shed door and he falls, on his back, arms and legs akimbo.

Liv Gelman shoots Levkowitz in the back, then unscrews the sound suppressor from her gun and returns both to her purse. She stands in the doorway of the hotel, pushes the two studs on this side of her watch to send a burst transmission to Ray Harker. They are two for two.

And Liv smiles. Of course the padlock on the shed was in place. Locks always do her bidding.

CHAPTER 6

On the ground, behind the martini bar, Dez hunkers low and studies the map of the grounds he'd taken from his hotel's lobby. From where they crouch, Cat Valdivia can't see the body of the sniper Dez killed, but she knows it's behind a small, grassy hillock. She can't drag her eyes off that hillock, knowing what's there.

Dez points to his map. "There's a theater here, inside the Delphi Center," he whispers. "Two buildings over. There'll be sound equipment, mixing boards, what not. Get lucky, I might be able to rig two-way communications with that. Get word out to the plod."

"The who?"

"Police, sorry. You ready?"

She removes her hot red lambskin biker jacket and begins pulling the sleeves inside out. Her jacket is fully reversable. The inside is matte black and it has a double-sided zipper. She pulls it back on, zips it over her white tank all the way to her neck. "Rule number one for a thief: Always be prepared to skulk."

Dez grins. "God but you're grand!" He rises, but still bent low. "Right. Follow my lead, kindly. Only move when I tell ye to."

She nods, scared but keeping her emotions in check.

Dez moves to the right rear corner of the building, stops, and slowly peeks around. Cat is right behind him.

He spots a high, wire fence with a locked gate and the words STAFF ONLY NO ADMITTANCE. Narrow, green, wooden slats have been slid into the wire links, vertically, to make the fence less ugly and imposing. It's eight feet high.

Dez draws the folding knife from his messenger bag. A pocket on the sheath contains his lockpicking tools. He peers up at the roofs, checks his sight lines. The Liberty is an absolutely mammoth site, and the bad guys are, at the very least, twelve men deep. Probably a lot more. But it would take scores of men, maybe a hundred, to cover every square foot of this place.

"Stay here till I get that lock open."

Cat moves up next to him and shows him her own set of lock-picks. She whispers, "Bet I'm faster."

"Bet I've been shot at more times than you."

"Here's an idea: You pick that lock. I'll wait here."

"Splendid, love. Ta."

Dez checks the roofs one last time, then duck-runs to the gate.

The gate features a standard, commercial padlock. He's worked with its kind a thousand times. He gets it picked inside of four seconds.

He checks the roofs again, then waves her over.

Cat does the classic under-the-helicopter-blades, bent-over run. But even running in that awkward position, she shows grace.

Inside the fenced-off area, they find groundskeeping equipment: mowers, trimmers, barrels of fertilizer and flower food. Dez spots an agricultural device with two handles and spike-lined metal wheels. "Harrower," he whispers. "Use it to level plowed land, break up clods."

"Is there any possible way you can imagine me giving a damn?"

"Honestly, no."

"Then let's shelve the guided tour of the farm museum."

He grins at her. She's pissed, which is a much better emotion than fright in a situation like this.

Dez turns the big implement over—it weighs northward of three hundred pounds—and starts digging around in its innards. "This is interesting," he whispers. He glances around, finds a screwdriver, and begins disassembling the harrowing device.

He pulls out an iron section a foot in length and Y-shaped. He slides the screwdriver in his left boot—he already has a paring knife from the bar's kitchen in his right boot. He digs around more gardening equipment, then stuffs his messenger bag with sturdy, stretchy rubber gaskets and a handful of big, one-inch-in-diameter nuts and their respective bolts.

"What the hell are you doing?"

"Slingshot."

"No. Seriously."

Dez grins at her. "If I found a shotgun lying about, I'd take that. This will have t'do."

"You could have taken the sniper's gun."

Dez says, "Ye find your mate fallen off a roof, with both his guns still there, well, it's possible he just slipped, yeah? Find either of his weapons missing, and he was definitely assaulted. Them guns are serving us quite well where they are."

Cat says, "You are certifiably bonkers."

"Won't argue that. Come along, love."

Back at the gate, they spot a roving guard a hundred yards away. The man carries an automatic rifle and wears Kevlar, knee and elbow pads, and a balaclava mask.

They peer through the wooden slats in the metal mesh fence. "Now, that's interesting," he whispers.

"What?"

Dez juts his chin in the general direction of the guard. "That rifle. SR-3 Vikhr. Nine millimeter."

She says, "Vicker? Who names a gun Vicker?"

"It's Russian for 'whirlwind,' love. An' that's the point, aye? Russian."

Cat thinks about it. "The handgun of the guy on the roof?"

"A GSh-18. Takes a nine-by-nineteen round. In this case, the seven-N-twenty-one round, not the NATO parabellum round."

"Russian?" she asks.

"Aye. His sniper rifle, too. Them lads is Russian."

"The guy on the PA sounded Slavic."

"Did, aye."

"Question." Cat raises her hand.

"Yeah?"

"In what fucked-up scenario does Russia invade Jersey?"

"Don't know their endgame, love. But now we've a better idea of who we're facin'. Let's us skedaddle."

CHAPTER 7

It's slow going. Dez and Cat Valdivia stop every few yards and check the likely locations for rooftop snipers, also watching for wandering soldiers on the ground level. It would be an easy, ninety-second walk, but today takes them ten minutes.

They move to the rear of the Delphi Insurance Center, where Dez is scheduled to perform on Tuesday.

"I'll watch for the villainous. You get the door," he whispers, taking one knee and drawing his makeshift slingshot out of his messenger bag. He rigs one of the stretchy gaskets over the upright ends of the Y-shaped device and hefts a thick metal nut and bolt, an inch in diameter, in his palm, along with the center of the gasket.

"That's the silliest thing I've ever seen," Cat whispers.

"Ye lot tried t'pass off the recipe for a feckin' macchiato as the endgame of the war on drugs, love."

The rear door pops open. On her haunches, Cat peeks in, then quick-ducks back out.

A guard! She mouths the silent word.

Dez nods. He gestures her out of the way. Still down on one knee, he shoulders open the metal door, right arm outstretched, left hand back by his ear, the gasket stretched taut. He spots a man in fatigues with a mask and an assault weapon. He's turning their way as Dez releases his hold on the iron nut and bolt.

Cat peeks over Dez's shoulder and sees the soles of the man's boots, visible for a moment, as he falls straight back. He lands hard on the poured cement floor, his masked head ricocheting once, his arms outstretched.

Dez hustles into the backstage area, Cat on his heels. He spots a door that reads PROPS, pops it open, glances inside, then squats and picks up the guard by his ankles, dragging him into the darkened room. His automatic weapon is attached to his ballistic vest by a strap, so the gun comes along for the ride.

Cat glances down at the man. Her hands rise to cover her nose and mouth, her eyes popping wide.

Dez drags him into the storage room. When he steps back out, Cat is leaning over a large metal sink, her back hunched. She's trying not to throw up.

"You all right?" he whispers.

"His . . . face," she says. "I thought that slingshot was a toy."

"It's not, love. We're a fair bit past the fun-and-games part of the day. But aye, I should've warned you. Force equals mass times acceleration. An estimated eight ounces of iron traveling upward of sixty miles an hour—"

"Yes." She holds up a palm to stop him. "I saw."

Dez holds out a Russian-made GSh-18 pistol. "Want this?"

A little color is returning to Cat's face. "I told you: I never touch them. I'm superstitious."

"Men might be shooting at you soon, love. Superstition be damned."

She shakes her head.

Dez shrugs and slides the weapon into his belt, snug against his spine.

They creep through the corridors until they come to an area that appears to be backstage. They spot curtains, both down and raised, along with sandbags, painted flats, a crudely constructed control panel for the rising and lowering of curtain-laden pipes, and a lectern with a small, gooseneck lamp, plus a headset and microphone hanging from a hook in the wall. Likely where a stage manager does his or her thing, Dez guesses.

They hear voices.

Moving slowly, they peek past one blue velvet curtain. Then a matte-black one. Then another of horizontally ruched burgundy velvet. Beyond that is a proscenium stage. Several people are sitting cross-legged on the stage. Others are seated in the first three rows of fold-down seating.

Dez spots a man on the stage, standing. The same getup as the others: Kevlar, balaclava, assault weapon. He watches as the man reaches for a communications rig on his belt and types in a four-digit code. He speaks in what Dez assumes is Russian.

A regular comms-check. Good unit discipline, this.

Dez spots a fifty-pound sandbag, leaning against an unpainted brick wall. He bends at the knees, picks it up in both hands, holding it against his chest, and starts marching onto the stage.

"What are . . . ?" Cat hisses softly but with shock.

Onstage, Dez whistles, high-low.

The terrorist turns and Dez uses both arms to throw the sandbag directly into the man's chest from four feet away while running toward him.

The bag hits him and hurls him back five feet. The terrorist lands on his shoulders, still sliding. His head collides with the pedals of a grand piano on the stage.

People are gasping, looking up in shock, wondering what just happened.

Dez draws the Russian pistol and checks the audience area, the balcony, the backstage-left area; he and Cat had arrived backstage-right.

This guard appears to have been alone.

One of the hostages takes a knee next to the gunman. A deep bass voice with a molasses-like Southern drawl says, "Fucker's alive. But you broke a shit ton of his ribs, dude."

Dez returns the gun to his belt. "Hoped t'take him alive, sir. Need some answers to—*holy hell! You're Calvin Willow!*"

The other man stands, wincing, rubbing his knee. He's in his late sixties, painfully thin, with long gray hair tied back in a ponytail, wearing jeans and cowboy boots and a cheap plaid shirt. Calvin Willow, one of the finest rock guitarists of the twentieth century, is worth tens of millions of dollars, but his clothes are even cheaper than Dez's. And Dez buys his wholesale.

Dez rushes his way and offers a hand. The guitarist takes it, pumps it once. "Who're you?"

"Desmond Limerick, sir. Huge fan of your work. Always have been. Just a feckin' pleasure, this."

Cat Valdivia says, "We've got a terrorist assault going on and you're fanboying some musician?"

Dez spins on her, as the other people seated on the stage begin to rise. Those in the audience climb to their feet, too. In total, Dez thinks thirty hostages or so were being held here.

"Some musician?" Dez is aghast. *"Some musician?"*

"Could be she's right, bud," the guitarist says, his voice heavy with a smoker's rasp. He offers Cat his hand. "Hey. Calvin."

"I'm Cat. Are there any more of these men in here?"

"Was," Calvin says around a wad of chewing gum. "Three of them assholes ushered a bunch of us in here. Two searched the place, then left this guy to guard us."

Cat says, "Broken ribs or not, we should get his weapons. We should take that body armor, too." She gets to her knees and unhooks the assault weapon from the man's ballistic vest. She hands it to someone who appears to be a stagehand. The soldier's sidearm goes next.

Cat says, "Why didn't his vest stop the sandbag?"

"It did. The sandbag didn't go through his chest. The hydrostatic shock of the sandbag did. Human body's mostly water, love. An' I just made his slosh around a bit."

She looks up at him. "Force equals mass times acceleration. Again."

"Sir Isaac's second law of motion. The classics never go out of style."

He turns to the crowd on the stage. "Can two of yez go watch the lobby, please. Sing out sharply if more of these feckin' tossers head our way. You"—he turns to another stagehand—"is there another exit beside the one to the rear?"

"I've worked here two full days," the kid says. "I can go find out."

"Do, aye, but not alone. Buddy system, people. Move in groups of two, please. Miss?" He spots a woman with a T-shirt that reads MY STAGE MY RULES. "Stage manager, you?"

"Yes."

"Get a medical kit, kindly. Don't want this bastard dyin' on me just yet. Go with someone else."

"Right," she says.

"You two." Dez picks guys who look like maybe they won't throw up at the site of gore. "Another guard in the back, in a room marked storage. He's dead. I'd like his rifle, please, an' also his ballistic vest. Cat: Did you spot them backstage ladders? I'd like t'know if there's roof access."

She says, "Right back."

"Ta. Calvin?"

The guitarist nods.

"That riff you done on the bridge between second an' third verse, 'Memphis Morning.' Were you influenced by Jimmy Raney's fretwork with Stan Getz on—"

"Desmond!"

"Right. She's right. Sorry. Terrible. I'm horrified at meself. Won't happen again. D'you know the riff I mean . . . ?"

Elsewhere around The Liberty, a group of three guys in their early twenties decide to try getting to the airport parking lot adjacent to The Liberty. They make it to within ten steps of the fencing before posted Russian guards cut them down.

Meanwhile, in the lobby of the largest hotel, a decidedly drunk guest starts arguing with one of the terrorists, who shoots him in the chest.

The Russians' body count is growing.

The same can be said of Liv Gelman and Ray Harker. In the basement of The Liberty's administration building, Liv walks up to a man, smiles, and says, "Are you Jacob Gaetano?"

Just as she'd done earlier with Dr. Levkowitz.

CHAPTER 8

Calvin Willow's face is a complex canvas of deep, leathery wrinkles from years of playing outdoor concerts and, before that, spending his youth working construction. He has thick, powerful hands on a tall, lanky frame. He's sixty-nine if Dez remembers correctly.

He's with Dez now, up at the back-of-the-balcony sound controls of the main auditorium of the Delphi Center concert hall. Dez keeps a small packet of tools in his messenger bag, including screwdrivers, tiny alligator clips and a small spool of wire. He doesn't need that stuff every day, but when he does, they're invaluable. He also has the larger screwdriver he stole from the maintenance area.

"Whatcha doing?" the singer-songwriter asks. His voice sounds like the guy gargles tarmac.

Dez has both his phone and his tablet computer out. He's also opened the top of the sound-mixing board, exposing its wiring. "Know what Bluetooth is?"

Calvin shrugs. "Got it on my phones. Dunno what it is."

Dez connects his phone to a component within the mixing board. "Short-range wireless technology. Lets us exchange data between devices, both fixed an' mobile, but only over short distances. My phone? Yours? Both limited to transmission power of, say, two-point-five milliwatts."

"I'm guessin' that ain't much." Calvin folds a stick of gum in two and shoves it in his mouth. Dez notes that it's a brand for people trying to quit smoking.

"Aye. Good for ten, twelve meters, tops. But if I give me phone a boost with this equipment, maybe I can goose the power up a bit."

"Most phones wouldn't let you do that sorta thing," the musician drawls.

"This ain't most phones, mate."

"You ain't most guys."

Dez shrugs. "I'm supposed to be sitting in for one of the bands opening for you tomorrow."

Calvin nods. "Sorry. I usually don't know shit about the bands opening for us. The venues pick 'em."

"I know."

"I'm just here for a sound check tonight."

"Figured."

Calvin says, "You're a gee-tar man, or you wouldn't know the name Jimmy Raney."

"Guitar, aye, an' keyboards."

Calvin waves toward the man on the stage, down below, who remains unconscious. "Know who these asswipes are?"

Dez clips two wires together. "Russian. Which isn't as much information as I'd like, but beggars an' choosers, as it were."

They glance up as Cat Valdivia jogs up the stairs to the balcony and joins them. Calvin says, "What's your part in all this?"

"Damned if I know." She turns to Dez. "You know what a fly tower is?"

"Don't."

"The area above a stage where stagehands can help raise and lower flats, or if there's a Peter Pan rig. Anyway, this theater's fly tower is pretty big. I think we should move everyone up there. If the terrorists come back, they'll think people fled. They won't think to look up."

Dez nods to Calvin. "She's a peach, this one. Helping me foil the ungodly."

"No, I'm with him because he's built like my daddy's pickup truck and I'm safer with him than not with him," she corrects.

"Could go get yourself one of them vests t'wear, love."

"I'm an alley cat, not an armadillo," she counters. "I'm quick and quiet."

"'Course. Did the soldier boy I hit wake up?"

She shakes her head. "One of the stagehands is an EMT. Says you not only broke the guy's ribs, you probably concussed him against the piano, too."

"Pity. Had questions for the lad." Dez reaches for his phone and brings it alive.

Calvin Willow says, "You reckon you can get a signal past the walls of this big ol' mall?"

"Might. A wee bit past, aye."

He dials a number and sets it on speaker mode.

"D-Ops." It's a woman's voice.

"Crisis call," Dez says. "Comin' from inside The Liberty Convention Center, New Jersey."

"Good lord!"

"Aye. Desmond Limerick, calling for Sir Richard. Ye've my voiceprint on file, so . . ."

"Yes, voiceprint confirms, Sergeant. Please hold."

Calvin draws a flask and takes a sip. "Who the hell you call, bud?"

"Sir Richard Corbyn-Smith. Director of operations, British Military Intelligence Six. London."

Cat's eyebrows rise in surprise.

"Limerick?" A man's voice with a posh London accent.

"Sir Richard."

"You're in that skirmish in New Jersey?"

"Am, sir. I've some intel for the local constabulary, but I'm trapped inside. Dunno how to reach 'em. Was hoping you could grease the skids."

"Give us a moment, Sergeant."

He's put on hold.

"You're a spy?"

"No! Don't trust 'em, spooks. Not as far as I can throw 'em."

Calvin Willow says, "They called you sergeant. You a soldier?"

"Me? Marching around, taking bloody orders? Not hardly! Just a musician trying to make a quid or two."

"Uh-huh. That sounds like twenty pounds of horseshit in a ten-pound bag, bud. But also: none of my goddamn business."

The phone crackled. "Sergeant? We're clearing you a path to the chief hostage negotiator."

"Ta, sir."

"I've no idea how you got your message in a bottle out, but you saved my people on more than one occasion, Limerick. We owe you. And I'm quite keen on paying debts."

Dez winces and puts the phone on mute. "Wasn't as dramatic as all that. Bloody drama queen." He undoes the mute. "Thank you, sir. We'll stand by."

Cat laughs as Dez puts it on mute again. "Well, you don't think small."

"Get everyone up in the fly tower, love. Brilliant idea, that."

Calvin Willow turns to her. "You a musician, too?"

"No. I'm a cat burglar." She walks away.

Calvin chews his nicotine gum. He grins, a long hank of gray hair bobbing before his blue eyes.

"For real?"

"Yeah."

"She any good?"

Dez laughs. "She done a lift of me wallet an' watch earlier today. Best I ever seen. Her hands are more impressive than yours, mate, and yours are in the Rock and Roll Hall of Fame!"

Calvin chuckles, a deep, resonant note. "Goddamn dumb luck's kept me alive and successful for decades, bud. Then I run into you two. Guess I still got a little of that luck running through me."

"Luck is the residue of hard work," Dez opines.

Calvin slaps him on the shoulder. "Hope you like bourbon, Mr. Dez Limerick, the non-spy non-soldier. You get my wrinkled old ass outta this, I'm buyin' by the barrel-full."

Dez beams. "Deal."

Newark police has jurisdiction over the hostage situation, nominally, but they're working with state police, the National Guard, and the FBI, among other agencies. The Liberty is owned and financed by a European-based banking consortium, so representatives are flying in from Berlin. And the city's most decorated hostage negotiator just landed in a hospital with a ruptured appendix. Due to the size and scope of the attack on The Liberty, the senior-most hostage negotiator in a three-state region, an NYPD captain, is called in. But he quickly asks if the Feds want to take over working with the hostage-takers, since they appear to be terrorists.

The FBI's Hostage Rescue Team and Crisis Negotiation Unit already are present. Special Agent Stella Ansara of the FBI's New York field office has crisis negotiation training, and she's present, so she gets the nod. She's well-versed in antiterrorism work, and she also has a master's in psychology.

The other agencies agree to give Stella Ansara command of the situation.

The task force had set up shop in Newark International's economy long-term parking P6. It's far enough away to not take direct gunfire, but The Liberty is visible from their hastily thrown together third-floor headquarters. Incident Command trailers have been hauled in, along with police cars, to create a sort of RV village.

Barely an hour into her new position, the chief assistant to Stella Ansara emerges from her IC trailer, waving over the other team leaders. "We've got radio contact with someone inside!"

The department leaders began sprinting toward the trailer.

In the subbasement of The Liberty's administration building, Olivia Gelman has just shot Jacob Gaetano. That's three down. She sends the pulse message via her watch to Ray Harker.

She immediately gets pinged by another of their associates.

They have assumed from the start that the entire mall would be under an umbrella of the nation's top signal-intelligence organizations, from the National Security Agency, to the National Geospatial-Intelligence Agency, to Homeland Security. The decision was made early on to stay off their highly encrypted, burst-transmission radios. But that signal tells her she needs to prick up her ears.

Liv slides her earpiece into place and activates the vox channel. "Go."

They've had one of their team running reconnaissance on law enforcement comms since three hours before the takeover began. The woman on the line says, "The chief hostage negotiator is FBI Special Agent Stella Ansara. She's getting a call, right now, from Desmond Limerick."

Liv shakes her head and smiles. But of course they are! If anyone could manage to cobble together a communications system that could beat these Russians, it would be Dez.

"I'm tracing his signal to the Delphi Center. He's in there. I also pulled up an image of Limerick, dining with a girl when the situation began."

"Show me."

Liv checks her smartwatch. A high-res, black-and-white image appears. It's from a CC camera in one of the restaurants, and it shows Dez smiling and chatting up a beautiful woman with dark, flowing hair.

"Have you ID'd her?"

"Yes, and she could be an X factor. Her name is Catalina Valdivia. And she's believed to be some sort of thief."

"Believed?"

"Never convicted. But a whole lot of smoke."

Liv laughs. "Talented and beautiful. No wonder she fell into Desmond's orbit! All right. Alert our Russian friends. Let them know where he is. Tell our friend the colonel that I'd like Señora Valdivia taken alive, please. I've questions for her."

Their surveillance expert says, "You sure? I know how you feel about Limerick. They'll kill him on sight."

Liv says, "Well, they'll certainly try. Out."

She shuts down the vox band, hoping their brief, burst-streamed conversation flew under the federal radar.

CHAPTER 9

Dez and Calvin Willow sit in the balcony, behind the soundboard, and wait.

Dez's phone pings. "This is FBI Special Agent Stella Ansara. To whom am I speaking?"

The woman on the line sounds all business.

"Name's Dez Limerick, ma'am. I'm hopin' British Intelligence is enough of an icebreaker, we can dispense with the pleasantries."

"If you're asking: Do I trust you? The answer is no. The terrorists control The Liberty. This is the first transmission we've received from The Liberty. I'm inclined to think I'm being led down a path, sir."

Dez reaches into his wallet and draws two business cards. "I've police officers in Los Angeles and Portland, Oregon, who can vouch for me. Got a pen?"

He recites the details on the cards, then slips them back in his wallet.

"While we attempt to confirm your bona fides, Mr. Limerick, tell me how this transmission is happening."

"Using the sound system in one of the theaters to boost my signal, ma'am."

"That doesn't sound plausible."

Dez laughs. "Terrorists taking a ten-acre mall made o' glass doesn't seem plausible, either, but there you have it. Also, let's assume they're monitoring all communications. I propose I tell you what I can, you write it down, you choose not to believe me until ye've checked my background, then you act accordingly. Yeah? Because we've only a little tempus an' it's fugiting like mad."

He waits.

"Go ahead, Mr. Limerick. No promises."

"I've spotted well over a dozen of them so far. Taken out a couple. Men are carrying SR-3 rifles and GSh-18 pistols. Both are Russian made. I've heard 'em speak to each other in a Slavic tongue. Don't speak it meself, but it could be Russian."

"Why would Russians invade a conference center in New Jersey?"

"Dunno. Can tell you they're soldiers, them. Good discipline. Their comms are key-code locked. They do regular comms checks. Snipers on roofs have picked off some of the civilians. I've seen the bodies."

They wait. Calvin Willow takes a swallow from his thin, metal flask.

"We've seen the bodies, too, Mr. Limerick," Agent Ansara says. "We've heard no demands."

"You're a hostage negotiator?"

A beat. "I am."

"Then you know they're playing a slow hand t'put you off your game. Make you anxious to hear from them."

"Maybe I'm hearing from them now."

"Possibly, aye. I'm not law enforcement. Wouldn't dream of tellin' you how to do your job, ma'am."

They wait.

They hear sneakers beating a hasty path up the stairs toward them. Cat rounds the corner, twin strands of her ink-black hair hanging like parentheses around her face.

"Soldiers coming!"

"Everyone up in the what-do-ye-call-it?"

"Fly tower." She nods.

"Good. Get backstage and douse all the lights ye can. I spotted the circuit breakers to the left of—"

She says, "So did I," and disappears down the stairs.

"Brave kiddo," Calvin says.

"Aye. Agent Ansara? Did you hear any of that?"

"Is your position compromised, Mr. Limerick?"

"Is, aye. Might not be able to try this trick again. Signing off. Good luck t'ye."

Calvin stands. "What do we do?"

The working lights and stage lights of the theater begin blinking off. They hear the dull *boom-boom-boom* of Cat Valdivia, hitting the breaker switches.

"Hope for the best," Dez says, disassembling his phone and the soundboard. "Plan for the worst."

CHAPTER 10

FBI Special Agent Stella Ansara looks around the Incident Command trailer in the Newark International P6 parking lot. One of her agents is on the phone to either Los Angeles or Portland, attempting to prove their caller is who he says he is. His call was recorded, of course, but Stella also took copious notes on a legal pad. She's Lebanese American, midforties, well-respected and well-liked (those are two very different accolades) within her ranks.

"Think he's legit?" one of her guys asks.

"I'm making no assumptions."

"He's got British spooks vouching for him."

Stella reaches for the Incident Command's coffee maker. "Yeah, guys who lie for a living. Not sure I'm buying that, either. We—"

The IC's primary phone rings again. The recording device and its backups are activated. "FBI Special Agent Stella Ansara."

It's not Limerick—or whomever the first caller was. This man sounds Russian.

"We are the forces that have taken The Liberty Convention Center. Several hostages have been killed and we estimate two thousand more are under our command. All egresses have been wired with explosives, but only the detonators are near the doors and tunnels and windows. The explosives themselves have been distributed to random hostages. If you attempt to enter The Liberty, you will trigger the death of one civilian, plus whoever is in near proximity to that person. Is this understood, FBI Special Agent Stella Ansara?"

"To whom am I speaking?"

The man says, "Inform the Office of Naval Intelligence that this incident is in regard to the *Kocatka.*" He spells it for her.

"What is that?"

"Inform the Office of Naval Intelligence that this incident is in regard to the *Kocatka.* Alert them that we will reach out to you again in exactly thirty minutes. At which time, the Office of Naval Intelligence will have given you a vital piece of information, which you will share with us."

"I don't even know what—"

The man hangs up.

Stella says, "Trace?"

"Not even trying to hide it," an aide says from her workstation. "That call came from the office of the CEO of The Liberty Convention Center. Right in the heart of that big, fat, glass target over there."

In fact, a former captain in the Russian army named Oborin is in the office of the chief executive officer of The Liberty Convention Center. But not the ringleader of the assault, Colonel Maksim Baranov. He's calling from elsewhere, and routing the call through Oborin and his men. Once the connection to the FBI is severed, Oborin speaks across the line to his colonel. The former captain is smoking a long Cuban cigar. He'd found the cigars after killing the CEO and his staff, who'd been on their knees, fingers laced behind their heads.

"Is everything under control there?" Colonel Baranov asks from afar.

"Going exactly according to the schedule, sir." Oborin blows a smoke ring. "I have a unit prepared to enter the Delphi theater. Proceed?"

He listens, knowing the colonel is calculating the angles. Oborin is a barrel-chested man with no neck and with a massive mustache, his hair slicked back.

The colonel says, "Our ally wants some girl taken alive, but he doesn't care about this Limerick's life? I find that odd. Get Thiago on the line."

The captain draws a satellite phone. He enters the lock-out numbers, then hits the only number stored in the phone's memory. He makes it a conference call with Thiago and the colonel.

An electronically distorted voice replies. The voice is male, and possibly South American. "Trouble, colonel?"

Oborin listens as Colonel Baranov replies, "We are ready to hit this Limerick. You want him alive or dead?"

Olivia Gelman replies, knowing the electronic distortion field will make her sound male and South American. "It is of no importance, either way. Secure Catalina Valdivia."

She waits as Colonel Baranov considers this. "You went to great trouble to get Limerick to The Liberty, Thiago. But seem uninterested in his fate. This intrigues me."

"I have promised to get you the *Kocatka*, Colonel. And I have an exit strategy for your men. Nothing else should concern you at this time."

Liv disconnected.

CHAPTER 11

Dez studies the soundboard desk and realizes it's basically a wooden box, five feet wide and two feet deep, behind which sits a swiveling office chair. He stands and attempts to lift the desk. It's heavy but movable. He goes to his knees and unplugs everything from the floor, then stands.

Calvin Willow grabs one of the short ends. "Where you want this?"

Dez laughs. "First, your hands are too feckin' valuable to be hauling furniture about! Second, you're nigh on seventy. I've got this."

Calvin gives him a look that would freeze rubbing alcohol. "Shut the fuck up, England. I got this end. Where the fuck you want this?"

Dez shrugs and takes the other short end. Together, they lift the wooden frame.

"Over that way," Dez says. "If you've a mind to flee, this would be the time."

"Flee where?" Calvin grits his teeth, veins standing out in his neck as they move the sturdy wooden desk. "My knees barely made it up a dozen steps to the balcony, bud. No way I'm climbing a ladder to the fly tower."

They position the desk where Dez wants it.

He returns to the swivel chair and now empty space before it. He kneels again and begins pulling wires up from a recess under the floor. "Could get interesting up here right soon."

"Some dumb son of a bitch was gonna pop a cap in my ass sometime, bud. I've been too drunk and too ornery in too many saloons. Shoulda happened years ago."

Dez laughs. "Now, that's a lyric you should record."

Dez hauls up as much electrical cable as he can, then gets it where he wants it.

He moves to the curved edge of the balcony and peers down. No work lights, no stage lights. It's not perfectly dark in here, but it's fairly shrouded. Dez has no way of reaching Cat to know if everyone's escaped to the area high above the stage; the gimmick that let him call London still won't work for short-distance calls, not with the Russians blocking Wi-Fi and jamming frequencies. He has to hope she's done her part.

Calvin Willow steps up next to him. He whispers, "You got a plan?"

"Do, aye, but not a good one."

Calvin snorts a rough laugh. "You just described my whole life, bud."

They hear a noise. It's coming from directly beneath them; from the lobby.

"I need a head count," Dez says, ducking low with just his eyes above the balcony edge. "How many of them bastards enter."

To his right, Calvin nods.

They hear voices. Men, speaking in what Dez assumes is Russian.

Flashlights pop on. They begin sweeping the audience seats.

Soon men appear. They're walking down both aisles, between the seats, toward the proscenium stage. Their lights bob. They whisper to each other. Dez can spot the glint of light off their automatic rifles.

Each aisle ends at a portable, five-step wooden stairway that leads to the stage. Men start mounting both stairs. One guy shines his light down into the empty orchestra pit at the foot of the stage.

Someone shines his light up toward the balcony. Dez and Calvin duck.

The soldiers find their unconscious and concussed fellow fighter, stripped of his ballistic vest and his weapons. His head still leans against the pedals of the grand piano.

Calvin taps Dez on the shoulder, then holds up four fingers.

Dez nods.

One man remains down in the audience area. Three are up on the stage. They consult each other, then head backstage.

Dez taps the singer on the shoulder and juts his chin back toward the rear of the balcony. Both men scuttle that way, moving silently. They're down on their haunches, heads close together.

"Best case: They check the place an' find naught," Dez whispers as softly as he can. "Then all four report in, pick up their playmate, an' leave."

Calvin says, "Worst case?"

Dez looks him in the eye. "Four entered. Nobody leaves."

"Fuck me."

Dez shrugs. "If they call the tune, I'll play. But it's them what called it, not I."

They head back down to the front of the balcony, crouching low.

One man remained behind. That leaves three checking the rear of the theater, the offices, the storage spaces.

Dez and the singer wait. Dez has left a corpse of one of their men in a storage room. That could complicate the story they're hoping to sell—that everyone escaped out the back, and the theater's empty.

They wait.

The men return, one of them on his comms set, speaking Russian. They begin removing their uncomfortable ski masks. They must have come to the conclusion Dez had hoped for.

They don't look particularly angry. Could be they haven't spotted the corpse of their friend.

Two of the men sling rifles over their shoulders and, together, pick up the concussed man.

It looks as if they're bugging out.

Dez makes a *stay here* gesture to Calvin Willow. Then he moves to the head of the balcony stairs and crouches low.

He's drawn his makeshift slingshot and a bolt from his messenger bag.

The soldiers seem to have moved off the stage and out of the seating area. If Dez is hearing this correctly, they're back in the lobby now. He can hear them muttering; no idea what they're saying.

There are brass handrails to either side of the stairs. One of the handrails jiggles a little and Dez hears a man grunt. Then stutter. Then fall.

Dez had dragged over the cables from the floor recess, where the soundboard is plugged in, and wrapped them around both railings. Anyone touches them gets a lethal dose of electricity.

And unfortunately, someone just did.

He waits. He hears mutterings. Hears treads on the stairs. Men coming up. How many? One for sure. No, two.

Dez has been hiding behind a short end of the soundboard table, which he and Calvin had lined up with the stairs. Dez puts his shoulder to it and gives the thick, heavy desk a mighty shove.

It goes sailing down the stairs. Catching both soldiers in transit.

Dez rises and moves to the head of the stairs. The bottom of the stairs is blocked by the table. He spots the leg of one man, mown over by it. He hears moaning.

A human head appears, above the desk, looking perplexed and more than a little scared.

Using the slingshot, Dez puts a one-inch-diameter bolt and its companion nut through the man's forehead.

Dez is moving down the stairs now. He leaps and makes a base-ball runner's slide, on one hip, boots leading, gliding across the top of the desk.

He emerges on his feet in the lobby. Three men lie around him—electrocuted, smashed by a runaway desk, or hit with a flying bolt.

One man still stands, his gun slung over his shoulder holding up his concussed mate.

Dez puts a second iron bolt into the soldier's chest and he falls.

He checks the men around and under the desk and the foot of the stairs. Three dead.

He checks the man he'd just hit in the chest. That shot killed him, too.

He checks the pulse of the man he'd concussed earlier. That guy's alive but Dez lifts his eyelid with the pad of one thumb. He's not coming around anytime soon.

Dez takes a moment. It's a distasteful thing, killing these men he'd never even met. But it's as he told Calvin Willow:

These men called the tune.

CHAPTER 12

Dez drags the desk the rest of the way into the lobby. He carries the four dead bodies, two at a time, up to the balcony. He carries the concussed man up as well. Calvin Willow watches, sipping from his flask, saying nothing, a grim scowl on his weathered face.

Dez retrieves the mechanisms of the soundboard from the ruined desk and brings the bits upstairs, too. He sits cross-legged on the floor and begins rewiring it. "Might've ruined this. With any luck, we'll get one more bite of the apple."

Calvin speaks softly. Almost reverentially. "I done a lot of shit in my life, bud, but I never had to kill a man."

"And the gods willing, ye never have to. It's vile work."

The soundboard, sans desk, lights up. "I'll be damned." Dez attaches his phone and puts it on speaker mode. He locked in the number for the police during the first call.

"Incident Command," a guy says.

"It's Limerick. Put Agent Ansara on. *Tout de suite,* kindly."

He waited. Calvin watched him.

They hear, "Limerick?"

"Aye, ma'am."

"We've contacted the police in LA and Portland. They vouch for the assistance you've recently given them. My man asked a Detective Swanson how we could prove you're you. She asked if you're being an unparalleled pain in the ass. So I guess you're in."

"Cheers, then. Our position was attacked an' I was forced to defend the place. Which means the Russians are down a few men, an' they'll figure it out in time. Gotta move, which means no more comms, ma'am."

"We don't know how big their force is. Did you take out more than one of them?"

"Aye, four. Well, six, dependin' on how you count 'em. Four just now, two a bit earlier."

He waits. Stella says, "You took six of their people off the board."

"Now that ye mention it, I removed the sniper from the roof of this cocktail bar, as well."

"So that's seven."

"Ma'am."

He waits.

"Well, that's . . . ah, all right."

"Have ye heard from the bastards yet? Excuse me language."

Stella says, "We have. They told me to contact the Office of Naval Intelligence and to tell them this has to do with something called the *Kocatka*. We don't know what that is. We've sent the info on to Naval Intelligence. But I've never banked on any of those spy agencies actually being useful or fast."

"Smart, you. Three-fourths foolish and a quarter flash, the lot of 'em. *Kocatka* don't mean squat to me, sorry to say."

"Something else. They claim they put sensors for their explosives in the doors and the light-rail tunnel, but the explosives themselves aren't there. They're attached to random hostages. Any incursion attempt by us would result in a hostage somewhere else in the complex being killed. Plus whoever's near them."

Calvin Willow mutters, "Jesus, Joseph, and Mary."

"Vicious, aye," Dez says, then smiles. "On t'other hand, this could be a godsend, yeah?"

A pause, and Stella says, "How?"

"This lot's not just taken down the Wi-Fi, ma'am. Too many people have satellite phones and voice-over-internet-protocol devices. Means the Russians are blocking a lot of frequencies, as well."

"We can confirm that, yes."

"Splendid! Then all me mate and me have to do is get one of them sensors you mentioned. Figure out its frequency, then get to the frequency-jamming tech the Russians are using. Use their own tech to block the explosives' frequencies! And Bob's your uncle!"

Calvin laughs without mirth. "That sounds like a pretty deep crock of zebra shit you got there, bud."

Stella says, "I don't know who's with you, Limerick, but there's no daylight between us on that assessment."

"Shouldn't be that hard, ma'am. D'you know where they're bunkered?"

"The call to us came from The Liberty Convention Center administration building. It's in the—"

"I've a map, thank you, ma'am. It's better'n even money, that's where their jamming equipment is. I eyeball one of them sensors, then get into the admin building. Should be able to make their bombs useless, an' reopen comms for you an' your lot. And after that, your momma's rich an' your daddy's good-looking. Cakewalk, this."

Stella's tone is as rigid as rebar. "I am the chief negotiator here, Limerick. There's me, then there's God. I am not authorizing you to mess with their bombs and sensors, for the simple reason that I don't know you. So you are to stand down and to go into hiding. We're doing this my way, mister. How clear am I being at this point?"

"Crystal, ma'am. But with a heaping truckload of respect, we're on the inside with them fuckers—excuse me language—and you're not. I'll play it your way for as long as I can. But this is their song and dance. Not yours, an' not mine. If it looks like the situation's going pear-shaped, me mate and me will do what I can t'stop 'em. How clear am *I* being at this point, ma'am?"

He waits. He looks up at Calvin Willow, who shrugs.

Stella says, "Act if—and only if—you see no other alternatives, Limerick. Are we on the same page?"

"We are, ma'am. And when the time comes t'make your move, I've nearly thirty civilians hiding up in the fly tower and rigging of the Delphi theater. So far, the ungodly haven't thought t'look up that way."

"That's thirty hostages out of immediate harm's way, Mr. Limerick, which brings us to a total of thirty safe hostages. You have my gratitude. And my respect."

"Cheers, ma'am. Signin' off."

Dez disconnects his phone.

They move into the seating area, then up onto the stage. Dez goes to the wall-mounted circuit breakers and pops on a few work lights. He cups his hands around his mouth and speaks upward.

"Cat! Coast is clear, but not forever. You lot: I've reached out to the police an' told 'em where you're hiding. They recommend you shelter in place, aye?"

He hears a general muttering coming from the dark well above his head.

Cat Valdivia begins climbing into the light. He sees her legs, first, then her derriere. Now isn't the time to dwell on it, Dez thinks, but she's sporting world-class bits of feminine anatomy, truth be told. And of course he wouldn't be so rude as to mention that out loud.

"They've agreed to stay put," she says, clapping dust off her palms. "I'm going with you. Mr. Willow?"

"The only people call me Mr. Willow are my ex-wives' lawyers." The musician raps his thigh with a fist. "These knees ain't what they used to be. Doubt I could haul ass up there if I wanted to. But I don't wanna slow you guys down, either. And truth is, I'm damn good at smacking around some drunk loudmouth in a bar, but a gunfight ain't in my wheelhouse and never was. Limerick?"

Dez draws his phone. "We'll hide you someplace safe. Give me your number."

"Phones are out," Cat reminds him.

"Phones are out now, love. Might not be forever. Give me your digits, too, please."

All three of them share their cell numbers. "When we get the all clear, I'll ring you up."

The musician says, "I owe you big time, bud."

Dez grins. "Want to pay me back? With interest? Thirty minutes, tops. My hotel room or yours. Just our two guitars, yeah? Nobody else ever has to hear it, but I want to jam with you, squire. Would love nothin' more."

Calvin Willow holds out a calloused hand. "Done."

CHAPTER 13

It takes Dez and Cat about ten minutes to sneak back to the outdoor, padlocked area that the grounds crew uses to store equipment. Dez re-ups his supply of iron ammunition, screwing together five bolts and five nuts, and stowing them in his bag. He discards the first of the stretchy gaskets he'd used for his makeshift slingshot, replacing it with a new one.

"Where to now?" she asks.

"Can I say—an' if this comes across as sexism, then I truly apologize—but can I say you're handlin' all this well?"

She studies him, eyes narrowed, to figure out if he's making fun of her. Both of them are down on their haunches, balanced on the balls of their feet, heads close together and speaking softly.

"The decisions in my life that led me to becoming a professional thief are none of your business. But let's just say I was evading violent situations before I turned fifteen."

"Fair that."

"Also, I steal for the money. And for the kick of doing something I'm really, really good at. But I won't deny it: The adrenaline is a good high. Always has been."

"It is, aye. Not that many people I meet figure out the trick to balancing the high of an adrenaline-producing lifestyle, without becoming an adrenaline junkie and taking stupid risks."

Again, she studies his eyes to see if he's teasing her. He isn't.

"Thank you. You know, there's a possibility we've made things worse."

"By killing them Russians an' potentially riling them up worse than they are? Aye. That's the reason I hid the bodies, best I could, given the time constraints."

"So what do we do now?"

"The Russians reached out to the gendarmes. They say this has something or other t'do with the U.S. Office of Naval Intelligence. I don't know what and don't much care. Also told 'em there are motion sensors in the exterior doors and the tunnels of the convention center. Them sensors will trip explosives, yeah? But the explosives aren't there, to kill or injure the cops. The explosives are strapped to random hostages. Try an incursion, and the plod will just get some poor innocents blown to bits."

Cat blanches. "That's sick."

"Aye."

"Can you get me near one of these sensors? If it's the kind I've seen before, on other capers, I might be able to deactivate one. Then if we figure out what frequency they're using . . . Why are you grinning like an idiot?"

"Because I had the exact same thought. Told the guvnor as much. She told me t'stand down and do nothing. But doing nothing's no guarantee of saving the hostages. So I'm thinking of ignoring her sage advice."

"Good." Cat nods once, decisively.

"What tools would you need?"

"Can I see that packet you carry around?"

Dez produces the small pack of tools, clips and wire, usually tucked into his messenger bag.

"This should work. Dez?"

"Aye?"

"The reason I came to find you, before all this started, is because I was casing The Liberty, planning out a high-stakes heist. I spotted your face in an ad for a band opening for Calvin Willows."

"Aha. Wasn't happenstance, then."

"Nope."

"An' this grand caper ye was planning?"

"Souvenir shops. The places selling the T-shirts and hats and mugs for the inaugural first few weeks of The Liberty. I have a friend who's really, really good with computers. She managed to slow the transmissions to a crawl between the merch shops and the credit card companies. Means more people got frustrated and just paid with cash. The Liberty hadn't planned on that, and had to come up with a place to store all that cash until they could call up an armored car company to take it to their bank."

Dez grins. "That's fair brilliant, that."

"The people making minimum wage, working the merch shops, would get paid. And the conference center itself is insured. So nobody gets hurt but I make bank."

"You've a nefarious streak in you. I quite like it."

"The reason I'm telling you this is: I did my reconnaissance. There are maintenance shafts and airflow ducts running parallel to the light-rail tunnel between here and the airport. They dead-end before they reach the airport, so we can't get out that way. But if we can get into the maintenance shafts, and if I can see one of the bomb sensors, I might be able to deactivate it."

"What would ye need?"

She gives him a shopping list.

Dez covers his mouth with one massive palm to avoid laughing out loud. He wipes tears from the corners of his eyes.

"Jay-sus, but you're a smashing bit! Ye know that?"

"There's a compliment lurking in there somewhere."

"That there is. Shall we fore to go?"

ADMINISTRATION OFFICES
THE LIBERTY

The former Russian army captain, Oborin, returns from a scouting expedition and calls Colonel Maksim Baranov, who is running the operation from afar.

"Sergei's dead, all right. We found him next to that bar. It looks like he fell off the roof and broke his neck."

Baranov's guttural voice cuts through the lines, "He was attacked, obviously."

The captain shrugs. "I thought so, too, but his weapons and armor were still there. If he'd been attacked, surely whoever it was would have taken them."

He lets the colonel ponder that. It does make sense to Oborin, but he still finds it hard to believe that a seasoned soldier and sniper would trip and fall off a roof.

"This seems . . . doubtful," the colonel says, but leaves it at that.

Oborin checks his watch. "When do you call the Americans back?"

"Fifteen minutes."

"Very good, sir. I tasked Dmitri with covering the roof over that bar. We should have no blind spots for the public areas outside the buildings now."

"Good. And the men you sent to that theater? For that British fellow?"

"They called in. No sign of this Brit. Limerick, was it? Or of a thief named Valdivia. Also, no hostages. And the man I left watching them had been attacked, stripped of his weaponry, and probably is concussed."

"Then the sheep are showing some spine. Well, good for them."

"They're not the only ones, sir. We've reports that some hostages moved into the kitchen of a martini bar and the door to the kitchen's been barricaded. We can't get to them without redeploying some of the explosives to get that door open."

Colonel Baranov laughs over the line. "So what? They can't leave the mall. As long as they make no more trouble for us, I say let them hide."

"Understood, sir."

"Thank you, Captain. Let me know when your team is back from that theater."

"Aye, sir." Oborin hangs up.

CHAPTER 14

It takes them seemingly forever, but Dez and Cat move quietly and cautiously through The Liberty, backtracking when they have no other choice, lying low when necessary, but eventually making it to the exterior of two of the convention center's eateries: a run-of-the-mill O'Malley Burgers and a Michelin-starred restaurant featuring French cuisine. Again, Dez watches Cat's back as she picks a rear door to get them into the French restaurant.

"The longer this thing goes on, the more chance of—*dios!*" Cat comes up short as they spot a cadaver in a rear hallway of the restaurant. This one is a woman wearing a Ms. Marvel T-shirt and a paper wrist bracelet for the comic book convention. So a hostage, not a terrorist. Dez takes a knee and checks for a pulse. She was shot twice in the chest.

He takes Cat's hand and helps her step over the corpse but not to step in blood. Cat avoids looking at the body.

They get to the spacious and clean kitchen and find eight hostages;

an array of customers, cooks, and front-of-the-house staff. Dez enters, slingshot leading, but finds no guards here.

"Who are you?" a man in a chef's white jacket asks. He hoists a wicked-looking meat cleaver.

Dez puts away his weapon. "We're the good guys, mate. We've been in contact with the police outside. We need t'get a few items, then we're off again."

The chef doesn't look like he's buying it. "Bullshit. He shot the last person who tried to step out of here."

"He?" Dez tenses. "The guard who shot that woman outside. Where is he now?"

Everyone glances around and shrugs. Someone, possibly the restaurant hostess, says, "He took a call on his radio. He was speaking what sounded like . . . Russian? I don't know. Then he left and told us, if we so much as peek out the door, he'll kill us."

Dez and Cat exchange looks. It could be that Dez's hit-and-run tactics are whittling away at the Russians forces, and they've had to move their men around to cover the ground. Dez nods to her, and Cat starts gathering what she needs.

The chef says, "What are you planning?"

"A distraction of sorts. You lot stay here until the police tell ye otherwise, please."

The big man waves the meat cleaver toward Cat, whose eyes go wide. She stops in her tracks. "This is my kitchen. She goes nowhere until you tell me what the fuck's going on!"

"Don't wave that thing, my son. Isn't a toy."

The man moves pugnaciously toward Dez. He's a good five inches taller. As he approaches, Dez smells whiskey. The chef's been seeking Dutch courage. "You give me some straight answers! Right this second! Tell me—"

Dez grabs the wrist holding the cleaver and applies pressure with the pads of his index and middle fingers to a nerve cluster on the inside of his wrist. The man's hand spasms open and he drops the cleaver.

Dez snatches it in midair. He twists the man's wrist before releasing it. The chef stumbles backward, holding his pained arm to his chest.

"Here." Dez reverses the cleaver and hands it to the hostess. "Gingerly, love. 'Tis sharp, this."

Cat has the supplies she needs and nervously swipes at the twin, curved strands of hair that bracket her face.

"We're off," Dez tells the hostess. "Stay here. The police know about the situation and a hostage negotiator is doing her magic. Be patient. And make sure t'pass around some of that whiskey, aye? Do everyone a bit of good."

Dez does the heavy lifting of the goods Cat will need, and they exit the kitchen.

The least attractive building within the glass walls of The Liberty is the administration building, well off the beaten paths of the tourists, tucked into a corner nearest the airport. Unlike everything else in this pristine, new, artificial environment, this building is a middle child, hiding away from the luster of its siblings.

An understated plaque by the front door reads THE LIBERTY—A FLAG FAMILY EXPERIENCE.

Dez whispers, "What's the Flag Family?"

"Just a European holding company. They finance super-big projects like this. See? I wasn't even trying to rip off Americans with my heist."

Dez grins at her.

Try as they might, it doesn't seem as if Dez and Cat can get to this building through subterfuge alone. Especially since, every time they hide, Dez has to set down the kitchen goods he's hauling, which include a canister of liquid nitrogen, used for some frozen desserts, a five-gallon jug of water, and a hemp bag filled with dry ice.

Finally, seeing no other alternative, Dez is forced to take down a roving guard with one of the flying bolts from his slingshot. He hides the body in a wheeled garbage bin as Cat picks yet another lock and gets them inside.

"Why aren't you taking their guns?" she asks softly, peering into the dim light of the building.

"No silencers. Can't fire 'em without giving me location away." He hefts the makeshift slingshot. "This works just as well but quieter."

They spot a door marked STAIRS. Dez goes first, opening the door gingerly, checking up and down. Then steps back to let Cat lead the way. She takes him down beneath the admin building.

"The slingshot works as well as a pistol," she whispers. "But there's going to come a time when you'll need one of those assault rifles. And no offense to your David-and-Goliath act, but when that day comes, the slingshot's going to be a joke."

She leads him unerringly through a warren of dimly lit corridors.

"David used a sling, not a slingshot. An' I'm hoping your crystal ball is cloudy, Cat. If we get to a position where we need one of them rifles, it'll be because we're facing a lot more rifles. And that'll be a fight we won't win."

"This way," she says, and uses her picks to open yet another door. This one is marked ENVIRONMENTAL SYSTEMS—LIGHT RAIL.

They round a corner and she skids to a halt, throwing her hand over her mouth.

Dez looks past her at another corpse. A man, this time. Shot in the chest. He goes to his haunches and checks for a pulse. Nothing.

He glances up and sees a bullet embedded in the wall, not four feet from the dead man's head. He frowns, draws his folding knife, and pries the bullet out of the wall.

He rolls the ruined bit of metal in his palm.

"What?" he hears over his shoulder.

"Wrong sort of bullet, Cat. This here's a forty-five. Russians been using the Russian nine-millimeter seven-N-twenty-one round."

"So what?"

Dez reaches for the dead man's wallet and checks his ID. The name means nothing to him. On a hunch, he slips the Maryland driver's license into his messenger bag. "Dunno. But every last one of them fuckers we've met used the same gun, the same round. Which makes tactical sense. You send a unit into hostile territory, all your forces should be able to swap ammunition as needed. Yeah? Why would someone be waltzing 'round here with a forty-five?"

He stands and scratches his head. "A mystery for another day. Which way?"

Not looking directly at the corpse, Cat leads the way.

The maintenance shaft they're inside is a nearly tubular tunnel, eight feet high and wide, with a flat walking surface. The walls and ceiling are one curved face. Dangling work lights are set every twenty feet. A great deal of equipment needed for the maintenance of a light-rail train system is stored herein. They spot flashlights set in a charging station. Also largish tool kits.

"I wish we could get all the way to the airport this way," she says.

Cat takes a flashlight, then leans in close to Dez. She wears no perfume, he notices. When this thief breaks into a room, she leaves no evidence behind. Not even a scent. "There are air vents along the way," she whispers. "We're parallel with the light-rail tunnel to the airport. If they've posted guards, we'll have to do this quiet—"

"As a Cat?"

"Now you're getting it."

Dez carries the heavy stuff. Cat leads, using the flashlight only sporadically.

They don't hear anything coming from the train tunnel. No trains, obviously. Public transportation systems have been shut down since the hostage crisis began.

Cat softly kneels at each wire-mesh enclosed air vent and listens for a moment. Then shines her flashlight through, looking for something. She makes it to the fifth air vent, down on one knee, peering in. She nods. "There it is."

Dez goes down on his haunches and looks at the circle of light she's shining into the train tunnel. He spots the electronic sensor, less than three feet away, on the far side of the mesh screen. It rests on a standing barrel of deicer. The device is no larger than a domestic smoke alarm.

"Seen its kind," he says. "Motion sensor. Not audio-tripped."

"So have I. Let's set this up."

With his own flashlight, Dez goes back to some of the maintenance equipment they'd passed. He finds a small array of wheelbarrows and rolls two of them to Cat's position. She's spotted a mess of transparent plastic tubing.

Dez sets the dry ice in the belly of one of the wheelbarrows. Cat sets one end of her tubing against the ice, then feeds the tube through the mesh, slowly, slowly drawing nearer to the sensor.

Dez uncaps the water jug he's been hauling around and glugs the water into the wheelbarrow.

As the water touches the dry ice, fog begins to roil.

Dez upends the second wheelbarrow and sets it atop the first, as a lid.

In almost no time, they spot dry ice fog flowing through the tube and out into the train tunnel.

"Feckin' brilliant," Dez whispers.

Cat grins but tries to hide it.

When the fog has blinded the bomb sensor, Dez takes the screwdriver he'd hidden in his boot and undoes the screws holding the wire mesh screen in place. He slowly removes it.

Cat takes the canister of liquid nitrogen and reaches into the train tunnel. Her arms disappear into the fog, invisible past her elbows.

"Liquid nitrogen. I swiped this trick from you in Madrid."

Dez hears the sizzle as they begin coating the fog-blinded sensor with the super-cold nitrogen.

Dez hears the crackle of the sensor and the barrel it's resting on as they freeze.

"Work gloves?"

Dez spotted some earlier, thick and well-used leather; on her small hands they look enormous and comical.

She reaches into the fog again and, a moment later, draws out the frozen sensor.

She moves slowly but without hesitation. To Dez, it looks like she's practicing tai chi.

She holds the sensor between her thickly gloved hands. Dez shines his flash on it.

"Turn it over."

She does, slowly.

Dez peers at it.

"Okay. Let's leave it on this side, aye?"

He removes the upended wheelbarrow, a fog bank spilling free. Cat gingerly sets the bomb sensor next to the dry ice, and Dez covers it again.

"You know the frequency they're using for the sensors?"

"Do," he says, smiling. "If I can get to these feckers' frequency jammers, I can unblock communications but block the bomb sensors."

Cat removes one glove and makes a fist.

Dez knuckle-bumps her.

She starts back down the maintenance shaft, the way they came. "I haven't had much luck with partners, Limerick. But you don't totally suck at this."

CHAPTER 15

NEWARK INTERNATIONAL P6 PARKING LOT

FBI Special Agent Stella Ansara is talking to a man in civilian clothes who looks like they chafe and are alien to him. His bearing and haircut scream career military. Stella herself looks fairly unhappy, even by the standards of being the woman in charge at ground zero of the biggest news story on the planet.

She and the Pentagon guy are standing outside the Incident Command truck, arguing. One of her guys leans out of the rear door of the big vehicle. "Chief? Russians are on the horn."

Stella Ansara and the Pentagon Guy—who won't even tell her his goddamn name—head into the trailer.

The hostage-taker's call is on speaker and all three redundant recording devices are activated.

"This is Special Agent Ansara."

She hears the same male, Russian voice as before. "Special Agent. By now, you will have heard from the Office of Naval Intelligence.

I suspect one of their officers has even been flown to New Jersey, and is with you now."

Stella and the Pentagon Guy exchange looks. The guy shakes his head: *Tell him nothing.*

"I can confirm that is accurate," Stella says, enjoying the Pentagon Guy's flash of anger.

"I told you that the Office of Naval Intelligence would bring you valuable information, yes?"

"You did say that, yes."

"Here is what he told you: He told you that he has never heard of the *Kocatka* and has nothing helpful to share with you."

The Pentagon Guy mutters, "Jesus."

"That's exactly right," Stella says, now realizing that she's the chief negotiator with the Russian terrorists, and also with a military intelligence unit. The taxpayers do not pay her enough for this job.

The Russian sounds pleased with himself. "You are a highly intelligent woman, Special Agent. So you are asking yourself the obvious question: A secretary on a telephone call could have told you that Naval Intelligence knows nothing. They could have emailed that to you. They could have texted it to you."

"But," she cuts in, for Pentagon Guy's benefit, and to help establish rapport with the Russian, "if a guy flies here from Virginia, to tell me the Pentagon knows nothing about the *Kocatka,* then of course they know everything there is to know about the *Kocatka.*"

She delivers this line staring into Pentagon Guy's eyes.

The Russian laughs. "Very good! I am grateful the powers-that-be sent you to negotiate, Special Agent. If I were dealing with a fool, this would take longer. Since I am not, we can move more quickly."

Stella says, "We heard shots fired. Several times."

"Yes," he says with chilling candor. "We had a civilian try to break free from one of the gift shops, and so of course one of my snipers shot her. We had a man dressed as a chef emerge from a restaurant, telling us he had information to exchange for his freedom. So one of my ground forces killed him. When people do not obey us to the letter, they die. This is a very simple rule."

Stella says, "Understand me. We want to find a way out of this. A way that serves your needs, and also ours. But every time you kill a civilian you move the goalposts. You keep killing people, and there may be no way out of this that doesn't involve the deaths of your people."

The Russian laughs. "Excellent. You do understand the rules of engagement. I am grateful. Yes, you are looking for a way out of this that serves your needs, and also ours. But that is not what we want. We want a way out of this that serves our needs only. And now you understand this. Any effort on your part to reach any other end will increase the number of dead hostages. Now we are, as you Americans say, on the same page."

Stella wills herself to calm down.

The Russian says, "The person from the Office of Naval Intelligence. I will speak to that person now?"

"Hold on. He's outside my trailer. I'll have him shown in."

She mutes her end of the call.

Pentagon Guy says, "Clear the room and stop the audio recording, I think I can—"

Stella steps into his space and drops her voice. She says, "Bitch, listen to me very carefully."

Pentagon Guy takes an involuntary step back. Stella can see no rank or insignia, but she assumes this guy is a full-bird colonel or better. Likely no one has challenged him like this in a very long time.

"At this very moment, I do not give two shits about national security. My goal—my only goal—is to get the remainder of the hostages out of there. I'm a hostage negotiator. The Russians are my opponent and are keeping facts from me. That's a given. You're either in alliance with me, and are not keeping secrets. Or you're an opponent, and you are."

She waits to see how he'll react. He tries a *now, now calm down* patriarchal smile and stiffens when he sees her give him a glare as abrasive as sandpaper. He changes tack, holds up both palms. "Pax. All right. I hear you."

Without looking at her control panel, Stella stabs the Mute button. "He's here," she tells the Russian, without stepping out of Pentagon Guy's space. "Go ahead."

"Sir," says the Russian. "You are holding the *Kocatka* and her crew somewhere in the Aegean. With the help of the Turks. We suspect it is moored near the island of Lesbos or near Izmir. You will release the ship and her crew—and her captain—within twenty-four hours. When she has reached Russian waters at the port of Sevastopol, we will begin releasing hostages from The Liberty. Ten at a time. If the *Kocatka* and all hands are not accounted for in twenty-four hours, we begin executing hostages in The Liberty. Ten at a time."

The Pentagon Guy clears his throat. "Well, there's a lot to unpack there. I'm from the U.S. Department of Defense and we don't know about this . . . is it a ship? Or its crew, or captain, or whatever. As for whether the port of Sevastopol is in, quote, 'Russian waters,' well, let's agree to disagree. If you can tell me more about this situation, I'll run it up the flagpole and see if anyone knows anything about it. Does that sound doable?"

The Russian says, "Twenty-three hours, fifty-eight minutes."

And disconnects.

CHAPTER 16

Dez and Cat are in the subbasement of the administration building of The Liberty. Dez has stopped to ponder their situation. Besides, they found a twenty-four pack of bottled water and both realize they're in need of a break. They sit five feet apart in the darkened room, atop huge boxes of what appear to be napkins and placemats embossed with the convention center's logo.

"This," Dez says, making a rounded, all-encompassing gesture with his water bottle, "is the admin building. Likely where the fuckers are headquartered."

She sips water, wipes her lips with the back of her hand. "Makes sense."

"Indisputable fact: Runnin' around out there, in the wild, means we'll be targets. We could take down a couple more of the Russians. Maybe more than a couple more. But that's small ball."

She nods. "Low-percentage play. There are too many of them, too well armed. We could cut their numbers down a little, but that's not the same as stopping them. And when I say, *we,* I mean *you.*"

"Exactly."

"Whereas . . ." Cat makes the same all-encompassing gesture with her water bottle.

"Aye. This building is ground zero."

They sit and sip.

"Their frequency jammers are here," she says. "I've used freq-jammers on heists. I know what they look like, how they work."

"As do I. Them jammers is what's keeping the bomb sensors connected t'the bombs. *If*—and this is a mighty big *if*—if the Russians told Agent Ansara the truth."

Cat shakes her head. She undoes her ponytail, shakes her hair out. "I wouldn't bluff with something like that. Bluff and they call you even once, then the cops are making their incursion through the light-rail tunnel."

Dez smiles. "I've met few people think as tactically as you. At least outside of the military."

She takes the compliment, then she sobers up. Her box of napkins and placemats is so large, her sneakers dangle a couple inches off the floor. She bounces her heels off the stiff packing material, contemplating.

"A few things you should know," she says. "One is: I am not the good guy here. I'm not a heroine. I'm a criminal. I'm self-centered. If I saw a good way of getting out of this and leaving everyone behind, you included, I would take it."

"Nothing wrong with that," Dez says. "Ye are helping, an' that's a fact. Even if it's an act of enlightened self-interest."

"Second thing to know about me: I do not like the cops. I do not trust them. In my life, I can't think of one time any cop has ever acted in genuine human concern for me, or the kids I grew up with, or any member of my family."

Dez says, "I've met more'n my fair share of police I trust, and who've had me back."

"Then you didn't grow up Hispanic in LA."

"Truth," Dez concedes, nodding. "Let me put it another way: I don't trust anyone based on their job title. But I always start from a position of trust. I've met more good people than I have bad in this world. Tons more. So I start by trusting, an' based on how that's greeted—if it's paid back, or if it's abused—then I adjust my reaction accordingly."

She stares across the space at him. "That's why you trusted me from the jump."

"That's right."

Cat thinks about that. She says, "I start from a position of assuming no one can be trusted and nobody has my back. I was prepared to doubt you in Madrid, but you let my ex-partner and me escape with you from those gunmen. Then you didn't turn me in to British Intelligence when you could have. We're exactly opposites, but we reach the same place. We react: you from a position of trust, me from a position of doubt. We see how it's met. And we act accordingly."

"Sounds about right."

"So the calculus for either of us is the same. We should do what we can to block the bombs and the bomb sensors. And to let the cops know."

Dez shrugs. "How it pencils out for me, too."

She says, "We could get killed doing this."

Dez says, "You steal things, ofttimes from armed people. Yeah? You could get killed doing that."

A beat, and Cat smiles. She sips water to cover it.

"It's just vaguely possible, Desmond Limerick, that we both have psyches fucked up beyond any possible recovery."

Dez grins. "That'd be the fun part, then!"

CHAPTER 17

Dez caps his water bottle and draws his tablet computer. He subconsciously kisses the well-nicked and scratched leather cover before opening it.

Cat notices and smiles.

"Once we get upstairs, might be able to map a grid of strong and weak electromagnetic fields. If I can deduce the pattern, might tell us where the frequency-jamming equipment is."

She says, "It'll be well guarded."

Dez shrugs. "Will it? Outside the walls of this whacking great convention center, there's the police an' federal authorities. Within the walls, the Russians came thinkin' they'd be dealin' with sheep. No idea how many of the opposition's in here, but best guess is: They need their men spread out widely."

Cat's thinking. Dez can tell by the way her eyes dart around, as if seeking clues in the low ceiling of the basement storage room.

"What?"

"I staked this place out before you got here. Remember?"

He nods.

"I know where the master control is for the building security system. If I can get to it, I might be able to set off alarms all over; on every floor. Lure them away from you."

"That'd help mightily, aye. Shall we?"

Dez packs his tablet away and moves to the door. Cat follows.

He opens the door and peers out. Sees no one.

From his shoulder, Cat whispers, "Remember what I said: If I see a way out of this for myself, I'm taking it. I'll wish you all the luck in the world, big guy. But I look out for numero uno first."

"Fair."

They sneak up to the first basement floor.

There, Dez takes a knee and draws his tablet. He begins typing away on it as it rests on his upturned other knee.

"I've never seen a computer like that."

"Bespoke," he says, typing.

Soon, looking over his shoulder, Cat begins to see the three-dimensional outline of the mall's admin building; the four stories aboveground, the two below.

Overlaid on this is a warping and waving set of lines and curves that look, to Cat, like nothing so much as a meteorologist's radar map of high- and low-pressure systems. She says as much.

"Very good analogy. These are strong and weak areas of electromagnetic energy," he whispers. "Watch what happens as I slide it from lower frequencies to higher ones."

The bubbles overlaid on the building shift and change. Some grow and some shrink. Again, like a weather map.

"There it is," Dez says. "Mobile phones in the States use cellular bands between, say, six hundred megahertz to thirty-nine gigahertz. Yeah? Now, your voice-over-internet system runs in the range of, say, two an' a half gigs to a bit less than six gigs. Them fuckers is blockin' both. And as I swing back an' forth between the higher an' lower bands, I can spot . . . there."

He points to his screen.

"It looks like Jackson Pollock's cat barfed a hairball on your screen. These squiggles don't mean anything to me."

"Third floor," Dez explains. "Southwest corner. That's where the jammers are."

"If you say so, Reed Richards."

He grins and stands. "That'd make you the Invisible Woman, yeah? Where d'you have to be to play merry hob with the building security?"

"This level. Over that direction. And I can do it by crawling around inside the walls."

"Still don't want to take a gun with you?"

"Never," she says. "Let's go before I talk myself out of this."

Dez leads the way. They spot a sentry and lie low as the man passes. He's jiggling doorknobs; on basic foot patrol, not looking for them specifically.

"Access to the maintenance tunnel is in the valve room," Cat whispers. "That way."

Dez still leads. They get to metal door she mentioned. Cat quickly picks the lock.

"Right, love. I'll be on the third floor. Give me fifteen minutes t'get up there."

She nods. "I'll have them chasing their tails."

"Good." He starts to back off. Cat touches his shoulder, then impetuously leans in and kisses him on the cheek.

"*Buena suerte.*"

Dez winks at her. "It's good to be good but better to be lucky. Ta. When ye get in there, stay put as long as ye can. I'll fetch you when the coast's clear."

She nods and closes the valve room door, separating them.

Dez gets moving.

It's as he guessed: He still has no idea how many troops the Russians brought, but he runs into precious few of them inside the administration building. The Liberty Convention Center is far too vast to condense their forces here. He spots one roving guard on the ground floor and evades him.

In the southwest corner of the third floor, he happens upon a door marked CONFERENCE CENTER SECURITY. Makes sense. This will be where all of the mall's closed-circuit camera feeds are sent. Plus, like as not, the central distribution hub for the mall's Wi-Fi routers.

Dez draws his slingshot and a quarter of a pound of iron in the form of a blended nut and bolt, nocked into the stretchy rubber gasket. He inhales and shoulders open the door.

Only one Russian guard is in here, and his rifle rests a good five feet away from him. Dez puts the bolt in the middle of the man's chest and he falls out of his rolling chair, hitting the floor hard.

Dez closes the door behind him and rams another chair under the door handle. He crosses to the man on the ground, who is holding his chest, moaning in pain. Dez relieves him of his pistol.

"My guess is, whoever's behind this feckin' flea circus, they'd've picked men who speak English. Do you, my son?"

The guy has at least one broken rib, but manages to generate enough lung capacity to hiss, "Fuck . . . you . . ."

"Splendid! Mind telling me what the end goal here is?"

"Will . . . kill . . . you . . ."

"Or not." Dez makes a fist and pops the guy in the head. Dez knows how to put some power into a short, choppy blow. The guy loses consciousness.

Dez takes a quick look around the room. A closet door is open and he finds two dead men therein, both shot in the head, both wearing shirts with The Liberty's logo over their breasts.

Dez takes the seat of the unconscious Russian and studies the monitors before him. It's a wide array of high-resolution, black-and-white images from cameras. The monitors themselves stretch out four feet in either direction of the chair, and each monitor can show the feed of nine security cameras, all of which appear to be mounted on high and peering down at the public spaces, the conference facilities, the restaurants, hotels, and shops that make up this place.

He also spots the very thing he's been looking for: a high-end device with Cyrillic lettering has been plugged into another monitor, which itself is marked WI-FI SERVICES. This lovely thing, the size of a toaster, is what's jamming the frequencies for all communications in and out of The Liberty.

Dez is still studying it when an alarm goes off. He rolls the chair to his left and checks.

The security alarm just began bleating in the second subbasement of the admin building, the level that includes access to the light-rail tunnel to the airport.

As Dez starts to grin, a second alarm goes off in the ground-floor lobby of the building.

Cat. Fucking with the admin building's alarm system. With luck, that should send the Russians scrambling away from Dez's current location.

He's starting to really admire Cat Valdivia. Her habit of stealing that which belongs to others seems like a bit of a moral failing, but who is Dez to judge?

Dez pulls out his tablet computer and brings up a program that lets him do quick mathematical equations. He checks his sums, then rolls his chair back to the Russian frequency jammer.

He notes the frequencies that serve American mobile phones,

and also voice-over-internet services. Those are the ones he wants to reopen.

Which is when he spots a small, yellow Post-it note on one of the frequency jammer's dials. It reads TEAГO.

Whatever that means—and Dez neither speaks nor reads Russian—the frequency beneath that Post-it note is open.

Cat's fake alarms in the lobby and second subbasement are still blaring, drawing the Russians away, so Dez gets busy. He reestablishes the frequencies for telecommunications. Then shuts down the frequency used by the bomb sensors in the light-rail tunnel.

Next, he removes the radio from the belt of the man he decked. The Russians' comms include a four-digit lock-out code, so Dez hasn't been tempted to take one before this; he couldn't listen to it if he'd wanted to. But he pries the backing off the communications device and, right above the recess for its twin AA batteries, he spots the frequency they use.

He draws his phone and calls the hostage negotiator back.

"This is the FBI. Is this the man with whom I've been speaking?"

"It's Dez Limerick, ma'am. I'm in the admin building and I've a terrible apology t'make. I completely disobeyed your orders. Brazenly, if I'm being honest. You've every right to be angry with me. Wouldn't blame you in the least."

He can hear Stella Ansara sigh over the line. "If you don't put me into cardiac arrest, Mr. Limerick, it won't be for lack of trying."

"The communications are back up. Cell phones an' internet." Dez glances at the frequency jammer again, and the Post-it note. TEAГO. What the hell is that, he wonders, and why is it bugging him? "Also, ma'am, I've isolated the frequency used by the bombs and their sensors. If the Russian bastards—language, sorry—if they're tellin' ye the truth, the hostages wired to bombs should be safe. That's a huge helping of *if*, mind ye."

He waits.

Stella says, "My God. Yes, Mr. Limerick. We're showing that the communications bands are wide open again! Do the Russians know this?"

"Not yet but they will, soon, when the hostages' phones start ringing."

"All right. This gives us an edge. Albeit it a brief one. Thank you, Mr. Limerick."

He hears her issuing orders to her people.

"Special Agent, ma'am?"

"I'm listening."

"The Russians are sporting communications rigs. I've not yet done it, but I can block their own frequency, as well. If ye were to make an incursion, I can cut off their comms. Just let me know when. But I won't be able t'hold this position forever. And if I'm overrun, they'll get the comms back."

"Understood, Mr. Limerick. Hold on a second."

Dez waits.

The Cyrillic note, TEAГО. That's really bothering him. He takes a telephone snapshot of it.

Just as he does, his phone vibrates. He has an incoming call from the New York City Police Department.

He glances down and sees the unconscious Russian's phone, partially visible in his trouser pocket, light up.

Dez puts Stella Ansara on hold and answers the new call.

It's a male voice on this call, and it's a recording.

"Attention, all civilians. This is the police. A combination of police forces and the National Guard will begin to retake The Liberty Convention Center in thirty seconds. All civilians: Get on the ground and cover your heads. If you can blockade doors, do so first. Repeat: all civilians. This is the police. A combination of police forces and the National—"

Dez calls the rock 'n' roll legend Calvin Willow. "'Tis Limerick. Ye heard?"

"I did, bud. Still where you left me, backstage."

"Stay down. This'll be over, for good or ill, shortly." He hangs up and calls Cat Valdivia.

"Cat, you heard?"

"Yup," she whispers. "Do the Russians know?"

"They will soon. Stay hidden."

"That's what alley cats do, Dez."

She hangs up.

Dez's phone pulses. He returns to the call to the Incident Command.

"It's Ansara. We are go for incursion in thirty seconds."

Dez reaches for the Russians' frequency jammer and shuts down their own communications grid.

He wheels back to the CC camera monitors. "I've got eyes on all of the security monitors, ma'am. The largest contingent of Russians I'm seeing are, ah . . ." He squints at the black-and-white images, scanning through them quickly. "At least six of the fuckers are outside the largest of the assembly halls. Ye've got four more in the lobby of the five-star hotel. And, ah, looks like four more . . . Scratch that, five more in the lobby of the admin buildin' itself."

Drawn there, he knows, by Cat and her false-flag alarms.

"We appreciate this, Limerick. Go for incursion in fifteen seconds. Keep your head down."

"Always do, ma'am."

Another lie. Dez really is due for some kind of act of contrition.

Just a few years back, a lot of public places in America underwent riots. He has an idea. He stands and studies all of the control panels and monitors throughout the security room. And he spots what he's looking for.

RIOT LOCK-OUT, ADMIN, LOBBY.

Dez flips three switches. He returns to the camera monitors.

If he's guessed right, the five Russians in the lobby are now trapped there, held in by reinforced doors that are designed to hold back mass protesters. Grinning, he peers at the screen. One of the trapped Russians is a barrel-chested man with no neck and a massive mustache, his hair slicked back. He appears to be shouting orders.

This next bit should be fun to watch.

CHAPTER 18

Oborin, the former Russian captain, and four of his men are in the lobby of The Liberty admin building. Glass and steel panels have slid shut over the exterior exit, and also over the route back to the elevators and stairs. Oborin has tried shooting the glass, to no effect.

Their forces, spread out around the conference center, do have explosives. But Oborin and his crew didn't keep any for themselves. Why should they have?

Dez takes the stairs to the ground floor and spots the glass-and-steel panels that he'd tripped into place. He places a palm on one pane; it's vaguely oily to the touch, and the light coming through it is slightly too blue. This is high-grade bulletproof Plexiglas, he knows.

He spots an intercom. He opens the cover with his tools, pulls out a few wires, cuts and crosses them.

"Excuse me?"

The five Russians turn and spot him. All five carry automatic rifles.

Dez waves enthusiastically through the partition. "An' which of ye might have the biggest swingin' cock of the lot?"

Oborin storms his way.

"Ah! You'd be the leader of this here panto! How d'ye do, sir. Desmond Aloysius Limerick, at your service."

Oborin braces his automatic rifle against his hip and rakes the Plexiglas panel. The bullets tumble away, barely scratching the material.

"D'you mind?" Dez holds his hands over his ears. "Bit loud that! Was tryin' to tell yez something!"

Oborin glowers at him.

"FBI an' the U.S. military are storming the convention center, sir. Ye've no comms, no way t'reach your men. 'Fraid this is the end of the line for you lot."

Oborin responds in English. "Who the fuck are you?"

"No one of import. Mind tellin' me what this was all about then, guv'nor?"

Oborin draws his handgun from off his hip, steps up to the Plexiglas, and aims at Dez's forehead. The barrel of his gun is two inches from the glass.

"Are you positive we are defenseless, little man?"

"Not positive, no."

Oborin fires.

The bullet ricochets off the Plexiglas and slams back into his hand and his gun. The gun goes spinning away. Several of Oborin fingers go with it.

"Feelin' a bit more positive of late, though."

★　★　★

As the FBI's Hostage Rescue Team, the state National Guard, and local law enforcement forces storm the convention center, Liv Gelman calls Ray Harker.

"Time's up, love. Rendezvous, plan A."

Ray says, "We didn't get them all. We gotta stay."

"Stay and die, and we won't get them all. Stay and live, and we might, yet. Rendezvous, plan A."

A pause. "I am not putting it on."

"Rendezvous," she says slowly. "Plan A. Kindly."

By the time FBI agents spot Ray Harker, he's wearing a horizontally striped shirt and a paper hat and a bubblegum pink apron. Stitched across his chest is the logo for the Polar Bear Ice Cream Shoppe.

Liv stands next to him in an identical shirt and cap and apron. Plus, she stopped to get a single-scoop cone. Pistachio.

"It adds to the overall je ne sais quoi," she whispers to Ray, licking her cone.

They're escorted out with the other civilian survivors of the terrorist attack on The Liberty.

CHAPTER 19

"The news at the top of the hour: It's been half a day since a combination of city, county and state police, plus the National Guard, ended the terrorist attack on The Liberty Convention Center in Newark, New Jersey. A spokesperson for the governor of New Jersey addressed the media less than ninety minutes ago and reported that eleven civilians were killed. Making this the deadliest foreign terrorist attack on U.S. soil since nine-eleven.

"A total of thirty people with Russian, Georgian, or Hungarian citizenship were involved in the attack. Of that group, twenty-two were killed and eight are in custody. Officials, speaking on condition of anonymity, say most of the mercenaries are former members of the Russian army and currently serve in a semi-independent military organization, the Leningrad Konsortsium, which has been linked to violence, military incursions, and terrorism in several African and Middle Eastern nations.

"The Leningrad Konsortsium was in the news recently when Russian media reported its only warship, the Killer Whale—*or Kocatka, in*

Russian—was allegedly lost in the Black Sea with no survivors. The Russian government has claimed the American Navy captured the Kocatka, with the aid of the Turkish navy, but officials in Washington and Ankara have denied that."

CHAPTER 20

Dez is taken into custody but it's done gently. Handcuffed, yes. Held in an interrogation cell, yes. But Dez has been arrested and handcuffed and interrogated by several police agencies since arriving in the States.

FBI Special Agent Stella Ansara tells Newark investigators about Dez's contributions to the ending of the hostage crisis, and Sir Richard Corbyn-Smith, director of operations for British MI6, vouches for him, too, and so he's held for just a little over an hour and given a perfectly fine cup of coffee and, oddly enough, some surprisingly good snickerdoodle cookies while he's inside. As interrogations go, this one is top drawer.

They ask Dez to stay around the Newark area for a while, and that's okay by him. He's got a head stuffed with questions and too few answers, so he wasn't planning on going anywhere anyway. He can't stay at The Liberty Suites hotel because the convention center is now the world's largest crime scene. He asks them if staying in

Manhattan is the equivalent of *don't leave town for a while* and they assure him it is.

He also sends a note to Stella Ansara, asking her if she'll let someone in federal law enforcement circles know that he'd like to talk to them about something he saw at the convention center.

As the combined local and federal SWAT teams invaded the center, finding the Russians in disarray and without their communications or leadership, Dez had texted Cat and told her to lie low where she was—hidden in the walls of the first basement level of the admin building. She hadn't responded. When Dez was taken into custody for questioning, he hadn't had a chance to check on her.

He does so now, as he takes the train from Newark to New York's Penn Station. He alerts her to where he's staying. He checks in with just his messenger bag. His bass guitar and all the rest of his clothes are under seal at the crime scene.

He sleeps like the dead. Monday was, by pretty much anyone's definition, one hell of a day.

Dez scopes out a big-and-tall men's shop on his mobile, buys extra T-shirts and underwear. Also a waterproof, waxed denim jacket because it's getting cooler, and an extra pair of black jeans. He settles into a not-too-pricy boutique hotel within walking distance of Penn Station.

As he swipes the key card and enters for the first time, his phone vibrates. He doesn't recognize the number, but it's got the Washington, DC, 202 area code.

"Dez Limerick."

"It's me. Ansara." He recognizes the special agent's voice. "If I didn't say it before, thank for playing eyes and ears for us at The Liberty yesterday."

"Helped a bit. Mostly hid and quaked in fear."

"You've got something you want to discuss?"

He tells her where he is, and they agree to meet at a coffee shop only a few blocks away.

The coffee joint is one of those perfectly pleasant places Dez has found throughout the United States: quiet, a little bit hipsterish, with a cool Spotify vibe and about a dozen types of coffees and teas. He gets a light roast coffee with sugar and cream and waits.

The woman who walks in and spots him—she was given his description, likely—is tall and athletic, dark of skin and hair, of Middle Eastern descent, he's guessing, and possibly midforties. She's quite lovely, her hair straight and to her shoulders, wearing a power suit with black sneakers that have been cleverly camouflaged to look like dress shoes. Her fitted jacket rides in such a way that he spots the outline of the holster clipped to her belt in back.

He rises, offers a hand. "Dez Limerick."

"Stella Ansara. And it's nice to finally put a face to the voice." She produces ID to prove she is who she says she is.

"Can I get ye a—"

"I'll get it."

She gets a plain black tea, joining him at his window-side table.

"The leader of them Russians? Colonel Baranov?"

Stella shakes her head. "He's gone. We don't think he was ever there. He was running that mission from elsewhere. But we've locked down the U.S. borders. He's not going anywhere."

Dez has drawn his tablet computer from his messenger bag. He brings up the photo he shot of the Russians' frequency jammer. He explains to her what the device is and how it works. She nods a lot.

"Take a wee look at this Post-it note." He uses his thumb and forefinger to zoom in on the photo. Printed on the note is the word ТЕАГО.

Stella squints at the image. She draws cheaters out of her purse and squints at it again. "What's that say?"

"It's Cyrillic. I don't read Russian so I had to look it up. For the most part, it's a lot like English. The T is a T, the E is an E, the A is an A, the O is an O.

"This letter?" she uses the tip of her pen to point to the *Г*.

"Turns out, that's a G. At least, according to Google."

Stella studies the image a bit. "T-E-A-G-O . . ." Then sits up straight. She turns her nutmeg brown eyes to Dez.

"Thiago."

"Aye. That's it."

"Like the assassin."

"What I was thinkin', aye."

He has her undivided attention. "I looked you up, Mr. Limerick."

"Dez to me friends."

"Earlier this summer, you helped MI6 identify a former CIA officer, a Ray Harker, as Thiago. And because of that, MI6 and the CIA stopped the assassination of . . . ?"

"The Tanzanian president, aye. Didn't capture that bastard, Harker, though."

Stella studies the image some more. "The Russians blocked out one specific frequency and marked it as *Thiago*?"

"No, they kept one specific frequency *open* and marked it thus."

"Why would they do that?"

Dez pulls a Kleenex out of his jeans pocket, sets it on the table. He unfolds it to reveal the .45 slug he pried out of a wall in the basement of The Liberty's admin building. He tells her the story.

"You tampered with evidence, Mr. Limerick."

"People were shooting guns at us, ma'am. Wasn't a lot of time t'worry about protocol."

"Us?" she says. "Over the radio, you said you and a, quote, 'mate,' unquote, were screwing with the Russians. Who else do we have to thank?"

Dez manages not to wince. He doesn't remember saying that to

Stella, but he could well have. He has no intention of bringing Cat into this.

"A lot of hostages did their bit to get us out of there. My contributions weren't as great as all that."

"Uh-huh," she says, and picks up the Kleenex and the slug, peering at it up close through her glasses. "This isn't the same caliber as the other bullets taken from the scene."

"Aye. That's right. Russians was firin' seven-N-twenty-one rounds. This is a forty-five."

She's making notes in the Notes field of her phone.

"Are you saying . . . ? Wait . . . do you believe Ray Harker, or Thiago, was at The Liberty?"

"Dunno. Speculation at best, a patchwork of misinformation at worst. Someone was there, firing a weapon unlike those of the Russians. That someone might've had a communications frequency left open, and it might've been the one marked *Thiago*. I know I'm stringin' together bits and bobs, seein' patterns where there may be none."

He reaches into his messenger bag and produces a Maryland driver's license, sliding it across the table to her side. "Jacob Gaetano. Died in the first basement level of the admin building. Shot with that bullet. Took his driving license."

She looks annoyed now. "You removed evidence, and you searched one of the dead bodies?"

"Did, aye."

"Limerick, for Christ's sake."

He smiles. "I'm no cop. Never trained to be one, have no interest in being one. Don't have to put together legal cases for the crown. I was tryin' to avoid getting meself shot, and tryin' to put a stop to these feckin' Russians, you should excuse me language. This was information worth holding on to whilst I was on the move. They're yours now, if you want 'em."

Stella Ansara clearly wants to admonish him more, but stops herself. She removes a plastic baggie the size of a sandwich bag from her jacket. She adds the slug and the driver's license. She makes notes in her pad, regarding the time and location at which she was given these items.

"This guy, Gaetano, was killed in the first basement level of the admin building?"

Dez nods.

"Okay. I'll coordinate with the Jersey authorities. Get a look at the body. Find out what I can about this guy. But . . ."

"But what I'm suggestin' here sounds far-fetched," Dez concedes. "A host of Russians take over a whacking great conference center an' start killin' hostages. An' in the midst of this, an American assassin goes by the nom de plume Thiago is inside this very same conference center, fulfilling a contract hit? It's comical. It's a farce."

She says, "It's ludicrous."

Dez nods. "Is."

She eyes him. He waits.

She hands him her card. "Send me that photo of the frequency jammer?"

Dez reads her email address, then sends the photo.

She stands, so Dez does, too. "This is worth looking into, Mr. Limerick. And yes, I'm supposed to read you the riot act about removing evidence and moving bodies. But it was essentially a war zone. If this turns out to be anything, we're going to be damn lucky you spotted the anomalies of the bullet and the Post-it note."

Dez sips his doctored coffee. "If it helps, I'll be well pleased. An if it don't, I apologize for wasting your time."

Stella Ansara offers her hand and they shake. She turns and leaves. She's out the door three seconds before she enters again and walks up to him.

"You go by Dez?"

"I do."

She offers her hand again, and again, they shake. "Stella."

Then she leaves for real.

Dez returns to his boutique hotel. He goes to his room and swipes open the door, steps in, and spots Catalina Valdivia cracking open a bottle of Four Roses Single Barrel bourbon. She has two expensive, crystal snifters, into which she pours the amber liquid. Dez is quite sure the only glasses in the room when he left were generic water glasses.

She looks back over her shoulder at him. She gives him the up and down. "New clothes?"

"Aye."

"Ditch them."

CHAPTER 21

Dez is really quite enthusiastic when it comes to having sex with pretty girls. If he were to rate his experience with Catalina Valdivia on a scale of one to ten, with ten being the best, Dez would give his afternoon in bed a three hundred and seven.

He orders room service, telling her she can have anything she likes but, for Dez, brekkers is the only acceptable postcoital food. "Oh!" She looks up from the bedside menu, eyes wide. "Yes! Eggs! Bacon! Absolutely!"

Dez thinks he could fall heavily for any woman who says *Bacon!* with that much enthusiasm.

They sit in bed—Dez in his shreddies, Cat in panties and one of his T-shirts—drinking bourbon and eating scrambled eggs with chives and sourdough toast and crispy bacon. In England, Dez prefers his bacon limply fried and dripping in grease next to baked beans and a grease-soaked tomato slice, but this is the States, and he's just not gonna get that here.

Cat holds up her glass in his direction. Dez lifts his and tinks his glass against hers.

"You saved my life," she says. "Nobody's ever saved my life before."

"That stunt with the false alarms likely saved mine, too, so we're even."

His phone vibes. He checks the incoming. Kansas Jack O'Herlihy. Likely checking to make sure Dez is okay. He can call him back later.

Cat runs a slim hand over some of the bullet and knife scars on his beefy torso. "You've seen some trouble in your life."

He barks a laugh. "I'm sitting up in bed with a gorgeous woman! Drinkin' top-drawer whiskey. I've no complaints."

She studies him. "You're a positive kinda dude."

He chews his food briskly. "Am."

"The cops haven't broken down my door, so . . ."

"Failed t'mention your contributions to that mad business. Typical male: hoggin' all the glory."

She smiles. "Thank you."

"You lost out on your heist. The merchandise cash."

Her eyes twinkle. "Don't be too sure of that."

"You didn't!" He laughs. "Russians shootin' it out, cops barging in, National Guard backin' 'em up. And you made it to the cash stash through all that?"

Cat shrugs. "Girl's gotta eat."

They shower—which leads to more sex—then shower again. By the time Dez has dried off, Cat is gone, leaving behind the expensive bourbon and a dopey smile plastered on Dez's face.

He sets the plates and flatware out in the hallway, and calls back his bandmate Jack O'Herlihy.

"Dez? Hey, how're you doing?"

"Never better."

"Are you in LA?"

The question surprises him. True, Los Angeles is where the men last met and played together. "Manhattan, 'course."

There's a longish pause. Jack says, "The weirdest thing happened."

"Aye?"

"You probably heard about that insanity over in New Jersey? That terrorist attack?"

Dez's mental alarms are going off. "Ye could say that, aye."

"Believe it or not, the Blacktop was supposed to play there. Tonight. We were opening for Calvin Willow, I shit you not."

Dez waits.

"I just checked my band's website. Dez, I can't explain this, but somebody photoshopped your image into a shot of the band. Added your name, too. Like you'd be playing with us."

Dez says, "You someplace I can drop by, mate? I've something t'show you."

CHAPTER 22

Kansas Jack and the Blacktop are still opening for Calvin Willow, but the concert's been moved from The Liberty to the Quagmire, a smaller but well-storied music venue in Midtown Manhattan. Dez knows of the place but hasn't been there before. He takes a cab. Someone at the alley entrance has his name on a clipboard, and Dez is escorted into the venue.

The place is gritty and dark, and smells of booze. Dez is madly in love with it in seconds.

Jack O'Herlihy is a scarecrow of a man, tall and painfully thin, his long hair slicked back with a Suavecito ducktail, and with sideburns. He fancies white shirts, inch-narrow black ties, and suits with high-water trousers. His look is very on-point: early sixties hipster rock star. The harsh house lights are on, and Jack's onstage setting up with his eight-piece band; Jack prefers his bebop with a horn section and cello. Old-school. Dez hugs the front man, then shakes hands or hugs the rest of the band, most of whom remember him from his guest gigs with them in Los Angeles.

Dez is well aware that Kansas Jack O'Herlihy has never once stepped foot in the state of Kansas; he picked the band name because it sounds cool.

Jack shows Dez the publicity still for the now-canceled show at The Liberty. There's Dez's grinning face, and Dez's name in the cutline. "I don't have any idea who could've done this, man. I am so, so sorry if you came out here for this."

"Show ye something." Dez draws his phone and shows Jack a string of texts:

Disaster! Big big big show Tuesday! In Newark. Bassist has covid. BEGGING for your help. KJack

Set me up with place to stay, I'm in.

Could kiss you!

Please don't.

Jack reads it, slack-jawed. He looks up, eyes wide.
"This isn't me! I didn't send this!"
Dez hits Reply on his phone and types XXX.
Jack's mobile pings. His eyes go very wide. "Swear to God, man, I—"
"I believe you, lad. You was hacked."
Other members of the band take Dez's phone and pass it around, reading it, too.
Jack says, "I owe you a huge apology, man."
Dez shrugs. "Not your fault. But it does beggar a few thousand questions. Like: Who wanted me here?"

An African American dynamo named Harlow—she plays electric guitar, bass, and banjo for the Blacktop, as needed—hands Dez back his phone. "Holy shit! Were you at The Liberty yesterday?"

"Me! No! Safe and sound. Ye know what a lucky bloke I am. You lot wasn't there either?"

"No way, Jose." Jack exhales, a hand on Dez's shoulder. "But . . . I don't know what to do about all this," he says, gesturing to the promo photo of the band plus Dez. "I feel terrible. We could—"

"Just put Limerick in the fuckin' lineup, bud."

Everyone turns as the legendary Calvin Willow strolls onto the stage, strap over one shoulder, a guitar flush against his back. The band gasps in unison.

Calvin offers his hand to Dez. "Lookin' good."

They shake. "Ta, mate."

Jack gulps. "You two know each other? Jesus, Joseph, and Curly!"

Dez jumps in. "Met donkey's years ago. Some nightclub."

Calvin takes the lead. If Dez wants his name out of that incident at The Liberty, he's willing to go there. "Good to see you again, bud." He turns to Jack. "I heard you guys just now. Your sound's tight."

Which is like Michael Jordan telling someone they can hoop.

"I sometimes throw 'Knock on Wood' into the show. Anyone here know it?"

Dez says, "The Eddie Floyd number, aye, 'course. An R an' B classic."

Jack and more than half the band nod, too.

"Takes more of a band than I'm packin' these days. Horns, keyboards. The Blacktop wanna sit in tonight for that?"

Jack says, "Do we . . . ? Could we . . . ? Is this . . . ? I'm, ah . . ."

Harlow open-palm whacks him on the back of his head. "Brain-Dead is saying yes, Mr. Willow. We *all* the way in."

Calvin nods to Dez. "You, too, bud?"

They shake.

Hours later, after all the bands work their way through the sound check, Dez, Calvin Willow, and Kansas Jack and the Blacktop go out drinking, because that's what band people do. They find a disreputable honky-tonk, which isn't easy to do in Manhattan. They've barely ordered the first round—Calvin's buying—when Dez's phone lights up. He checks the name, then excuses himself, steps out into the cool evening air.

"Special Agent Ansara?"

Stella Ansara says, "Mr. Limerick?"

"Dez."

"I'm just back from the New Jersey coroner's office. I wanted you to know: Jacob Gaetano was shot with a forty-five slug, likely fired from a SIG."

"Russians was firin' Russian-made guns, ma'am."

"We know. And no SIG Sauers have been found anywhere at The Liberty. We also found where the Russians were staging before the attack. In a warehouse in Kearny, a suburb of Newark. No SIGs there. No forty-five ammo. Just plenty of Russian-made firepower."

"So we've an extra player in this feckin' circus. Excuse me language."

"We have an extra player, yes. Whom we have not identified. And the New Jersey cops found that frequency jammer with the note about Thiago. So this is me calling to say thank you. And it's me calling to unofficially ask for your help, sir. From the file I read, you've tangled with the assassin known as Thiago. Nobody in my field office has."

"It's actually a bit more interesting than even that," Dez says. Then tells her about the mysterious text allegedly from Jack O'Herlihy, which drew Dez to the East Coast and to The Liberty Convention Center.

"This friend of yours didn't actually invite you to play with them?"

"That's right. Somebody hacked him. Added me name and photo to his website, too. Reserved a room for me. I've tried hackin' the account for that reservation, but it's through a bank in the Caymans. Not a hope in hell."

"Someone wanted you there."

"Aye. No coincidence, that."

"Thiago?"

"AKA disgraced CIA officer Ray Harker? Dunno. I've met Harker. He's got the brains God gave a rabid hamster. This whole thing feels complicated. Lots of moving parts. 'Sides, the name Thiago on the freq jammer suggests that Harker an' the Russians might've been in cahoots. Why throw a five-foot-eight spanner like me into the works? Makes no sense."

He listens to silence. Harlow and a couple other bandmates pop outside to smoke. She waggles her pack at Dez, who shakes his head no.

Over the line, Stella Ansara says, "Every time I think you're shining me on, Mr. Limerick, you say something like *makes no sense.* Which it doesn't. But the fact that you admit that makes me suspect you're telling me the truth."

"Am. An' there may be a bit more ye need to hear about."

She says, "I'm booked tomorrow. Can you come into the field office on Thursday?"

Dez says, "Ever hear of a Midtown music venue called the Quagmire?"

There's a beat. "I saw Ani DiFranco play there. Maybe ten years ago."

"One of the greatest lyricists of her era, that one. Doing a set tonight. Drop by. We can talk after the show."

"Or you can come by the field office on Thursday." She recites the address. "Call first, to let me know when you're coming. Thank you, Mr. Limerick. The FBI appreciates the help."

Stella hangs up.

CHAPTER 23

Olivia Gelman and Ray Harker are enjoying a little drink on the lesser deck of a two-hundred-and-forty-foot mega-yacht moored at the North Cove Marina, under the shadow of the new World Trade Center. The Lloyd's Register Ice Class ID yacht would sell for upward of eighty million euros, were it not stolen, the original owners somewhere at the bottom of the Mediterranean.

Liv is making them both a vodka martini. She has lately taken to mixology and has found enjoyment in the science and art of classic cocktails.

"We got three," Ray grumbles, speaking around a cigarette. "Just three. Fuck."

She smiles from across the wet bar. "Yes."

"That's not the contract. The contract calls for getting all six. Everyone on the list. Goddamn it, we spent nearly a million bucks setting this up! Just to net half of them? Fuck."

She adds orange zest and a cocktail cherry to both glasses and walks them over to him. Ray hesitates, then takes the drink she's proffered.

They toast. "We'll get the rest. Do not worry."

"We spent nearly a million—"

"Thiago spent nearly a million dollars. We're not Thiago. Just part of it. It wasn't our money to lose, and the organization peer-reviewed the hits and voted for us to go ahead. Everything is fine, Ray. You worry too much."

She rests a hand on his chest.

"We wouldn't be in this bullshit situation if you hadn't gotten that asshole Limerick to The Liberty."

She ignores the comment, tastes her drink, nods in satisfaction.

"Why? Seriously, Liv. Why did you do that?"

She smiles up at him. "You worry too much. I had my reasons. And you cannot say that wasn't fun! The Russians never met us face-to-face. They could just as easily have killed either of us, skulking around like we were, moving from building to building! God. That was the most alive I have felt in years!"

Ray would like to think she's nuts, but he has to admit that the thrill of manipulating the Russians, avoiding them, working their way through the hit list, was one hell of a challenge.

"Nobody alive but us coulda pulled that off," he admits.

"Absolutely!" She beams up at him and twirls on the balls of her sneakers. Her dark hair flying. She's giddy.

"Hey. I spoke to that Oborin. The colonel's top guy? He says he spoke to Thiago, who ordered a hit squad to kill Limerick but to bring back that chick he was running with. How come?"

She cocks her head, looking out through the glass at the Manhattan skyline and the other yachts in the harbor. "To understand one's enemy, it is important to know everything possible about them. Their wants, their fears, their hopes. Who they are attracted to. And this woman! This Catalina Valdivia? She is a thief. Like me."

Ray gulps down his drink. "Thief? You're an assassin, babe. Same as me."

Liv rolls her eyes. "Not the same as you. You kill because it is what you are the very, very best at. And you enjoy it. I kill only in the pursuit of profit. You would take on pro bono assassinations if you could. My killing is entirely profit-motivated."

"Why are you fixated on that dipshit Limerick?"

"Because Desmond is brilliant, innovative, and most impossible to predict. He is an X factor."

Ray's face darkens. "How come you always call him *Desmond*?"

She sips, staring out at Lower Manhattan. "Because we were lovers once."

A beat, and Ray says, "What the fuck? You never told me that."

She smiles over her shoulder at him. "Oh, don't worry, darling. That was a long time ago." She sips her vodka martini. "That was before Desmond killed me."

CHAPTER 24

Dez is sweat-soaked, his black T-shirt clinging to his barrel chest. He and Harlow are both on bass guitar, both sharing the same mic, both six feet to stage left of Calvin Willow. And when the front man growls his guttural ". . . it's like thunder . . ." Dez and Harlow lean into their mic with the same practiced move, dipping their respective shoulders—Dez's left, Harlow's right—and perform the call-and-response that the R&B classic calls for.

"*Thunder!*"

And when Calvin growls the word "lightning," the bass duo hit him back. "*Lightning!*"

Calvin Willow is center stage, backed up by his two guys on strings and his drummer, plus Kansas Jack and the Blacktop, eight musicians deep, complete with horn section, keyboards, and a cellist. They're blowing the doors off the Quagmire, rocking hard on Eddie Floyd and Steve Cropper's "Knock on Wood."

Dez has rarely had such a good time on any stage. And working in close-order formation with Harlow is a pure joy. She's maybe fifty-five, Black, and has played backup strings for everyone from Kings of Leon to Queen Latifah to Rascal Flatts. She's nearly as fit as Dez and sexy as hell, and they've been grinning at each other, laughing, deep into their groove, in their zone—in Calvin Willow's zone, more precisely—and Jesus if that rangy old bastard isn't every bit as amazing onstage as he's always been on the radio or streaming services.

The sold-out house is going nuts, dancing in the aisles, singing along. Harlow is gay and proud, and her own hard-core fandom crowd is losing their collective shit at the edge of the stage.

After Calvin's final chord, it takes a good thirty seconds for the cheering to cool down. Calvin leans into his mic and growls, "Kansas Jack and the Blacktop! Give it *up*!"

And the cheering continues.

Dez washes up in the absolutely disgusting backstage bathroom. He'd wisely brought a fresh black T-shirt. Harlow and he now share the same lime-stained sink, the same silvered mirror, as she washes sweat off her abdomen, runs fingers through her kinky hair, and switches to a T-shirt emblazoned with BUCKAROO BANZAI AND THE HONG KONG CAVALIERS.

"You goddamn amazing out there, big guy." She winks at him through the mirror.

"Anytime, any stage, anywhere in the world, love. Hand t'god. I'd play next to you if they paid me in cat litter."

Harlow hip-checks him before heading out to find her horde of uber-fans.

Dez weaves his way to the bar portion of the Quagmire and orders, first, a bottle of water. He drains it in a go. He'll get to the booze in due course, but hydrating first is an imperative. It's as crowded in the bar as it was having a dozen musicians crowded onto that tiny stage, complete with baby grand and a full drum kit. Dez still has no idea how they shoehorned everyone into that space. God, but that was a lovely set.

He's about to order a stout when a pretty bird approaches him, smiling softly. She's wearing a tank under a biker jacket, boot-cut jeans and cowboy boots, and she's looking splendid.

"That wasn't half bad," she speaks over the din.

"Ta, then. I'm Dez."

Her smile notches up a degree.

"Jay-sus! Stella! Sorry! I didn't recognize you looking so bloody . . . ah . . ."

Well, this is a cul-de-sac Dez wishes he hasn't ambled into.

Stella Ansara just smiles tolerantly and leans in to be heard over the susurrus of the bar. "Decided to take you up on the offer. I liked the song. I'd never heard it before."

"A classic, that. R an' B handed down by the gods. 'Tis good to see ye, then."

She says, "Can we talk?"

Stella is drinking a light beer from a bottle and Dez grabs a Harp, and they head out to the side street around the corner from the Quagmire. Maybe two dozen other people are out here, too, catching some fresh air, or smoking weed, or making out.

"Any luck tracking down our missing Russian colonel?"

"Maksim Baranov," she says, "and no. But we think it unlikely he got out of the country. The search continues."

They find an isolated spot to speak. Stella says, "You and the other bassist look very close."

"Harlow. Performed onstage with her a bit in Los Angeles. As good on strings as anyone I know. Better'n me, an' that's a fact. I'm pleased ye came."

"I wanted to ask you some questions, and I didn't want it to be in a formal setting. No microphones, no notes. Just us."

Dez sips his beer, waits. Stella takes a dainty sip of her beer. At this rate, she's likely to finish it sometime in the second quarter of the coming year. "We conducted an after-action this morning. City, state, federal agencies. And from what we can narrow down, you took out nine of the Russians. Killed or incapacitated."

Dez shrugs. "Wasn't exactly keeping score."

"How?"

"Luck, mostly."

She says, "Dez, I'm thinking about telling you some stuff, and maybe asking you some stuff, and my decision—do so or don't—hinges on my trusting you. And right now, I don't know enough about you to trust you."

Dez really doesn't like talking about his past. He even asked a foreign intelligence service to help obfuscate his past. A fact that, likely, Stella Ansara herself has recently discovered.

Sure enough. "There are no records on you that precede this year," she says. "I'm ex–Air Force. I called in a favor. Air Force intelligence found the same thing. Prior to moving to LA, you're a ghost."

"Served for a bit with a covert unit overseas," he admits. "Them fuckwits—pardon me—at the convention center weren't the first terrorists I've waltzed with."

"Which unit?"

"See, it's the word 'covert' you're having trouble interpreting."

She says, "Don't be a wiseass, Limerick."

He laughs and gulps beer. "I done my bit at The Liberty. Far as I'm concerned, it's in the rearview. I'm happy never thinkin' about them lot ever again. You don't trust me enough to ask me something, that's fine by me. I'll be sleeping like a baby tonight."

She glares at him. They're the same height, and she's wearing two-inch heels, so she's got the advantage. Dez suspects that glare could peel the paint off a warship.

Then the ice breaks and she allows a cock-eyed smile to peek through, if only for a second. She sips her beer. "Sleeping with the other bassist, maybe?"

"Harlow? I wish! Dead sexy, her. But I'm not exactly her flavor." Dez nods to something over her shoulder and Ansara turns to see the bassist surrounded by her all-girl groupie cluster.

"Ah."

Dez sips beer, waits.

"You know, she actually is my flavor. I didn't realize she was gay because the two of you were so hot together onstage and—"

She suddenly looks shocked. "I didn't mean you were hot, Mr. Limerick. I meant . . . that came out wrong. I meant . . ."

"If we agree that I experienced a sudden and inexplicable loss of hearing, an' that all of that was lost to me, could we go back to talking about violence and mayhem?"

She blushes and smiles. "You're a nice man. Thank you. And . . . and I think maybe you were trained as a breach expert."

Dez shows her the tattoo of Janus on his forearm. "That's right. Beginnings an' gates. Transitions an' time. Duality an' doors. Passages an' endings."

"You were a breacher. A doorman."

"We used the term 'gatekeeper' in me outfit, but aye."

"Okay." She looks around to make sure no one else can overhear them. "The Russians at The Liberty: What was their exit strategy? You must have thought about it."

Dez shrugs. "Wasn't one. An' them arseholes—sorry—they didn't have the mien of suicide bombers. Weren't plannin' on going down with the ship, them. They was acting as if they had an exit." Dez sips his beer. "An' near as I can tell, there was none."

"That's what I think, too. One of my guys interrogated one of the terrorists. This low-life is wanted for drug dealing in Mother Russia. He gets expatriated back, he's ending up in a Russian prison, which, I'm told, they're not much fun."

"Heard the same."

"He was singing his lungs out to get a deal. He said their leader, this Colonel Baranov, wanted to set up a hostage situation so the U.S. would give this private military contractor, the Leningrad Konsortsium, back a battleship our Navy and the Turks commandeered a couple of weeks ago. Baranov was contacted by Thiago, the assassin, and together, they hatched the hostage crisis at The Liberty. Thiago promised them a way out when they'd gotten the Navy to back down. We're still trying to pin down the details of this so-called exit strategy."

"At least that answers the *why* question."

"We don't think Baranov skipped clear, we think he was never in The Liberty. He was the guy I spoke to during the hostage negotiations, but I think he was calling into The Liberty, and his calls rerouted to me."

"Whilst he was sunning himself on some beach, maybe? Profiles in courage."

Stella smiles and nods.

Dez asks, "What d'you know about this Thiago?"

"Maybe more than you. You think it's a CIA dropout named Ray Harker. But the name Thiago has been associated with assassinations for over a decade."

"Since well before Harker done a runner in Chechnya."

"Right. Current theory: Thiago is the name of a collective of assassins. Law enforcement sometimes call it the Thiago group."

"That'd make Harker a drone."

Stella nods, glancing around again. "Could he have been the brains behind the attack on The Liberty?"

"Not one chance in fecking hell, excuse me French. If he's

a master planner, I'm a prima ballerina. Lad's more the blunt-instrument type."

Stella thinks about that for a bit. Dez gives her the time.

"So Thiago—which could be a fraternal order of killers, or a combine—helps Baranov and his guys stage the hostage crisis. Thiago tells them there's an exit strategy. A strategy that none of the law enforcement types I met with today can figure out. Myself included. And neither can an ex-gatekeeper."

Dez drinks.

"And thanks to the forty-five slug you found, we have reason to suspect that an as-yet-unknown killer was in The Liberty as well. Maybe someone associated with Thiago. Thing is: The Russian fentanyl slinger who's singing his heart out? He says the colonel and his guys never met face-to-face with the assassin. All Colonel Baranov knew was: Thiago would get him and his guys free of The Liberty, once the U.S. Navy caved."

Dez says, "Why? Why help the Russkies to pull off that crazy stunt? Why trick 'em into thinking there was some sort of backdoor way out? I'm fairly certain there wasn't. You're fairly certain there wasn't. So that gets it back to the big question: Why?"

Stella says, "Cui bono."

"Who benefits; aye."

She's thinking. She subconsciously taps the beer bottle against a button on her jacket, rhythmically, while she works through the problem.

Dez says, "Fella whose name I now forget was shot with a forty-five. Possibly a Glock."

She says, "Jacob Gaetano."

"Who was he?"

She sips. "A high school teacher and coach."

They both ponder the situation for a moment.

"I've two questions," Dez says. "His killing wasn't random.

Thiago—whosoever that may be—didn't kill the lad for giggles, yeah? He was targeted. So how did our lad Jacob Gaetano end up at The Liberty on Monday? Figure that out, and ye might get a step closer to figuring out the cui bono part."

She nods. "You think he was lured there by his killer. Yeah, could be. That's logical. What's your second question?"

"Press is sayin' eleven civilians died at The Liberty. One of 'em, Gaetano, maybe wasn't killed by the Russians. So if one of the civilian deaths is an anomaly . . ."

The special agent's eyes light up. "Maybe others weren't killed by the Russians, either. Maybe there's more than one anomalous homicide."

"Could be."

"Which would suggest Thiago set up the Russians to cover . . . multiple hits?"

Dez shrugs. "Where d'you hide a plaid rose?"

She says, "There's no such thing as a plaid rose."

"Right. An' if ye had one, where would you hide it?"

She studies his eyes. She slowly nods. "In a bouquet of plaid roses."

Dez taps his beer bottle against hers. "Well, cheers then."

CHAPTER 25

Calvin Willow is heading on to a music festival in Australia.

Kansas Jack and the Blacktop had a handful of lackluster gigs lined up in the New York/Philadelphia area, spaced out over the next month or so. But the word spreads about the band backing up Calvin Willow, and suddenly venues are tripping over each other to sign them up. The new gigs will pay better than the ones that were on the schedule, so Jack O'Herlihy gobbles them up as fast as they're offered. He also asks Dez if he'd like to stay on for a couple of weeks. Dez has nothing else lined up, so he agrees.

Dez is curious as to why someone impersonated Jack and lured him to the hostage crisis in Newark in the first place. Gigging with the band for a couple of weeks will be fun, but it also might be an opportunity to figure out who's behind all this.

The morning after the performance at the Quagmire is when Dez first realizes he's picked up a tail. He walks from his boutique hotel to a Puerto Rican breakfast joint that makes an amazing *huevos revuelto con salchicha* with *pan de agua* and café con leche. He spots a guy in a fancy sports car following him to the restaurant, and another guy in another flash car following him as he returns to the hotel. Using cars to follow a man on foot is daft. The pursuers stand out like idiots.

Dez goes online and finds a gym that offers day rates, and heads there to work off the food. Again: the tail. And again, heading back.

Dez doesn't think these guys are law enforcement. First, because so far there are just two skulkers. And they've two sort of fancy-looking cars between them. If they were cops, their rides would be dingy and unremarkable. Also, parking is murder in Midtown, and these lads likely spend more time moving their cars than watching Dez.

On his way back from the gym, Dez checks the subway times online, then quickly dashes down into a subterranean station and catches a train just as it's pulling out. Losing his pursuers.

He gets off at the next station and hustles back toward his hotel. He stops in a stationery store across the street and half a block down. It has a good window view of his hotel. He's essentially staking out the stakeout.

Sure enough, the guys who'd been following him cruise past the store, looking for parking. Dez notes that one of them is on a walkie-talkie. That's not, like, suspicious-looking whatsoever.

Dez's phone vibrates. He draws it. "Cat?"

Catalina Valdivia says, "Did you tell the cops about me?"

"Not a word. Honest."

"So how come I've picked up a shadow?"

"Oh ho."

"Oh ho?"

"I know. It sounded better in me head 'fore I said it out loud."

"Why are you oh-hoing me?"

"Because I picked up a shadow as well, love. Two gents outside me hotel. Look like extras in a Scorsese flick."

She doesn't reply immediately. "They have to be connected."

"Have to be, aye."

"Well, I'm getting outta Dodge. I have a place I can hole up until this passes."

"Wise, that."

"Want to come along?"

"Is it far?"

"It's in Italy."

"Me mate, Jack O'Herlihy, asked me t'sit in with his band for a bit, so I'll be stayin' here. 'Sides, I want to have a word with the lads tailing me."

"That's your answer?" she says. "We're both being surveilled, so you want to go confront them?"

"Well, I'm an extrovert, love. I make friends easily."

"What if they're connected to the Russians and they're out for revenge?"

"Best to find out either way, yeah?"

"What about lying low in a picturesque Italian village with a hot *chica*?"

"Told me mate I'd back up his band for two weeks, or there-abouts. If the offer still stands after that, ring me up. How many people in your surveillance team?"

Cat says, "Three that I've spotted so far."

Dez is sure he can handle his followers. But getting Cat clear of all this seems the higher priority. "Tell me where you are. I'll come chat your lot up. If I like what I hear, I'll come back an' do the same with my lot."

"I don't like owing anyone anything. I don't like depending on anyone. This rescuing-me thing is getting on my nerves."

"This is self-interest at its grandest, love. Promise. Someone lured me to The Liberty. Someone wanted me there, an' went to extraordinary steps to make it happen. I'm dyin' to find out who. And why. Chatting up the lads following you serves my needs."

After a beat, Cat gives him an address for a hotel in Brooklyn. It's a fancy, four-star hotel. Far grander than the place Dez is staying. Dez stands in the stationer as she describes the trio who has her under surveillance. They're using a white Mazda SUV. There must be three zillion identical vehicles in the greater New York area; they're ubiquitous. Her team consists of two men and a woman. They'd followed Cat to Dez's hotel when she came to visit him, and they followed her back.

"Three blocks from my hotel is a park with a jogging trail," she says. "Parts of the trail are pretty isolated. Bet I could lure them there."

Dez beams. "That's just the thing! Give me directions."

She does.

The sun's getting low in the sky as Catalina Valdivia emerges from her hotel in yoga pants, sneakers, a Nike tank, and a baseball cap, her ponytail threaded through the gap in the rear of the cap. She slips in earbuds, warms up with some stretching, then starts jogging toward the park.

The Mazda SUV falls in behind her.

Cat runs cleanly and smoothly. She obviously does this a lot. She has true power in her legs and excellent balance. And her lithe form draws a lot of admiring glances as she sets a solid pace.

Three blocks away, she cuts into the park.

The SUV pulls over. A man and a woman emerge. The woman is still getting into her own jogging togs. She's blond and fit. She starts moving in Cat's wake.

The guy, wearing jeans and a hoodie, walks the other direction. They've obviously checked out this venue in advance; they know where to catch Cat in a pincer.

The driver stays in the Mazda, in a parking lot adjacent to the park.

The blonde keeps Cat in sight as the trail begins winding between and around a few amorphous clusters of trees. Warning signs line the track, telling people not to jog here after dark. Cat ignores them.

She puts on a little burst of speed and disappears.

The blonde puts on the afterburners to catch up.

A minute later, she spots her partner, the guy in the hoodie, who'd been coming up the trail from the opposite side.

Both of them come to a halt amid a cluster of trees.

"Where is she?" the guy asks, approaching the blonde.

Where she is, is behind a tree, nodding to Dez, who is behind another tree. Dez steps out now.

"Hallo, friends! Lovely night."

The duo turn his way. The blonde isn't carrying a gun; there's nowhere on her togs to hide one. The hoodie could be. Dez smiles disarmingly.

He didn't keep the makeshift slingshot he jury-rigged at the conference center, but those inch-in-diameter nuts and bolts had seemed too good to waste. He'd slid three of them into his messenger bag before the police raided the center. Now he holds one in his loosely closed right hand.

"What do you want?" the guy asks. Dez is now about eight feet away.

"Fried eggs. Blood sausage. A thick beefsteak tomato, fairly swimmin' in grease. An' baked beans."

"What?"

"A couple million acres of land in the U.S. of A., and not one decent fry-up in the whole country. A crime, that. Heart-healthy egg substitutes? Multi-seed bread? Jay-sus, ye've no idea how to do breakfast in this country, an' that's a fact."

"Dude, get the fuck out of here," the hoodie says.

Dude? There is a possibility that this couple doesn't know who Dez is. They seem genuinely annoyed right now, rather than surprised by his appearance.

Could it be these watchers aren't connected to the watchers outside Dez's hotel?

"I've a question for ye," he says, all smiles. "Regardin' me mate. Catalina Valdivia."

Hoodie reaches behind himself and begins to draw a gun from a belt holster.

Dez sidearms the heavy iron bolt, hard as he can, into the lad's noggin.

Hoodie grunts and falls into shrubbery adjacent to the trail.

The blonde draws a switchblade knife.

And Cat materializes behind her. Dez never saw the thief move from the tree behind which she'd been hiding. He hadn't heard a sound. Yet here she is, on the far side of the blonde with the knife.

"Psst."

The blonde turns and Cat goes for a spin kick, planting the sole of her right Nike in the blonde's abs.

The woman's face contorts to a rictus of pain. She folds like a cutthroat razor and drops to the trail.

As Dez approaches, the blonde touches her ear. "We're made!"

She had an earjack. And she's likely just alerted the fella back in the SUV.

Dez picks up the switchblade and sends it spiraling off into a copse of trees. Same for Hoodie's gun. He squats and begins patting down the unconscious guy bleeding from his temple.

He beams up at Cat. "Is it sexist to say that watchin' you jog is one of the finest sights of the week?" He turns to the blonde. "I was speakin' to Cat, love. Not you."

Cat says, "Run now, flirt later. She alerted their third guy."

"I know, darlin'." Dez picks up the thrown bolt and uses Hoodie's hoodie to wipe blood off it. He takes the man's wallet. "Was counting on that. Let's go. Back the way you came."

The blonde holds her gut, keening in agony.

"Who sent ye?"

"Fuck . . . your . . . self . . ."

Dez says to Cat, "I'll be honest; I get that a lot."

"I imagine."

"D'you know who I am, then?" he asks the blonde.

He can tell from her eyes. She does not.

"Come along, love. People to be, places to do." Dez leads Cat back down the trail, heading the opposite way.

They get back to the trailhead and the adjacent parking lot. Sure enough, the driver's missing from the Mazda. He would have taken the shorter route, the route Hoodie took.

"I'd like their wheels, please."

Cat figures out his game plan. "I didn't pack my lockpicks."

Dez shows her a palm with Mazda keys in it. "Ta-da. Basic tradecraft. Everyone on the snatch team has copies of the keys."

He unlocks the SUV. They climb in. He gets it in gear and pulls out of the parking lot.

"Is that who you thought they'd be?" Cat asks from the passenger seat. "A snatch team? Was this a kidnapping?"

Dez shrugs. "Dunno. But the oddest part: I don't think they knew who I am. I'd assumed these fuckers were part and parcel of the lot running surveillance on me. If they had been, they'd've recognized me, aye?"

They're moving through the dusk-darkened streets of Brooklyn at a fair clip.

"Better'n even money, they have this car LoJacked, love. We haven't all night. See if there're any paperwork in back. Flash drives, anything."

She climbs between the seats as Dez keeps driving.

"I'm a better driver than you," she calls to him. "We should be doing this in a different order."

"If we was in hot pursuit, I'd make sure it's you behind the wheel."

She slides back up front. "Three backpacks. I found a cheap flip phone in one of them."

Dez hands her the wallet he stole from Hoodie. She goes through it. "Lots of money. No ID. Also a swipe card. Maybe from a hotel?"

"I might be able t'do something with that." He reaches for it.

A moment later, Dez has taken a wildly circuitous route back to Cat's own hotel. "Check out. Get to the airport. You trust this place ye have in Italy?"

"I own it through four cutout false identities," she says. "Give me your phone."

Dez unlocks it and hands it over. She types. "You can always reach me through this website. Also owned under several false IDs. I'll head to Italy. If the coast is clear, I'll text you."

"I'd rather you sexted me."

She smiles. "Well, that, too. Dez?"

She leans over and kisses him. "I do hate owing anyone. I hate being rescued. Let's not make a habit of this, okay?"

"Done."

She climbs out.

CHAPTER 26

Dez doesn't know if the Mazda's LoJacked but he drives it across the Brooklyn Bridge and into Manhattan. He parks it in a lot nearest to One Police Plaza. He removes enough bits of the engine that the thing won't ever run again.

He shoulders the three backpacks Cat spotted in the rear of the SUV, then takes the subway to Midtown.

He looks odd, carrying three backpacks, but everyone in the train minds their own business.

Dez emerges from the underground and does a quick recce. He spots both of his shadows; one parked a block east of his hotel in a Nissan Z, one a block west in an Audi R8. The guy in the Audi has his window rolled down, his elbow out of the car. He's smoking.

Dez waits until no pedestrians will notice, then puts an iron bolt and nut into the side of the man's head from fifteen paces.

He walks to the guy's fancy Audi, opens the driver's door, pushes the unconscious man into the passenger seat. He stores the three backpacks in the passenger-side footwell. He gets behind the wheel and pats the man down, taking his wallet and disassembling his automatic handgun.

He's pretty sure both guys could see Dez's hotel but they can't see each other. This man has a walkie-talkie on the dashboard of his car.

The guy moans as Dez puts the Audi into gear. "Who . . . ?"

"Dez Limerick, squire. D'ye know who Catalina Valdivia is, then?"

The guy puts his hand to his temple, then looks at the blood on his fingertips. "What . . . happened . . . ?"

The man has a strong New England accent.

"Valdivia," Dez says, pulling out into traffic. "Catalina Valdivia."

The guy's still groggy from the hit. "Don't know any . . . Valdivia . . ."

Dez thinks the man's telling the truth.

He picks up the walkie-talkie and toggles it.

"Hallo, then. It's me. Dez Limerick."

He assumes the guy in the Nissan Z has the same walkie-talkie. A beat, then he hears a voice. "Where the fuck are you, asshole?" Another New England accent.

"I'm here, my son." Dez veers out of traffic and slams into the driver's-side door of the Nissan. He sees the driver take the stunning impact.

Dez climbs out of the Audi, takes his three backpacks, and saunters over to his hotel, ignoring the honking and the traffic jam he's just created.

Outside the door to his room, Dez finds his bass guitar in its case and his duffel bag, which was left in his room at The Liberty. Also a note from the FBI's Stella Ansara. THANK YOU AGAIN FOR YOUR HELP. COFFEE TOMORROW?

In the room, Dez pours himself a dollop of the booze Cat brought him. Then searches the wallet taken from the Audi and the three backpacks gathered in Brooklyn.

The trio in Brooklyn had a manila folder with a dozen photos of Cat. They'd been taking meticulous notes about her day; where she went, and when.

He puts the flip phone next to his hip on the bed.

The guy following Dez in the lovely Audi—well, formerly lovely, before the T-bone crash—is carrying eight hundred dollars and a Connecticut driver's license.

The trio in the park hadn't sounded particularly like New Englanders. Hoodie and the Blonde—now, there's a band name, he thinks—sounded Californian, if anything.

The trio staking out Cat hadn't known about Dez.

The lad in the Audi claimed he didn't know about Cat.

Curious.

Dez opens his tablet computer, subconsciously kissing the well-nicked leather cover. He draws his little tool kit. From his duffel, he gets a credit card reader and attaches it to his bespoke mobile phone. He swipes Hoodie's card through it and discovers the guy was staying at a Radisson near JFK.

Anonymous-looking SUV, cheap hotel with easy access to a busy airport. No one carrying IDs. Using earbuds to stay in contact with each other. Those three seemed to be pros.

The guys staking out Dez looked a little too flashy, a little too conspicuous, what with their cars and walkie-talkies. Not pros. More like thugs.

Dez takes the back off the snatch team's burner and uses alligator clips and wires to connect it to his own phone.

He runs a program on his tablet.

The burner has only ever called one number. It has only ever received calls from that same number.

Dez runs GPS on the other phone but is surprised to find it's blocked. That should have worked.

Shrugging, he sips his bourbon and calls the number.

He can hear the chirping of an anti-surveillance suite. He recognizes the sound. Dez uses the same suite on his own phone. All of Dez's calls are routed through an anonymous server farm in Estonia.

The call connects.

He hears nothing.

"Hallo?" he says. "This is Desmond Limerick. To whom do I have the pleasure of speaking?"

A few seconds of silence, then the line disconnects.

Olivia Gelman steps out onto the flying deck of the mega-yacht she's stolen and sends her burner phone into the dark of the Hudson River.

She begins laughing. God, the thrill of hearing Dez's voice again! After all that time! The laughter just keeps bubbling up.

Ray Harker ducks out of the aft galley, wearing only boxer shorts. The doors are too short for his height. His body is a bronze statue, his form chiseled. "What're you grinning about?"

"Oh God." Liv uses a knuckle to wipe a tear from under her eye. "I sent a team to find Miss Valdivia. They found Desmond instead. Or he found them, as the case may be."

She spots a phone in Ray's hand. "Anything important?"

"Hmm? Oh." He waggles the phone. "You know the New Haven Boys I use sometimes. I sent them on an errand."

"An important one?"

"If it was an important one, I wouldn't have sent those thugs. They're just muscle."

Liv nods, stares out at the Manhattan skyline, made more glamorous by its proximity and by the low angle, as seen from a yacht.

"It's a lovely night," she observes.

"Yeah. The team you sent: Do they know about you?"

It's a stupid question, but Liv allows it. "No, darling. No face-to-face meeting, and my calls are all routed through Estonia. They know nothing to tell. But Desmond's response tells me a great deal."

"Which is?"

Liv smiles warmly. "Catalina Valdivia is important to our Desmond. Which means she's important to me, as well."

Behind her back, Ray Harker grinds his teeth. "You're obsessed with that asshole."

Liv stares at the city. "I suppose I am."

CHAPTER 27

Thursday morning, Dez meets with Stella Ansara at a coffee shop near Grand Central. She gets decaf. Dez doesn't understand decaf coffee any more than he understands nonalcoholic beer. A thing is what it is and it isn't something else.

When they're settled at a table with a little privacy, Stella says, "Still no sign of the Russian leader, Colonel Baranov. But more of the Russians are spilling their guts. Here, I have something new to show you."

She goes to her phone and whistles up a PDF. She hands the phone to Dez. He holds it in landscape, using his thumb pads to zoom in and out. It's a blueprint.

"What is this?"

"The sub-sub-basement level of The Liberty's administration building, which includes tunnels leading away from the convention center and the airport."

Dez looks up. "Weren't no such level."

"I know. Whoever Thiago is, they worked up an elaborate fake sub-sub-basement, with maps and schematics, and construction information. And they used that to convince the Russians there was a way out."

Dez zooms in, peers at it. He changes to a different sector of the PDF and studies it, then another and another. "This stuff is fantastically detailed."

"My best friend's a civil engineer. I had her look at it. She said the same thing."

"All this would've taken donkey's years to design!"

"Agreed. Whoever's behind this, they've been pulling strings for weeks. Maybe longer."

Dez hands the phone back. Stella says, "I'm going to assume you haven't been sitting on your duff."

"No, ma'am."

He tells her that someone hacked into the website of the band Kansas Jack and the Blacktop, as well as Jack O'Herlihy's phone, all for the sole purpose of drawing Dez to The Liberty.

"Someone wanted you there."

Dez nods. He produces the card of the guy from Connecticut. "Stole this driving license of a lad had me under surveillance. He had a gun and a walkie-talkie. Was two of 'em. In their haste, the poor sods managed to hit each other's cars. Sloppy driving, that."

Dez tells her when and where. She takes two-thumb notes on the Notes app on her phone, typing as quickly as Dez speaks. "I'll call NYPD, find out if a squad car showed up."

She takes a cell phone picture of the driver's license, then slides on her cheaters. She types again. "Let's see if this guy's got a colorful history."

As she does that, Dez says, "I lied to ye."

Stella looks up quickly.

"Ye asked if a mate was at The Liberty with me, an' she'd asked me to keep her out of it. Won't tell ye who she is because it's not my tale to tell. But she was staying in Brooklyn last night, an' she, too, was under surveillance. Three of 'em, and I think they were attempting to kidnap her."

Stella gives him the bent eye. "Attempting. You intervened?"

"Seemed the thing t'do, aye. Also stole a Mazda SUV of theirs." He tells her where he parked the SUV. She recognizes the address and smiles. "You parked it in front of police headquarters."

"Disabled it, too. Should still be there." He hands her the Mazda keys.

"We can run prints on it."

"It'll turn up stolen, dollars to doughnuts. Left them idiots in a park in Brooklyn."

"Alive?"

"Of course, alive! What d'ye take me for?"

"Somebody who's really good at killing armed men."

Dez sips his doctored coffee. "I've killed, yeah. Not something I do with pride. Not something I do if there are ways t'avoid it."

"That's fair, Dez. And I'm sorry for suggesting otherwise." She nods to her phone. "Okay, here's what just popped: A couple of NYPD uniforms rolled on a car crash near Penn Station yesterday. They found two guys dazed. Both from Connecticut, both with unregistered handguns. They're both part of a mob in that state, sometimes known as the New Haven Boys. They're low-level hoods. And as far as the FBI knows, they're not connected with Russia, or that Russian para-military organization that hit the convention center."

"Hoods for hire, yeah? Didn't seem like the most well-organized bunch, them."

Stella checks to make sure no one can hear them. "Here's an interesting tidbit. The CIA is forbidden from operating on U.S. soil, right? The Bureau has always suspected that some CIA officers have sourced-out domestic black-bag jobs to organized crime. Maybe to the New Haven Boys. It's been a long-standing rumor; not anything we could ever prove."

Dez says, "An' Ray Harker is ex-CIA. That's an interesting coincidence, that. Worth lookin' into."

Stella stares him in the eye. The moment lasts. She says, "Dez, I really, really do not want that croissant up at the cash register. Truly. I truly do not."

"Well, then buy it and give me half, yeah?"

Stella does just that. Once the croissant is back at the table and evenly divided between them, she says, "We put together what's called an after-action task force. Representing every agency that had any jurisdiction whatsoever. We've been going through the murders at The Liberty. We found a couple of anomalies, just like you predicted."

Dez chews, nods. Stella checks the Notes on her telephone.

"A guy named . . . Let's see . . . Peter Garvey was at one of the conference buildings. He stepped out onto a balcony and either jumped or fell to his death."

"Weren't no Russians up on that balcony?"

"No. Just a room full of academics from a private college. Garvey was a member of the college board of trustees. One of the Jersey cops talked to the college president and other members of the board. None of them believe this guy would commit suicide. So it looks like he was pushed."

"Which wasn't how the Russkies was maintaining hostage discipline, yeah?" Dez has drawn his tablet computer from his messenger bag and writes down the name Peter Garvey. "Was this fella important on the geopolitical stage?"

"Not that we can tell. A medium-sized fish in a small pond. Known around York, Pennsylvania, as an attorney but mostly did real estate, estate planning, that sort of thing. A big deal in the Catholic Church. Someone did tell one of the cops that Garvey had been a delinquent and a drug abuser well into his twenties, but then found religion."

Dez takes notes.

"We might have one more anomaly but the after-action group is split on this one."

Again using her phone, she brings up crime-scene photos. She hands Dez her phone. He spots an image of a well-dressed gentleman lying on his back on the ground. He was shot. In front of him is a sort of metal shed, and it's splotched with the man's blood. From the way his legs and arms are positioned, Dez is willing to bet he was running for cover when one of the Russian roof snipers tagged him.

"This is Adam Levkowitz. A former pediatrician from Westchester, New York."

"Back shot," Dez says. "Exactly how them Russian fuckers was doing it. Sorry for me language."

Stella smiles. "No, I think we can all get on the same page with *Russian fuckers*. The after-action group flagged this one as an anomaly for two reasons. One: Witnesses said Dr. Levkowitz had been inside one of the hotels. He was killed out back of the hotel. The door he had to go through isn't a fire door, or a door for the guests. It's staff only, and it's locked twenty-four seven. Locked from the inside and the outside, to keep guests from getting back into this area."

She gestures to the photo. "So how'd a former pediatrician get that door open?"

Dez says, "Former? What's he do now?"

"Admin for an association of family-practice doctors. He's no longer licensed to practice."

Dez thinks about that a minute. "Second question, why was he running toward a shed, had a whacking great padlock on it?"

"Exactly. He shouldn't have been able to open one door, and he wouldn't have been able to open the other. So what was he doing?

Panicking? Maybe. Maybe a hotel staffer opened the rear door in his or her own attempt to flee. This might be a nothingburger."

"Might. Was he shot with a Russian slug?"

She shakes her head. "Too much damage to tell and the Jersey cops haven't found the slug yet."

"How tall was Dr. Levkowitz?"

Stella checks her notes. "Ahh . . . five–nine, five–ten. Why?"

"That blood spatter on the shed door. Looks like the blood hit at the same height as that exit wound on his chest, yeah? If so . . ."

"If he was shot by a sniper from above, the exit wound would have been lower on his abdomen, and the blood splotch lower, too." Stella nods. "Because the bullet would have been traveling downward. From this spray, Levkowitz was shot from behind, all right, but not from above."

"Did see some Russians trollin' the paths between buildings. But not that many. Anything interesting about the good doctor?"

"His father–in–law is in the U.S. House."

Dez shrugs. "Could be something. But thin gruel at best." He ticks off the points. "Jacob Gaetano, shot with a forty–five, was a high school teacher. Peter Garvey, who took the high jump off a balcony, was a no–name lawyer from a small city in Pennsylvania. Adam Levkowitz made it magically through a door he shouldn't've been able t'open, and was shot by someone standing on the ground, behind the hotel. An' him, an ex–pediatrician from upstate New York, who's the son–in–law of a congressman."

"The cops haven't fine–toothed any of them yet. But at first blush, they don't appear to have anything in common. It's worth giving these guys a better look."

They sit and think. Dez licks the pad of his index finger and uses it to whisk up flaky bits of the croissant.

Stella finishes her decaf and stands. "I'll ask the police in our task force to get the ball rolling on our three unusual homicides:

Garvey, Gaetano, and Levkowitz. I'll have the Bureau look into the Connecticut mob. To see if there's any connection between them and this ex-CIA killer."

Dez stands, too. "I've a connection or two in that world as well. Want t'thank ye for not freezing me out of this. Want t'know who lured me into that hostage fandango. And who sicced them hoodlums on me and a snatch team on me mate."

Stella says, "Okay. Well, let's say we gather again in a couple of days, see what we each dug up?"

Dez agrees. And he's now an unofficial part of the investigation.

CHAPTER 28

Dez calls London and this time he goes through the proper channels, contacting a low-level officer of British MI6 and asking if he might have a moment of time with the director of operations, Sir Richard Corbyn-Smith.

Dez has considered moving to a different hotel after the thugs found his place but thought, no, maybe it's better to stay and see if another couple of Mulligans show up. He's barely back to the hotel when his phone vibrates. "Please hold for Sir Richard."

Dez is just entering his room when he hears the familiar patrician voice. "Limerick? We're being told you did yeoman work with those Russians in New Jersey. You know you have an open invitation to join our operation."

Dez believes he'd be better suited working as a female impressionist in a cabaret than serving as a spook, but he keeps that to himself. "Thank you, sir. And I'm embarrassed to say I'm calling with another favor."

"Ask away."

"You've got lads what keep a watch on the CIA, yeah? I'm hearing rumors that, when the Agency wants t'get fingers dirty Stateside, they sometimes employ organized criminals, maybe out of Connecticut."

"Yes. I believe we've heard the same. And yes, I've someone who makes it a bit of a hobby keeping track of the CIA's penchant for breaking rules. Can I have him call you back?"

"Greatly appreciate it, Sir Richard."

"We have a long-standing if informal policy, Limerick. Any chance MI6 gets to tinkle in the CIA's wading pool is time well spent."

Dez barks a laugh. "A policy I, meself, adhere to, sir! Thank you again."

Ray Harker is standing on the flying deck of their mega-yacht, on his phone, a cup of coffee in hand. "What the fuck. Seriously. What. The fuck."

The man on the other end of the line has a New England accent. "This fucker, Limerick. He sent two of my guys to jail. Both of them seriously hurt."

Ray is furious. He's used the New Haven Boys in the past for dirty deeds on domestic soil. He knew a couple of other CIA officers who'd used them, too, before Ray left the Agency for much, much more lucrative work as an assassin and part of the Thiago group. These guys are good. Ruthless thugs, mind you, but if ruthless thug was the ingredient you needed, you couldn't do better than them.

"My men, they are arrested on charge of—"

"Briggs. Briggs! I do not give a fuck. Okay? I want you to send as many guys as you need. Hit this asshole. I want him dead. I'm upping the payout. Two hundred grand. Put him in the earth. Am I clear here?"

"Asshole will have moved. How do we find—"

"I've got a couple of guys at the FBI willing to take a buck on the side, keep their ears open. Okay? Limerick didn't move. He's right where he was before. Limerick's too stupid to realize the danger he's in. Get it done, Briggs. Quickly."

He hangs up.

Limerick once embarrassed Ray Harker during a CIA op in Chechnya. That had been long enough ago, Ray would be willing to let it slide, because Limerick's unimportant in the greater scheme.

But Ray's been partnered with Olivia Gelman for several weeks now. And there's no question that she's put the two of them—put the Thiago group—onto the most lucrative hit ever. A world-class hit can pay upward of a million dollars. This one? Much higher.

Liv also was the mastermind behind luring those Russians to The Liberty. And luring all of the targets to The Liberty, as well. And making it all come together like it was designed by some sort of Swiss clockmaker. It was perfect. Complicated, but perfect.

But for all that Liv did with utmost perfection to set up this hit, she also lured Limerick to the site. And Limerick managed to help end the threat of the Russians before all the other hits could take place.

Liv put at risk a record-setting (if records were kept for this sort of thing) payoff, and the kind of hit that would cement their reputation as the premier assassins. A hit so good they wouldn't simply be part of the Thiago organization. They'd *be* the organization. And she risked it because she's obsessed with that Brit runt.

Well, fuck him, Ray thinks. And fuck her for being infatuated with Limerick.

It's time to end Limerick and to end Liv's obsession with him. Once and for all.

CHAPTER 29

Dez plays another gig with Kansas Jack and the Blacktop. This time in Jersey City. Jack O'Herlihy is a terrific front man, in his super-narrow ties and his pompadour. They hit the rockabilly staples and hit them hard: "Red Hot" by Billy Lee Riley and Link Wray. "Race with the Devil" from Gene Vincent and His Blue Caps. "Rock This Town" by the Stray Cats. They glide over Carl Perkins and Roy Orbison and Charlie Feathers tunes, avoiding Elvis because Jack's got a superstitious thing about playing any of the King's hits.

Jack buys the first round at a bar after the show and Dez buys the second.

Dez gets back to his hotel around 2 A.M. and does a quick recce. Sure enough, more guys who might or might not be from Connecticut, staking him out. Dez is gobsmacked. He didn't expect his ploy—of staying right where he is—to work. But there they are.

He's also more than a bit tipsy, so he leaves the surveillance unit where they are and rents a room at another hotel two blocks away, using a credit card and an ID under a false name. He has a few such IDs, all linked to corrupt banks in corrupt countries, making them nigh impossible to verify.

He sleeps well, awaking refreshed at eight. He exercises and showers, pays up for his room, then begins figuring out how best to screw with the guys staking out his other hotel.

But before he can do that, he gets a text on his phone.

If this is Limerick, Sir Richard sends his best.

Dez calls the number back.

"Is this Mr. Limerick?" The man sounds Scottish.

"Dunno about the *mister* part, but ye've the right lad."

"Name's Stewart. Buy me a cup of dreadful American coffee, and I'll tell you tales of organized criminal assets and crooked-as-fuck American spooks."

Well, this sounds promising, so Dez decides to keep the watchers at his hotel waiting. "Pleasure, squire!"

The man going by the in-field pseudonym of Stewart turns out to be in his midsixties, balding and pudgy. He has a doughy, lopsided face and an easy smile. He shakes Dez's hand and they order coffee in a place in SoHo. Dez is still doctoring his when Stewart says, "Mate of mine, whom his sainted mother did *not* name Jamison, says you saved his pale and pathetic arse outside of Madrid. He says you're something of a genius."

"He's wrong about that, but yeah. Remember Jamison. Good man. I'm Dez."

They shake. "Pleased. And now you wish to hear tales of Connecticuters?"

"That really is a word? I'll be damned. I'm looking for an ex-spook name of Ray Harker. A right twat who ditched the Agency and became a gun for hire."

Stewart nods. "I've heard of him. Sir Richard himself put me in the States five years ago, with the clear and clearly illegal mandate of spying on the CIA. Sir Richard's never trusted 'em, and I'm of a mind he's right. The *special relationship,* my arse. Some of the CIA lot are brave and true. But much of the rest are crooked, corrupt, or crazy. My remit's to figure out which is which."

"Never taken to them meself," Dez says. "An' by the way, I'm currently owing a big favor to one of your own. Arabella Satti. Did me a solid, few weeks back."

Stewart nods. "Belle. Yes, I asked her about you when Sir Richard rang me up. She claims you're a conceited son of a bitch and a pain in her shapely backside—my description of her backside, not hers, you understand. She also said to trust you with my life."

Dez nods.

Stewart leans across the table, drops his voice. "Several years ago, a group of career criminals caught the eye of some crooked CIA officers. The thugs were all from New Haven, Connecticut. Many of them had been arrested and tried for various crimes, and not one of them had ever spoke a word against their compatriots. Not once. A subset of the CIA, not happy with the rule stating they cannot operate on U.S. soil, decided to put the so-called New Haven Boys on retainer. From time to time, and for a hefty pay, the Boys get their hands dirty on behalf of the CIA. They mostly spend their time running drugs and girls. Some protection operations. The classics. Then, when someone at the Agency whistles, they salute smartly and do Agency bidding. Leader's a nasty blighter name of Briggs. Was special forces, U.S. Army. He rules the mob with an iron fist."

"Jay-sus, but the CIA picks lovely dance partners, don't it?"

"Worth saying: Most CIA officers wouldn't come within a

league of these mad bastards. Only a few use 'em, near as I know. And your Ray Harker? I'd put him at the top of list, like as not."

Dez says, "And where would I find this charmer name of Briggs?"

Stewart smiles. "May I ask why?"

"Aye. Two gents from Connecticut staked out me hotel. I messed with them a bit. Got 'em in gaol. Then I stayed put t'see if they'd try again. And as of last night, they had. I'm thrilled, of course. Christmas come early. If I can get a quiet conversation with a decent and honest businessman, such as this Briggs, well, could be he'd lead me to Ray Harker."

"And your feud with Harker? If I may be so bold."

Dez sips his coffee. "I'd thought Harker was the assassin known as Thiago. A very smart lady tells me the name Thiago's been connected to the murder-for-hire world for ages. So it's likely not a fella, but an organization. And I've reason to believe the Thiago organization was part an' parcel of that Russian hostage situation in Newark."

"Good lord."

"So on one level, I want to find out what I can about this Thiago organization, to see how it fits with that Russian thing. And on another level, I want to track down Ray Harker in order to kick his kumquats up into his chest cavity. Two birds, one stone."

The man not named Stewart grins. He's got the kind of face that completely transforms when he grins: eyes, nose, ears, jawline; the lot. It's the kind of grin one cannot see and not also grin.

"Arabella Satti told me one more thing about you, matey."

"An' that is?"

"That you make friends easily. But when you make enemies, there's blood on the streets."

Dez smiles into his cup. "Exaggerates, Belle. 'Avoiding a fight is a mark of honor; only fools insist on quarreling.' Proverbs, twenty, three. I'm the peaceable sort, me."

CHAPTER 30

The leader of the New Haven Boys, Briggs, works out of a gentlemen's club in Queens, or so sayeth the Scots spy.

Dez took his messenger bag with his smaller knife, the sheath with lockpicks, and his tablet to the gig with Kansas Jack and the Blacktop. There's naught he needs immediately in his hotel room, so he stays away.

He calls FBI Special Agent Stella Ansara and asks her about this guy Briggs.

"Yes, that name has come up. He's supposed to be the capo of this group, but unlike his crew, the cops have never charged him with anything. Us, either."

"D'you have a photo of the lad? Also, a home address?"

Stella takes four minutes to dig one up and sends it to Dez's phone. "Can I ask what you're up to?"

"The surveillance is back on at me hotel, and I'm assumin' you don't want me creating another traffic crash just to mess with 'em."

"That'd be nice, thank you."

"So I'll chat up the good man an' see if we can't come to an understanding."

"This guy's a damn crime lord, Limerick. Plus, probably, a thug-for-hire for corrupt CIA officers. You're not going to get within a football field of him."

"Ye've underestimated me finest quality, Special Agent."

"Oh? And what's that?"

Dez says, "I'm convivial."

"Convivial?"

"It's me secret weapon. None can stand against it."

"You're not half as charming as you think you are, Limerick."

He barks a laugh. "I think I'm three times as charming as your average scoundrel! That still puts me well ahead of the pack, don't it?"

Step two, Dez uses Google Earth to find out exactly where Briggs's strip club is, and to get a look at the footprint of the building. Being a gatekeeper means getting through doors and locks, and websites are nothing more than virtual doors and locks. He's not an outstanding hacker, but he's good enough to get into the development services site of the nearest municipality, and to download the blueprints for the strip club. He goes to the website of the nearest fire brigade and does the same.

Within a couple of hours, he knows the building as well as Briggs and his staff.

He calls the club and asks for Briggs. When he hears a thick New England accent, saying, "Yo. Who's this?" Dez hangs up.

Now he knows where his target is.

Dez rents a jeep under a false ID that's connected to one of his overseas bank accounts. It's getting on 1 A.M. by the time Dez gets to the strip club in Queens, which has the helpful name Stripperz! The exclamation mark was added, Dez assumes, because the name alone seemed a shade too subtle.

He sits in the club parking lot until closing time. The last seven or eight customers drift out around the same time.

After closing time, he waits an additional thirty minutes. He watches as the dancers march out, always in groups of two and three, because no stripper with an ounce of experience walks into a night-time parking lot alone.

Two cooks leave next, having cleaned their stations. A couple of women who could be waitresses leave together and stand at a bus stop across the way. A guy who might or might not be a bartender makes his exit.

Well back from the other cars in the parking lot are five very loud, very bright, very aggressive-looking sports cars. Based on what Dez has seen of the New Haven Boys so far, those belong to Briggs and his people.

A minimum of five guys. Maybe more. Within minutes, two loud guys in silk shirts and gold chains leave the club and climb into the sports cars.

Three cars left. The math works out just about exactly as Dez has hoped.

Satisfied that civilians have fled, Dez picks the lock on the front door of Stripperz! and saunters in.

The place likely is lurid and revolting when all the lights are on and the crappy sound system is pumping out mideighties rock hits. With work lights glowing, the place has all the charm of sepsis but none of the glamor.

He peeks in the kitchen. Lights off and nobody here.

Dez makes a bet with himself: the featured music will include "Back That Azz Up" by Juvenile. He checks. Easy money. He cranks up the sound, loud as he can, gets it playing, then sits on the edge of the raised stage, his back to the stripper poles, his boots dangling.

Three men emerge from a hidden door. Three guys who look more or less like the dorks Dez met outside his hotel, down to the gold chains and silk shirts. The guy in the middle is Briggs, according to the photo Special Agent Ansara sent him.

Briggs and a total gorilla of a guy—six-five and bulky—watch as the third guy shuts off the music and gets in Dez's face.

"Hey! We're closed! Get the fuck out!"

Dez stands and, in doing so, plows his oversized fist into the midriff of the third guy.

The man folds and drops.

Briggs and his gorilla are still about ten feet away. Briggs says, "Hey! Who the fuck are you?"

Dez bends over and takes an automatic from a hip holster of the downed man, who moans in the fetal position.

"Just a lad lookin' for a quiet drink, innkeep." He disassembles the auto, tossing parts of it here and there, holding on to the now nearly useless frame.

Briggs turns to the gorilla, shaking his head. He says, "You mind?"

The gorilla advances on Dez, huge fists clenched. The gorilla growls, "Should have kept the gun, asshole."

"Kept as much as I need," Dez says, throwing the frame of the gun like a boomerang. It spins, the metal gouging into the gorilla's throat.

The man's hands go to his neck. Dez marches into his space and plows a boot sole into the outside of the man's knee. As he collapses that direction, Dez pushes him back so, when the gorilla falls, he falls on Briggs.

They tumble together, destroying one of the strip club's four-top tables. Dez takes a moment to scoop up both of their guns and toss them aside. He glances at the third guy, who still hasn't risen.

Dez bends his right arm in two and slams the point of his

elbow into a nerve cluster in the gorilla's neck. He's instantaneously unconscious.

Briggs is trapped under about 260 pounds of deadweight. Dez puts him in a choke hold and he quickly loses consciousness.

He returns to the third guy, gets him on his feet. Holding him by the collar of his very shiny shirt, Dez frog-marches the smaller guy into Briggs's office. He spots the controls for the building's alarm system and turns them off. He shoves the third guy in front of a hip-high safe and says, "Open it, lad."

The guy's still holding his midriff. "What . . . What the . . ."

"Open the feckin' safe, darlin', or I will disconnect your scrotum from your torso. Please."

The guy opens the safe.

Dez clocks him behind the ear and he folds.

Dez takes out about thirty thousand dollars in cash.

He checks on his unconscious men by the stage, then seeks out the dressing room. Finds it. Five chairs and tables, five vanities, lots of pasties and stilettos and thongs. Each dressing room table has a drawer, and each is locked. Gatekeepers love locks. When he's got the drawers open, he distributes the thirty thousand in cash to the dancers, with a note that reads BRIGGS BELIEVES THIS WAS STOLEN BY A GUY LAST NIGHT. WHAT YOU DO WITH IT IS UP TO YOU.

He relocks each drawer.

Dez checks into a storage closet and comes up with a longish spool of wire. He gets all three lads up on the stage—nearly throwing his back out, getting the gorilla up there—then wires their wrists behind their backs, and to each other, and twining the wire around one of the stripper poles. All three are on their knees.

He waits for all three to come to. He has them facing north, south, and west.

When all three are sufficiently conscious and aware of their situations, he prods the smallest of the three. "Tell 'em, my lad."

"He had me open the safe, boss. He stole from you."

Briggs is seething. He lets loose with a long string of crude hy-phenates. Ending with "You're a dead man!"

"What I am is Desmond Limerick, sir. I believe I met two more of your mates quite recently."

Dez can see the look of recognition on Briggs's face. The gorilla recognizes the name, too.

"This is in regards to me 'oul mate, Raymond Harker. Tall fella? Blond? He sent you lot 'round to find me hotel. Question is: Did he also send ye lot after my friend in Brooklyn?"

"Fuck you!"

Dez shrugs. He doesn't hit Briggs. He hits the third guy; the smallest of the three. In the nose. Cartilage crackles and blood flows.

The gorilla swears at him, fighting with the wire around his wrists.

Dez smiles at Briggs. "Mr. Briggs, sir. Did Ray Harker send ye to snatch my friend in Brooklyn?"

"You gonna die slow! I will fucking grind out your eyes!"

Dez hits the third guy in the nose. This time the man's head pings off the strippers' pole. The man grunts.

"Mr. Briggs, sir. Did Ray Harker send ye to snatch my friend?"

"Fuck you!"

He hits the third guy. More blood pours down the guy's chin, staining his silk shirt. The gorilla watches, quiet now, no longer threatening, taking measure of the situation.

"Mr. Briggs, sir. Did Ray Harker send ye to snatch my friend?"

"You have no idea how much trouble I bring to—"

Bam. The third guy's nose is smashed. His eyes roll up into his skull and he slumps down, unconscious against the pole.

Dez takes his time moving in front of the gorilla and making a fist. He asks, sweetly, "Mr. Briggs, sir. Did Ray Harker send ye to snatch my friend?"

The gorilla says, "Tell him."

Briggs is stunned. "What? Fuck you! I ain't tell this bastard—"

The gorilla says, "I don't give a fuck about Ray Harker. Tell this bastard or I'll kill you."

"You work for me!"

"I worked for you and then I decided to kill you. We're from New Haven." The gorilla shrugs. "Ain't exactly unheard of."

A beat, and Briggs turns to Dez. "We were told only about you, asshole. Told to find you and kill you."

So whomsoever the snatch team was outside Cat's hotel, it wasn't these guys. Dez suspected as much.

"Thank you, gentlemen. 'Twas a pleasure doin' business with you."

Dez hops off the stage and, with that bandy-legged, seafaring gait of his, strolls into Briggs's office and reactivates the alarms. Then he calls for both the police and fire response.

Dez and his jeep are two blocks away from Stripperz! when the first fire truck passes him, lights and sirens all a dither.

CHAPTER 31

It's dawn as the mob boss called Briggs arrives home. He and his men were interrogated for hours. It was beyond humiliating, being found, tied up, robbed, by both firefighters and the police Briggs has been diligently paying off. It made him look weak. It made him look like prey.

And the insubordination he received from his finest fighter is more than a little frightening. Briggs has kept dominance over his small band of criminals through a combination of fear and greed.

Last night's affair shook his reputation.

He drives home as the sun rises. He still doesn't know for sure who this Limerick guy is, but he tore through Briggs's troops the way a tornado seeks a trailer park.

Briggs lives in a small, ranch-style house five miles from the strip club, surrounded by a high fence. He paid very good money to electrify the fence. He lives alone with just his violent and well-trained attack dog, a Doberman pinscher.

He gets home, unlocks the gate, unlocks the front door, and de-activates his top-of-the-line security system. He turns on the lights in his living room.

Dez sits on his couch. A frosty six-pack of Harp Lager rests on his glass-and-bamboo coffee table. One of the six bottles is missing, and Dez is drinking from it. Dez sits on the right-hand side of the couch. Briggs's attack dog is curled up on the left-hand cushion. On the floor sits a plate and the gnawed remains of a T-bone steak.

Dez doesn't often drink beer at dawn but he can't honestly say this is the first time, either.

Having been interrogated earlier, Briggs is, of course, unarmed. He stands awhile, fists bunched near his hips, trying to control his emotions.

Dez says, "Beer, then?"

Nearly two minutes pass. Briggs considers the situation. He walks out of the living room, checks his kitchen and both bedrooms and the bathroom, but finds nobody else. He checks his bed stand but the Colt revolver normally there is missing. He's sure the SIG in the living room is, as well.

He returns to the living room. He takes a bottle, uses the edge of his fireplace mantel to pop the cap, and drinks half of it.

He sits in an armchair, lights a cigarette, smokes it down, snubs it out, lights another.

He says, "You ain't allowed on the couch."

Dez rises and moves to the room's other chair.

"I was talking to the fucking dog."

"Ah. Sorry, 'course." Dez moves back to the couch.

"You stole my money. Beat my guys. Made me lose face. So tell me how come it is I ain't killing you, you son of a bitch."

Dez sips his beer. "Because I know something you don't. You think the magic sauce for your crew's success in the States is you're protected by the CIA. Because you do their bidding, they keep law enforcement types off you, I'm guessing."

Briggs doesn't deny it.

"You was thinking Ray Harker is CIA. My guess is, the arsehole told you he was still working with the Agency, an' killin' me was company business."

Briggs neither confirms nor denies, but sips and smokes.

"'Twasn't, my lad. Harker done a runner. Been on the CIA's most-wanted list for donkey's years. An' now, so are you and yours. There'll be no more covert contracts. No more clandestine, domestic ops to keep the Company boys' hands clean. Harker fucked ye, bruv. You're in it now."

They sit for a spell. The sun's fully up. They drink, and Briggs smokes. The couch smells of smoke, and Dez is fairly certain his clothes will, too.

Briggs locks his eyes on Dez. "What do you want?"

"Harker, 'course."

Dez couldn't ask Briggs this in front of his men. There's no way the mob boss would have given him jack with his guys watching.

Briggs says, "Why?"

"I've a fine and burning hatred for that prick. It is my intention to find him and to beat him to death."

Briggs just studies him. He was seething with anger when he entered, but that's gone now. Now he's just tired. He secretly suspected Harker had stopped representing the CIA, but he hadn't done anything to prove it. Now he suspects Limerick is right, and in one evening, Briggs has lost his reputation for toughness and unit discipline, and his intelligence agency shield.

He takes another measured swallow of his beer.

"I've known and worked for Harker for, shit, a dozen years. Hell, more. He lied to me. If I find him first, you won't get the chance to lay a hand on him, fucker."

"I can live with that."

Briggs pauses, then nods, and draws his cell phone. He unlocks it with his face, goes to contacts, and hands it to Dez.

Dez copies the contact into his own phone. It's Harker's, but is logged into Briggs's contacts as RH.

He hands the phone back. He holds up his empty bottle. "Do you recycle?"

Briggs takes the bottle.

Dez leaves.

Briggs glowers at his dog. But doesn't make her get down.

CHAPTER 32

Later that morning, Dez calls Stella Ansara and tells her about the New Haven Boys staking out his hotel. She agrees to let NYPD know.

About forty minutes later, she calls Dez back. "The cops just chased them off. No one's watching your hotel now."

"Ta, that."

"Also, the Newark police unearthed the slug that killed that pediatrician, Adam Levkowitz. The guy who was shot in the back. It was a forty-five."

"So not the Russians," Dez says.

"One anomaly's an oddity. Two is a pattern. There was another killer at The Liberty."

"Good to know we wasn't seeing patterns where they weren't. Any idea how Dr. Levkowitz ended up at The Liberty?"

"Hang on." Dez can practically hear her scrolling through the notes field of her phone. "Ah . . . yes. He's been in group counseling. A PTSD group. Anyway, they all got free passes to the opening of the convention center. Made it a group outing."

That seems particularly unhelpful. Dez says, "Peter Garvey?"

"He was there because he's on a college board of trustees. They had a quarterly meeting. The Liberty apparently was giving away free conference rooms all this month, to dredge up interest in their smaller meeting facilities."

"And Gaetano? The high school teacher?"

"He's a comic book collector. He got a free ticket to a comic con that was taking place there."

Dez hears the neurons in his brain ping. "Garvey, Levkowitz, and Gaetano. All got free tickets to events at the convention center."

"Which lends credence to your idea that they were targeted. That they were lured there. Same as you."

"Does, aye."

Stella says, "Now I've got a question for you."

"Fire away."

"The thugs who we suspect sometimes worked for the CIA? They have a strip club on Long Island. Last night, someone robbed it and beat one of the hoods pretty badly."

"You know what I blame for all the incivility in America? Social media."

"You don't say." Stella's voice is laden with irony. "Because I was about to say that that has a certain Desmond Limerick touch to it."

"Violence holds no place in me life."

"Are your knuckles swollen this morning?"

"A little, aye."

She laughs. "You do you. Just don't let us catch you doing it." And hangs up.

Dez eats at a local breakfast joint and showers and changes—his hair still smells a little of Briggs's cigarette smoke. Then he boots up his tablet, and an app invented by the Israeli Mossad. He types in the number that Briggs had given him for Ray Harker's mobile.

The app takes nearly ninety seconds, then gives Dez the exact GPS coordinates for that mobile.

Personal privacy isn't really one of things the Mossad loses a lot of sleep over.

Harker is here in New York. Or at least his phone is.

Another spy—Arabella Satti of MI6—hates Ray Harker even more than Dez does. He sends a text to her mobile: Have lead on Harker. New York area. You around?

Five minutes later, his phone vibrates.

In Prague. All yours. Nail the bastard. A

Well, it was polite to invite her, but he hadn't expected her to be in the States.

Dez takes his mobile and his bespoke tablet computer, plus both of his knives; a 290-millimeter fixed-blade fighting knife, made by Coltellerie Maserin, and his folding Raptor blade, with its steel cutting surface that glides into the anodized aluminum handle.

Handguns are literally everywhere in the States but Dez has no intention of finding one. He has no gun-carry permit in the United States and he's making this country his home; at least for the time being. He'd prefer not to get crosswise with the police on that issue.

Also, the GPS coordinates for Ray Harker's phone put him in a highly populated portion of Greenwich Village and Dez would like to avoid a gunfight in such a setting.

He does take along three of the inch-in-diameter nuts and bolts. They're certainly not illegal to carry.

The knives and bolts should serve in the event of trouble. And with any luck, he won't need them at all. He just wants to see what the situation is. If the phone number really leads to Harker, Dez can leave the task of capturing him to Stella and the FBI. That's their job.

It's time to see what his old mate is up to.

CHAPTER 33

Mark Ivanson is where Mark Ivanson can often be found; in a bar and well into his cups.

Ivanson's been telling the bartender and three other patrons in the Greenwich Village tavern about his harrowing ordeal at The Liberty. He'd been there after netting free tickets to hear the legendary Calvin Willow perform.

Several drinking buddies and the bartender gather in to hear every gory detail. Ivanson was holed up in one of the convention center's eateries, an ice-cream shop, with about seven other hostages. He'd seen one woman shot by a sniper and killed. He was sure he was going to die that day.

The bartender knows Ivanson's good for it, so he refills his scotch rocks. A secretary at the Ivanson family business covers Mark's bar tab at the end of every month.

Someone asks, "Did your life flash in front of your eyes?"

"No, but every hot babe I *didn't* lay sure did!"

The others laugh. Someone slaps him on the shoulder. Ivanson's one of those guys, his storytelling skills go up with his blood-alcohol content.

At one point, two of the regular drinkers check their watches and head off for the night. When they do, Olivia Gelman slides onto the stool next to Ivanson. She's wearing a backless dress that ties off behind her neck and three-inch heels. Her deep mahogany hair frames her face in rich waves. "Oh my God, I heard you talking! You were at that terrorist thing?"

Ivanson literally does a double take. She's beautiful.

"Yeah. Lucky to have walked away from that one."

Liv makes eye contact with the bartender, then glances at Ivanson's glass. "Same," she says. "But the Balvenie, please. For both of us."

That's a much, much nicer scotch than Mark Ivanson usually drinks. His night is looking up.

When the bartender crosses to get the better bottle, Liv makes eye contact with Ray Harker, drinking at a table by the windows, watching her work. He tips his beer her direction.

Liv says, "And you got a ticket to hear Calvin Willow play?"

"Sure did. But, of course, he didn't. Play. I wish. That would have been . . ." He knows he's blathering, but this truly is a gorgeous woman leaning his way, making eye contact and smiling.

"How did that happen?" she asks. "The free tickets."

He frowns. "Ah . . . I don't really know. Some radio station said I was randomly selected."

She holds up her rocks glass, and Mark Ivanson does the same.

"To being lucky," Liv says, letting the lilt of innuendo shade her phrasing.

"I'll drink to that."

They do. She offers a hand. "I'm Janice."

"Janice, hi. Mark."

"What do you do, Mark?"

"My family's trucking business. I'm, I guess, the CFO."

"Lucky and good with math," she says.

He grins stupidly. "Not that good. Dad promoted me about twelve years ago. Said I could get into less trouble if he knew where I was all day."

"Ah. A bad boy." She sips the single malt. "Girls always go for the bad boys."

Ivanson's having some trouble believing that this hottie is hitting on him. He says, "Your accent is beautiful. Where are you from?"

"Many places. Mark? Do you want to get out of here?"

Not getting killed in a major terrorist situation was lucky. But not this lucky. He grins. "Yes, I do."

Liv produces a black Amex and pays for all his drinks, plus hers, which she barely touched. She set her purse on the floor by her stool when she sat down. When she bends to pick it up, Ivanson spots the tattoo on her right rear shoulder of a two-faced Roman god.

That tattoo rings a bell. Something funny. He almost has it when she takes his arm and leads him to the bar exit and the elevator to the lobby of this building.

The elevator is glass-sided. Beyond the tavern, the building also hosts an array of businesses, a chain bookstore, a sushi restaurant, and a small hotel, all with a shared lobby.

And as they descend toward the lobby, Liv spots Desmond Limerick, swinging through the rotating doors with that usual dumb grin of his plastered over his roundish face.

Liv turns so her back is to the elevator windows and she touches her ear. Twice.

"Desmond is in the lobby."

Mark Ivanson smiles. "I don't know what that means."

Without turning back, Liv hits the 2 button—the building's mezzanine level.

She brushes lint off his shoulder and smiles warmly. "Just something all the kids are saying these days."

CHAPTER 34

Dez enters the lobby of the fifteen-story building. It's dark out now but brightly lit in here. The place is bustling, the lobby serving a wide array of establishments.

When he's in close proximity, the Mossad app works as a direction finder. The problem being, the direction finder only works in two dimensions, not three. He glances at his mobile and sees that Harker's phone is directly ahead of him. But on this floor? Or one of the other fourteen?

A flaw in the programming, that.

He spots a large and backlit map shaped like a canted desk, showing the various businesses that use this lobby. He strolls that way to get a sense of the layout of the place.

It would take him forever to search the entire building. He's thinking the better bet is to hang out in the lobby and hope that Harker comes to him. Because with this many floors . . .

As Dez thinks this, he glances at the twin, glass-sided elevators. One is heading down now.

And there's Ray Harker. Tall, blond, tanned, handsome. And staring directly at Dez. He pulls back his windbreaker to reveal a shoulder holster and a Glock.

Sometimes, Dez's plans work out better than what's actually good for him. This would be one of those times.

Harker is on the third level, heading down. Dez has maybe five seconds. He could lead the bastard outside, but there are as many civilians there as there are in the lobby. That move wouldn't reduce the likelihood of collateral injuries or deaths.

He studies the building map for a moment and decides the bookstore is his best bet. And it's got an entry on the ground floor.

Dez is halfway there as the elevator arrives on the first floor and the doors hiss open.

On the mezzanine level, Liv Gelman guides Mark Ivanson back toward the restrooms. She studied the building at length after Ray Harker had tracked the target to this, one of the drunk's favorite booze halls.

They pass the stairs on their way to the restrooms. Ivanson veers toward the stairs and Liv—who is stronger than she looks—drags him back.

"Hey. Aren't we going somewhere else?" he slurs, stumbling a little.

She has her arm entwined with his. "Yes. I have a very naughty idea. Are you up for some fun?"

He grins. "Lead on!"

They get to the restrooms—ladies' on the left, men's on the right—and Liv directs him to the men's bathroom. They're a step away when a voice rings out, "Hey, lady."

She turns. A janitor has just come up the stairs.

"Bathrooms are closed on this side. I just cleaned them. There's two more, on the west side of this floor."

"That's all right." She smiles brightly. "We won't be a minute."

"Yeah, but you can't—"

Liv releases Ivanson's arm. She draws a Glock from her purse, plus a sound suppressor, which she adroitly screws into place. Then turns and shoots the janitor.

Ivanson's back is to the action. Plus, he's pretty drunk. He hears the *phut phut* of the bullets but doesn't know what it is. He glances around, perplexed.

"Hey!"

Two security guards have just climbed up the stairs. One has his eyes on the janitor with two center-body-mass shots to his chest, the wounds an inch apart.

The other spots Liv.

Who turns and begins racing down the corridor, away from the restrooms and Mark Ivanson.

Dez turns his head a second before entering the bookstore.

Ray Harker has spotted him.

Dez notes two people working cash registers. One is maybe a college student, and the other is a woman in her forties whose name tag reads MANAGER. Dez muscles his way past a paying customer and steps in front of the manager.

"Tall, blond lad, about to enter this bookstore, is a criminal, an' he's armed. Call nine-one-one, will ye kindly? Thank ye, ma'am."

Then he heads deeper into the bookstore.

The place is quite a labyrinth and, as hoped, the stacks are taller than Dez. It's got both new and used books, plus calendars and stationery and vintage CDs and vinyl records, and what have you. About a thousand types of cute and unusual pens. Dez has no idea there was such a market for cute and unusual pens. Goes to show what he knows.

He cuts an immediate left into cookbooks and sprints the distance, avoiding running anyone over. He takes a right into spiritual.

Now Harker will have to hunt him down. And Harker won't have the luxury of taking his eyes off the entrance, for fear that Dez will backtrack to the lobby.

It's much easier being chased in a public maze than it is chasing in a public maze. Provided Harker doesn't have a partner. And so far, Dez hasn't spotted one.

The store manager looked properly shocked. Dez hopes she took him seriously and the police are on their way. Dez wishes he'd either kept that slingshot or conjured up another one from somewhere. He's mad good at throwing things, thanks to a lifetime of cricket and darts. But against a Glock auto, he's at the disadvantage of distance.

He realizes for the first time that there's a basement level. The signage over the down-escalator reads USED MYSTERIES/SCI-FI/ROMANCE. And like a lot of shops, the up-escalator isn't adjacent to the down; it's on the far side of the store.

He waits, eyeing a spinner rack of reading glasses and beaded lanyards.

He's got an iron bolt in his right fist.

He hears a woman say, "Hey!" as if someone bumped into her. Which, likely, someone just did.

As Dez spots the broad shoulder of Ray Harker turning a corner, twenty feet away, he quickly sweeps down the escalator to the next level, running, hitting every fourth step.

He moves quickly across the space, around people and tabletop displays of books and board games, and reaches the up-elevator.

With luck, he'll emerge in Harker's blind spot.

Luck isn't with him, and as his head clears the escalator walls, Harker spots him, cleanly draws his Glock, and gets a shot off.

Dez ducks and sprints back down the up-elevator. A young man has just stepped on.

"Look out, dude, this is the up—"

"Fella up there with a gun. Call nine-one-one," Dez says, grabbing the kid by the lapels and forcefully lifting him off the escalator and into a corner aisle lined with graphic novels.

"For real?"

"Very."

Harker's using a quick-draw, snap-open shoulder holster designed to take a gun that already has a sound suppressor in place. Dez's impressed how quickly Harker got the long, ungainly package out from beneath his coat.

And now it's a standoff.

Will Harker come down the up-escalator, as Dez did? Or will he take the down-escalator?

Dez picks a place near an exhibit of Doctor Who books and games and paraphernalia. From here, he can watch both egresses.

Nothing happens.

Harker may have porridge for brains, but he's realized the same thing Dez has: Choose either escalator, and you might pick wrong.

On the mezzanine level, Liv Gelman deftly picks the lock to the building's security room. One person is on duty, staring at a bank of monitors. She looks up, startled, before Liv shoots her in the chest. The guard is rocked back, her rolling chair flipping over.

Liv has done her reconnoiter. She knows that there's another door on the far side of this room, and it leads to the other end of the mezzanine level and a second set of stairs.

She gets there and is quick-walking down the stairs, having been spotted by neither of the other guards. She touches her earjack again.

"I'm being chased. Ivanson's alive. Where are you?"

She waits a half second.

"Bookstore. Limerick's in the basement area. I can't tell which escalator he'll use. We—"

"I hear sirens," she says. And indeed she does. "Get out now. Rendezvous point beta. Go."

Then she's in the lobby and moving quickly out into the evening and rush-hour traffic and blending neatly into the flow of pedestrians.

On the ground floor of the bookstore, Harker hears Liv's command but hesitates.

Putting a bullet in that cocky Brit son of a bitch would make him sleep better. And since this is the second time Limerick has interfered with these hits, putting a bullet in him also would make their payoff more likely.

Liv is right. But Harker's tempted.

Dez waits. It's a standoff now. And if Ray Harker has the patience of Job and all the time in the world, he can make the standoff work in his favor.

But Dez is fairly certain Harker has neither.

Dez glances at the sci-fi display and notes a bowl full of glittery superballs, the size of an average garlic bulb.

Which gives him a wicked idea.

He grabs the bowl and walks to the up-escalator. "Raymond, my lad! Is that you, then?"

Harker either has left ahead of the police arrival, or he's still up there. If so, Harker can hear where Dez is.

The escalators both have long, narrow walls to the left and the right, so customers can't fall over the sides as they ride up or down.

"I read an article once, in *Wired*. D'you know what polybuta-diene is?"

He waits.

"You talk too fucking much, asshole."

From the sound of his voice, Harker is directly above Dez.

Dez rears back and throws a superball, hard as he can.

It bounces off one wall of the escalator, then its opposite wall, then disappears from sight.

On the ground floor, Harker hears something and sees something streaking past his head. It's moving too fast to see. He ducks and the silent thing whizzes past his ear.

Could Limerick have a silenced gun?

"Polybutadiene is a synthetic polymer, my son! Extreme elasticity. Invented in the 1960s. Mostly used for the makin' of tyre treads and sidewalls, yeah?"

He throws another superball. It pings madly up the escalator well. He throws another, then another and another.

He hears, "The fuck?"

"Know what else they're used in?"

Dez throws five more of the sparkly, ultra-elastic globes. Then draws one of the iron bolts out of his messenger bag and dares the quick sprint up the stairs.

On the ground floor, the superballs are still pinging madly about. Harker has drawn his silenced weapon and Dez spots customers and staff scrambling for safety. Harker has his arm up, covering his head, as dense balls of rubber fling themselves in random patterns. They whiz past and around him like bees, confusing him.

Well, Dez thinks, the superballs are smarter than Ray Harker. That tracks.

Harker spots Dez just as Dez sidearms the combined bolt and screw toward the gunman.

It connects.

Harker grunts and stumbles backward.

But doesn't release his grip on his gun.

Dez jukes behind a long, tall bookshelf—self-help—and a second later, two forty-five slugs rip through the metal shelving and a handful of books. Paper scrap flies in every direction. An overhead florescent light shorts out and pops free of its moorings.

Dez sees people hunkered down in the aisle. "Move! Move! Move!"

He sprints toward them and they move indeed.

He gets to the end of the aisle and glances back.

Harker rounds the corner and fires off two more shots, but Dez has ducked back with plenty of time.

The shots go wild anyway. Dez sees Harker's face for only a split second, but that's long enough to show a deep gouge across the man's forehead. The right side of his face is bathed in blood and it looks as if his right eye is plastered shut with it.

Dez remembers that Harker is right-hand dominant and also right-eye dominant. If Harker's lost his binocular vision, even for the moment, it's advantage Limerick.

He's about to celebrate that when another bullet rips a chunk out of the floor carpeting, two inches from Dez's left boot.

That bullet came from a different angle.

Harker has an ally.

Dez scrambles fast down his current aisle, and juts quickly to his right, gaining some distance on them.

He thinks the other shooter is a woman. He spotted high heels and well-shaped legs, and the hem of a dress.

Whoever she is, she changes the math of this thing, and not in a good way. One-on-one, it's easier to hide than to seek in a tall and twisty labyrinth like a bookstore. One-on-two, it's easier to seek than to hide.

He's snatched up another iron bolt from his bag, hoping for the best.

In his ear, Ray Harker hears Liv Gelman, speaking low. "Police are nearly here. We exit! Now!"

But he hasn't killed Limerick yet. He has to get that limey bastard before—

A bullet slams into the wall four inches from Harker's head. He winces and ducks. It came from his right, and he's been blood-blinded on his right. He hunkers behind a cashier's kiosk and glances that way.

The bullet came from Liv.

She all but shouts through his earjack, "I said *now*!"

She's right. He knows she's right.

He torques out the sound suppressor and stores both it and his gun in his shoulder rig. He rises and moves quickly her direction, blood pulsing from the wound on his face, trickling down his cheek and neck, under his sweater.

She takes his arm and leads him out of the bookstore and toward the back of the lobby, and an alley she scouted out in advance. They hear sirens, right outside the building.

Limerick will have to die later.

By the time the police arrive, Dez realizes Harker and the bird who's helping him have slipped free.

But that's okay. Because it *was* Harker. Raymond Fucking Harker. Ex-CIA. Associated with the Thiago group of assassins.

Ray Harker. A right legend in the annals of assholery, and an ulcerated wound on the buttocks of the planet.

CHAPTER 35

Dez is interviewed by the police but not arrested. They never saw him throw the bolt—or the bouncy little balls—at Harker. He's just another civilian caught up in the violence.

But he also texts Stella Ansara, and she arrives before the police get everyone's statements. Stella wears her hair in a ponytail and she's got the standard windbreaker with the letters FBI, twelve-inches tall, scrawled across her back. She also uses driving glasses, Dez notes. She badges her way in, speaks to the senior-most cop on the scene, then gestures for Dez to join her.

"Ray Harker," he says without preamble. "This whole thing is a Thiago fiasco, and we know that now for certain an' for sure."

"Are you all right?"

"Me? Never better. I tagged Harker, though. He's bleeding from his forehead. Dunno how much blood he lost, but some."

Stella calls over a New York cop and asks for a BOLO on a tall, blond white male, in his thirties, bleeding from his forehead. "Last scene in this vicinity."

"An' there's a woman with him," Dez adds. "Also armed."

Stella says, "A woman?"

"Aye. Ye'll find her slug down that aisle there. She hit the floor." He points it out to the uniformed cop, who makes a note. "Them other shots? Up in the shelving? Them's Harker."

Another cop enters and whispers to the lead investigator. He nods to Stella, who brings Dez with her.

"Ma'am? We had a janitor and a security guard shot, up on two. Double-tap to the chest, both of them. Very pro. Two other guards chased her."

Dez and Stella exchange looks. Stella says, "Her?"

"Yeah, and they got a description. Brunette, white, maybe five-five, long curled hair. Very pretty."

"In a dress and heels?" Dez asks.

"Yeah."

To Stella, he says, "Harker's little helper."

"Okay. Anything else?"

"Got a drunk from the upstairs bar. The security guards think the woman was about to kill him."

"Are you holding him?"

"The building security office is a crime scene. We put him in an extra room on the second."

Stella asks, "You talked to him?"

"He's pretty drunk, but not out of it. Yeah. I got five bucks says this is either the luckiest week of his life, or the unluckiest."

"Because," Dez steps in, "our lad survived that terrorist incident in New Jersey?"

The cop says, "Jesus. How'd you know?"

Stella nods to Dez. "This pretty much locks up the multiple-targets theory. You were right all along."

"C'mon," the cop says. "I'll take you to him."

He turns and twists his ankle a little. He's just stepped on a superball. He spots two more. "The hell's this?"

Dez nudges him with his elbow and grins. "Used me balls. Ofttimes, that's better'n using your brains."

Stella shakes her head. "So thinks every man I ever met."

The cops have found a large black coffee for Mark Ivanson and that, plus the adrenaline spike from his fear, has sobered him up. When Stella and Dez arrive, he tells them about the hot lady who hit on him at the bar and asked if he wanted to get out of there.

Stella says, "Can you describe her, sir?"

Dez jumps in. "Did the barkeep serve her?"

"Huh? Yeah. And she bought really pricey booze."

Dez touches Stella on the forearm. "You don't mind, I'll run up and ask the bartender to describe her. My experience: Bartenders have excellent situational awareness. Plus, he was sober."

"Thanks. I'll meet you up there."

Dez leaves and takes the elevator to fifteen.

He gets out and saunters to the bar. It takes the bartender, a twentysomething guy with a top knot and waxed mustache, a minute to get to him.

"Ye know what I haven't had in years? A vodka gimlet."

"Got a fave vodka?" the guy says, wiping down the bar.

"Belvedere."

"Good choice, my man. Hold on."

He brings the drink in a couple of minutes. Dez takes a sip and sighs. "You are a man what knows his craft."

"Thanks, dude."

"Ye heard about the commotion downstairs, then?"

"Some idiot shooting up the bookstore? Yeah. Fuck, this town just gets crazier and crazier."

"Name's Dez. I'm helping the FBI on this matter. Guy who was attacked was one of your clients."

"Holy shit. He all right?"

"He is. Name of Mark Ivanson."

"Oh! Shit!" The bartender clearly knows Ivanson and smacks the bar with an open palm. "No way! Dude was here for a couple of hours today! Well, I mean, he's here a couple of hours a couple of days a week. Every week."

"Said he was with a right flash bird."

The bartender blinks at him.

"A pretty woman."

"Whoa, yeah! That was some world-class talent. I'm . . . can I say this? Not trying to be mean here, but she could do better than Mark Ivanson. She could do better than a *sober* Mark Ivanson."

"Aye, got ye. Describe her?"

He does, and as expected, his memory is sharp. Bartenders tend to remember people who spend well on expensive drinks. Mark Ivanson's date, Dez discovers, was about five-five, dressed to the nines, a dark brunette, her curly hair worn down, curvy, and with big eyes. "Great heels. I got a thing for high heels."

"An' who doesn't?"

"Her dress was Prada."

Dez raises his eyebrows.

"I've got a master's in fashion design. Can't get a job in the industry, so . . ." He gestures around the bar.

Dez glances back and sees Stella Ansara moving toward him. She looks dead serious.

"Seen her before, have ye?"

"Absolutely not. Her, I'd remember."

The bartender notices Stella's FBI windbreaker and stops smiling. She steps up next to Dez, glances at his drink. "What is that?"

"Vodka gimlet."

"Same," she says, and nods to the bartender.

"Ye're on duty, love?"

"I'm not working today. I'm here because you called." She gestures to her windbreaker. "I keep this in my hallway closet in case I need it."

Before her drink arrives, Dez describes the woman who picked up Mark Ivanson. "Matches the description Ivanson gave ye? An' the security cops?"

Stella drops her voice. "And you don't know who she is?"

Dez blinks. "Don't. If I knew, I'd tell ye."

"You're sure."

Her drink arrives. They wait for the bartender to move away. Dez says, "Said I got a glimpse of her legs, is all. Out with it, love. What'd Ivanson tell ye?"

"Show me your right forearm."

He does. It's the tattoo of Janus, the Roman god of doors.

"Dez, the woman called herself Janice. Ivanson says he thought that was funny, because she had a tattoo on her right shoulder. Of Janus, the Roman god of doors."

The color drains from Dez's face.

"You're sure you don't know who that is?"

"There's no one it could be," he says. "Honest. The tattoo has t'be a coincidence."

Stella sips her drink. Her eyes pop open. "The bartender's good."

"Aye."

"Did you get the tattoo when you became, what was the term? A gatekeeper?"

"Did, aye. Rite of passage."

"And there's no woman out there who got the same training you did."

"Not anymore," he says. He's suddenly more serious than Stella has ever seen him.

"Someone who flunked out of the training? Or got discharged?"

"I've no idea who this mysterious woman could be. Hand t'god. There was a woman, trained to be keeper. Same as me. But she died."

"Died how?"

Dez says, "I killed her."

CHAPTER 36

Stella's really not on duty, so they order smash burgers at the bar with charred, lemony brussels sprouts, plus another round.

"Ivanson lied to me down there," she tells Dez, removing her FBI jacket and shoving it into a tote bag. The terra-cotta red of her sweater goes well with her Middle Eastern complexion and hair color. "I asked him about the other suspicious deaths at The Liberty. Garvey, Gaetano, and Levkowitz. He says he doesn't know them. The guy's a lousy liar."

"An' how was it our lad got an invite to the conference center?"

"Just as you suspected. He got picked at random by a radio station to get a free tour of the place and to catch Calvin Willow's show. We called the radio station. There was no such promotion."

"He was lured there. The lawyer serving on the college board of trustees was there 'cause his board got a free deal to use the site for their retreat. The former pediatrician and the high school teacher . . . them, I don't remember."

Stella does. "The doc was in a PTSD support group that got a free pass. The teacher was a comic book collector, there for the comics show."

"Right right. So that's three deaths, one near-death, and four free passes to lure the victims there. And behind it all, Ray Harker."

"And a woman with the same tattoo you have."

"Who is not a gatekeeper."

"So you say."

Dez chomps on a brussels sprout. "So I do. There's much of them days I can't discuss with you because it's classified. Ye'll have t'trust me when I say, there once was a woman gatekeeper, but she has shuffled off this mortal coil."

"At your hands."

"Aye," he says simply, eyes on his food.

"Who was she?"

"Unimportant in this context." He sips his drink. He eats a bit. Stella waits.

"Liv. Her name was Liv."

"From that tone of voice, I'm thinking you two might have been . . . close?"

"Was lovers for a bit. Which gets us t'the end of the road, as far as that particular story is concerned."

"You're positive she's dead."

Dez sighs. "I am."

Liv Gelman has two cars standing by, facing north and south, a half block in either direction of the building that houses the bookstore. Once clear of the bookstore, she gets Ray Harker into the passenger seat of one and roars away.

They can't get far with him bleeding like that. Every cop in this part of Manhattan is moving in their direction. So Liv pulls into an alley six blocks from the shooting, and waits.

Ray has taken off his jacket, wadded it up, and is holding it against the gash on his right forehead. That has stanched the bleeding, for now, but his face and neck and shoulders are caked in blood. "Keep low," she says, and he lowers his seatback. He's woozy from blood loss and, for all Liv knows, a concussion.

"What did he hit you with?"

"I have no fucking idea."

Liv is well aware of Dez's eye-hand coordination and his strength. Whatever projectile he was using, it had to be hard and sharp.

She gets out and walks the scene a few times. She waits until most of the police are gone, then drives Ray to the marina. She helps him get aboard their stolen mega-yacht without anyone stopping them to ask what happened.

The organization to which they belong, the Thiago group, has access to a wide and disparate array of assets. Including physicians who get paid not to ask too many questions. Liv takes a look at the jagged gouge on Ray's face, then places the calls to get such a doctor to them.

"You didn't get Ivanson," he says, lying on a couch. They've swapped out his blood-ruined jacket with a towel and an ice pack.

"I did not."

"He can describe you."

"And has by now," she says with little emotion. She brings him an unlidded bottle of aspirin, a decanter of whiskey, and a glass. "*Je suis désolée,* but we were not to remain anonymous forever."

He drains some whiskey and gives it a five-aspirin chaser, then refills his glass. She holds the ice pack in place. The bleeding has stopped but that cut will require stitches.

"We still gotta get Selkirk and O'Malley," he says.

"I know."

"How the fuck did that fucking fucker get to Ivanson?"

"I do not know."

"If he's somehow got the list . . ."

"He hasn't."

"Well, he was goddamn there."

"Yes," she says, keeping icily calm. Her phone vibrates. "I have to go. I'm to meet a physician. I'll have to get him here blindfolded, or else kill him after he's treated your wound."

"Okay."

She has taken Ray's cell phone from his blood-ruined jacket, although he hasn't yet realized it.

There is no written list of the people she and Ray have taken a contract to kill. And the link between the targets is far too obscured for even Desmond Limerick to have figured it out. Which means he wasn't there following Mark Ivanson.

He was there following Ray Harker or herself.

While she's waiting to meet the physician, she wants to check both of their phones to see if they've been compromised.

She has washed blood off her hands and forearms, and she's shrugging on a biker jacket, when Ray says, "Babe?"

"Yes?"

"We gotta kill Limerick."

"Far, far easier said than done. And possibly not necessary."

"Not necessary? Jesus fuck, babe. You're the one lured him into this. You got a plan to get him out?"

"I do and it already has begun."

"Wanna clue me in?"

She grabs the keys to the stolen car. "Thiago. One of our assets is tracking down this thief, this Catalina Valdivia. She seems important to Desmond. Find her, and she'll be our leveler."

CHAPTER 37

Dez and Stella are just finishing their meal when Dez says, "I'm on me way to talk to our lad Ivanson."

Stella says, "No. You're not."

"Met a most impressive police captain in Los Angeles who explained t'me the concept of the silver tray. If you send me to talk to Ivanson, then anything he tells me could be compromised in court. But if I go under me own steam, anything I relate t'you will be free an' clear. Yeah?"

"Yes, that is the legal doctrine, and no, I don't want you talking to him outside of my presence."

"May I ask why?"

"Because it's my case, Dez. You're assisting me, and I'm glad of it. But I also cannot ignore the tattoos. You say you don't know the woman helping Harker. And I believe you. But I'm too good an investigator to think that my instincts are somehow perfect. Okay?"

Dez wants to argue that she's wrong. But is she? It would be rude, wrong, and sexist to insist. "It's your call."

She says, "Good. Then we're going together."

They get to Mark Ivanson's brownstone and, on the stoop, press the ringer button.

"Ah . . . hello?"

"Mr. Ivanson? FBI Special Agent Ansara. My associate and I have a few more questions to ask you. May we come up?"

"I'm . . . not feeling that well. Can it wait?"

"I'm afraid it can't, sir."

"I'm . . . all right."

The door clacks open.

On the walk up, Stella says, "You talk. I'll listen. I think you have a way of getting people to open up. I'll stop you if I think you cross any lines."

"Fair."

Ivanson lets them into an apartment big enough for two but occupied by one. They spot the remnants of a feminine touch, but well faded. There is no tan line on Ivanson's ring finger, so if a marriage dissolved, it was some time back.

The man's shirt is untucked and his eyes are red rimmed. "I'm having a drink. Do you . . . ?"

Stella says, "No, thank you," as Dez says, "Why not?"

Ivanson pours Dez some cheap blended Scotch, and tops his own off as well. The apartment is messy but not dirty. Dez peeks in the kitchen, which is spotless. His guess: Ivanson uses a maid service.

The man clears room on his couch, and his guests sit. Ivanson sits on the flat stone surface in front of his room's fake fireplace, facing them. He keeps the bottle of scotch at his side. He addresses Dez.

"Hey, I heard that the people who tried to, you know . . . that they went after you, too. In a bookstore."

"Did, aye. Them lot's naught-for-two on the day. Tossers."

"Well, cheers, I guess. Welcome to a pretty crappy fraternity: guys who were almost shot today."

Dez lifts his T-shirt and shows Ivanson an exit wound in his flank. "Been shot. More'n once. It's not as bad as ye hear."

"Unless it kills you."

"Well, yeah. There's that."

They drink in silence. Stella takes no notes.

Ivanson turns to her. "You had some questions?"

Dez sips and sighs. "Garvey, Gaetano, an' Levkowitz."

Ivanson twitches a little. He tries to maintain a poker face, sips his drink. "I don't know those names."

"Ye do."

"Ah, Mister . . . ?"

"Limerick, Desmond Limerick, but me mates call me Dez. And aye, yeah. Ye do know 'em."

Ivanson sips his drink. His face has turned red.

"You're, what, from England? What're you, Interpol?"

"I'm no sort of law enforcement whatsoever, mate. Just a citizen helpin' out."

He turns to Stella. "So then I don't, you know, like, technically have to answer his questions?"

Stella shrugs. "It would be helpful if you did, sir."

Dez sips and Ivanson refills his own glass.

"I wish I could help you guys. But I was in that thing in New Jersey. That terrorist thing? I was one of the hostages. And I'm, like . . ." He mimes an explosion near his temple.

"As was I. Started in a martini bar. You was in the ice-cream shop, yeah?"

Ivanson's eyes pop. "Whoa! You were there?"

Dez nods.

"Yeah. Wow. Okay. So you know. It was crazy!"

"'Twas."

Dez leans back, one ankle thrown across his knee. "There's a lyric. Donald Fagan an' Walter Becker. Brilliant them."

"Steely Dan! Oh, sure."

"The song 'Hey Nineteen.' One lyric always stands out for me. *'It's hard times befallen / The sole survivors.'*"

"Good stuff. Steely Dan. Dire Straits. I love that era."

Dez says, "I've an innate sense of pattern recognition, me. Been handy in me line of work. And as far as you four go, it's this: hard times befallen."

"Four of who?" Ivanson says. His right leg is shaking, his heel bouncing off the carpet, three beats a second.

"Garvey, the lawyer? Police say he used t'be a hellion as a youth, then found religion. Levkowitz, the former doc? PTSD. An' you, you're a divorced drunk."

Ivanson sips his whiskey. His leg is still bouncing. "I think you need to leave now."

"Gaetano was a teacher, yeah? No trauma in his past; least, not that the gendarmes have discovered so far."

"I don't know these people. Can you leave?"

"Haven't finished me drink, mate."

"I . . . sure. Yeah. No problem. But seriously. I wish I could help you."

"Could be three inciting incidents. Or, could be you was mates, yeah? And it was one inciting incident. One friend gets religion. One gets PTSD an' drops out of medicine. One gets chased into a bottle. The teacher seems fine."

Ivanson's leg bounces. "Can't help you. Don't know these names. Sorry."

He splashes more whiskey in his glass.

"Me question's this: If the four of you was pals, once, a long time ago, and if something went disastrously bad, that'd explain where ye all ended up."

"Can we talk about something else?"

Dez sips. "Peter Garvey was at The Liberty."

Ivanson starts so suddenly he spills a little whiskey on his thigh. He unrolls the sleeve of his shirt, bunches it in his fist, and uses the sleeve to sop up the spill.

"He . . ." His voice breaks a little.

"Aye. Adam Levkowitz was, too."

"I don't . . . you're lying. What are you saying?"

"Jacob Gaetano, too."

"Stop it. Shut up."

"Said ye didn't know 'em."

"I didn't. Don't. I . . . what are you saying?"

Dez glances at Stella and she gives him the subtlest of nods.

He leans forward, elbows on his knees. "Them Russians was using Russian weapons, yeah? With Russian ammunition. Levkowitz and Gaetano got shot with standard NATO rounds. Garvey, on t'other hand, got pushed off a balcony."

Ivanson is staring at him, open-mouthed.

Dez waits.

"They're dead?"

"They're dead. At the hands of the same people tried to kill you an' me this afternoon."

Ivanson drains his glass. His leg won't stop hopping.

"It's hard time befallen the sole survivors."

Ivanson whispers, "Shut up."

"Tellin' ye the truth."

"Shut up. Shut the fuck . . . What are you saying? They're dead?" He's close to tears.

"So ye did know 'em."

"No. No, no, no. I didn't know them. Don't know them. I . . . can you leave? Please? Both of you?"

Dez sets his glass down on the glass-and-brass coffee table. He reaches out. "Give me your phone, lad. I'll input me number. You may want to reach me later."

A beat, and Ivanson hands it over. Dez types quickly and hands it back. He stands, and so does Stella.

"Two thoughts I shall leave you with, mate. One: We've linked the four of you to them assassins. An' if there's four, there could be more. Anything you're not tellin' Special Agent Ansara here could get other people killed, yeah? If it's only you four, then no worries. Nobody's at risk. Except you."

Ivanson shudders, staring up at him with red eyes.

"And that'd be thought number two: Them killers went to a lot of trouble to take you lot out. D'you honestly think, just because they missed once, they'll give up?"

He heads to the door. Stella takes one of her business cards and sets it on the coffee table. At the door, she says, "Thank you for your time, sir."

They're all the way to the ground floor before Stella Ansara whispers, "That was a master class in head-fuckery, Mr. Limerick."

"Always pleased to lend John Law a hand, ma'am."

CHAPTER 38

POSITANO, ITALY

Catalina Valdivia does her morning Pilates-yoga blend, listening to Lana Del Rey. She showers, puts on a brief dress and sunhat and sandals, grabs her massive tote bag, and begins her walk to the local grocer.

Positano is among the world's most vertical villages. It's perched on a cliff overlooking the Mediterranean, in central Italy, part of the Amalfi Coast, south of Naples. And it's almost impossible to get from any given point A to any given point B without either ascending or descending.

Cat's villa is about midway between the top and the bottom of the colorfully painted village. She begins walking upward along the Viale Pasitea, the winding, switchback road. It's the only road that leads down into Positano, then continues on, up again, out of Positano. It's a closed loop.

A techie friend of hers set her villa up with a camera that scans the license plates and windshields of cars that pass, heading downward. Any car that has been captured more than two weeks apart gets catalogued by the computer as a local. Any car that passes two or more times in a day, but is not yet registered as a local, gets catalogued as suspicious. Every night, she sits on her balcony with a glass of the local, lemony white wine, watches the bobbing lights of the boats in the bay, and studies the batch of suspicious vehicles, looking for surveillance.

She also knows who owns the villas above and below her, which would make good surveillance of her place. She speaks fluent Italian and, being of Mexican descent, has the looks to pass as an Italian.

She believes her bolt-hole to be the perfect place to hide and relax between heists.

The grocer is tiny and, one would think, would pass as the local version of a 7-Eleven. Like most things in Italy (Catalina Valdivia included), there's more to it than meets the eye. Whatever she needs, she will find here. Meat or seafood. Vegetables or fruits (the Amalfi Coast's lemons and oranges are not to be believed). Bread and pastries. Desserts. Liquor. Cleaning supplies. Toiletries. Basic home repair essentials. Light bulbs, mosquito-repellant plugs, air filters. She once laughed herself silly, noticing a carburetor on a shelf. This place is Aladdin's cave, disguised as an ampm mini-mart.

For that evening, she has decided on a lemon pasta and a spinach salad with pine nuts. She finds every single ingredient she has hoped to find. It's madness. She has no idea how the once-taciturn and now-jovial couple who own the place do it.

Grocery shopping done, she joins the droves of tourists and walks down about a thousand stone steps into the village to visit the pharmacy. She passes many dozing cats. She stops to enjoy a vanilla bean gelato, to people-watch, to check out the amazing array of yachts, super-yachts, and mega-yachts in Covo dei

Saraceni—Saracens' cove. In Italy, even places named for marauders sound romantic.

That night, she makes her pasta and listens to music and dances alone in her kitchen. She eats out on her deck, watching the sunset.

She opens her laptop and checks the surveillance footage of the cars that pass on this town's only road.

She spots—not one—but three possible surveillance vehicles.

There is a six-hour difference between Italy and New York City. It's going on nine here; only three in the afternoon there.

She calls Desmond Limerick.

He picks up on the first ring.

"They're here."

"Cat?"

"Yes, Cat. They're here."

"Two questions, then."

"Fire."

"Who's them? And where's here?"

CHAPTER 39

Sunday morning, Dez calls Stella Ansara. "I told you I had a mate at The Liberty. Well, she's in trouble. The same lot that had her under surveillance in Brooklyn is back now."

"Where is she?"

"Europe. Said she was hiding. Apparently not well enough."

Stella says, "Are you going to go help her?"

"'Course I am. Wouldn't be in this mess, weren't for me."

"Dez, before you go: Remember the high school coach who got killed at the convention center? He was the only one without any obvious trauma in his past? Turns out he was born rich, in a family that made its bucks in the pet food, pet supplies industry. He blew through a trust fund before he turned twenty-five, did time for cocaine use and sales. Ended up living in a trailer and teaching gym at a local high school for about thirty-five thousand a year."

"So all four of the targets have trauma in their backgrounds."

"So it seems. I've got half the law enforcement agencies on the Eastern Seaboard helping search the backgrounds of these guys. Come to find out: When you're primary on the terrorist incident of the year, every other agency is quick to answer your calls."

"One would think so."

"We haven't found any connection between the four of them yet, but we're looking. And you put the fear of God, the Devil, and the Russians into Mark Ivanson last night. My guess is, that could pay off, too."

"Ta, then. I'm off to help me friend. Will let ye know when I'm back. Stella?"

"Yes?"

"Want me to introduce you to Harlow? Me fellow bass player?"

Stella laughs. "Dez, that woman is way, way cool. But you gotta punch your weight. You know what I mean?"

"I do. Will be back sharpish. Cheers."

Dez calls the bass player for Kansas Jack and the Blacktop. "Harlow. You seein' anyone these days?"

"Not currently. Why?"

"Want to meet a smart an' lovely lass has a steady job, good income, and parking privileges in Manhattan? And who owns her own handcuffs?"

Harlow says, "Straight white boys are just so weird."

Dez uses one of his false passports and flies United to Rome, departing from Newark—the terrorist incident at the adjacent Liberty Convention Center is over, and the airport now is open but there are still national TV newspeople doing standups outside the terminal. He doesn't have time to worry about checked luggage, which means he's without his knives. He can't even come up with a good excuse for carrying iron nuts and bolts, so they stay behind, too.

He lands in Rome at dawn. He texts Catalina Valdivia: In Rome
now.

The three bubbles on his phone start bouncing immediately. I'm
hiding in Naples. They broke into my place. It's them.

Dez has fast fingers. He types back. Where do we meet?

L'Antica Pizzeria da Michele. Within walking distance of train
station.

Fast as I can.

He takes the train to Naples and looks up the pizzeria on his phone.
It's an easy walk. Dez vacationed in Italy often and he knows the
north region well, and Rome sort of well. But he's never been farther south than Rome. This is terra incognita.

Naples is rough. Rougher than he'd anticipated, being used to
places like Florence and Venice. The downtown core is dirty and
graffiti-ridden. It's working class, but with a vibe of mafiosi, organized crime. Mount Vesuvius isn't the only thing looming over this
none-too-bucolic city.

Dez steps over trash and sidesteps fentanyl zombies on his way to
the famed, old pizzeria. He waits with others to get inside; people are
admitted in groups of twenty, and wait in the alley for their chance.
Once he's inside and seated, Catalina Valdivia appears as if teleported,
taking the second seat at his small wooden table.

"How do you do that?"

She says, "Do what?"

"Appear an' disappear, as if by magic!"

She says, "Magic."

"In retrospect, I should've guessed that."

Cat kisses him and whisks away his menu. "They only offer

marinara or margherita, and the margherita is better. Get it with double cheese."

"Will do," he says.

Her face is a rictus of anger and fear. "They're in my home. In my home! Positano is where I go between jobs. It's my haven! They . . . fuck!"

Dez orders beers for them both—the only Italian restaurant in the entire bloody country that doesn't serve wine, Dez thinks—and a pizza. "Pizza was invented in Naples, ye now. During a cholera epidemic. They—"

"Could you, please? With the Rick Steves?" She's near tears. Dez takes her hand and squeezes.

"I'm sorry, love. When girls cry, I get wordy."

She wipes tears from her cheek with both thumbs. "I'm not crying. Fuck you. What are we going to do?"

"Are they inside your home?"

"Yeah. I have a GoPro. I checked it. They . . . they went through my things. My clothes. Fuck!"

"Do they think you're coming back?"

"Yes. I'd bought groceries."

"All right, then. We enjoy a nice pie and some beer, then we go beat the ever-loving hell out of them."

Cat squeezes his hand. "You promise?"

"Promise, love."

CHAPTER 40

The doctor who occasionally does house visits for the Thiago group studies Ray Harker's eyes, then recleans the head wound and applies a bandage over it.

He talks to Liv Gelman out of Ray's hearing. "Look, the guy's concussed. Let him sleep for a couple of days."

They have a timeline to complete their killings. Sleeping for a couple of days does not fit in well with that timeline. Liv checks her watch. She has teams of people converging in Italy right now.

"How many stitches will he need?"

"That's the thing. Whatever he was hit with, it gouged out some of the skin. I can't just stitch it. Barring plastic surgery, that's going to be an ugly scar forever."

"Thank you. Some painkillers?"

"I left a bottle. Do I have to ride back in the trunk of your car again?"

She smiles. "It was that or dump your body at sea."

"The trunk was pretty roomy, now that I think about it."

Dez and Cat drive from Naples to Positano. She explains about the layout of the vertical village, with one road in and one road out. All cars passing her villa are heading downhill. "And there's limited parking along much of that road."

"Then they'll be staking you out from a building. A home or a business that's closed."

"I saw them plant hidden cameras in my place," she says, glowering through her designer sunglasses.

"That's helpful. If I can get their transmission frequency, should show me where their bivouac is."

They ride in silence awhile.

"I recognized the blonde. The bitch whose ass I kicked in the park in Brooklyn."

"So definitely the same snatch team."

"But more of them. I counted five."

"The easiest way to get them out in the open is for you to waltz into your place and, dunno, make an omelet or something. That'd bring 'em to your door right quick. The problem being—"

"It wouldn't bring all five. They'd leave their backup watching the video."

"And they may have more than five. That's why it's better we hit 'em where they are. I'll have to figure a way to whittle that number down."

Cat says, "Are you armed?"

"I am not. But something will turn up. Always does."

She addresses the side window, her head turned from him. "People with excessive positivity really piss me off."

"Can't help it, love. Was gifted with an attitude of gratitude, me. Always seein' the sunny side of life."

"Yeah, well, see it quietly for a while."

He knows she's not mad at him. She's angry that someone's been inside her house, touching her things.

"Why Italy?" he asks. Meaning: Why hide in this specific nation between jobs?

"It's pretty. The food's good. The wine's good."

"Why Positano?" he asks.

"Wait till you see it."

She's not wrong. They stop at a lay-by above the village where locals are selling oranges and lemons, or orange juice and lemonade, and she shows him the jewel box of a village as seen from a distance. The bay is crowded with everything from rowboats to mega-yachts. The beach is cheek by jowl with people sunbathing or throwing Frisbees, or drying off from a swim.

"Magnificent."

The one road that travels through Positano contains a series of narrow switchbacks. From their angle, it's tough to tell where the road is. The layout of the homes seems totally chaotic from this angle. The curve of the cliffside means they can see much of the town from up here. Cat points to a villa painted a pale blush pink. "That's my place."

"What a view."

"Yeah." She sounds sad now; less angry about her home being invaded.

"What were the ungodly driving?"

"A small Audi coupe and a couple of vans. All three were white."

They stay where they are a bit. Dez keenly studies the gaily painted town. He nudges Cat's shoulder. "That them?"

He's pointing to a parking lot below her place with two vans.

"I think so. I know that place. It used to be a gift shop but it went under. Yeah, those look like their vans."

"If I'm reading this town right, I'm betting you can climb up on roofs and move between levels. Yeah?"

"I could. But I'm a cat burglar."

"That's how they plan to snatch you, would be my guess. Have someone sneak up onto your balcony whilst someone else rings your front door."

"Fuckers."

"Quite. Want an orange?"

She says, "Knock yourself out."

He buys an orange. He peels it and splits it into iridescent crescents. It's exquisite.

"There's a minimum of five people trying to kidnap me," Cat tells him. "I don't do violence. That means you're on your own."

"The other option is to up stakes and just leave. Never look back."

She shoots him a scalding look.

"No, I don't much like it, either. Do you have, like, a panic room in there?"

"No, but I have exits that are impossible to see if you don't know they're there."

"Good. Then we'll get you in your villa. Let the bastards see you. You sneak out. I'll take their bivouac when their forces are spread thin. After the others can't find ye, likely they'll return to their hideout. And I take the remainder of 'em. Neat as a pin."

"You'll need weapons."

"Let me worry about that, love. Want some of this?"

She takes a wedge of orange. It really is fantastic.

"I've a play in mind, love. 'Twill be dangerous. Ye should know that before I pitch it."

Cat nods. "I've got a play in mind, too. And I'll betcha mine's more dangerous than yours. You in?"

CHAPTER 41

Dez acquires the makings of the weapons he'll need in the neighboring town of Amalfi.

Inside the former gift shop, the snatch team has set up four small, black-and-white monitors for the four cameras they hid in Catalina Valdivia's home. Their vans, stolen in Rome, feature the name of a painting and remodeling company; any villagers passing by will assume the gift shop has a new owner.

There are six people on this team. Five have worked together before and their employer, who they know only as Thiago, has arranged a sixth, an Italian thug who doesn't look too much like a thug and who speaks the local lingo. In case any townspeople drop by to welcome them.

The blond woman whom Cat kicked in the Brooklyn park is in charge. She's aching to pay the thief back for that kick.

One of her guys checks his watch. He's been monitoring the feeds from Cat's villa. "Where the fuck is this bitch?"

"Maybe she's got a lover?" the blonde says. "She's damn hot. I'm kinda doubting she sleeps in her own bed alone here in Italy."

"Heard that," another guy says. "She bought groceries, so we know she's com—whoa!"

A shadowy figure flits across one of the monitors. "Boss?"

The blonde moves closer. She's carrying a take-out box of Chinese food and chopsticks. She thinks Italian cuisine is overrated.

They watch. "Did you see . . . ?"

There it is again.

Cat. Dressed in all black. She moves quickly past one of the hidden cameras.

The blonde picks up her walkie-talkie. "Team One: she's in the house. Move via the roofs. Report when you're ready. Team Two: Move into position."

Two of her six-person team begins climbing onto the roof of the former gift shop. Both have handguns but they're hidden. Because of the way the town's only road hairpins so wildly, they're looking straight up, a mere five feet above their heads, at the patio of another villa. They sneak up that far and glance around. The owners haven't spotted them.

They hurry to a sturdy-looking lattice supporting very old lemon trees and deftly but silently climb to the roof of this villa.

Catalina Valdivia's place now is only six feet above them.

Two more members of the snatch team get into one of the white vans and begin heading downhill. They already realized they couldn't drive even one hundred feet *up* the town's only road; too much traffic. So this requires them driving all the way to the bottom of the touristy town, then back up, then taking the left that takes them back to Cat's place, and not the right that leads on to Naples and Rome.

"Fucking stupid way to design a town," one of the kidnappers grouses as they inch through heavy traffic down into the village.

The blonde and her guy on monitor duty watch the cameras. They see Cat only one more time, and briefly at that.

"She spotted the goddamn cameras?" the blonde asks.

"Maybe. The truck?"

The blonde checks in with the guys in the van. They're maybe twenty minutes out.

They'll get to Cat's villa and ring the doorbell. But now they suspect that Cat knows they've been inside her place. Which means she'll run out to her balcony and try to climb down toward the village.

And into the arms of Team One.

This is going like clockwork.

Or it is until Dez Limerick steps out of hiding, uses a screwdriver to jam open the controls of a fire extinguisher he just purchased, and throws it into the former gift shop.

The metal canister hits the cement floor with a clang and the particulate begins to discharge. Every action has an equal and opposite reaction. The flow of retardant acts like a rocket. The metal tube swirls and spins madly around on the floor, breakdancing, gushing a thick fog of white smoke.

The blonde and her guy on monitor duty are shocked, caught off guard. They both begin to tear up and choke as the pressurized stream of particulate engulfs them.

Dez enters with his goggles and KN95 mask. And also his spanking new cricket bat.

Moving faster than they can react, he punches the woman in the gut with one end of the bat, reverses thrust, and sends the other end into her mate's jaw. As he's falling backward, Dez hits the woman on a nerve cluster behind the ear.

They lie toppled over each other, fully unconscious. Dez takes a moment to make sure they're alive; all things in moderation.

He texts Cat.

Got 2 of them.

In her villa, Cat moves to one of her couches, slides it aside, lifts up the all-but-invisible trapdoor beneath it, and climbs in.

There's a rope in this little crawlspace. She pulls on it and the couch moves back to where it was before. Hiding the trapdoor.

"Ring again," one of the guys from the van says.

His partner, the Italian, rings the bell at the front door of Cat's villa again.

Nothing.

The other lifts his walkie-talkie. "Anyone on your side, One?"

Crackle. Then they hear, "No."

"She's onto us. Get inside. Now."

Team One climbs onto Cat's sea-view patio. Her patio door is un-locked. Both draw their weapons and enter.

One of them clicks his radio. "We're in."

The other unlocks and opens the front door for his compatriots.

They silently search the premises. Top to bottom.

They regather in Cat's central living room, with its vaulted, mural-adorned ceiling.

One of them calls base. "Teams One and Two are inside. She's not here."

They wait.

He hits the Send button again. "Base? Repeat, target is not here."

They wait.

"Base?"

Someone says, "Something's wrong."

"No shit, Sherlock. You two guys, take the van. We'll go back via the roofs. Move."

The van gets there before the guys sneaking over the neighbors' roof and the lemon tree trellis. They pull into the parking lot, hide their guns, and enter the former gift shop.

The space is still filled with smoke from the extinguisher, and a fine white particulate lies everywhere.

Dez emerges from behind the door they just barged through, cricket bad awhirl. He takes out the kneecap of one lad in a manner that sends him toppling into his mate. With both of them down, Dez drops the bat, takes a knee, and punches both in the face.

No need of a fine bat for such pedestrian violence. His fist will do.

Two more down.

Dez calls the last two members of the snatch team on their walkie-talkie.

"We've taken out four of yez so far, mates." That "we" is a nice bit of misdirection. They have no idea the size of their opposition. "Wouldn't mind making it a full house. But if ye've a mind to flee an' report back that ye failed, that'd suit us just as well. Your call."

From a window, he spots two guys climb down off the roof of the gift shop, climb into the other van, and peel out.

Smart of them. Clearly the brains of this outfit.

He texts Cat: You're clear, love.

He heads out. Cricket bat over his shoulder, whistling a jaunty tune, Dez saunters back up the one-way road to Cat's villa. It's another lovely day in Positano and he wonders if there are any other kind.

He gets to Cat's place. The front door is still open.

"Cat?"

Dez lowers the cricket bat off his shoulder.

He waits, listening.

He spots a mobile phone on the round, wooden, antique table in the middle of Cat's living room.

It isn't the kind of phone Cat uses.

Dez checks the kitchen and the balcony and spots no one. He moves to the phone on the round table.

A light is blinking. A call on hold.

He depresses it.

An electronically distorted male voice says, "I didn't send just one team, Desmond."

He says, "Thiago."

"Yes. And we've decided you should stop meddling in our affairs. Miss Valdivia is no threat to us. If you back off, she lives. It's quite simple."

The voice sounds Latino, but Dez knows the distortion field can create that illusion.

"And if I don't play nice?"

"Then bits of Catalina Valdivia will begin washing up on the shores of the Mediterranean. And will do so for weeks to come."

He wills himself to calm down. "This was a very bad play on your part. I was helpin' the FBI, is all. Now I've a stake in this thing."

"We'll see. Why not stay in Italy? Enjoy the food, the wine, the views. Relax. You've more than earned it."

Dez says, "I'll be seeing ye soon, squire."

"Your call, Desmond."

Dez walks out, locking Cat's place up. He climbs into his rental and drives back to Rome. He schedules a flight back to the States.

The man on the phone—and he has no particular reason to think it was a *man*—called him Desmond. Twice.

Very few people call him that.

He had an ex-lover who used to. Olivia Gelman. But she's dead.

Dez is 99.9 percent certain.

CHAPTER 42

Liv Gelman's second snatch team takes a powerboat to the marina at Lido del Faro, and from there hauls an unconscious Catalina Valdivia into a van with a logo, phone number, and URL of a laundry service. They drive due east into Rome.

The Thiago group has a safe house in the bohemian Trastevere neighborhood west of the Tiber. The three men back the van into a little garage, lower the big door, and haul Cat up the stairs and into the safe house. They deactivate the security and dump her on a bed in one of two bedrooms.

One of the guys cuffs Cat's right wrist to the brass bed frame.

They move to the living room, order take-out food, and set up the kitchen table for a long night of poker.

Thiago pays very, very well. And they've been told they might be babysitting the Latina American for several days.

It takes thirty minutes for the food to arrive. They draw; low card has to go downstairs to get it. A thug named Viktor draws a three, swears a bloody oath, drains his beer, and heads down.

The food delivery guy knocks, then knocks again, then knocks again.

"Show some fucking patience!" Viktor bellows, jogging down a floor, throwing open the door.

Dez hits the man with a lot more anger than he meant to. The blow doesn't knock Viktor unconscious. It kills him.

Emotion is a bad thing in a fight. Dez reins it in, takes the man's handgun, racks the slide, mounts the stairs two at a time, and enters the safe house, gun in his left, right palm supporting his left.

The other two guys don't have time to react.

"Guns, lad. D'you speak English?"

They do not. Dez repeats it in French. Nothing. Repeats it in Spanish.

The guys gingerly remove their weapons from their holsters and place them on the ground.

"The lass?"

One of the men gestures to the bedroom. "She is cuffed."

"On your knees, kindly. Fingers laced behind your heads."

They do.

Dez reverses the gun, makes sure the safety's on, and slams the butt into their skulls.

Both lie face down, well and truly out of the fight.

Dez flicks off the safety. He moves to the bedroom, gun leading. He kicks in the door.

His eyes adjust to the dark. He takes in the form of Cat. Standing by the bed, holding the makeshift tracker that Dez crafted from a burner phone they bought with the fire extinguisher.

His eyes dart to the handcuffs, hanging from the bed frame, one cuff open and forming a capital E.

Cat looks that way, too, and rolls her eyes. "Oh please. I was picking those in junior high."

It was Cat who predicted that there would be more than one snatch team. "You've been picking off these guys, and the Russian terrorists, like you're picking daisies. No way do they send only one team after me."

This was spoken while Dez and Cat had stood on the parapet over Positano, taking in the spectacular view and sharing a fresh orange from a roadside van.

"You take out the first set, so as not to be too obvious. I let the second team take me."

Dez says, "You could be killed."

"Nope. They'll need me alive and healthy to keep you toeing the line. You'll ask for proof of life, right? No way they'll off me."

"There are fates worse than death."

Cat looks him in the eye. "If you're talking about sexual assault, that's a line from the eighteen century. It's also the work of amateurs. Do these seem like amateurs to you?"

"This is dangerous."

Cat takes another wedge of orange from his palm. "I'm a thief, Big Dee. This is what I do."

At the safe house in Trastevere, Dez carries the dead man upstairs. He and Cat check the pockets of the trio, and Cat uses the cords from lamps to hog-tie the two Dez hasn't killed. She glances at the man whose neck Dez broke and whose jaw was unhinged by the blow.

"What did you hit this guy with?" she whispers.

"Unbridled grievance."

They search the entire safe house. Cat heads down and searches the laundry truck in the garage.

When she returns Dez is on his knees, on the hardwood floor, gingerly taking apart a contraption.

"What's that?"

Dez doesn't look up. "Bomb. Self-destruct mechanism, in case they needed to abandon this site."

"Jesús y María."

"Aye . . . There. Done." He glances up, just the smallest indication of sweat on his brow. He removes a packet of C4 the size of a flue brick. "Harmless now. Big beastie, this. Would've taken out the entire block."

"Who the hell are these assholes?"

Dez says, "Familiar with the name Thiago?"

Cat's mouth drops open. "Like, the assassin?"

"Good lord. How d'ye know that?"

"I stole a whole lot of money from a guy one time. He'd been fixing mixed martial arts fights in Vegas. Before I am-scrayed, he threatened to send Thiago after me. The cops found him the next day, his throat slit. I called some underworld connections, asked about the name."

"It's likely a group, not a fella," Dez says, and sighs. "Here's the part I haven't told ye yet."

And then he does. He tells her about FBI Special Agent Stella Ansara, and about them working on the theory that former CIA officer Ray Harker, who is part of the Thiago group, was killing people at The Liberty.

"You found a bullet that didn't match the others. When we were in the basement of the admin building."

"That's right. There was a thread of killings going on at The Liberty, hidden amidst the killings by the Russians."

He tells her about the fake escape route that someone called Thiago had sold, hook, line, and sinker, to Colonel Baranov of the Russian forces.

She says, "There is no sub-sub-basement. Thiago led those Russians into a kill box."

"Exactly." He's impressed by how quickly she's picking all this up.

"Is this Harker dude behind everything?"

"See that bottle of dish soap by the kitchen sink?"

She turns, does.

"That's smarter'n Harker. When it's having an off day. No way he's behind this."

"Who then?"

They're on the floor. Dez leans back against a wall, knees up, elbows on his knees. Cat sits cross-legged facing him.

Dez takes his time. Something about his face leads her to show some patience.

"Someone found a way to get all sorts of guns into The Liberty. Found a way to bollux the entries, so the law couldn't follow 'em in. Found a way to bollux most comms whilst leaving some open."

"Yeah?"

"I've not told ye much about the trainin' I've had. But that insanity at the convention center? That's how I'd've staged it, too."

Cat gives this a couple of beats. "Someone with the same training as you."

"Shouldn't be anyone like that. Not in North America, at any rate. Time was, there was a woman who had the same trainin' as me. Every bit as good at it as I am. But she's dead."

Something in the way he says that catches her attention. "And yet . . . ?"

Dez leans forward and draws the mechanical remnants of the self-destruct mechanism into the space between them. The C4 stays well separated.

He draws the burner phone he found in Cat's living room, hits Redial.

The mechanical voice sounds after a single ring. "You doubt my resolve, Desmond?"

"Doubt your competence. Doubt them three lads at the safe house in Rome have what it takes t'keep Cat from me."

They wait, both sitting on the floor. Dez's eyes are on the bomb resting on the floor between his legs.

A switch at the top of the dismantled bomb clicks into place. And, of course, nothing happens. Because the explosive has been dismantled.

"Strike two, love. No bomb. No boom."

They wait. Then hear a laugh. "Oh dear."

"Was a time you was better than this, Liv."

Again they wait.

It stretches on.

They hear the exaggerated sound of a kiss. Followed by the sound of someone blowing that kiss to him. *Wooooo.*

Liv's unaltered laugh comes across the line. And then her unaltered voice.

"Well played, Desmond. But the name of the game is still Catch Me If You Can."

Olivia Gelman disconnects.

CHAPTER 43

Dez and Cat fly back to the States. Dez expects to fly coach.

Coach is not how Catalina Valdivia rolls.

Stella Ansara is asked to chair a meeting at New York's One Police Plaza, featuring representatives of the municipal, county, state, and federal law enforcement agencies that responded to the terrorist attack on the convention center. The goal is to update all parties—and later the media—on the investigation. Officials of the convention center, the European consortium funding it, and Newark Liberty International Airport take part as well.

Stella carefully explains that some of the killings appear to have a connection other than the obvious: unfortunate bystanders at the wrong place and the wrong time. Several police agencies are helping her look into the murders of Garvey, Gaetano, and Levkowitz. She doesn't go into details about how they're connected.

She is introduced to a man who looks minutes, not hours, away from a myocardial infarction, who has been brought in from another convention site to be interim executive director of The Liberty. The former executive director was executed on his knees, along with his top staff. This interim director looks like he'd rather wrestle a polar bear, and Stella can't really blame him.

The interim director introduces her to Jonas Diedrich, North American operations director for the FLAG Family Holdings, which financed the construction and opening of the convention center. Diedrich is a sallow, well-dressed German fellow, perhaps sixty, with a taut smile and slicked-back hair. He shakes her hand, and his grip is firm. "I'm sorry we don't have someone of more authority here for this, Special Agent. My position as North American operations director is, ah, how would you say . . . a cheerleader."

She laughs. "I've had jobs like that, too. FLAG Family Holdings is . . . ?"

"The real estate acquisitions arm of a consortium of European banks. My interest in The Liberty is entirely financial, I'm afraid. Just looking after our investment."

"I see." A motion over Diedrich's left shoulder catches her eye. "Can you excuse me a second?"

She hurries over to a New Jersey State Police inspector she met during the hostage standoff. He was gesturing to her. They shake hands. "Bill?"

"I heard about someone taking a swing at one of The Liberty survivors in Manhattan? Your case?"

Stella nods. "A guy named Mark Ivanson. He wasn't killed at The Liberty but he damn near was the next day. Looks like a team of pro hitters, too. We're trying to see if there's a connection to what went on at the convention center."

The statie says, "So you're gonna love this. We got a homicide in Jersey City. Earlier today. The name Gene O'Malley mean anything to you?"

Stella shakes his head.

"His family runs O'Malley Burgers, all up and down the East Coast."

"I've had them. They're . . . okay."

"I've had 'em and I think you're being generous."

Stella frowns. "There's an O'Malley Burgers franchise at The Liberty."

"That's right. And Gene O'Malley was there. He was one of the hostages. He survived, only to get a double-tap to the back of his head at his home in Jersey City."

Stella's on high alert. "That's too damn close to what happened to my guy in Manhattan. Can I . . . ?"

"I got a car out front ready to take us there. Figured you'd want in."

She shakes his hand again. "Owe you."

Dez and Cat are over the Atlantic. She's paid for business class accommodations, and they have two aisle seats, both isolation pods but with screens that can be raised and lowered between them. They can either have total privacy, even from each other, or they can talk to each other while enjoying privacy from the other passengers.

Cat orders champagne for herself and Dez gets a beer. Both get small bowls of warm, assorted nuts. Dez thinks business class might not be terrible. Cat says, "So tell me about this Liv."

He's tempted to tell her to mind her own business. Dez rarely talks about his past. But Cat just risked her own life to get Dez a step closer to whoever's behind all this, and he's a compulsive payer of debts.

"I'll not go into me own background, except to say I served overseas in a military unit, and I learned t'be a gatekeeper."

"Doors, portals, transitions; right." She remembers his mantra and the tattoo of Janus on his arm.

"A woman name of Olivia Gelman had the training. Took to it like she'd been born to it. She was Swiss but of Jewish background. Left Switzerland to do her turn in the Israel Defense Force. Ye have to understand, Liv's family was rich and powerful in Switzerland. She was under no obligation to do her time in the IDF. Did it anyway. Used t'think that made her brave. Now I think it made her an adrenaline junkie."

"You met her learning to do . . . whatever it is you do?"

"Aye. We trained together. She's as good with a gun or in hand-to-hand combat as I am. An' she's as good at the gatekeeping stuff as well. The science of it all. She was brilliant."

Cat sips her bubbles. "What happened to her?"

Dez pauses, eyes giving her the thousand-yard stare. Cat waits.

"Me unit was in Tunisia. Tryin' to get a bead on a warlord sittin' on a stash of heroin. Maybe upwards of twenty million euros' worth."

Cat whistles, high-low.

"Aye. This lad was a major distributor of heroin into Europe an' the Middle East. We found him holed up in an eighteenth-century French fort. Got there, got in, and found the warlord an' his mates dead."

"Someone else got to them first?"

"Aye, and not lookin' to stop the heroin. Looking to take over. We caught 'em on their way out. Was a fight. Most of me men was pinned down. I tussled with one of the thieves, wearing a balaclava and ballistic vest. She—"

Cat says, "She."

Dez gives her a tired smile. "Pleased to see you're ahead of the narrative here. Aye, that's right. Liv. She had a grenade. I slid a knife into her chest. Up to the bolster, through the arm of her vest. Best case, nicked her heart. Worst case, tore open a lung. Was fair certain she was dead. One of her mates drove me back with a barrage of cover fire, got her out, got her mask off. That's when I saw it was Liv. They got away but we got the heroin. From the way her lad threw her body in the back of their truck, I was dead certain I'd killed her."

"She was part of the crew lifting the heroin?"

"Was, aye. Had taken all this training"—Dez slides up his sleeve to reveal Janus—"and used it to become a bloody thief. We'd lost touch, oh, two years afore this incident. I thought she was working undercover for the IDF. Turns out, she'd done her turn an' hadn't re-upped, and they'd not heard from her, either. Only later realized she and her mates had become, possibly, the leading criminal theft ring in the Arab Maghreb."

"The . . . ?"

"Algeria, Libya, Mauritania, Morocco, Tunisia. That area. They'd taken advantage of the war-torn bits of that Northern African region to run their own high-stakes, high-risk cartel."

"I've never heard any of that, but I never worked that part of the world, either." She taps her glass against his and smiles. "I don't run in the same circles as violent thieves, or people working in the drug trade. And besides, thieves with a reputation are doing it wrong. The whole point is to *not* have any reputation."

"Fair, that. Near as we could tell, the cartel broke up after that Tunisian gambit. No one ever found Liv's body but I was sure she was dead."

He's giving her the thousand-yard stare again. Cat reaches across the barrier between their pods and lightly touches his shoulder to gain his attention, then takes his hand in hers, their elbows up on the partition.

"You'd been lovers."

"For a bit," he says. "Yeah."

"Were you angry she'd taken the training with you and turned it to being a thief?"

Dez thinks about it a bit. He sips his beer to hide a shy smile. "Would you be insulted if I said yes?"

"Nah. I get that. You got about the worst case of Galahad complex I ever saw."

He says, "I never go looking for trouble, love."

She clinks her glass against his, squeezes his hand warmly, and smiles. "That there's what we call coyote shit, big guy."

CHAPTER 44

Dez takes his phone off airplane mode while they're rolling up to the terminal at JFK, and he immediately gets a message ping from Special Agent Stella Ansara. He informs Cat.

She's releasing her seat belt. "Law enforcement and I don't see eye to eye. Leave me out of whatever you've got going with the Fed. *¿Comprende?*"

He nods and waits until they're in the terminal and clear of the other passengers before returning Stella's call.

"Hey." Stella sounds as serious as a cyclone. "I'm in Jersey City. A survivor of the Russians' attack on the convention center just got himself assassinated in his home."

Dez says, "À la Mark Ivanson."

"Oh, it gets a lot better than that. My vic had a good, old-fashioned landline phone, and we've got a voicemail. Listen."

He puts the phone on speaker and Cat huddles close to listen.

Beep. "*Gene? Gene, I don't know if you remember . . . I mean, fuck, of course you remember. It's Mark. Mark Ivanson. Look, I just talked to an FBI agent and, I don't know, a British guy from Interpol or something."*

Cat gives Dez a quick, molten glance and he shakes his head no.

"Look, I was at The Liberty when those Russians attacked. The FBI agent, she's saying Peter Garvey was there, and Adam Levkowitz, and Jacob Gaetano. And she's saying they're dead. They're all dead. And I'm calling after all these years because, Jesus, man. If four of us were there, maybe we all were. This is way too big to be a coincidence, you know? And to make matters worse, someone tried to fucking kill me yesterday, here in Manhattan. I shit you not. So anyway, look, if you get this, call me back. Not to, you know, whatever. Hash over old times. Fuck, nobody wants that. But . . . just call me back."

Ivanson left his phone number and disconnected.

It's Stella's voice on the line again. "I was sure you were right about the connection, Dez. And now Ivanson's just confirmed it for us."

"Aye. Garvey, Gaetano, and Levkowitz killed at The Liberty. One took a header off a balcony, an' two shot with very non-Russian munitions. Ivanson survives, then Ray Harker tries to off him in Manhattan. This . . . ?"

"Gene O'Malley. CEO of O'Malley Burgers."

"This Gene O'Malley takes two to the brainpan in Jersey City."

Cat scrounges a newspaper up from near one of the plastic chairs in the waiting area. She grabs a pen from her purse and begins scribbling.

Over the line, Stella says, "An NYPD black-and-white and one of my guys are en route to Ivanson's now. We've got enough to take him into custody and to get some answers. You want to be there when I talk to him?"

"Do, aye."

Cat shows him what she's scratched on the newspaper: LIST OF

ASSASSINATIONS. DIDN'T GET THEM ALL BECAUSE YOU ENDED THE SIEGE BEFORE THEY WERE DONE!!

Dez nods to her.

Stella Ansara says, "If I were a betting gal, I'd say this Thiago—Ray Harker and whoever's helping him—wanted to get all five of them at the convention center. Only got three, because you helped us put an end to it before they were ready. So now they're batting cleanup."

Cat gives him a silent, *See! That's what I just said!*

Dez grins and winks at her. "The voicemail. Our mate, Ivanson, didn't say, 'If four of us were there, maybe you were, too.' He said, 'If four of us were there, maybe we all were.'"

"Meaning O'Malley and maybe others? I caught that, too. We have four dead and one who the assassins missed, but there could be at least one more on the list."

Dez says, "Aye."

"Dez, we've asked city and state police to conduct thorough background checks on Ivanson and the first three who died. Not all the work is done, but as of a couple of minutes ago, I can tell you that multiple agencies have found no connection to these men, whatsoever."

"Yet Ivanson clearly lied to us."

She says, "I know. There *is* a connection. I'm just telling you, it's not going to be an obvious one. If it was, investigators would have spotted it by now."

Dez can see that she's right. "Can't wait t'hear what our lad Ivanson's got to say. Thanks for the call, mate."

"Also, Dez. Hold on." He waits and the audio signature on the call changes, as if Stella has moved. "Dez?" she says softly. "I got a . . . pretty flirty text from your fellow bass player. Harlow. This is your doing, isn't it?"

"I plead the fifth, onna grounds of anything I say might incriminate me."

Her voice takes on the resonance of a warm smile. "If it works out, you and me are buddies for life. It doesn't, oh man, I'm going to abuse my authority and make your life hell."

"Seems fair. Cheers."

They hang up.

"Did you just set up a Fed on a blind date?" Cat asks, fists on her hips.

"Maybe."

"Jesus, and I thought I took stupid risks."

CHAPTER 45

Liv Gelman sends two of her guys to drive Ray Harker to their on-call physician, who recleans Ray's head wound and checks his concussion. The new pressure bandage begins bleeding through before they even leave the guy's clinic (CLOSED FOR REPAIRS says the hastily written note on the door), so the doc cleans the wound again and applies a new bandage.

Before he does, Ray insists on seeing the wound in a mirror. It's shaped like a sideways V, taking up half of the right side of his forehead. A large chunk of flesh was torn out by whatever the hell projectile hit him.

"You should get scheduled for plastic surgery," the doc informs Ray.

"I gotta kill a guy first."

The doctor pinches the bridge of his nose. "See. You people can't be telling me stuff like that, okay? I can't know that."

He goes to a cabinet and takes out a vial of pills. "These are powerful, so only take—"

Ray takes the vial from him, reaches past him, and takes two more vials.

"C'mon, man!"

Ray glances at his two guys. "Move."

On the ride back to the yacht, Ray takes four of the painkillers with a generous gulp of whiskey from a flask.

Liv Gelman turns and sees Ray enter the yacht's lower deck living quarters, with his fine new bandage and his grim glower.

She smiles. "Gene O'Malley has gone to that great drive-through in the sky."

"You got him."

She says, "Indeed. In the end, it turns out he did not want fries with that."

Ray exhales something that might be a mirthless laugh.

"I've been thinking: That little minx, Miss Valdivia? I think she let herself get caught, whilst wearing a tracker, so Desmond could find the Thiago safe house in Rome."

Ray sloppily pours whiskey into a glass and gulps it, along with a couple more pills. "The sooner that fucker finds us, the sooner I can kill him." His voice is thick and he slurs his words a little.

Liv stares into his dilated eyes. "Much pain?"

"Less than Limerick's gonna feel."

Dez helps Cat get checked into a hotel using one of Dez's false IDs and the accompanying bank account. "Liv tracked ye to Positano. Let's assume she's still tracking you."

The hotel is lovely, in Midtown, small and quiet, and Dez can tell Cat hates everything about the situation. He pours them both a drink from the minibar and she paces.

Dez says, "Gilded cage syndrome?"

"I don't like being in anyone's debt," she says, scowling. "I don't like men seeing me as a damsel in distress. I don't like living on someone else's dime. I don't like that bitch who had me kidnapped and who had men invade my goddamn home."

About halfway through that she slipped subconsciously into Spanish, but Dez was able to follow along. *"Lo lamento, love."*

She looks startled, shaking her head, then allowing a swift smile to sneak through. "Sorry about that. I only do that when I'm angry, and I'm not even aware of it."

"You've money saved up from your, ah, vocation, I'm assuming?"

"Yeah, but, like you said . . ."

"Liv. She tracked ye once. Could again, if you use your own resources. So gilded cage or not, ye've two options. Let me help, or go to some other friend and ask for help. Just till I put a stop to this mad business."

She stands at the room's window, looking out at the sea of foot traffic on the sidewalks and the wash of yellow from all the cabs.

"The fastest way out for me is to help you. But goddamn it, I am not a crime fighter. I'm the opposite of that. This should be none of my fucking business. I should be as far from here as possible, enjoying a drink with an umbrella and planning my next heist."

"Agreed."

She sets down her drink, turns to him, and hugs him. She stays like that, her head on his shoulder, for half a minute. She's shaking. Dez holds her.

Cat murmurs into his neck, "Let's get this bitch."

"Let's."

His phone vibrates. They separate and he checks. "It's Stella."

Cat turns away from him and uses a knuckle to collect unshed tears from her lashes, hoping he doesn't spot it.

Dez connects. "Special Agent?"

"We've got a problem." Stella doesn't bother with any preambles. "Mark Ivanson. He's gone. Cleaning out an account with stacks of paper cash. He owns a company car, and it hasn't been moved. I don't think he's dumb enough to use a credit card. So for now, he's in the wind."

Dez ponders that a moment. Cat cocks one eyebrow, studying. She's starting to identify his tells, and she knows when he's calculating a play.

"You hit Ivanson pretty hard at his place," Stella says, then hurriedly adds, "And, yes, I let you. So that's on me. But it looks like you put the fear of God into him and he's bolted."

"I was a bit afraid of that, if I'm bein' honest."

"Me, too."

They're both silent for a moment. Stella says, "Oh, and more of the police agencies that are assisting us have gotten back to us about the dead guys. All lived in this basic Northeastern area. All white guys. All between the ages of forty-seven and fifty. But beyond that, no connections yet. These aren't Barney Fife agencies. They're good. Whatever the connection between these guys, it's really well hidden."

"All right. Thanks, mate. I'm sure Ivanson will turn up. Cheers."

He disconnects, then turns to Cat. "An' who's Barney Fife, then?"

Cat shakes her head. "Wait, I . . . Did you *not* have Nick at Nite growing up?"

"Misspent youth."

She says, "It's like you're from Mars or something. Hey: You almost told the Fed something, then you clammed up."

He grins. "Did, aye. She and me went to this lad Ivanson's place and I may've spooked him a bit."

"I've seen how you spook people 'a bit.'"

"Was afraid he'd do a runner. Before we left, I asked for his phone so I could input me number. I got his as well, and better yet, I input it in an app that'll let me track him."

Cat makes the T-for-timeout symbol. "I'm all for lying to the cops. Hell, I lettered in that. But why not tell your buddy? She seems to trust you."

"Because I'd rather find Mr. Ivanson on me lonesome, whilst not playing by Edmond Hoyle's rules, yeah?"

"So you find this dude, you can ask him using your own particular physicality, as opposed to Miranda rights."

"Exactly." Dez smiles at her, waiting.

"What?"

"Edmond Hoyle. He—"

"Eighteenth-century Englishman. Wrote treatises on the rules of games."

Dez smile morphs into a grin. "Jay-sus but you're astoundin'!"

She rolls her eyes. "I risk my life by breaking rules, big guy. You gotta know *all* the rules before you can break them properly."

CHAPTER 46

Dez and Cat rustle up some room service, and Dez uses one of the apps on his tablet computer to access the GPS coordinates of Mark Ivanson's phone. "He's travelin' north. Likely in a car. He's on Highway 81."

"Fleeing to Canada," she says, spearing bits of her salad. They eat sitting on the bed, shoulder to shoulder.

"Memorized all the exits, have ye?"

She reaches for a glass of the wine she ordered. "Oh, hell yes."

"He may be heading that way. Best to give him a long tether and see where he stops. That'll tell me if I can go after him by car or by air."

"When do you think he'll stop?"

Dez chews his own salad and swallows. "No idea."

"Then wouldn't our time be better spent with less clothing?"

Dez sets down his plate and fork. "An' why the hell didn't I think of that!"

They make love, and shower, and sleep, and the wine's gone warm when they wake up, so Dez orders another bottle. It's grown dark out. He checks his tablet.

"Mark Ivanson's stopped."

"Where?" Cat asks languidly.

"Jasperson, New York."

"Never heard of it."

Dez goes to Google Earth. They sit side by side on the bed and find the tiny village, not too far from Lake Ontario and the town of Oswego. Dez snorts a little laugh.

"What?"

"I was just in a town called Astoria. Other side of the continent."

"What happened there."

"Nothing that I recall," he says, subconsciously touching the bullet wound on his flank.

"Your guy Ivanson didn't cross into Canada. It'll probably be faster to fly to Syracuse and get a rental car there. Be on the dude in a couple of hours."

"Aye."

"I'm coming, too."

"Ye don't have to."

She turns to him, their bare shoulders touching. "Dez? I don't ever, ever have to do anything I don't want to. Understood? If I come with you, it's because I choose to."

"More than fair."

"Then get your ass moving, Rudyard. We both need to buy some warmer clothes."

The next morning, both wearing thicker coats and sporting stocking caps and gloves, Dez and Cat catch a commercial flight to Syracuse and rent a Jeep. Another commercial flight: another reason to leave Dez's knives back in the hotel. This time, Cat isn't worried about him being unarmed. She's seen for herself that he can find weapons whenever and wherever he needs them.

It's early afternoon by the time they arrive. The weather is in the midforties as they drive north and west toward the hamlet of Jasperson, but the wind whipping off the Great Lakes makes it feel a good ten degrees colder than that. In Fulton, Dez spots a sporting goods store and pulls over. He nods to a nearby diner. "Get us some coffee, an' something warm t'go, will ye?"

He peels off three twenties from his pocket and holds them her direction. Cat bristles.

"Jay-sus, love, you—"

"Shut the hell up. I know I can't use my credit cards." She snatches the money from him and reaches for the passenger's-side door. "You know, I'd rather just lift your wallet than take your handouts."

"Understood."

She says, "Yankee imperialist," and slams the door shut.

Dez steps out and yells over the top of the Jeep. "Yankee? I'm bloody British!"

She returns with two lidded coffees, plus a little paper bag of creamers and sugar and stir sticks. Also two warm panini in foil wrap, and cups of tomato-orange soup. They sit in the car and finish the soup. Cat returned first and chose the driver's side, and Dez doesn't balk. She checks the bag he brought.

"What's this?"

"Professional slingshot," he says. "For hunting small game. Better made than the one I jury-rigged."

She studies it. It's made of a tough aluminum, fifteen inches high when held by its rubber grip. There's an extension at the bottom of the handle, angled at forty-five degrees, that fits over the user's fore-arm. "For stability?"

"Aye. Hadn't used one of these much before, but I liked how the last one worked. Give ye distance but without noise."

He also has a bag with a shoulder strap for it, and a packet of one-inch-diameter ball bearings. "These'll sting," Cat says.

She revs up the car.

"I didn't get you a weapon because—"

"—because I never touch them. Bad luck. Thanks."

They drive another hour to Jasperson. Dez checks his tablet as they travel. "He's not in Jasperson. He's just a bit to the north, love. Take this next exit."

Dez is a very good driver but he realizes Cat is quite comfort-able behind the wheel. He suspects that if they get into a chase, she should drive.

They travel in silence, leaving the radio off.

Cat says, "What's that?"

A form looms in the distance. At first, it appears to be a moun-tain range.

Soon they realize it's man-made.

It's a factory.

But not just a factory. It's an industrial campus. And it appears to take up square miles of acreage.

"Our lad's there."

Dez goes online and inputs the GPS coordinates.

Cat checks her rearview. "We're the only traffic on this road."

"Aye. This was a factory. Says here, 'twas built in the seventies an' went bankrupt in the seventies. Built to manufacture Panthera cars."

She wrinkles her nose. "Never heard of them."

"I remember them. A bit. Was supposed to be this grand exper-iment in makin' European-style cars in America. Overseas banks poured huge amounts of money into it. Tryin' to shake up the Big Three automakers. The Japanese were tryin' t'do the same. Only this effort? The Panthera brand? Ran smack-dab into the chipper-shredder of the 1973 recession."

He reads more as their Jeep draws closer. They realize the plant as the footprint of a fair-sized town. "It would have employed thousands," Cat says as the compound grows closer and higher. They spot a tall, chain-link fence with concertina wire around the perimeter.

"Aye. Tens of thousands. Says here, they was over-financed an', when the recession hit, the project folded in less than a month. Added considerably to the recession in Europe, accordin' to Wikipedia."

She smiles at him. "You know a lot about cars?"

"Done some work as a mechanic. I find engines fascinatin'."

They're moving through a vast sea of abandoned parking lots. Sun and frost have taken their toll on the tarmac. Weeds have destroyed much of the once-impermeable surface. Even small trees have cracked through. Cat says, "Mark Ivanson?"

Dez points to a car parked near the main, front gate of the compound.

Cat parks their Jeep next to it.

They climb out and Dez peers up at the rusty metal banner, curved like a rainbow over the big, four-lane-wide main gate.

PANTHERA WORKS—A DIVISION OF FRANKFURT LANDESBANK AG.

Dez stuffs the new professional hunting slingshot into the small backpack it came with, and adds ball bearings to his coat pocket. Cat zips her coat up and digs out the stocking cap. "This is spooky. Where's Waldo?"

Dez has switched from his tablet to his bespoke phone. He juts his chin in the direction of the Panthera Works factory.

"So, if this was a monster movie . . ."

"It isn't, love."

"You don't know that."

They find a gap where the big, sideways-rolling gate meets the fence. They spot a fresh shoeprint in a puddle. Mark Ivanson.

Cat slips through nimbly. Dez pushes his way through, grunting.

"If you weren't built like *mi papi's* GMC, this wouldn't be a problem."

Dez points to her frame, then to his own. "Alley cat. Bull in a China shop. From each according to his ability."

They trudge into the industrial complex.

Many of the buildings are cinder block, and others are metal. Most are at least three stories tall and as long and wide as a city block. The streets are wide enough to take truck-and-trailer rigs and cargo loaders. It's quiet. They hear birds and the wind, but not much else. They spot some feral cats. She wears gloves but has jammed her fists into her coat pocket, the faux-fur collar up.

Dez alternates taking in the scene, checking his corners and potential ambush spots, and watching the GPS directions on his phone. He nudges Cat and they angle to their right.

They find themselves whispering. "Does this dude seem like the type to be armed?" she asks.

"He does not."

"Then again . . ."

Dez nods. "Then again."

They creep silently forward.

They come to an absolutely massive manufacturing building. The vertical doors are a good twenty-five feet high and closed—rusted closed, from the looks of them. The building is five stories tall and, at a guess, six hundred yards long and wide. They spot the rusty Panthera brand logo over the doors, with PCI. Also the name of the German bank that owned the place.

They spot Mark Ivanson.

He's standing. Wearing a winter coat and a stocking cap, hands in his pockets, staring up at the building. Not moving.

They approach stealthily.

They're maybe two hundred feet from him when another man steps out from behind the corner of building PC1. He stands next to Ivanson. Also looking up.

Dez gestures, and they duck behind an empty dumpster.

This new fellow looks a bit like Mark Ivanson. Not family-related, but similar, as in: a white guy, nearing fifty. Which is to say, this guy looks like every one of the men that Liv Gelman and Ray Harker have targeted for assassination. His vivid red hair sets him off from the others. His coat looks designer, and his shoes look expensive, so he's got money. Cat holds up a hand, fingers splayed wide, plus one more finger, and silently mouths the word, *Six?*

A sixth target of the Thiago group? Could be. Dez shrugs.

He nods and they start to inch closer. There's not much coverage here, and it takes a while.

The wind shifts a bit, and they hear snippets of dialogue. They crouch behind an old boxcar-like trailer from a truck-and-trailer rig. It features the sun-faded Panthera logo.

". . . come back . . . ?" This, from Mark Ivanson.

"No. You?"

"Nope."

The wind ebbs and they lose the track. It picks up again.

". . . figured it out . . . ?" the newcomer says.

"I didn't. FBI told me."

". . . why now and . . ."

They see Ivanson shrug. "I don't know, man."

Dez feels the wind shift around from the other direction. That's all they're going to get.

Cat has drawn her iPhone and is getting photos of the new guy.

Clever; Dez had meant to ask her to do that. She takes a few images, then frowns. She nudges Dez and ducks back into hiding.

She shows him her phone. No bars, no reception.

Dez draws his bespoke phone, checks. He has no reception, either, and, compared with commercial phones, his mobile is ruggedized and robust. He can almost always find a signal when others around him can't. Portions of his mobile operate as a satellite phone, but even that isn't receiving now.

Nothing to be done about it. Dez touches her shoulder, head gestures to the guys. Cat nods.

Dez stands but makes a *stay hidden* gesture.

He steps out from behind the trailer. He begins strolling closer with that bandy-legged gait of his.

"Gentlemen?"

Mark Ivanson gasps and spins so fast he stumbles and almost falls.

The other guy turns and sprints in the opposite direction.

Dez is about to say something when a flash of motion at the corner of his eye catches his attention.

Cat. Sprinting after the new guy.

He wishes she hadn't done that.

"Y . . . you!" Ivanson's eyes are wide.

"Dez Limerick. Fancy runnin' into you here! How's tricks, Mark, my son?"

"How . . . how did you . . . ?" Ivanson glances around in a manic manner, likely looking for FBI blazers and drawn guns.

"People often give skulkin' a bad name, but I find that's unfair, that. Often a very useful skill, skulkin'. Did ye know that a group of foxes is known as a skulk?"

"You followed me."

"Did, aye." Dez has drawn closer but keeps his hands in his coat pocket, smiling, attempting to look harmless. Dez is quick but not fast. There are few who can beat him in a ten-foot race and many who can beat him in a hundred-yard dash. He'd rather not chase this lad, especially since Ivanson looks like he's about ready for a heart attack.

"Why here, mate? This place? Of all the space to run in North America, why come here?"

"I . . . go away! I don't have to tell you shit!"

Ivanson pulls his right hand out of his pocket.

He has a twenty-two pistol.

Well, Dez read that one wrong.

He grips one of the ball bearings in his coat pocket. "Oh, please, Marcus, my lad. I've mates in the FBI! You're in the shite up to your neck, an' that's the fact. But ye don't want to shoot someone works with the Feds, now, do ye? That'd be stupid. And stupid, you're not."

Ivanson hasn't pointed the gun at him yet.

"Get out of here!" Ivanson says, imploringly.

"Your family owns a trucking firm, yeah? That your link to Panthera?"

Which makes little sense; from what Dez remembers, the long-gone and long-forgotten carmaker never went in for trucks. Only sedans. Mostly, Dez just wants Ivanson talking.

"Get out. You . . . you don't have any idea. . . . Get away from me." The man is close to tears.

"Who's your mate, then?"

"Leave me alone!" Now the gun is raised in Dez's general direction. But Ivanson's hand is shaking so bad, there's little chance he can aim accurately.

That's the good news. The bad news: Ivanson's finger isn't indexed; it's on the trigger.

"Gently, my son," Dez croons, smiling. "You're in the thick of it, aye. But shootin' me's no answer. I'm one of the few alive who wants to help ye, an' who can help ye."

Dez wishes Cat would return. But he's heard nothing from the direction she and the stranger ran.

Ivanson thrusts the gun forward like it was a rapier, in time with each word. "Just! Go! Just! *Go!*"

"Can't, mate." The gun, and the gun hand, are shaking badly. "The lovely lass tried to kill you? Name's Olivia. Once upon a time, she was me mate. Trained together. Need t'find her. Need to stop her."

"Leave me alone!"

"I know Liv like I know meself. I also know the two-hundred-and-forty-pound pot roast, calls himself her partner. They will not stop, mate. They will not let you live. Can't, them. Dunno why. But with your help, I will. An' then it'll be me doin' the stopping."

Mark Ivanson's arm drops like the razor arm of a printer's cutting block. It scythes down and then hangs limply at his side. He almost drops the gun.

"I . . . I don't know what to do."

Dez doesn't release the ball bearing in his grip. Not yet. "FBI Special Agent Stella Ansara. She's dead brilliant, that one. Honest, an' tough as hardtack. Between us, we can keep you safe."

Ivanson snorts a sharp laugh. Mucus escapes his nose. Tears glitter behind his eyelashes.

"Safe." He burps the almost-laugh again. "Fuck you. Safe from what? Safe from the past?"

Ivan raises the gun.

Aiming it at his own temple.

Dez's release is lightning fast.

The ball bearing thuds into Ivanson's chest. It's got enough force to make him stumble backward, his arms pinwheeling.

He fires and the bullet flies almost straight up into the air.

Dez is on him in a flash, taking the gun from him, but gently; not hurting Ivanson's hand. Ivanson is a threat to nobody, now. Not even himself.

Dez hugs the man. Tight as he can.

"Got ye. Got ye. S'all right."

Ivanson's legs give out. He becomes deadweight, and Dez goes to his knees, too. Maintaining the bear hug.

Ivanson sobs into his shoulder. Great, racking sobs that shake his whole body; that batter his diaphragm.

Dez glances to his right.

Cat stands, eighty feet away, boots spread wide, eyes wide with fear, breathing deep. She heard the shot.

Dez nods to her.

She makes the sign of the cross and mouths something in Spanish.

CHAPTER 47

CIA officer Brent Yamada is at home, in his garage, trying to fix a weed whacker; the monofilament's all knotted. He's been working on it nonstop for forty minutes and it's more knotted than when he began.

He steps inside and grabs a longneck beer. He walks back to the garage, glances at the beer, realizes he forgot to get the bottle opener. He sighs. Man, it's been that kinda week.

He returns to the kitchen and shudders to a stop. "Jesus!"

Ray Harker stands behind his butcher-block island, drinking a frosty Michelob from Yamada's fridge. Ray is wearing a long rain-coat. He has an off-white bandage covering half of his forehead. His eyes are red-rimmed, and he's unshaven.

"Ray! You about made me piss my pants, man!"

Ray drains a third of the beer in his fist.

"What . . . what happened to your face, man?"

Ray wipes his lips with the back of his hand. "Need you to find two guys."

"What?"

"Need you to find two guys."

Yamada stands there. "Ah. I don't know. I mean, I've helped where I could. But everyone at Langley's looking for you. Shit, everyone in every agency in America is looking for your ass right now. I don't—"

From his raincoat pocket, Ray produces a large stack of money, rubber-banded. Brent Yamada has taken enough bribes to know that that many inches of green equals fifty thousand dollars.

"Holy shit."

Ray drains the beer.

"Which guys?"

Ray reaches into his coat again and produces two photos. He flicks one onto the butcher block, and it lands face up. "Mark Ivanson. His Social Security's on the back."

He tosses the other. Another white guy, more or less the same age as Ivanson. With vivid red hair.

"And this asshole's Wade Selkirk."

Dez, Cat, and Mark Ivanson check in to a freeway motel in Astoria, New York. Dez drives the Jeep with Ivanson, and Cat drives the car he borrowed from a college friend in Syracuse. Ivanson has been smart enough to avoid using his credit cards and filling out any forms while running from the FBI. And the assassins.

Dez notes that, the moment they're away from Panthera Works, they both have mobile reception. "My phone's closer akin to a satellite phone than a traditional mobile," he tells Cat. "That shouldn't've happened."

He wonders if all of the metal buildings at the auto plant created some sort of super-interference.

Dez gets them checked in using one of his aliases. Ivanson is emotionless now, his face blank, eyes focused on nothing. Cat takes the Jeep and returns with a bag of burgers and fries, and bottled waters.

In the room, she gets one set of food unwrapped and puts it in front of Ivanson, who stares at it as if it were an abstract painting.

"Didn't catch the redheaded fella?" Dez asks, but kindly.

"He had a gun, too. I better-part-of-valored the hell out of there."

"Good. Smart. Can ye send me the best photo ye got of him?"

Cat sends it to Dez's phone.

He calls Special Agent Ansara.

"Where are you?"

"Upstate New York, an' I've Mark Ivanson with me."

"You're kidding! How the heck . . . ?"

"When I input his number into me phone, I fed it into an app I've got, lets me track another phone."

"And you didn't tell me."

"That's right. Thought I might have to do something nefarious when I caught up with our lad. Didn't want it reflectin' on you."

Stella sighs. "Okay. Fill me in."

Dez tells her about the auto manufacturing plant abandoned in the 1970s, Panthera Works, and its owner, Frankfurt Landesbank.

"Why did Ivanson go there?"

"Dunno yet. We've squirreled him into a motel. Fella tried to shoot himself."

Cat glances up quickly from the bottle of water she just cracked open. Dez hasn't told her that, yet. She'd just heard the shot.

"He met a man here. White fella, his age."

Stella says, "Like the other vics."

"That's right. Sending ye a phone photo. A bit blurry. Might not be good enough for an ID."

He hits a few keys.

Stella says, "Ah . . . okay, I've got it."

"This one ran before I could chat him up."

"We'll run facial recog. It's a long shot, but it might work."

"D'you see any connection twixt any of this and a defunct auto-maker from the seventies?"

"No, and our vics would have been children or infants when Panthera Works went under. If there's a connection, I'm not seeing it."

"Same here."

She says, "More of the police agencies looking into our victims have gotten back to me. Fine-tooth combs, across the board, and not a single thing linking these guys. Not schools, not clubs, not memberships. No links between their parents or grandparents or great-grandparents. Not the hospitals they were born in. Not the military—in fact, none of them served. They're men of different faiths or no faith at all. Men of different political parties and those who've never registered, never voted. Their companies haven't sought the same venture capital money, or the same investors. They don't even like the same NFL or NBA teams. Dez? I say this guardedly: There may be no connection between them. Other than Thiago wanting them dead."

"Unlikely, that."

"If there's a connection, some of the best investigators east of the Mississippi can't find it. At some point, that just means there isn't one."

Dez ponders that. He looks over at Ivanson, who finally picks up a French fry and bites into it. He chews without emotion. He might not be tasting it.

"Our lad's nearly catatonic, but I'll see if he's getting chattier. Then we'll head back t'New York City. Soon as we can."

Stella says, "Thank you. Seriously. Again."

She hangs up.

Dez pockets his phone. He grabs one of the burgers and eats a third of it, then drains some of his water. He sighs, contented.

"Americans do many things badly. The fast-food hamburger just ain't one of 'em."

Cat says, "Well, English food sucks, so the bar's set kinda low."

Dez sits opposite Ivanson, who's in the room's only chair. "Feel like tellin' us what's going on, mate?"

Ivanson bites into his burger. He chews thoughtfully. He swallows.

He whispers, "No."

"Why are them lot tryin' to kill you?"

"I don't . . . I honestly don't know."

"Who was your pal at the factory?"

Ivanson doesn't answer. He slowly eats another French fry.

"The more I know, the better I can protect you. Me an' the FBI both."

Ivanson looks at him. "You want to help me?"

"'Course."

He bites into his burger, chews, swallows. His red eyes on Dez. He sips his water.

"You should have let me shoot."

CHAPTER 48

They finish their meal. Cat also had stopped for a fifth of whiskey, and she'd asked the manager for a third plastic cup for the room.

Mark Ivanson hasn't said another word.

Dez sits on the floor, his back to the bed. Cat sits on the bed cross-legged above and behind him.

"I've an idea." Dez pulls his phone and dials a number, puts it on speaker.

"Hey!" It's a male voice, American, and sounds happy. "It's not so tall, not so dark, and not so handsome! How are you?"

Dez laughs. "Alonzo, me lad! Was in need of some superglue. Was wonderin' if ye'd made your béchamel lately."

"And yo mama. My béchamel brings all the boys to the yard."

Dez covers the phone with his oversized mitt. "Best chef I ever met," he whispers to Cat. Then, into the phone, "I've a favor t'ask of herself. But I don't want to bother her if she's in the deep of it."

The other man sighs. "She's working sixteen-hour days. You

ask me, she could use the distraction. Give me two minutes, we'll call you back."

He disconnects.

Cat says, "Alonzo?"

"Mate of mine from California. Wee bit back, I got meself shot a bit. Alonzo stayed with me, fed me till I was on me feet. There's not a door on Earth I wouldn't go through with that man."

Cat smiles quizzically down at him. "Who's the *she*?"

"Alonzo's house staff for Petra Alexandris of Triton Expediters. Also her consiglieri. I—"

His phone vibes.

Cat draws her own phone and looks up the name Petra Alexandris.

Dez answers. The woman on the other end says, almost dreamily, "Dez!"

"Wotcher, love. Fixed all of the world's problems?"

"Creating more of them every day," Petra Alexandris says. "Are you in LA?"

"I wish. Upstate New York, an' it's as cold as a toad's testicles up here."

Behind him on the bed, Cat studies her phone and starts to frown.

"Alonzo said you need some help?"

"Do. Regardin' banks."

"You came to the right girl."

Dez says, "What's a *landesbank*?"

"*Landesbanken* are, as the name implies, German banks of the land. Banks operating in autonomous territorial subdivisions."

"Okay. An' what's AG in a bank title mean?"

"I can never remember the German word. It's got a couple dozen consonants. But basically it means stock corporation. What's this about?"

"D'you know Frankfurt Landesbank AG?"

On the bed, Cat's frown has grown. In the room's only chair, Mark Ivanson has seemingly fallen asleep sitting up.

"I do. They've been around since the 1800s, in one iteration or another. Triton Expeditors does plenty of deals with them. Why?"

"They financed a car manufacturing plant in Upstate New York in the 1970s and it failed spectacularly."

Petra said, "Panthera Works. It was one of the case studies when I was getting my master's. It's famous. Or infamous, I suppose. The 1970s saw a horrible recession, but the failure of Panthera Works worsened the recession in Western Europe considerably."

"Okay. This is helpful. Can't help but note that the initials for Frankfurt Landesbank AG are FLAG."

Petra says, "Right. FLAG Family Holdings is the American subdivision of the Frankfurt Landesbank."

"They financed The Liberty Convention Center."

"Yes, and also . . ." Petra pauses. "Oh, hell. You were there. Weren't you? That terrorist incident in Newark, with those Russians."

"Yeah, but ye know me. I hunkered in a corner and waited for rescue. Not one for takin' chances, me."

Petra snorts a little laugh. "Yeah, that's the Desmond Aloysius Limerick we all know and love. Are you in the middle of this thing?"

"Am. But I'm safe. You?"

"I'd be better if you were here," she says softly. "But I also couldn't concentrate on what I'm trying to achieve, if you were here. So . . ."

"Take care of yourself, love. Listen to Alonzo. Nobody alive loves ye more than he does."

"I do, and I will. Stay safe. And Dez?"

"Aye?"

"Come visit. Please."

Petra hangs up. Dez does, too, smiling.

From behind him, on the bed, Cat Valdivia says, "Petra Alexandris. CEO of Triton Expediters."

"Aye."

"The multinational. The financing institution for half of the world's militaries."

"Aye."

When she doesn't say anything more, Dez turns quizzically, looking up at her.

"You were lovers. It was in her voice."

"We were. For a time."

Cat looks serious. She says, "I try never to compare myself to any other women. Women do that all the time, and it's toxic."

"Men do it, too, and it is toxic, aye."

"Dez? I am nowhere near in this woman's league."

Dez laughs. "Well, there's your error, right there."

Cat looks at him.

Dez says, "There are no leagues. There's only the moment. An' in the moment, you're nonpareil."

He turns back to the remains of the fast food and starts gathering napkins and wrappers in the bag. He's unaware that Cat is studying him anew.

CHAPTER 49

There's enough information in the glove box of Mark Ivanson's borrowed car to get it back to its owner. Cat searched it first and found Ivanson's satchel of extra clothes.

Cat jacks her thumb in the direction of Ivanson and says, "Do you really want to put Crazy Boy in a pressurized airplane?"

"I do not." Dez calls the agency and asks if they can change the rental agreement and drive the Jeep to New York City. Turns out, they can drop it off at JFK, so that's the new plan.

Once they're on the highway, heading south, Ivanson curls up in the backseat and falls asleep. Cat drives.

Dez calls Stella Ansara again.

"I've a connection," he says. "It's tenuous, but it's somethin'."

"Fire."

"The American arm of a German bank financed The Liberty. The same bank also financed the auto plant that went belly up in the 1970s, Panthera Works."

"Where you found Ivanson and the redheaded guy."

"Aye."

Stella sighs. "Well, it's a damn sight more than we've got so far. Worth checking. Is Ivanson talking?"

Dez turns in his seat and checks the sleeping man. "Hardly a bloody word. The terrorist incident, the near assassination, tryin' to kill himself up here: I think the lad's as near the breakin' point as anyone I ever met. I'm not willin' to push him. Just bringin' him back. The rest is up to your lot."

Stella says, "Thank you. I have the feeling that's the right call. What are the names of the banks?"

"The German one's Frankfurt Landesbank AG. The American arm is FLAG Family Holdings."

There's a pause. "I met a guy from there. He's . . . Hold on . . ."

Stella likely is scrolling through the Notes field of her phone, Dez thinks.

"Jonas Diedrich, North American operations director, FLAG Family Holdings. It was at a multiagency debrief on the terrorist incident."

"This is as thin a thread as any I've ever encountered, mate. Could be a heapin' helping of hope, an' not much more."

"Your thin thread's the only thread I've got worth pulling right now. I'll talk to this Diedrich again. Thank you . . . mate."

She says that with a laugh and disconnects.

They drive for a while.

Cat says, "You know, it dawns on me that you haven't told your very special special agent that you've identified Ray Harker's partner."

A good mile passes under their tires before he responds, "Aye. Tryin' to figure out how to play that. I'll have to tell her, eventually. Still. Won't be easy."

Cat smiles. "I'm a lifelong outlaw and I'm damn, damn good at it. And now I find myself helping stop criminals, while beholden to a mysterious Brit who uses information from one ex-lover to help us track down another ex-lover. Do I have that right?"

Dez laughs. "Well, it's sordid as hell, the way you say it."

Cat changes lanes and blows past a Tesla doing seventy. "It's like a Tarantino movie on the fucking Lifetime channel."

CHAPTER 50

That afternoon in New York City, Dez hands the still–unspeaking Mark Ivanson over to the FBI, where Stella Ansara orders a psych eval and a protective hold.

Catalina Valdivia stays away from the meeting. She's not yet on the FBI's radar and would like it to stay that way.

Stella shakes Dez's hand. "You did really good, finding this guy. Thank you. Oh, and hacking his phone's GPS is illegal, so, you know, knock that shit off."

He says, "Yes, ma'am. Oh, any luck with the redheaded fella?"

Stella shakes her head. "The shot was too fuzzy. Facial recog came back negative."

"Feared as much."

She glances around, then draws him a few steps farther from her cohort. "I, ah, had coffee with Harlow," she says, smiling. "It was nice. I don't know if it's going anywhere but . . . thank you."

"She's as talented a musician as any I ever met. Nothing with strings she can't play. Glad ye had fun."

Stella pauses, then shrugs. "I don't . . . connect well with women I'm interested in. You know? Like, hardly ever. It comes from . . . It doesn't matter where it comes from, Dez, it's just part of me. And ever since you reached out to Incident Command, from within The Liberty, you've been nothing but helpful. And kind. And I want you to know it's noted and appreciated."

They shake hands again. Dez goes to find Cat in a wine bar, three blocks away. She's ordered a sparkling prosecco for herself— "All things Italian," she explains—and Dez gets an Oregon pinot noir, because he's tried them in Portland and thinks they're money in the bank. When he's seated at the small, high bistro table, she says, "So we lure out your Olivia Gelman, right? Question: Am I the bait, or are you?"

"Since when are you so eager to play the bait?"

She says, "Since this bitch isn't going away anytime soon, so the sooner I can hasten her exit, stage left, the better I like it, okay?"

Dez sips his wine and ponders the problem. "Liv is smart. Smarter'n me."

"So am I."

"Granted. We used you as the lure in Positano. Doubt she'd fall for the same trick twice. And . . ."

She gives him some time. "And . . . ?"

"I still dunno why she lured me to The Liberty in the first place. I'm dead certain it was her. Had t'be. But the way of it? Baffles me."

Cat smiles and sips her bubbles. "Not me."

"Do tell."

"You said you'd trained together. That you became lovers."

"Aye."

"Then she took your training and became a thief. She ran into you on a heist. You beat her. Damn near killed her."

"Aye."

Cat says, "I know what she's thinking. I've thought the same. There's a security company called the Adagio Group. They're good. Best of the best. And the woman who fronts them is famous. A genius."

"Aye?"

"And anytime I get a chance to steal anything protected by the Adagio Group, I go for it. I can steal from chumps and chowderheads standing on my head. Gimme a real challenge, and my blood gets pumping."

"You think she lured me into this just to say she beat me? She had to beat a Russian paramilitary group an' every law enforcement agency on the East Coast! But she needed to beat me, too?"

"I think so. I think she owes you. Big-time. She went one-on-one with you that one time. In Tunisia, I think you said? You won, she lost. You stopped the big drug heist and damn near stopped her heart. Who knows? Maybe you did stop her heart, and she had to be resuscitated. You're her white whale, big guy. She could defeat the Pentagon, the Holy Roman Empire, the '27 Yankees, and the fucking Disney corporation! But you're the prize in her Cracker Jack box."

They sit and sip and think. Dez shrugs. "Could be you're right. It tracks. Makes me feel egotistical, admitting that. Can't imagine this fecking shite revolving around me of all people."

Cat holds up her glass. Dez touches his glass to hers. "To white whales," she says.

"To white whales. So how do we get Liv to come after me?"

"Her partner. You said his name is Ray Harker?"

"Aye, the gobshite."

"You don't think much of him."

"Don't. If the lad were on fire, I wouldn't cross the street to piss on the flames, for fear of wasting good urine."

"You were tracking his phone to that bookstore, where he almost killed you."

"Oh, please. I was in more danger of getting a paper cut than I was of him. And the next time I tried trackin' his phone, I couldn't. If I were to bet, I think Liv figured out how I got there and added a patch to his comms security."

"So we don't get to him through his phone, but we do get to him. Somehow. Goad him? If she's the brain and he's the brawn, he's their weak point."

Dez grins. "That's brilliant, that."

Cat sips her wine and gives him a smile that is, well, catlike. "That's because I'm the brains and you're the brawn."

CHAPTER 51

Dez contacts the man working under the alias of Stewart, the Scotsman employed by MI6 to keep tabs on the CIA. He leaves a number and, ninety seconds later, Stewart calls him back. Cat leans in close, her shoulder pressing into Dez's, so she can hear.

"Limerick? In need of a wallah, are you?"

"Aye, an' full disclosure, I'm sittin' with an ally I trust."

"Any luck hunting down that Harker fella?"

"Aye, some. We tangled an' I hurt him. But didn't finish him off. Need to lure him out. How do I go about that?"

"No idea, but I know people who know people, who know people. Give a lad a couple of hours, and I'll see if I can find something in Harker's life to use as a hook."

"You're a lifesaver, mate. Cheers."

Dez hangs up.

"My thinking's this: Liv an' that right twat, Harker, get hired t'kill six men, an' they lure 'em to The Liberty to hide their deaths among many, aye?" Dez draws out his tablet and goes to a notes list. "We got, ah, Garvey, Gaetano, and Levkowitz. Killed in situ. We got Mark Ivanson, who survives via what I think we can all agree is sheer dumb luck. We got Gene O'Malley, who is shot an' killed in his home. An' we've got the redheaded lad that Mark met up with at the Panthera Works auto plant."

Cat says, "With you so far."

"Ivanson looks fairly catatonic. That leaves us with Redhead. Alas, the snap you got was too fuzzy for facial recognition."

"Damn it. Sorry."

"No worries. The problem is: The FBI's using a massive image database. Billions of images. But all of the dead men and Ivanson were at The Liberty. Which means Redhead had to be, too. If I can get back into the security feeds of The Liberty, an' run your photo against those images, we might get lucky. Not one snap versus billions, but one versus a few thousand. If nothing else, I can write an algorithm to track down all redheaded males who were there on Monday."

She frowns. "All right. So maybe I'm the brawn and you're the brains."

"You're a trip to the moon on gossamer wings."

She winks at him. "Corny, but you make it work."

They return to the fancy hotel, where Cat is registered under one of Dez's false IDs. Dez sits at the desk and begins pounding away on his tablet. "When I was in The Liberty's security system, I left a backdoor. Almost always do, just in case I forgot something."

"I've done the same. I'm not a hacker, but I have one I trust."

Dez types in silence for maybe twenty minutes. Cat showers.

When she emerges, wearing one towel and her hair wrapped in another, Dez says, "My algorithm's runnin'. Now let's see . . ."

He glances up. She's barefoot, water pearling on her legs and shoulders, and she's without makeup. She looks younger, and more innocent, and incandescent. "God, but you're a beauty."

"If every time we shower, we end up having to re-shower afterwards, the New York City hotels are going to register us as a nuisance."

Dez stands and kisses her. "I'm willin' to risk it."

She shoves him backward onto the bed and straddles him.

They make love, and shower, and—this was predictable—order eggs and toast and bacon from room service. They tuck into their food as Dez's tablet pings.

They sit up against the pillows, shoulder to shoulder, and check the images on his computer. There are seventeen of them, all showing Caucasian men in their thirties, forties, or fifties, with red hair and a full head of it.

They discard most of them after a brief examination. One of the Russian mercenaries was a redhead, but his nose and ears are all wrong for their guy. They narrow it down to five images that might be the guy they saw, briefly, at the Panthera Works plant.

The images all come from security cameras, which means they all come from about ten to twenty feet above the hostages. This red-headed guy—could be *their* redheaded guy—was being held in what appears to be a gift shop, along with a dozen or so other hostages. In one of the images, all of the hostages have turned, as one, and are staring out a window. Their faces show surprise and shock.

Dez blows that image up to take the full screen. Cat points to the lower right-hand corner of the photo. "What's that? Outside?"

"That's the police an' National Guard. This was taken during the endgame. After you an' me had bolluxed the Russians' systems an' let in the good guys. Mister Redhead must've . . ."

His voice drains away.

"What?"

Dez uses the pad of his index finger and thumb to blow the photo up. He points. "Tall, blond fella? A couple of meters behind Mister Redhead? That's Ray Harker."

"He was that close to killing number six," she whispers.

"Maybe. The goal was t'make their assassinations look like part of the Russians' mad scheme, yeah? Harker wasn't about to just throttle Mister Redhead like a chicken, right there in front of the other hostages. He likely was plannin' on moving our lad somewhere private, an' doing him quiet-like."

"But this proves that this guy"—Cat points to the redheaded hostage—"is our guy."

"Aye. I'm sendin' this to Stella. Likely she can identify some of the other hostages in the gift shop. Maybe one of them recognizes our lad."

He does that. Stella Ansara is not going to be happy that Dez snuck back into the security feeds of The Liberty, but to date, she's been giving him a pretty long leash.

As he finishes his text to her, attaching the photo and identifying Ray Harker, his phone vibrates.

It's Stewart, the Scots spook from MI6.

"Squire! Any luck?"

Stewart gives them a low, deep chuckle. "Sorry for so late a call, but I do believe so. And if you were to bestow such accolades as genius, or brilliant, or stellar, why, who would I be to disagree with you?"

Dez winks at Cat. "We're listening."

"So Raymond Harker, bless his soul, has an ex-wife."

"Who'd marry that lump of brick dust?"

Stewart takes on an ironic tone. "Tall, blond, blue-eyed, strongly built. Wonders just ceased."

"Fair point. An' the ex-wife, squire?"

Stewart laughs again and Cat has to cover her mouth with her palm to stop from joining him. Some people's laughs are just contagious.

"Oh, you will love this! She obtained—not one, mind you, and not two—but *three* restraining orders against Harker for spying on her after their divorce! The restraining orders are spaced out: three years between the first two, and four years between the latter two."

"So he spied on her for the better part of a decade."

"Yes. Planted minicams in or around her home. Planted a tracker on her car. Got well written up by the Agency's internal affairs, but 'twas never enough to get him the sack. Which is yet another reason to adore the CIA."

"Ye've a name an' address for the ex?"

Stewart does.

There is no guarantee that Ray Harker is still spying on his ex-wife. This could be no lead whatsoever.

But the Ray Harker that Dez knows and loves is just creepy enough. This might work.

CHAPTER 52

Dez and Cat send a text to Ellen Turner, and she agrees to meet with them regarding her ex-husband, Ray Harker. She lives in Arlington, Virginia, and Dez flies down early Friday to meet her. Cat comes along under the theory that Ms. Turner will be more likely to meet this strange man if he's with a woman.

Cat and Dez sit on her couch and Ellen Turner sits opposite them and cries. She's a petite blonde and she's wearing hospital scrubs, but Dez hasn't asked what she does. "Of course he has cameras watching me," she says miserably. "I've moved six times since I filed for divorce. That was over twelve years ago!"

Cat does a lot of the talking. "My friend here is good with electronics. Would you allow him to do a sweep of your home? To see if your ex is still spying on you?"

Ellen says, "I'm sorry. Who are you again?"

"We're helping the FBI to track Ray down."

"But he works for, ah, a government agency that—"

"He doesn't," Cat says, gently. "He was CIA but he left and became a, ah, sort of mercenary, I guess you'd say."

Ellen nods. "That really, really sounds like Ray. Of course he did. Please, help yourself around."

Dez uses an app on his phone to sweep for electronic bugs, and sure enough, he finds a tiny camera in her garage. He finds another in her kitchen and a third facing her shower in the bathroom. He tells Ellen about the first two and doesn't tell her about the third. He just hopes she never finds out.

Cat stays with Ellen in the living room as Dez borrows a black marker and a legal pad from their hostess's second-bedroom-turned-office. He writes two messages on the pad—held in landscape—then turns and holds the first message up to the garage camera.

HOLSTEINS ARE CATTLE.

VULTURES ARE BIRDS

RAY HARKER'S AS DUMB

AS RHINOCEROS TURDS

Then he shows the other one. It includes a telephone number. Below which is written:

LIV SAVED YOUR ASS LAST TIME BUT YOU CAN'T HIDE BEHIND HER SKIRTS FOREVER. BE A MAN FOR ONCE.

Dez clears out the cameras after that and destroys them. He also shows Ellen Turner a website for a device not unlike a router, which will detect unwanted transmissions and electrical signals within the geometry of her property lines.

"Why didn't the police ever show me this?" she asks, hugging Dez, then Cat.

On the flight back to New York, Dez shows Cat the legal pad notes. She's laughing so hard, other people in first class are throwing eye darts at her. She doesn't care.

CHAPTER 53

Liv Gelman says, "Problem?"

Ray is standing at a window of the yacht's deck three, amidships lounge, drinking a tall whiskey. He's staring out at, apparently, not a damn thing. His shoulders rise high, and she knows her lover's body language well enough to know that equates as tension.

She spots his phone curled up in his other fist.

He hasn't responded.

"Ray? Problem?"

Nothing.

"Ray?"

He starts, turns, sees her. "Nothing. No, I'm fine."

"Is there a—"

"I said I'm fine."

He watches her, standing in the stateroom doorway.

She says, "I have a consortium of hackers I use. In Hong Kong. They're doing a high-resolution search for Wade Selkirk and Mark

Ivanson. They're brilliant, and wonderfully criminal in their endeavors. I've high hopes."

Ray drinks whiskey. "I got a crooked guy in the Agency looking for them, too."

Liv pretends she doesn't already know this, and the ID of his crooked guy. "Great news. We'll find them."

"We wouldn't have lost them except for you. And Limerick."

They stand like that for a bit. The bandages on his forehead have yellowed from the disinfectant, and possibly from blood.

Liv turns and walks away.

Ray listens to her fading boot steps. Then lifts his phone and dials with his thumb while draining his glass. He's pouring another when he hears the click.

"Raymond, my lad! How's tricks?"

He drinks half of the new one. Refills his glass.

Limerick apparently has no problem waiting.

"I am. Going to. Kill you."

"Well, that's why I reached out, my son! Enough chitchat. We should get on about that, yeah?"

"You are fucking dead."

"For *dead,* read *bored.*"

"You think you can be with my ex-wife? You think you can hit that, you little shit?"

Dez says, "Soooo . . . booooored . . ."

"You'll meet? You and me? When and where I say?"

"Wouldn't miss it for love nor money!"

Ray thinks about. He drains his glass. "There's a warehouse, closed because of a fire in a meth lab. Five blocks from Pier Ninety-nine. West of Fordham."

"I can find it, darlin'."

"Midnight."

"Of course."

"Just you."

"How else?"

"Fuck you."

Liv skips down the stairs to the lower deck, and to the bedroom suite she retrofitted for communications. She has a man working there, sitting amidst a mass of technology, wearing a foam headset. He's Chinese and works directly as part of the Thiago group.

He doffs his headset. "Harker made the call. Just as you said."

"He's meeting Desmond Limerick," Liv says. It isn't a question.

"Yes."

"When and where?"

Her comms guy tells her.

Liv draws her own phone and makes a call.

Briggs, leader of the New Haven Boys and owner of the Stripperz! club in Queens, answers immediately.

"Mr. Briggs? An opportunity for you to avenge yourself on Ray Harker for lying to you. And on Dez Limerick, for destroying your reputation. Interested?"

CHAPTER 54

A simple Google search turns up the warehouse closed by the NYPD and the fire department after a meth lab fire. Dez searches the grounds via Google Earth and takes the Street View.

He memorizes everything he can.

Catalina Valdivia says, "You're sure about this?"

"Of course. It's the best play, love."

Ray Harker sneaks off the yacht a little after ten without Liv noticing. He's brought his Glock and the vial of pain pills. The time has come to end Limerick as a threat, once and for all.

His head feels perfectly clear, the pain subsiding now that he has a clear mission. This is what he should have done in the first place. Liv's infatuation with the runty English dude stalled a brilliant and complicated plan to weave six assassinations into an ongoing terrorist assault. And it would have worked. *Should* have worked.

It still might. He and Liv got three of the six targets at The

Liberty, and eliminated number four, Gene O'Malley, in his home. Number five, Mark Ivanson, escaped—again, thanks to Limerick. And now he's apparently gone to ground. So has number six, Wade Selkirk.

Ray's plan is simplicity—unlike Liv and her byzantine, complicated schemes. One: Kill Limerick. Two: Hunt down the final two targets and kill them. Three: Take credit for the highest-paying hits in the history of the Thiago group.

Simple.

He rolls past the warehouse with its crime-scene tape around 10:40. The place is dark, a perfect cube of soot-stained cinder block and broken panes. Ray scouted the place out for another hit, eight months earlier. He ruled it out because the floorboards were broken through and just walking into the place could kill you. But scout it, he had, and he knows the building well enough. He can get in and get to a safe spot with sturdy floors. Limerick won't have that advantage.

Best case scenario: Wound Limerick. Just a little. Just enough that Ray can beat the man to death. He doesn't want to end this too quickly.

He rolls around the perimeter of the warehouse, spots nothing amiss.

He parks two blocks away and walks. He knows an entrance on the rear side of the warehouse, one he jimmied open earlier. He checks the shadows, checks corners and rooftops and open windows. He sees a few clusters of drug buyers and sellers, but nothing worth worrying about. They ignore him as he passes.

Something obscures his vision for a moment and he realizes it's blood. His forehead wound has begun to bleed. He applies pressure to the dirty bandage over it until it stops. There will be time to get it repatched up when he's finished.

Ray finds the window next to the door in the back. No glass.

He reaches through the window, stretches as far to his right as he can, and finds the crowbar he used to jam the door shut. He removes it, opens the door, and walks through.

Limerick fancies himself some sort of door expert. He'll find a way in. No question. But he won't find a way out.

Ray hears noises that could be rats. And noises that could be the old and battle-bruised building settling.

And he hears human noises.

He draws his SIG. Limerick might be here already.

Good.

This won't be a fair fight. Against Ray Harker, there is no such thing.

He creeps through the dark, his eyes adjusting quickly. He needs to be steady, so he downs two more painkillers.

He hears a muttering, somewhere above him and to the right. Second floor.

Maybe Limerick hasn't come alone?

Ray previously scouted a service stairwell, at the west end of the building. He moves that way, wary of rotting floorboards. He's in no hurry. The stairs are perfect because they were smashed through a long time ago. No risers or steps, but the supports are still there for each riser. He holsters his weapon and begins climbing, using his hands and feet to scale what remains of the old stairway.

He gets to the second floor, crouches, draws his weapon. He listens.

He wipes blood away from his right eye. The wound is seeping.

He hears the distinctive sound of a pistol being cocked. Dead ahead.

He creeps that way.

He scopes out every floorboard first, then applies a little weight to see if it will hold. Then advances. He'd been a Marine. He'd been CIA. This isn't his first go-around.

He comes to a corner, smells cologne. He pauses, back to the wall, listens.

He rounds the corner. Sights up on the back of a standing man who's peering down through broken floorboards at the ground floor.

"Don't," Ray says.

Briggs, Ray's pet thug from Connecticut, turns. A second thug turns, and a third.

Very, very bright lights pop on.

"THIS IS THE FBI! THE BUILDING IS SURROUNDED! EVERYONE DROP YOUR WEAPONS!"

"What is this?" Cat whispers.

"Musical version of *The Philadelphia Story*. Bing Crosby, Frank Sinatra, Grace Kelly. Brilliant."

They lie on the hotel room bed together. They got popcorn from the lobby gift shop and a bottle of bubbly. Dez has found a channel for classic movies on the room's TV and lucked into *High Society*, a favorite.

His phone buzzes. He puts the movie on mute.

"Dez? It's Stella. We got him. It's over."

Dez and Cat exchange looks. "Is Harker alive?"

"He is, but he took a bullet to the thigh. Guess what: We got four of the New Haven Boys, too. Including the guy Briggs who runs the gang."

Dez thinks: Liv. Cleaning up loose ends. "Cheers, that."

"Hey, you did more damage to Harker than we thought. The wound on his forehead is infected. He was taken to a level one trauma hospital. The EMTs said it looked bad."

"Understood. Ta, for lettin' me know."

Stella Ansara says, "You didn't want to be here for this? Curious."

"For Harker? He's a joke. I just wanted him off the board so whoever's really behind all this has fewer options."

Cat gives him a sly smile, realizing he still hasn't told the special agent about his ex-lover.

"Okay, Dez. Thanks for playing this one by the book. The takedown was clean. Multi-jurisdictional kudos all around. Mayor's happy, justice is happy, the damn attorney general's happy. I owe you another one."

"Well played, mate. Cheers, then."

He hangs up. He turns the sound back up.

"She doesn't know you're hunting a former gatekeeper."

"Shh," Dez says, nodding to the screen. "Louis Armstrong."

CHAPTER 55

Saturday morning, Liv Gelman checks in with the partner members of the Thiago group and informs them that Ray Harker's erratic behavior, following the wound he received in combat, has been dealt with. Ray no longer will be a diversion.

Also, that she had Ray followed when he went to meet the CIA officer who is being paid off to help them find the last two of six targets. Ray's bent officer is now Liv's bent officer.

And the Hong Kong collective of hackers she has hired is scraping the internet in a way no government intelligence agency could ever hope to match.

"They've already found one of our wayward sheep," she explains across the secure video conference server. "Mark Ivanson is in FBI custody. I'm working on a way to get to him now."

"And the sixth man?"

"Wade Selkirk. Either my hacker collective will find him, or Ray's corrupt CIA officer will. It's a matter of time."

"Good. Is Harker dead?"

Liv smiles into the pinhole camera on the one and only laptop on the entire planet Earth properly outfitted to receive this transmission. She cannot see the partners but they can see her. She knows that one of them resides in the south of France, one in Beijing, and one in Houston, Texas. She has met them, and they believe she does not know their names. They are wrong in this assumption, but Liv lets on nothing.

"He is not. But I worry about his diminishing mental capacity. Which is why I took the liberty of spiking his painkillers with polonium-210." She smiles mischievously. "I know. I walked him into a firefight with forces he was unprepared for. Poisoning him was a belt-and-braces thing. One can never be too sure."

"Very good. One last thing: This gatekeeper? This Englishman. Have you established how he caught wind of the events in Newark to begin with?"

Liv smiles into the camera and lies effervescently. "Ray has quite a hatred for this Limerick fellow. P'raps Ray lured him in to kill him?"

"Then it's a good thing you've relieved Harker from any further duties. Well done, Miss Gelman. Good hunting."

She disconnects.

The three principal partners are keeping their fingers out of the pie. She hopes that lasts.

Next: Contact the buyer who ordered the hit and pour more oil on troubled waters.

Dez meets Stella Ansara for coffee in the morning. He discovers that she currently is the flavor of the month among everyone who's anyone in the Justice Department, the Pentagon, and the U.S. Intelligence Community. Bagging the most wanted ex–CIA officer in existence—and alive—has added many, many feathers to her cap.

"I made my station chief look good and the FBI director look good. At the end of the day, this is a political job. Those things matter."

"Then very well done, indeed. Y'know that croissant you really don't want?"

"Screw that. Hit me with a pain au chocolat!"

"Now, that's how ye celebrate!"

He gets two and they're wondrous. But Stella grows serious quickly. "The docs say Ray Harker's health is failing and they haven't figured out why yet. They're not a hundred percent he's going to pull through."

Dez shrugs. "Shame, that. Any luck hunting down the missing sixth man?"

She shakes her head and smiles, wiping flaky crumbs off her lips with a napkin. "Yes, and it's thank you, again. We talked to some of the hostages who were being held in the gift shop at The Liberty. They identified a red-haired man who called himself Wade. That was enough for us to track him down. Wade Selkirk. He's in real estate. In Philadelphia. Roughly the same age as the other five. And so far, no hint of any connection between him and the others."

Dez asks, "Mark Ivanson?"

"I had a forensic psychiatrist give him the once-over. She's afraid he's very close to a full mental breakdown. She wants me soft-shoeing around Ivanson for the time being."

Dez thought much the same.

"Y'know, there's a collective of hackers in Hong Kong I've hired a time or two, to handle some sordid bits. They are to hackin' what Cirque du Soleil is to the trapeze. I could ask them to help hunt down this Selkirk fella."

"Let's hold off on breaking international law until my day of accolades are over, shall we?"

"Yes, ma'am."

"Oh! This is interesting," she says, suddenly remembering something. "I was wondering why experienced Russian mercenaries believed the Thiago group about there being a sub-sub-basement beneath The Liberty. I mean, we saw the fake schematics, and they were impeccable forgeries. But still: It's bothered me that the Russians were naïve."

"Bothered me, too."

"One of the FBI guys from Quantico has been interviewing the Russians. They talked to a top lieutenant, a guy named . . ." She scrolls through her smartphone notes. "Oborin. He says the Russians believed there was a sub-sub-basement because they got to practice in a replica of the thing."

Dez devours the last of his pastry. "A replica? A replica of a level that doesn't exist?"

Stella shrugs. "So says my guy from Quantico. And he taught me everything I know about interrogating hostiles in custody."

Dez's brain is pinging about in his skull. "That's . . . Does that make sense to ye? Thiago wanted the Russians t'believe there was a sub-sub-basement, so they crafted extremely convincing schematics for it. And when that alone wasn't enough they . . . they built a sub-sub-basement? Where?"

"The Russians say they don't know. Their Colonel Baranov and his top guys were flown to a site, and got to do a walk-through. They don't know where it was."

"That's daft. But likely unimportant. What's next for you, then?"

"Find the sixth missing victim, this Selkirk. Find out what the connection is to these six guys. A connection so weird none of our law enforcement agencies have figured it out yet."

"Talked to the executive of the German bank yet? The big wheel from FLAG Family Holdings?"

Stella thumbs through her notes again. Dez is amazed at how her brain categorizes facts. She now has days and days and days of interviews in the Notes field of her phone, and can find anything within seconds. "Jonas Diedrich. He's been in Berlin but should've just flown back. I'm meeting him next."

"I have strong doubts it'll lead to anything. But slim hope's better than none, yeah?"

Stella leaves the coffee shop and goes directly to the Financial District of Lower Manhattan. She'd never find parking down there, even with government plates on her official vehicle, so she takes a taxi.

If you take a map of the Financial District and draw a rectangle from the offices of JPMorgan to Citigroup, to Goldman Sachs, to the Bank of New York Mellon, you'd find the skyscraper owned by Frankfurt Landesbank AG smack in the middle. Its American real estate division, FLAG Family Holdings, occupies the seventeenth through twenty-fifth floors of the building.

Stella checks in with the security in the lobby—no mall cops, these, they look like the security she's seen in federal buildings in DC—and one of them unlocks an elevator to get her to twenty-five. The guard calls a younger guard who goes up with her.

"C suite," the guy in the elevator says. "Ever since nine-eleven, we've gotten pretty security conscious."

"You know escorting me up in the elevator wouldn't have mattered squat on nine-eleven. Right?"

The guy says, "I don't make the rules, ma'am."

Stella, herself, has told people that many a time.

The guard hands her off to a young and pretty woman in an expensive suit and heels. The aide gives Stella a lanyard with a pass and she's surprised to find her own photo on the card.

"There's a camera in the elevator," the aide says. "The passes are biodegradable. This will be mush by tomorrow."

She escorts Stella to the northwest corner of the executive level, a massive office with a burnished golden plaque by the door that reads JONAS DIEDRICH—DIREKTOR

A secretary with a German accent sits outside Diedrich's office and accepts the handoff. She nods the aide away. "Special Agent Ansara? Right this way, please."

She raps twice on the door and escorts Stella in. The office is opulent, with walls facing north and west, all window, with an unbelievable view of Manhattan. Stella is rocked back by the panorama.

"Herr Direktor?"

Jonas Diedrich stands by a sink in the far corner of the opulent office. His suit coat is off and he wears silver suspenders. His sleeves are rolled up and he's washing his hands and forearms. "This is Special Agent Ansara, Federal Bureau of Investigation," the secretary says. "And you have a meeting with the ophthalmologist next."

Diedrich looks up sharply. "I do? I totally forgot. Thank you, Lina."

The secretary gives him a little bow and exits. *Well, it coulda been a curtsey,* Stella muses to herself.

Diedrich dries off his hands and arms. "My apologies! I flew in from Germany and the pressurized air on airliners dries out my skin."

"I've experienced the same things."

They shake hands. As Stella remembered from their brief meeting earlier, Diedrich is a sallow and thin fellow, maybe sixty, his hair swept and slicked back. His shirt and tie and trousers and shoes all scream money. He says, "Coffee? Tea? Water?"

"No, thank you, and I'm not going to take up much of your time."

"I once met an Ansara in Davos, Switzerland. He was from Saudi Arabia but a Christian."

Stella says, "Then we could be related. That's my family background, too."

He gestures to the L-shaped couches that surround a low coffee table. "Sit sit sit. Please. How may I help you?"

She stays standing. "You're the director of an important bank, sir. I won't be here that long."

Diedrich laughs. "You saw the plaque outside my door, yes? *Direktor.* Which is quite funny, because I'm merely the director of North American Operations. Which is a tiny fraction of the holdings of Frankfurt Landesbank. If you met any of the *real* bank royalty, I assure you, they would not remember my name."

"Well, I appreciate your time, anyway. I have a . . . strange question to ask you."

Diedrich has draped his suit coat over the back of a chair. He shrugs into it, adjusts his shirt cuffs, his onyx cuff links glinting, as do his eyes. "Ah! Intriguing. I have seven meetings planned for today and absolutely none of them promise to be intriguing. Please be the exception, Special Agent Ansara."

She's pondered how to ask this. "One of the hostages from Monday's terrorist incident survived. Then, a few days later, someone attempted to assassinate him. Does the name Mark Ivanson mean anything to you?"

"No." Diedrich steps to his desk and reaches for his desk phone. In German, he says, "Lina? Do we know a . . . ?"

Stella repeats the name and spells it.

"One moment, Herr Direktor."

Stella speaks up loud enough for the secretary to hear. "Also, the name Wade Selkirk."

Diedrich says, "Search both, please," and disconnects. He straightens. "I don't know either names. But my children claim I forget their names half the time, so . . ." He shrugs apologetically.

"The reason I ask is: Mark Ivanson survived the assault on The Liberty. Then, after surviving an assassination attempt, he fled. We found him at the remains of Panthera Works in Upstate New York."

Diedrich's eyes go wide. "Frankfurt Landesbank owned Panthera!"

"We know, sir. And The Liberty."

"My God."

He goes to his desk phone again. "Lina: Find out if those two names are connected to the bank, please. And also, see if the name is connected in any way to Panthera Works."

"Panthera . . . ?"

"The automaker, Lina! From the seventies. It was our greatest failure! Surely you have not forgotten!"

"Of course, sir."

He says to Stella, "No one likes to recall the time we single-handedly decimated the European economy. My granddaughter would say: 'Our bad.'"

"I don't think that recession's all on you guys, sir."

"Gracious and accurate. We have extensive records on Panthera. I could inundate you with whatever we have, or we can do targeted searches. What do you need?"

"For now, if you could search for any connection between Ivanson and Selkirk, and Panthera, or Frankfurt Landesbank, that'd be a big help."

He shakes her hand. "Of course. I myself am useless with the archives, but what's the point of being *Direktor,* or making everyone spell it with the 'k,' if you don't have staff to make you look good, yes?"

Stella thanks him again and he walks her to the door. "I am having lunch with the mayor," he says. "But I'll be available all afternoon if you need me. Time is a vital ingredient when investigating terrorism, yes?"

Stella smiles at him. "Well, you've got an appointment with your ophthalmologist first."

Diedrich looks surprised, then makes a comical gesture of

smacking his forehead with the palm of his hand. "*Mein Gott!* I swear, I've got what you Americans call COVID brain, yes?"

She laughs. "Like airplanes drying out your skin. Yeah, I've experienced that one, too. Thank you, sir."

He draws his wallet and finds a business card. This one is buried back, behind the rest of his cards. "This is my private number. You can reach me day or night."

"Thank you, sir."

"Best of luck, Special Agent."

He escorts her out. The secretary has summoned the young aide in the tall heels, who walks Stella to the elevator.

Lina says, "The, ah, ophthalm—"

Jonas Diedrich waves her off and returns to his office. He locks the door. He moves to his desk, unlocks the bottom drawer on the left, and withdraws a remote control. He activates it and a maple wall panel retracts. Behind which is a private elevator that runs, without stops, from the privacy level of parking, deep beneath the Frankfurt Landesbank building, to the director's office.

Liv Gelman steps out.

"Thank you for seeing me."

"The FBI," Diedrich says, stone-faced. "They've asked about Mark and Wade. And Panthera Works."

Liv's eyes widen. "Goodness! They're further along than we'd imagined."

"I need these men dead, Thiago. I am paying an astronomical amount for it."

"And dead they shall be, *Direktor.* Everything is going according to plan."

CHAPTER 56

Dez does one more show with Kansas Jack and the Blacktop and enjoys it thoroughly. The band is off to Sarasota for a three-night stand, so Dez bids them goodbye.

They drank at a bar after the gig and he's walking back to Cat's hotel, 1 A.M., when he stops short. He can practically hear the thought pinging around inside his cranium.

He rushes back to the hotel. In the room, he finds no Catalina Valdivia, but a note that reads, GILDED OR NOT, A CAGE IS A CAGE. I'M OUT OF HERE FOR A WHILE. XOXOX

It was her call, and he doubted she'd stay long. Also, she's clever enough and criminal enough to know how to stay off the radar. Dez is a little worried that Liv will find her again, but he doesn't see a lot of options.

One in the morning in New York is two in the afternoon in Hong Kong. He uses a fifteen-key encryption code and reaches out to the Hong Kong collective of hackers he's used before. One of them is named Peng Shanshan but everyone calls her Spot. She's nineteen, stunningly amoral, and swears like a sailor.

Dez types: You read about Russian terrorists in New Jersey, in USA?

He waits. Ping: We don't work with fuck-dick terrorists. You know that. Fuck you.

Dez types: I know you don't, and you know you don't, but the person behind them needs to find a guy here in USA and, if I was her, I'd use you. But I wouldn't tell you who I was backing.

He waits. He grabs a tiny scotch bottle from the minifridge, cracks it open, sips it. He waits some more. He knows Spot, and knows the girl hates terrorists, even more than she dislikes governments. He checks out the classic movie channel he found the other day. He checks his email and messages and finds nothing worth reading.

Ping: Who is this fuckwad looking for?

Dez types: Wade Selkirk.

Ping: FUCKING BITCH! Qamar works for Russian mercs??? You 100%, D-Dog?

Dez smiles. Qamar. The Arabic word for moon. Olivia Gelman used the alias Yareakh—the Hebrew word for moon—back when they'd both been gatekeepers. He types: 100%.

Ping: Dez's screen is filled with lines of alphanumeric code. He grins, recognizing it. It's access to the router at an Estonian server farm that Liv must be using. Dez recognizes it because he uses the same server farm.

With this much information, Dez can track her down.

Ping: Do that bitch nasty, D-Dog!

Dez thinks a nineteen-year-old prodigy shouldn't have this much anger in her system. He wonders if she's ever considered yoga.

CHAPTER 57

Liv Gelman chose a master suite on the stolen mega-yacht. The king-sized bed is luxurious, the Egyptian cotton sheets the highest end you can order. She always sleeps soundly when on water, even on an anchored boat.

It's between three and four A.M., the hour of the wolf, as the Russians say. She blinks awake. Not drowsily; fully awake. She reaches for the gun under the bed's second pillow and sits up, thumbing off the safety.

Dez smiles from across the room.

Liv gasps. "Desmond!"

"Hallo, Liv. Wotcher."

A little laugh burbles up from within her, and eyes sparkle. "My God. You look good."

"You look naked."

She says, "Well, I could put clothes on or you could get naked. I'm really fine with either plan."

Dez stands and leans against an oak desk on the far side of the elegant suite. His butt is against the table, ankles are crossed, hands held in front of him, right hand holding his left wrist. It's a non-threatening position.

Liv's SIG is aimed at his center mass.

"I've missed you," she says softly.

"You've killed so many people."

"The killing is ancillary. I am working on something much bigger."

Dez studies her. She's radiant, her mahogany hair bed-tousled, her skin shining in the city lights from the windows that dominate two walls of the master suite. He says, "You graduated from thief to assassin."

"No, Desmond. I'm still a thief. I might be the greatest thief on Earth. The assassination is lucrative, yes, but it's the ends to a means."

"Will you be shooting me?" he asks softly.

"No." She lowers the gun. She makes no move to cover her breasts. "Will you be attempting to have me arrested?"

"Aye, will."

"Then understand, please, that Catalina Valdivia's parents are alive and living in a condo just off Avenue Republica de Uruguay in Mexico City's Colonia Centro district. And if I'm captured, I've ordered for them to be killed."

Liv smiles brightly. "You see, I assumed you'd find me."

Dez studies her. He knows she's not bluffing. "That's a strong move, love. Clever."

"You like her. Don't you. Catalina."

Dez shrugs. "We're sleeping together. We won't be when this is all over. We're ships passing—"

"—passing in the night, yes. As we were?" She smiles.

Dez speaks softly, "We was a bit more than that, love."

"Did you know I died when you stabbed me? I was dead for one minute, nineteen seconds."

"Wasn't my intention."

Liv shrugs and her breasts quiver. "I know. All's forgiven. How did you find me?"

"Luck."

Liv laughs. Then sighs. "You've cost me the use of this pretty, pretty boat. Bastard. I've enjoyed it. I'll have it scuttled in the morning."

"You've got to stop what you're doing."

She amps up the smile. "Won't."

"I will stop ye."

"You are the only person I have ever met who could. Playing against you at The Liberty was so thrilling."

Dez says, "Playing against? You think of it as a chess match?"

"It *is* a chess match. You beat me that time in Tunisia. We got four of the five targets at The Liberty but you interfered with our getting the perfect set."

Dez says, "Four of six."

She makes a pretend inhale of surprise. "You know about Wade Selkirk! Oh, you're good."

"Stop, love. Just stop."

Liv says, "No. We play the game until one of us topples our queen and concedes. You have no idea the stakes I'm playing for."

"Top killer in the company o' killers?"

Her smile grows incandescent. "Top. Gatekeeper. Ever."

Dez sighs.

"I'd like you to get off my boat now, Desmond. I have a dozen men on board and I'm willing to turn this into a gunfight, if that's what you want. I'm willing to have Catalina's parents killed. I'm willing to burn down the village to feel its warmth."

Dez has served in Africa and he knows the proverb. He stands up from off the desk. He studies her and she studies him.

"Don't doubt my resolve, Desmond. Don't."

"I don't. I'll stop ye."

She says, "There's my Desmond!"

Dez turns and leaves. He walks off the boat, onto the dock, and into Manhattan and the night.

CHAPTER 58

Dez returns to the hotel rented under a false name, leaves a message for Cat, and sleeps until nearly noon.

He's awakened when his phone chirps and he's hoping it's Cat. It's Special Agent Stella Ansara.

"Selkirk has emerged and it's bad. Very bad." She sounds out of breath.

Dez sits up in bed. "Tell me."

"We tracked him to a hotel he was staying in. He'd gone out for cigarettes, we think, and saw our units arrive. He fled. Well, this morning, he showed up and he's turned it into a hostage crisis."

Dez says, "Again?"

"He's in a home in Neponsit. Do you know it?"

"Don't." Dez is reaching for his tablet to look it up.

"Affluent community on Rockaway. He got into a house, and he got into the house's panic room. He has a girl with him and he's sounding incoherent."

"Ah, Jay-sus."

"You told me he'd had a handgun when you saw him at Panthera Works, so we're assuming he's not bluffing when he says he'll kill the girl if we don't give him what he wants."

"Which is . . . ?"

"You ready for this?"

Dez rubs sleep from his eyes. "Hit me."

"Herr Jonas Diedrich, director of North American holdings, Frankfurt Landesbank. The same Diedrich who told me he'd never, ever heard of Selkirk. The girl is his granddaughter."

So somehow, the German bank really is the connection between the assassination targets.

"Dez, when we met for drinks after that show at the Quagmire, you told me you'd been a gatekeeper. A military breach expert."

"Am."

"Selkirk sounds crazy. I want to get this girl out of that panic room alive. She's fifteen. Can you come take a look? Tell us what you see?"

"I can be there fast as I can whistle up a taxi."

"Tell me where you are. I'll have a black-and-white pick you up and take you to a heliport. Dez: thank you."

The Feds have blocked off a landing zone for the NYPD helo in the spacious backyard of a three-story, nineteenth-century mansion on Long Island, not two blocks from Jacob Riis Park. Stella's waiting for him in her FBI windbreaker, FBI ball cap, canvas trousers, and lace-up boots. Dez has his messenger bag and does the duckwalk under the helo rotors to join her.

She shakes his hand and starts marching toward the mansion. "We really appreciate this!" she shouts over the rotor whoosh. "It's been a crazy morning. Did you hear about the mega-yacht that caught fire and sank in the North Cove Marina?" She points out over Jamaica Bay, in the direction of the marina in which Liv moored her stolen yacht.

Dez says, "Didn't."

"The panic room is state of the art. We don't—"

"Wait." Dez stops, studying the great house. It looks much like the one to the left of it, and the one to the right of it. The house likely has six to ten bedrooms. It's massive and gothic and gorgeous. He spots a sign adhered to the window: WINTHROP SECURITY.

"Have field glasses, do ye?"

Liv lifts a small walkie-talkie and speaks into it.

A man in full SWAT regalia jogs their direction. He has binoculars and, on Stella's orders, hands them to Dez.

Dez studies the house to the left of this one, and the house to the right, then hands the glasses back. "Ta, mate. Shall we?"

More than a dozen law enforcement vehicles fill the cul-de-sac. Neighbors are being kept indoors. Police helicopters keep the media choppers at bay, but they hover in place out over Jamaica Bay.

Stella leads Dez in through the French doors to the kitchen and smaller dining room. "Diedrich is in the Incident Command vehicle, in the cul-de-sac. He's still claiming he knows nothing of Selkirk, and Ivanson, and the assassinations. Right now, I'm trusting that jackass about as far as I could throw him."

"I could throw him."

Stella flashes a grin. "You could, but let's hold off on that for a bit."

"How old's the girl, then? Fifteen?"

"Yes. Her name's Amalia."

A good fifteen FBI agents and police have crowded into the living room, entryway, and den of the great house. Most everyone's in full battle rattle. Stella points to a woman in her late twenties, in comfortable clothing and sneakers, who's crying in the foyer. They approach. "This is Maeve. Amalia's math tutor. She's the one who called us."

"You all right, love?" Dez asks.

His accent makes her glance up, hopefully. "Aye, I am." She's Irish, and sounds as if she's from Dublin. "This is my fault! Amalia turns off the security on the days I come by. I should've told her not to do that!"

The tutor subconsciously signs as she speaks. American Sign Language, Dez thinks.

Stella grips both of the tutor's upper arms, forces her to make eye contact. "Maeve. This is *not* your fault. Okay? And you called nine-one-one in record time. You did everything right."

"God, but I adore tha' girl! She's bright, an' inquisitive, an' sweet."

Dez says, "Is she deaf?"

"Not total. Had meningitis as a kiddo, lost seventy percent of her hearing. An' does it slow her down? It does hell!"

"Has hearing aids, does she?"

Maeve nods.

"Right then. Find the charging box for 'em. Likely in the girl's bedroom or bathroom, yeah? Bring it to Special Agent Ansara, if ye please. Fast as ye can."

The tutor has been dying to find some way to help. She tears out of the foyer and up the stairs so fast, she damn near knocks two FBI agents on their butts.

Another man in an FBI windbreaker steps in front of Dez. He's in his sixties, with silver hair. He holds up a palm. He addresses Stella but points to Dez. "I don't know who this civilian is, and I don't know why he's in my crime scene. You've earned some major kudos these last days, but—"

Stella says, "By stopping the Russian terrorist incident at The Liberty? And by capturing the CIA's most-wanted guy? While you were ordering the foie gras at Jean-Georges with the director of your new campaign finance committee?"

He blanches. "Don't push it, Stel. This isn't Ted Mack's *Amateur Hour*."

Dez grins. "Ted Mack! Jay-sus, pops, but how old are you?"

The silver-haired guy bristles. "Fine. *America's Got Talent*. I was dating myself."

Dez says, "Sister Agnes says ye'll go blind doing that."

"I—what!"

Stella steps into his personal space. "We have this . . . sir. Permission to proceed."

A couple of the other guys in Kevlar give the silver-haired gentleman the bent eye, and he quickly does the math. "Of course. Good luck, everyone."

He beats a hasty retreat.

Stella turns to a guy in full military getup. "Mitch? Dez Limerick."

The gym rat shakes Dez's hand. "Mitch Hernández. Any friend of Stella's."

Mitch Hernández points to a wall of beautiful maple wood paneling. "The safe room's behind here, Mister Limerick. It has its own air supply, weeks' worth of food, its own generator, its own stand-alone camera-and-mic system to monitor the rest of the house." He makes a fist and raps on the wood. It's lined with metal. "If the APCs we'd rode around Afghanistan had been made of this grade of metal, I wouldn't have lost so many guys to IEDs."

"This is fecked."

"Sums it up pretty good," Hernández says.

"Wiring that leads to the panic room?"

"Isn't any. It was built as a solid steel block and lowered into place with a crane. They have Bluetooth, so this Selkirk guy can see and hear us."

Dez gestures to Hernández and Stella Ansara, then leads them out of the room and out of the house, into the backyard again.

"Don't want Selkirk hearin' this. House to the left of us has a sign in the window reads Winthrop Security. Same as the house to the right. Want to bet one or both of 'em have matching panic rooms?"

Stella and Hernández exchange glances. Hernández says, "Son of a bitch."

Stella says, "Told you."

Hernández says, "Which one do you want, Mr. Limerick? Right or left."

"Left, for no other reason that it's twenty paces closer. And it's Dez to me mates."

A block from Jonas Diedrich's house, several of the neighbors have gathered outside to ogle and whisper and to get video for Insta and TikTok. In a neighborhood in which adding a new spin class at the fitness center is considered big news, today's action is seismic. One of the women living next door to Diedrich stands next to a woman in sunglasses whom she doesn't know. She points to her own gabled roof. "That one's mine."

"No way!" Olivia Gelman says, sounding perfectly American. "Really?"

"Yeah. I heard the police say the guy's in the panic room, and he has Amalia. God, this is awful."

"Panic room?"

"Yeah. It's the top of the line. From Winthrop Security. Super-expensive but, hey, what price do you put on your own personal safety?"

Liv says, "I hear that, sister!"

"We have the same panic room in our house. Winthrop did the entire neighborhood, all in the same summer, about four years ago."

Liv smiles. "You don't say!"

CHAPTER 59

The FBI tracks down the man who owns the house to the left of Jonas Diedrich, and they escort Dez and Stella to it. Dez's phone vibrates en route. He doesn't recognize the number.

It's Cat. I'm safe.

She's using a burner. "Hang on a bit," he says, and quickly texts her. Liv knows your parents live in Colonia Centro, Mexico City. Get them out.

He tucks his phone away. "Let's go."

The man who owns the house is an appellate lawyer with a sterling reputation. Hard to tell now, because he's decked out in gym clothes, high white socks, and a matching sweatband. He's holding a pickleball paddle. FBI agent Mitch Hernández explains the situation.

The attorney says, "I don't think I want anyone, FBI or civilian, digging around inside my panic room. Do you know how much I paid for that? Pick someone else's."

Stella says, "And you really don't want us telling the media that you had a chance to save Amalia Diedrich's life and didn't, because it was inconvenient."

The lawyer looks around, calculating.

"Of course," he says unenthusiastically, looking out toward Jamaica Bay. "Anything I can do to help."

"Thank you so much, sir. The FBI appreciates your cooperation in this matter."

He leads the three of them inside, and into his den. He shows them the fob on his key ring that, at a touch, makes the maple wall paneling slide back to expose the hardened steel door of his panic room.

He stands in such a way, with his left hand shielding his right, that the FBI agents and Dez can't see the PIN he enters in the ten-key pad on the door. He cranks the handle, and the door hisses open.

The inside is all steel: the floor, the walls, the ceiling. It's the size of a decent hotel room. One portion includes a bed big enough for two people and a little office space. Dez spots a bathroom and thinks, likely, it has a chemical toilet. The front part looks like the command booth of something NASA would build. It's a long table with a rolling chair, featuring an array of monitors and controls.

"I can watch the entire house, and the grounds, from here," the lawyer says. "We have weeks of freeze-dried food and a water recycler system. We could hold out here in the event of nuclear fallout."

Dez says, "My last place in LA had a hot plate and a camp cot. And mice."

He sits and begins studying the controls. He draws his long, black-coated steel knife from a belt sheath under his jacket and uses it to pry the faceplate off the master controls.

"Hey! That's expensive!"

"Ye can bill me," Dez says, removing the plate and studying the electronics beneath it.

"Bill you? I don't even know who you are, mister!"

Dez begins poking through the wiring. He draws his phone, adds an accessory via the USB-C outlet, and begins figuring out where all the electricity goes. He says, "Name's Pepe Nero, sir." He gestures to Stella. "Sally Iodato. Pleased t'meet you."

The lawyer has grabbed a pen and pad, and writes the names down. "Pepe. Sally. Believe you, me, you're going to get billed for any damage."

"Fair, that. We'd . . ." Dez pauses. He smiles. "Ah, but that's nifty. You can reach out to Diedrich's panic room, yeah?"

The lawyer in the pickleball getup shrugs. "To every panic room in the cul-de-sac. Why?"

"Could ye give us a second, sir?"

Hernández escorts the lawyer away. Stella pulls up a second rolling chair and sits next to Dez. She whispers, smiling, "Pepe Nero and Sale Iodato. *Black pepper* and *iodized salt* in Italian."

"Shut the fecker up, didn't it? Excuse me language."

The house to the left of Jonas Diedrich's is owned by an appellate lawyer, and the house to the right of Diedrich's is owned by a thoracic surgeon. And by sheer chance, that's the one Liv Gelman chooses.

No one could cut through the heavy police and FBI security and sneak into the home of the thoracic surgeon without being a master thief. Good thing Liv qualifies. She took the surgeon's wife aside, after they had chatted a couple blocks from here, and used a combination of fear and pain to get the fob and the PIN from her. She left the woman unconscious and concussed. Liv doesn't kill when there's a good enough reason to avoid it.

She gets inside the surgeon's home unnoticed—she preens, knowing few alive could have done that—then gets the panic room open. She studies the inside, marveling at it.

She uses a knife to pry open the facing of the main control panel and begins digging around to see how the thing works.

Dez draws his tablet computer from his messenger bag and begins attaching wires to it from within the console of the lawyer's panic room. Whispering, Stella says, "You didn't feel a need to be there when we grabbed Ray Harker."

Dez is prying around inside the master controls of the panic room. "Didn't."

"From the way you speak of him, I assume you really hate the guy."

Dez glances her way. "Harker's a twat. But I've no need t'beat him in a fight. I've nothing to prove. Getting him arrested takes him off the board. That's all I wanted."

She waits.

"Punchin' him in the balls would've been nice, 'course."

Stella grins. "Of course. Do you know what you're doing here?" She gestures at the controls.

"Aye. You have the charging box for Amalia's hearin' aids?"

Stella does.

Dez holds it under a desk lamp and reads information on the device.

"What are you thinking?"

"Most top-of-the-line hearin' aids these days are Bluetooth. I'm betting I can hack the frequency, speak t'the girl, an' Selkirk won't know."

Stella smiles. "Like you goosed the Bluetooth at the theater in The Liberty to call British intelligence."

"Exactly."

Stella says, "When this is all over, my treadmill's starting to squeak."

Dez winks at her. "Pleased t'take a look."

It takes Dez another thirty minutes to figure out a plan.

Two houses away, Liv Gelman now is monitoring Dez's every action, having highjacked the cameras in the attorney's panic room.

Jonas Diedrich's panic room is an exact replica of the ones that Dez and Stella are in, and that Liv Gelman is in. All three of them now have eyes on Wade Selkirk and his fifteen-year-old hostage, Amalia Diedrich. Selkirk has a handgun, all right. He's also pacing. He looks drunk or high or both, and inches from true panic.

Amalia sits in one of the two chairs at the command console. She sits rigidly, her sneakers together, knees together, shoulders high, her arms locked at her side and hands gripping the chair. She is not tied up, which, to Dez, seems a good thing. She looks like she has cried but isn't now. Now, she's just unmoving.

Amalia doesn't flinch when she hears a voice in her hearing aids. She's used to such things, because the Bluetooth in her aids is how she takes phone calls and watches YouTube, or TikTok and Instagram.

"Amalia? Please don't react. My name is Stella and I'm with the FBI. My friend and I are monitoring you from your neighbor's panic room. If you nod slightly, we will see it."

Amalia glances at the pacing man and, when his back is turned, nods.

"Excellent! This is great. Amalia, we've figured out how to get the door open. When we do, I want you to duck down under the control panel. Tuck the chair you're sitting in as close to you as you can. Can you do that, sweetie?"

Selkirk's pacing turns him away from Amalia and she nods.

"Dang, you are one brave kiddo! Okay, when we're ready, I will count down from five, like this: five, four, three, two, one, go. Just like that. When you hear 'go,' you duck. You with me?"

Amalia nods.

"You're crushing it, Amalia! We're all rooting for you. Okay, sweetie, hang on now."

Liv Gelman goes, "Pssst!"

A woman FBI agent spins at the sound and sees Liv standing at the kitchen entrance of the house to the right of Diedrich's. The door's only open about ten inches, Liv's pretty face framed by the wood and a glimpse of a terry cloth robe held tight around her frame. She gestures, *Come here,* to the FBI agent, then ducks back.

The agent puts a hand on her service weapon, holstered at her hip, and steps into the kitchen of the thoracic surgeon. "Ma'am? Ma'am, we evacuated the entire block. You can't be—"

Liv hits her with a spin kick, the sole of her boot clocking the agent right under her chin. The woman crashes to the floor, her skull ricocheting off the wall.

Liv kneels and begins removing her FBI jacket and ballistic vest.

Stella Ansara puts her cell phone on mute, so Amalia Diedrich can't hear her. "What are you doing?"

Dez is typing madly on his tablet computer, which is wired to the command console of the panic room. "Writing a virus. I can download it via the camera and microphone link. It'll open the door to Diedrich's panic room. Truth is, it'll open every door to every panic room in the cul-de-sac. Can't be helped. Aaaand . . ." He hits Enter. "Done."

"Mitch!"

Hernández sticks his head in the door. "Dez can unlock the panic room door. We think."

Dez says, "Hey!"

Stella ignores him. "We breach on my mark. You take point."

He simply nods and sprints out of the house, across both yards, and into Diedrich's house.

Stella's walkie-talkie crackles. Hernández. *"We're ready, boss."*

Dez likes that the big, beefy guy calls Stella "boss."

Stella holds her phone in her left hand and her walkie-talkie in her right. She nods to Dez.

Dez watches Wade Selkirk pacing and muttering to himself, his pistol tightly gripped in his hand. He walks five steps toward Amalia, then turns, five steps away. Turns and stalks toward her. Turns.

Dez nods to Stella. She unmutes her phone. "Amalia? It's Stella. We're ready. I'll count down from five. You go on 'go.' Nod if you've got that."

Selkirk stalks five steps toward the girl and turns. Amalia nods.

"You are absolutely awesome! Okay, here we go. Five. Four. Three."

Dez and Stella watch the pacing man.

"Two. One. *Go!*"

Dez hits a knuckle-buster combo on his keypad. They hear the locking mechanism of their own, open, door clack.

Stella toggles her walkie-talkie. "Mitch: Now!"

On-screen, Dez and Stella see Selkirk turn his back on Amalia, who ducks under the command console and squeezes her chair in with her. They watch as the door to that panic room swings open.

Selkirk turns, spots the missing girl, then spots Mitch Hernández and three other guys, guns drawn, storming in on him.

He drops his pistol and places his laced hands on his head.

CHAPTER 60

Dez raids the appellate lawyer's panic room stash and finds a bag of Pirate's Booty and little bottles of a nice cava.

"Hey! You can't do that."

Dez says, "No, Sally can't do that, she's a public servant. Pepe Nero is a famous outlaw, the hero of the commoners, and he scoffs at your quaint laws."

He sits and puts his feet up by the controls. Stella shakes her head in mock reprimand, then puts her boots up on the console, too. Dez cracks open one of the cavas and hands it to her. He proffers the snacks and she takes a handful.

"That was remarkable work," she says. "The FBI is in your debt, and so am I."

Dez activates one of the grounds cameras. This one gives them a view of the backyard of Jonas Diedrich's place. They see FBI agents frog-march Wade Selkirk out of the house. He's handcuffed. A woman FBI agent pats him down and nods to her cohorts, and he's escorted around to the front of the building and, Dez guesses, to a paddy wagon.

"Awww." Stella points to the screen. They see the tutor, Maeve, holding Amalia in a tight, prolonged hug.

"Good kid, her. Smart an' brave. Don't make 'em better."

"I hear that." Stella sips her bubbly. "I'll head over in a sec and congratulate her. With Selkirk in custody, we might finally get to the bottom of this."

"You . . . Hang on . . ."

Dez drops his boots to the floor and leans in to peer at the screen.

They see Wade Selkirk stumble and go to his knees. FBI agents gather around him, as he falls face-first into the grass.

Dez looks up but Stella already is halfway out of the steel room. Dez drops the stolen snacks and sprints after her.

Outside, Dez is more than a little impressed to see Stella leap over a hedge like a champion steeplechaser. Dez himself needs to sprint around the thing. She gets to the scrum of agents a dozen strides ahead of him.

They have Selkirk on his back, back arched over his cuffed wrists. One agent pats him down and his hands come away blood-soaked.

Stella says, "The hell?"

Dez stops and plays back the scene of Wade Selkirk's arrest in his head. They watched it on the monitor. He begins looking around at the agents outside the banker's house.

An agent, down on one knee, says, "He's bleeding from the chest!"

Someone begins doing the two-hand compressions on Selkirk's rib cage, doing the one-two-three-four-one-two-three-four fast count.

Dez says, "Stella?"

Crouching, she turns to him.

"A woman agent patted Selkirk down. Where is she?"

Stella rises and draws her walkie-talkie. She begins barking orders.

Dez knows what's happened now, so he stops looking around. There won't be anything to see. He stuffs his hands in his pockets and wonders why he left the cava and Pirate's Booty behind.

Ninety seconds later, Stella steps up to him. "It was a woman agent. We both saw her. Nobody can find her now."

"Aye. An' you'll find a dead or unconscious FBI agent somewhere's about. The assassin ambushed your agent, stole her jacket an' cap an' vest, got close enough to Selkirk, done him good."

"How?"

"Stiletto."

Stella blinks at him. "Like the shoe?"

"Like the fixed-blade, ultra-thin knife. More like a short, stiff fencing saber. Worn attached to a bracelet on her wrist. Touch of a button, the stiletto pops out and pops back in. Our lad Selkirk's been bleeding internally since she frisked him."

Stella stares at him. "That's a lot of very specific information, Dez. What do you know that I don't?"

He nods to her. "Sorry, aye. I'll fill ye in on Olivia Gelman. The spring-loaded stiletto's her weapon o' choice. An' then maybe we speak to Herr Diedrich."

They stand outside the Incident Command vehicle in the cul-de-sac of the village of Neponsit. Stella's arms are crossed, her body language radiating anger. A doctor has pronounced Wade Selkirk dead, and they're loading his body onto an ambulance.

Dez tells Stella as much as he can about the former gatekeeper, Olivia Gelman. He leaves out as much as he can, just as he omitted as much about his own covert training as he could.

"When were you going to tell me?"

"Wasn't sure it was her until recently. An' she and me got history. Was hopin' I could talk her down."

"We could have been looking for her if you'd told me."

Dez smiles at her. "Respectfully. Liv has the same trainin' I do. If I'm egotistical, I'm as good as she is. If I'm being honest, I'm not quite as good as she is. You'd have no better luck goin' up against her as ye would goin' up against me."

Stella opens her mouth to protest, then doesn't. She grinds her teeth, looks away, douses her anger.

"We wouldn't have gotten the Russians without you. Wouldn't have gotten Ray Harker, or Wade Selkirk, or Mark Ivanson. You really are as good as all that. But Dez, you cannot be keeping vital information from me. Absolutely cannot."

"You're right, an' I apologize."

She inhales deep. "Let's talk to Diedrich."

They step into the command vehicle. Jonas Diedrich is in a huddle with his granddaughter and her tutor. He looks up as Dez and Stella step aboard. He speaks to the others, and Maeve takes her student to the door of the massive RV.

"Hey." Stella stops them, and offers her hand. "Amalia? I'm Stella. We spoke on—"

Amalia ignores the outstretched hand and throws a bear hug around her, her shoulder to Stella's ballistic vest.

A beat, and Stella hugs her back. "You did really, really good, kiddo."

The hug lasts a bit. Then Maeve escorts the teenager out to the street.

Dez and Stella approach. "My daughter is on her way to collect her. Special Agent: I am as grateful as I have ever been. You and all of your team. That was a job done remarkably well."

Stella says, "Which makes your lying to me all the tougher to swallow, Mr. Diedrich."

"I have not lied to you," the older man says smoothly, smiling gently.

"You said you'd never heard of Wade Selkirk."

"And I have not. Is that the man who took my granddaughter?"

"I think you know damn well it is. I think you and Selkirk have history, and he came here for a very specific reason."

Diedrich says, "He might have, yes, but then again, he could be suffering from psychosis. Or drug addiction. Or he may be dual-diagnosed with both. God knows New York has been overrun with such people."

"You're still claiming you don't know him."

The German banker never raises his voice, nor stops smiling softly. "That is correct, Special Agent."

"Selkirk was seen at Panthera Works. Selkirk came here. We have him on tape in the panic room talking about paying you back, Mr. Diedrich. About forcing you to do something. What was it he wanted to pay you back for, sir?"

"I have no idea."

"What was he forcing you to do, taking Amalia hostage?"

"I have no idea."

Stella stares into the man's eyes and shuts up. Many people are uncomfortable with long periods of silence, and will start talking just to make the moment end. Jonas Diedrich doesn't appear to be one of those people. His maddeningly even smile never falters, and he keeps his pale blue eyes locked on hers.

He never asks who Dez is, and Dez stands one pace right flank rear to Stella, putting her clearly in command.

"We're going to continue the investigation. If we find out Selkirk had a connection is to you, well. . . . Sir, can we ask you not to leave the New York area for the foreseeable future?"

"You can ask that, but I am under no obligation to obey. I am a citizen of the Federal Republic of Germany. You could, of course, place me in custody. But the stakeholders of Frankfurt Landesbank AG would not take kindly to such an act. Nor would the German delegation to the United Nations, nor the German ambassador to the United States, who is both a great good friend of mine, and also a distant cousin. But of course, none of that matters to you, Special Agent. You will do your job to the best of your ability, despite any political pressure. I have that sense about you, and I am always right when it comes to people."

Stella does a masterful job of keeping her emotions off her face. She lets the moment go a few beats, then steps aside. "We'll be in touch, Mr. Diedrich. You can count on that."

"I have the utmost faith in you," he says, gathering his overcoat and heading toward the command vehicle's entrance.

Dez steps aside. "Died rich."

The banker just smiles. "It's pronounced *Diedrich,* sir. In German, the second of two consecutive vowels is dominant."

"Hmm? Oh, no, sorry. I'm just sayin' your obituary. It'll say you died rich."

Diedrich's smile finally falters. He locks eyes on Dez.

"Is that a threat?"

"'Tis a premonition."

"I didn't catch your name, sir."

Dez grins big. "Desmond Aloysius Limerick, sir. At your service."

Diedrich nods, then steps down out of the vehicle.

Stella sighs. "God, I hate privileged, rich, white pricks."

Dez uncrosses his massive arms. "With Selkirk dead, it may well be time to take off the kid gloves, as far as Mark Ivanson's concerned. See if he'll grass."

Stella studies him. "And by grass . . . ?"

Dez rolls his eyes. "Grass. Grass park. Narc."

"Is there going to come a time when you talk American?"

"Perish the thought."

"Whatever. My forensic shrink says I could put Ivanson in a psychotic fugue state if I push too hard."

"Which would be different from now, how exactly?"

She rubs at a kink in her neck, tilting her head left, then right. She sighs. "You're not wrong."

"Upside? The killings likely will stop now. We think there were only six targets. Five are dead and Ivanson's in custody."

"Yeah, but boy, do I want to know what's behind all this. And I really, really want to perp walk Herr Diedrich for something. For anything. For jaywalking. That would bring me so much personal joy."

Dez side-hugs her. "It's not doing what you love, it's loving what you do."

CHAPTER 61

That evening, Dez's phone vibes. It's Catalina Valdivia.

"When Liv Gelman told you my parents were living in Mexico City, you were with her. Face-to-face."

Dez says, "That's right. How d'you know?"

"Because my mom and dad haven't been in Mexico since the early 1970s. And neither of them has ever been to Mexico City. I bought them an Alpine-style condo in Aspen. Dad golfs every day and Mom's in every arts club known to mankind."

Dez laughs. "It was a fine an' details bluff, that. Liv's not lost a step, her."

"Better safe than sorry: I reached out to some guys I know who don't mind a little dirty work. They're watching my folks for me."

Dez is eating a Reuben in a comfy little diner not far from his hotel. He fills her in on the arrest and death of Wade Selkirk. Since she knows he found and confronted Liv Gelman, he details that meeting, too.

"And you didn't kill her."

"I kill when it's necessary but I'm no assassin."

"Just this once, you could've maybe broken that rule."

"I know ye want her dead, love. Don't blame ye. If the gods are willin', it won't be at my hands. But I do mean t'stop her."

He tells her about the German banker Jonas Diedrich.

"So Frankfurt Landesbank is part of this."

"Seems, aye."

"I'm heading back tomorrow."

"Could stay out there. Stay safe."

"The bitch took away my feeling of safety in my home in Italy. The bitch threatened *mi mamá y papá*. I didn't need your gilded cage, mister, and I'm not some goddamned damsel in distress. I'll be there tomorrow. I'm getting Liv Gelman. Help or stay out of my way."

Cat hangs up.

Dez grins. Alley cat, hell. That was an apex predator he just chatted up.

Monday morning, Dez hits a gym to pay penance for the Reuben. And to work off his growing sense of frustration.

Around noon, Stella Ansara calls him.

"We had an electronic incursion into the holding cells. Someone hacking in, looking for Mark Ivanson."

Dez says, "Liv Gelman."

"Your evil doppelganger, yeah, that's what I thought."

Dez says, "Stella . . ."

"I know, I know. If a guy with your training wanted to get to Ivanson, you'd succeed. Eventually. Because we're holding him behind gates, and gates are your thing."

"Aye. Liv's, too."

"So you know those kid gloves you mentioned? I'm thinking it's time."

Dez tells Stella that she can't keep Mark Ivanson in a holding cell, and she can't relocate him using any traditional FBI method, because Liv Gelman is counting on both moves.

"I'll have a vehicle pull up to your field office as soon as I can. You, an' you yourself, have Ivanson ready to transport."

"How will I know which vehicle is yours?"

"Oh, you'll know."

Dez starts hacking. He wishes he had Spot, the Hong Kong hacker, on hand. She could do what he's planning inside of five minutes. It takes Dez well over two hours to make it happen.

He takes a cab to a downtown garage. A man with a clipboard is waiting for him, scowling.

"This is highly irregular," the man says, handing the clipboard over.

Dez signs a false name. "I know what you're saying. Were I you, I'd question the orders. Take it up the chain of command."

The guy hands Dez a set of keys and then points over his shoulder at a massive truck. "Who the hell has time for that? Take it, brother."

Twenty minutes later, Dez is a block away from the FBI's New York field office, and he calls Stella Ansara to let her know he's near.

He pulls up and Stella steps out of the building with three other FBI agents, including Mitch Hernández. All wear Kevlar and are holding their firearms. With them is a sheepish-looking Mark Ivanson, wearing a ballistic vest and a helmet. They look comical on his thin frame.

Dez rolls down the window and sticks his elbow out. "The back's open. Hop in."

Stella studies the all-metal truck, featuring the logo of Frankfurt Landesbank AG. "You stole an armored car from Diedrich."

Dez frowns. "'Stole' is a bit pejorative. Borrowed."

Stella smiles at him through her Ray-Bans. "I can live with that."

Across the street, Liv Gelman sees Dez pull up in the bank's armored truck, and she doubles over laughing. "Oh, Desmond! I truly did not see that coming!"

Dez drives through Manhattan and, in his wake, NYPD blocks streets and routes drivers elsewhere. Dez isn't aware that Liv is behind him, or that he's shaken her, but he assumes both are true.

He drives the bank's armored truck out of New York, heading north toward New Rochelle. Dez has never been there and has no connections to the city. Stella has told him the same is true for her. No amount of backgrounding on either of them would point Liv to the town locals call New Ro.

FBI agent Mitch Hernández asked his sister in Kansas City, Kansas, to rent a couple of white Toyota RAV4s, and they switch the armored truck to the ubiquitous SUVs before finishing their trip to New Rochelle.

Hernández's sister has rented them an Airbnb in New Rochelle. Dez, Stella, and Mark Ivanson head into the home, while Hernández and the other two agents—whom Stella handpicked—guard the neighborhood.

The house is quaint and small, two bedrooms, bath and a half, stucco and cute, with old but well-cared-for parquetry floors and lots of house plants. Dez gets coffee going. Stella checks out the whole house, leading with her gun, then holsters it and gets Ivanson out of his oversized protective gear.

Dez brings coffee, sugar, half-and-half, cups, and a carafe to the living room. Ivanson sits, leaning forward, his knees and feet together, hands on his lap.

But—and Dez thinks this is a good sign—he reaches for a cup and the coffee carafe, and doctors himself a cup.

"I'm going to tell you how this started," he says softly.

Stella pours herself a cup. She takes her time, not pushing. "Thank you, Mark. It's really going to help."

Using his name, *Mark,* to make this more a conversation than an interrogation. Dez can see why she's a designated hostage negotiator for the FBI.

Dez sits back, his cup looking comically small in his massive mitt.

Mark Ivanson sips his coffee. He nods. He leans back on the couch and crosses his legs.

CHAPTER 62

TWENTY-FOUR YEARS AGO

Mark Ivanson and Wade Selkirk know each other from the New York club scene. Both are in their midtwenties, both buy coke off the same dealer, neither can stomach the hip-hop and house clubs that have been pushing out the rock venues in the city.

Wade has introduced Mark to some of the world's most expensive tequila and mescal. You can't even get some of this stuff legally in the States.

Mark has introduced Wade to the city's most elite escort service. Expensive? Hell, yes. But the quality of Hungarian girls is not to be believed.

They're a well-matched pair. Mark's father owns a trucking firm that dominates the Eastern Seaboard highways. Wade's grandfather, then his father, made their thick piles of cash in Philadelphia real estate. And neither of their dads believes their sons will grow up enough to take over the family business. Not ever.

Mark Ivanson is coked to the gills in a boho club on a Tuesday when Wade stumbles in and falls into the booth at his side, his shit-eating grin a thing of wonderment.

Mark waits, and when Wade keeps grinning, he says, "The fuck, dude?"

"Throw me a line, I'll tell you."

They both glance around. It's getting on midnight and the place is packed. The bouncers are paid not to care about white powdery lines on the tables. Mark dribbles out a shortie and Wade uses a rolled hundred to snort it up.

"Fuck. Oh that's good."

"I know. What do you got going?"

Wade is still grinning big-time. "Okay. So I know this guy. He . . . whoa."

The cocaine does its magic. Wade pauses, shakes his head, starts over. "Okay. So I know this guy. Last year, he paid a hundred and fifty grand to take part in this . . . thing."

Mark grins. "Well, that makes sense. A thing. A hundred and a half. Did it come with bucket seats?"

"Shut the fuck up, dude."

"Tell the fucking story, bro."

Wade tries to sober up. "Okay, okay, okay. This guy. I know him from college. Good guy. We shared a dealer. He's tight."

"Yeah?"

"So last year, this guy spent a hundred and fifty grand to go on this . . . wait for it . . . on a hunt!"

They sit, side by side, watching hot young things shimmy and bounce on the dance floor. The music booms, the gelled lights spiral.

Mark Ivanson says, "A hunt."

"A fucking hunt."

"For . . . giraffe, what? Elephants?"

Wade's grin actually increases to a point Mark's afraid his face will rupture.

"Nah, man. Way, way fuckin' cooler than that!"

Before Mark Ivanson gets his official invitation, he's become well acquainted with Jonas Diedrich.

They all have. Diedrich doesn't bring in anyone for the hunts he didn't get to know personally. Plus, his family's banking empire pays for a private investigator to vet everyone.

Jonas Diedrich has asked both Mark and Wade to dine with him in his Upper West Side apartment, which takes up the entirety of the ninth floor. The palm-print coded elevator stops in the foyer, not out in a shared hallway. The Diedrich clan has owned the apartment for going on eighty years. Or, to be more accurate, the apartment is owned by the charitable foundation of the American subdivision of the German-owned Frankfurt Landesbank AG, a bank founded by Diedrich's great-great-grandfather in the 1800s.

Diedrich is more or less a decade older than them; thirty-six at the time. He's sophisticated, a polyglot. He treats them to a catered meal of the finest food and wine either of them has experienced, along with every imaginable drug one could want, and three blond girls; one for the host and one each for the guests, and Diedrich lets his guests pick whom they bed.

The party lasts five hours. During which, Diedrich holds court on issues ranging from politics to the manufacturing brilliance of Mikhail Kalashnikov; from the plot weaknesses in *Tosca* to the Knicks chances that season; from the agricultural plans of the new Argentine prime minister to the collected works of porn star Briana Banks.

The official invitation comes to the guys exactly one week later. It's an oral invitation; nothing written down, not ever.

Mark and Wade show up at a small airfield in New Jersey with one overnight bag each. They've been told to dress warm, with comfortable hiking boots. They've been told nothing else. The airfield isn't much more than a rutted path in a field next to a rusty Quonset hut. A midsized, two-engine passenger plane is getting the once-over by its pilots.

Inside the Quonset hut, the guys meet the other guests. All guys, all more or less the same age as they, all affluent, all from the same New York/New Jersey/Pennsylvania area.

Peter Garvey, who's been legacied into his father's law school. Adam Levkowitz, studying medicine. Jacob Gaetano, a hard-charging Manhattan stockbroker. And Gene O'Malley, whose family owns the O'Malley Burgers outlets from Maine to South Carolina.

None of them know where they're headed. But each of them has paid $150,000 for a once-in-a-lifetime experience.

The plane takes off after dark. By the time they land, they have no idea which state they're in—or maybe it's Canada? It is colder, so maybe. They find themselves at another isolated airfield.

Two Range Rovers are waiting to whisk them away.

They drive for close to an hour through the dark. Both drivers appear to speak German but not English. They've seen no sign of their host.

At one point, Adam Levkowitz leans forward in his seat and points out the windshield. "What is that?"

He's riding with Mark and Wade. They lean forward, too. "A mountain range," Wade says. "I think."

It isn't.

They're almost inside the gargantuan and abandoned factory grounds before Mark makes out a rusty sign over a gate. PANTHERA WORKS—A DIVISION OF FRANKFURT LANDESBANK AG.

"You guys ever hear of Panthera Works?"

Levkowitz turns in his seat. "Yeah, I think they made cars in the . . . 1970s? Or were gonna make cars? Got blown out by the re-cession. I think they were, like, German or something."

The Range Rovers drive into a tall, dark, quiet village of indus-trial buildings, all abandoned. They were surrounded by acres and acres of rust and decay. It's dystopian.

They reach one building the length and width—Mark estimates—of six football fields. Over the door is the Panthera logo and PCI. "Jesus."

The cars park. The six guests emerge.

The inside of the five-story behemoth is lit up. It's the first lighted building they've spotted.

Jonas Diedrich himself stands in the twenty-foot-high doorway, wearing camo fatigues and lace-up boots.

The others join him. The drivers turn the Rovers around and exit the campus.

"This is Friday," Diedrich says in his rich baritone. "We shall be here until dawn Monday. There is food and drink. We've outfitted several of the original administrative offices into apartments with individual bathrooms."

Jacob Gaetano whispers, "What was this place?" His voice echoes in the high-ceilinged building and all the indescribable metal equipment they glimpse amid the gloom.

"Panthera Works was going to revolutionize the automobile in-dustry. My family's banks financed the project and lost untold mil-lions. Frankfurt Landesbank has held the property ever since, as the state of New York has sought to find a buyer for the property. We are as isolated as we can be within the United States, gentlemen. No security cameras. No guards. No media. No government. No rules."

Jonas Diedrich smiles warmly.

Gene O'Malley says, "So what's the game?"

Diedrich hands them six manila envelopes. He chuckles. "Look! I don't even have a secretary or aide to do this for me. I had to figure out how to use the photocopier. I even had to learn to change the toner! Ha!"

Their overnight bags at their feet, they open their packets.

Inside, they find an official U.S. Army photo of one Sergeant Steve Thackery. He's African American, all of twenty-two in this photo, tall and robust, standing at attention. They read his statistics in silence.

"The Gulf War was not kind to Sergeant Thackery," Diedrich intones, the German accent making his English crisp and precise. "First came the drugs. Then the post-traumatic stress disorder. Then the psychosis. He was a gifted soldier. A good fighter. Disciplined. He is . . . few of those things today."

Peter Garvey rubs his chin, looking queasy. "And we're going to . . . ?"

"The retired sergeant currently has no family and no known address. No friends. He has been drifting. The government cannot even find him to deliver his veteran benefits. And, of course"— Diedrich gestures around—"he is here."

Mark Ivanson gulps. "We're . . ."

"Hunting him. Yes. Oh, not to kill him. Dear no. This isn't the famed story by Richard Connell, 'The Most Dangerous Game.' No murders on my property, thank you very much." Diedrich laughs heartily.

Wade says, "So how's it work?" He sounds excited.

"The good sergeant has a paintball gun and a rather large knapsack of paintballs. He has been informed that you are here. He will hide and hunt you. You will hunt him. If he spots you and hits you with a paintball, you are *dead*. And your one hundred and fifty thousand American dollars is forfeit. If he gets all six of you, he has been told he will receive one thousand dollars and a very, very generous supply of crack cocaine. He was . . . most enthusiastic about the latter."

They look around at each other. Their assumptions are the same: Give a mind-blown vet with PTSD and addiction issues enough crack, and he'd be dead inside a week. Whatever transpires here, well, even if Sergeant Thackery survived, it would be the word of six affluent and productive members of society versus that of a drug-addicted drifter.

Peter Garvey raises his hand. "What happens to the last man standing?"

"You have all contributed one hundred and fifty thousand to the kitty. I have added one hundred thousand of my own, private fortune, to make the pot one million dollars, total. The last man jack of you standing wins the entire one million."

Mark looks at Wade, and the two of them start laughing. The other four soon join in. "Wow," Mark says through a grin. "This is fucking . . . wow."

Jonas Diedrich gives him a little bow and a smug smile. "I am pleased you find it to your liking."

Jacob Gaetano says, "And we'll have paintball guns, too?"

Diedrich steps away from them and, from behind an iron work-bench, produces a rucksack. He drops it at their feet.

Four of the six of them have played baseball in high school or college. Even before the sack opens and spills out its contents, they know that sound.

Aluminum baseball bats.

Jonas Diedrich says, "Well, Sergeant Thackery certainly believes you'll have paintball guns, yes."

This is the fourth such hunt that Jonas Diedrich has organized for rich, young, indolent Americans. One per year.

He has found nothing in this world quite as stimulating as watching rich, civilized Americans carrying bats, hunting men with the intent of beating them.

To date, he has picked four ex-soldiers, three African American and one Mexican American. Diedrich enjoys how the race play brings out an additional level of violence in his clientele.

The first three drug-addled soldiers survived, but were badly beaten. Diedrich's pilots flew them to three random airfields in America, then drove them to an abandoned building, and left them with plenty of crack.

All three had smoked themselves to death before telling anyone how they received their extensive beatings.

It would be no different for ex-Sergeant Thackery. The six clients will feel little remorse—their prey won't die on their watch, and they'll be told the hare is recovering nicely, thank you. And they've all seen inner-city violence change the American landscape in the 1980s and '90s. The clientele will avow to their dying day that they don't have a racist bone in their bodies. But, Dietrich believes, all of them will secretly enjoy a certain satisfaction on inflicting some of the violence that inner-city minorities seemed to inflict on each other and decent white families. He is constantly amused by the pains Americans go through to hide their prejudices.

The Primary Chassis Construction Building Number One—PC1—of Panthera Works is five stories tall, six hundred yards long and wide, and poorly lit. There are a million places to hide, but the hunters have teamwork and patience.

And almost immediately, the hunt goes badly.

Sergeant Thackery appears to be more able than Diedrich's private investigators had indicated. Perhaps his PTSD played in his favor, giving him a cagey caution. For whatever reason, he evades the hunters for the better part of five hours that first night.

The group gathers together—they have walkie-talkies—at the building's entrance and eats, gulping hot coffee, fatigue already showing on their unathletic frames. They are grease-stained and two of their number have cut their hands on rusty iron bits of machinery. The hunt, which started as exhilaration, has become a slog.

Diedrich tells them not to worry: In the entire building, this is the only egress that hasn't been welded shut. Sergeant Thackery isn't going anywhere.

They all sleep for four hours, then begin the hunt again on Saturday.

Sergeant Thackery gets the first one only forty-five minutes later, on the cavernous, echoic third floor. The medical student, Adam Levkowitz, takes a paintball square in the back.

Two others see it, but neither can tell where the sergeant has fired from.

"You're out, dude," Wade chides the med student, who slumps back to the entrance.

Sergeant Thackery gets two more before noon. One on the fourth floor, one on the ground floor. Pete Garvey, the law school student, and Gene O'Malley, heir to the burger chain.

O'Malley got some of the paint from the paintball in his eyes and Diedrich, who always considers every possibility, has an eye-wash station set up near their quarters.

Diedrich doesn't admit to any worry yet. None of the other three veterans, from the other hunts, managed to take out half of the six hunters. But the good sergeant is without food or water, and without his precious drugs. He won't last long.

The seven of them eat lunch in silent dejection that Saturday. Diedrich has brought in two of his own security personnel to guard the guests during the break. After, Jacob Gaetano, Wade Selkirk, and Mark Ivanson set out for the hunt.

Sergeant Thackery gets Mark on the top and fifth floor.

He paint-shoots Gaetano next.

Wade Selkirk is the last man standing. And looks to win one million, tax-free.

"But you still have to find and defeat the sergeant," Diedrich reminds him.

The dejected losers speak not one word during dinner. Selkirk sits a little away from them, on an overturned bucket, eating his preprepared sandwich and bag of chips and soft drink.

He resumes the hunt at seven o'clock.

He stops four hours later. He's exhausted, angry, surly.

Jonas Diedrich presents an air of sangfroid. But no hunt has ever lasted this long.

Thackery's lack of drugs should have broken him by now. Is it possible that the ghosts of his PTSD are stronger even than his demons of addiction?

The others grumble, "Would you just fucking get him . . . ? Jesus, Wade . . . Freezing my ass here . . ."

Sunday morning, the hunt begins again.

Five floors.

Thousands of square yards per floor.

The hours wear on.

Wade Selkirk checks his watch. Even lifting his arm to do that hurts. He aches everywhere.

It's an hour early for the Sunday lunch but fuck it. He's through.

Baseball bat dragging behind him, he trudges down the metal stairs to the ground floor and limps to the staging area.

He's within sight of the other five guests when Sergeant Thackery emerges behind him from the shadows of an obscure mechanical device. Paintball gun aimed at Selkirk's back.

The other five don't even have time to warn him. Selkirk grunts as the plastic ball slaps into his back.

Jonas Diedrich emerges from behind yet another unimaginable ironmongering monstrosity and hits Sergeant Thackery across the head with an iron crowbar.

"Enough!" Diedrich bellows. He raises the metal bar and brings it down again. *"Enough!"*

He hits Thackery again. Blood spatters his camo fatigue trousers and his lace-up boots. *"Wer bist du? Weißt du wer ich bin?"*

He raises the crowbar and slams it down again. Again.

Wade watches. All the frustration, the fatigue. The anger. The embarrassment of getting back-shot with the paintball. Wade hefts his baseball bat, steps toward the downed man, and swings hard.

Adam Levkowitz rises from his chair and reaches for a bat.

Gene O'Malley does, too.

Peter Garvey and Jacob Gaetano start laughing and shouting. "Hit him! Fuck yeah . . . ! Get him . . . !"

And Mark Ivanson joins in the shouting.

Diedrich has brought plenty of expensive booze for Sunday's final meal. So far, his guests have been served meals ready to eat, but that night they dine on steak and lobster and an assortment of fresh vegetables and fruits. There are good German Rieslings for the meal, followed by whiskey and vodka and schnapps and sake for after, and cigars, of course. Cubans.

Diedrich has changed into fresh fatigues. He's washed the blood off his hands.

None of the contestants sleep that night but several of them pass out drunk.

In the morning, the Range Rovers return.

Diedrich's men bring in six satchels and hand one each to a guest. Hesitantly, they each open theirs.

Cash.

Diedrich stands apart from them, hands clasped behind his back. His air of sangfroid is back. "The hunt did not go as planned. What occurred there, at the end, was, of course, an unfortunate accident."

The others, suffering from a ragout of guilt, exhaustion, and their hangovers, don't argue with his account.

"Since I was unable to bring this endeavor to its promised solution, I offer you this instead: Each of you gets your original one hundred and fifty thousand dollars back, plus one hundred and fifty thousand dollars from my personal account."

The others are trying to figure out why he's showing no remorse over the murder of Sergeant Thackery.

Diedrich smiles shyly. "I would have more for you, but I am relatively low on, as you Americans would say, the totem pole at Frankfurt Landesbank, yes? I have layers of parents and siblings and cousins to whom I still must answer. So: This is what I have to offer. I hope it makes amends for the unfortunate ending of our little game."

They've each run their fingers over their stacks of used hundred-dollar bills. Mark Ivanson says, "You said nobody would get killed. You told us—"

"Someone always gets killed, my dear Mark." Diedrich smiles benignly. "Do you know the difference between comedy and tragedy? Comedies end before the protagonist dies. But dies, he will. Always. That is human nature."

Wade says, "Yeah, but—"

"This also is human nature, yes? You, Wade, are heir to a real estate empire. You are, so long as your association with this weekend's enterprise never becomes public, yes? Jacob, you are on a meteoric rise within the realms of stock brokerage. Adam and Peter have postsecondary degrees to achieve, which will launch your careers. And Mark and Gene: In a nation built on capitalism, your families thrive."

Diedrich looks at each of them, in turn.

"All of which could be washed away by the incoming tide. Let us hope that never happens."

The six contestants look at the ground, or at each other, or at the satchels of money in their hands.

Then, one by one, they turn for their coats and hats, and the Range Rovers parked outside.

Jonas Diedrich says, "And with that, our weekend is concluded. Thank you, my friends."

That was twenty-four years ago. None of the six ever told a soul. Five married and divorced. Within ten years, Peter Garvey's legal career took off and he turned, strongly, to the church. He attended services four times per week, hoping to wash away his sins.

Adam Levkowitz became a pediatrician but his PTSD made it impossible to keep up his practice. He's got a thankless job as director of a physician's association, and he's been in group counseling, but has never told the other members of the group about the cause of his stress.

Jacob Gaetano dropped out of the stockbroker field within a year of the hunt. He's been in and out of Alcoholics Anonymous and inpatient programs. He took a low-paying job as a high school teacher.

Mark Ivanson still works for his father's interstate trucking company, and has risen to chief financial officer. But he spends nearly every night of every week in a drunken stupor.

Wade Selkirk still sells real estate in Philadelphia. He's been married three times, thrice divorced, and wakes up screaming a couple of times per week.

And Gene O'Malley slings burgers and fries and shakes, up and down the East Coast. He never married. He's never made friends. He's alienated his family. He's a successful, morose, and lonely man.

They have not kept in touch with each other. None of them have spoken to, or spoken of, Jonas Diedrich and the Frankfurt Landesbank AG, Panthera Works, and Sergeant Steve Thackery.

And twenty-four years later, none of them were aware that any of the others had been invited to the grand opening of the spanking new Liberty Convention Center in Newark.

CHAPTER 63

After telling Stella and Dez his story, Mark Ivanson falls asleep on the couch in the Airbnb. Who knows, maybe his first real sleep in years. Dez and Stella talk softly in the kitchen. The three FBI agents keep watch outside.

Dez's phone vibrates. He checks the incoming call ID. "D'you know what Triton Expediters is?"

"It's a big multinational. Part of the military-industrial complex."

"A big part of it, aye. CEO's Petra Alexandris, a friend. I'd asked her about the German bank. This is she."

Dez takes the call. "Petra. All's well?"

Petra Alexandris says. "Dez, Hi. I'm in Brussels. I've been asking around about Frankfurt Landesbank. Apparently, the International Criminal Court is going to unveil major, major indictments. Maybe as early as this weekend. I've got three different sources who tell me the indictments will decapitate the bank."

Dez says, "I'm standing with FBI Special Agent Stella Ansara. 'Tis her I've been assistin', best I can."

Stella speaks up. "Ms. Alexandris? Hello. Dez is more than assisting, he's basically saved my ass. A couple dozen times."

"But he's also driven you crazy?" They can hear the laughter in Petra's voice.

"Yep. That's him."

"I know the feeling. This isn't public knowledge yet, but apparently Frankfurt Landesbank has been selling Iranian crude on the black market. Despite dozens of restrictions put on them by the Americans, the European Union, NATO, and the United Nations. It's huge. All of the top brass has been swept up in it. And there are rumors that Iranian intelligence might already have had one of the next generation of the banking family—the Diedrichs—killed."

Dez and Stella stare at each other. Dez says, "I've a major ask, love. Can ye find out, when the dust settles, who'll be chief executive of the whole kit an' caboodle? Who'll be the top cheese at Frankfurt Landesbank?"

"I already have some inkling of that. Apparently, all of the bank divisions in Europe are up to their eyeballs in this Iranian thing. My sources tell me it'll be the subdivision that handles land acquisition and investments in the U.S. that remains untouched."

Dez says, "The FLAG Family Holdings."

"Right. One of the Diedrich clan is in charge there, I think, but he's so many rungs down the ladder, he hasn't been named in the indictments."

"Jonas Diedrich," Stella Ansara says. "We've met him. We think he's part of this thing that we've been investigating."

Petra says, "Is this helpful?"

"It is, Ms. Alexandris. Thank you."

Dez says, "Love? Ballpark it for us. What's Frankfurt Landesbank worth?"

"Don't quote me, but I'd guess a market cap of, oh . . . a hundred and fourteen billion. Plus or minus. That's in U.S. dollars, which is the currency Triton uses the most."

Stella says, "Ms. Alexandris, we have an FBI field office in Belgium. Advisers to Interpol. Can I have one of their agents get in touch with you to get further details?"

Petra gives the special agent her contacts and rings off.

Dez hoists himself up on a countertop, his boots dangling. "Quarter of a century ago, a young sociopath name of Jonas Diedrich was rich an' bored, an' he organized human hunts for other rich, bored, brain-fecked young twats, excuse me language."

Stella takes up the narrative. "He's personally rich by most people's standards, but not by Diedrich family standards. He has no real authority at the family's centuries-old banking establishment. So the hunts are a diversion. A sick entertainment."

"Bread an' circuses, aye. He's no one important within the bank hierarchy, our Jonas. And if he got himself into serious trouble, well, he's a German citizen. At worst, he'd get deported. Had little to lose, him."

"But jump-cut twenty-four years into the future, and he's about to be the CEO of a company with a net worth of a hundred and fourteen billion dollars."

"And six men watched him commit murder. Some of them *just* watched. Others joined in. All six took bribes to stay mum. Which they did, for two an' a half decades. But suddenly, our Jonas is about to become as fine a target for blackmail as ye'd ever hope for."

"Jonas knows this," Stella says, building the case in her head. "He knows the criminal court is going to unveil indictments. But the world at large doesn't. The six conspirators don't know he's about to become one of the world's wealthiest and most powerful bankers. So before they do . . ."

"He has to have 'em killed. But he's afraid. What if the six have kept in touch with each other? What if they're still mates? If they start dyin' off, one by one, will it spook the others? Get 'em to go to the plod for protective custody?"

Stella blinks at him.

"The plod. Police. Try'n keep up, mate."

"It's like talking to a J. K. Rowling character." She shakes her head. "So Jonas knows he's going to need these guys dead. He doesn't want to have it done one at a time. He needs them killed simultaneously."

"And an investigation into six assassinations could turn up a connection to him. Maybe one of the six kept a diary? Told a lover? Has a letter stashed away in a safe box for the Feds. He can't take that chance. He's a sociopath, but he's not stupid."

"So he hires one of the most infamous assassins, the Thiago group. In this case: Ray Harker and your Olivia Gelman."

Dez says, "She's not my Olivia Gelman."

Stella waves him off. "Yes, but you were lovers. It's in your face. In the way you say her name."

Dez opts not to deny it. He says, "Harker?"

"His condition's worsening. The docs are trying to figure out why."

Dez shrugs. "All right, then. Working under the nom de crime of Thiago, Harker an' Liv trick a bunch of idiot Russian mercs into invading a fecking conference center, sorry. They lure the six targets there. Take out the targets, lay the blame at the feet of the Russians. There's no separate assassination investigation. Everyone would buy that."

Stella smiles. "You didn't."

"Luck, that."

They both think for a while. Dez makes a second pot of coffee.

Stella radios the three agents outside, and they come in one at a time to take a cup back out with them.

"The Russians aren't naïve," Stella says at length. Dez begins cleaning the coffeepot and everything else. Stella grabs a towel to dry. "They had to be convinced—convinced!—that there was a back door to The Liberty."

"The extensive blueprints for a fantasy sub-sub-basement level."

"And this Colonel Maksim Baranov and his top men claim they actually toured a replica of the tunnels. A real sub-sub-basement. But where . . . ?"

"Someplace Jonas Diedrich could control, yeah? Someplace isolated, a bunch of Russians wouldn't stand out. Some . . ."

Dez's voice drifts away. He turns to Stella.

She gasps. "The Panthera Works plant! Upstate!"

"Has to be."

They stare at each other. Stella says, "We've locked down the U.S. border like I've never seen it. Despite that, we'd started to assume that Colonel Baranov and the remainder of his men somehow got free after The Liberty. But . . ."

"But maybe they're lyin' low, where they've got plenty of isolation."

Stella says, "Let me do you one better: Maybe the Russians are at the Panthera Works plant. But think about it: If you're the Thiago group, and you want to monitor the assassinations in and around New York . . ."

"Ye might want a nice, quiet, isolated spot to lie doggo. Yeah."

Stella says, "Dez? If we're right, it's possible that the missing Russian mercs are at Panthera Works. Or maybe the brains behind the Thiago group."

"I didn't search the place. That'd take weeks. And according to what I read, the state's been trying to find a buyer for the site for ages. It's too far out for kids to explore; too cold for the homeless. I'd bet, like as not, you could hide the House of Commons in there and nobody'd find 'em for years."

She says, "Are we saying the Russians could be there? Or the organizers of the Thiago group?"

Dex shrugs. "Maybe both. Only one way to find out."

CHAPTER 64

Back in New York City, Stella meets with Special Agent Tom Fairweather of the FBI's elite Hostage Rescue Team. He's something of a legend inside the Bureau. Not overly tall, not overly muscular, soft of voice, he looks like a high school civics teacher, and not the former Navy SEAL that he is. His unit is considered the agency's number-one antiterrorism force in all of America, and he would have taken point at The Liberty, if he and his forces hadn't been trying to take back a U.S.-owned tanker attacked by Houthi rebels in the Red Sea when the shooting started in Newark.

His team's back now, and when Stella makes the pitch to storm the abandoned Panthera Works auto plant in upstate New York, everyone agrees to put Tom Fairweather in charge.

Everyone, including Stella. "I'm a better investigator than I am a SWAT leader," she tells the special agent in charge of her field office. "Tom's great. Glad to follow his orders."

She meets with Fairweather at the New York field office, and she's expecting Dez to show up at any time. She lays out a scenario that she and Dez cooked up in advance.

"You and HRT enter however you think best, while my civilian adviser sneaks in from another side. He's got some pretty amazing skills at figuring the ins and outs of a dangerous situation."

Tom Fairweather says, "No." He's got a widow's peak, largish ears, and eyes that turn down at the corners, making him look perpetually sad. No one alive has ever heard him shout in anger. While talking to Stella, he faces her, eyes on her, hands clasped in front of him, giving her his undivided attention.

"Limerick's the guy who got us into The Liberty."

Fairweather says, "I've read the reports."

"He's solved much of this whole thing. He's been invaluable."

"I agree. He sounds amazing. But he's also a civilian and I won't have him at the site when we make our entrance." The decision is spoken softly.

"Tom, he's more than meets the eye."

He waits for her to finish speaking, then says, "No. Sorry."

Someone raps on the conference room door and escorts Dez in. He's wearing a visitor's badge on a lanyard, the ID bouncing off his barrel chest.

"Interrupting?"

Stella sighs. "Desmond Limerick, Special Agent Tom Fairweather."

Dez approaches the slight man and offers his mitt. Fairweather takes the handshake, glances down. He turns Dez's arm, studies the tattoo of Janus, the Roman god of doors.

He sighs.

"Special Agent Ansara wants you on-site, Mr. Limerick. You're in. Tell me how you want to do this."

Dez's phone vibes. He checks it. "Splendid, mate. Gimme half a mo?"

He steps aside.

A shocked Stella turns to Fairweather. "What the hell?"

He also drops his voice, his face devoid of emotion. "The tattoo. Limerick's a gatekeeper."

She's startled. "You know what that is?"

"Yes, but I've never had the privilege of working with a 'keeper. He's in."

She smiles. "Thank you, Tom."

She turns away.

"Stella?"

She turns back.

The soft-spoken ex-SEAL says, "You've got a dang gatekeeper in your hip pocket. Next time? Lead with that."

Dez takes the incoming call in the corner. It's Catalina Valdivia. "We're wheels down at JFK."

"Change of plan, love. We're decamping for Upstate New York. We think maybe we've found either the Thiago group, or the missing Russians. An' if we're fecking lucky: both."

"What's the play?"

"The FBI hard lads enter loud from one side, whilst you an' me enter quiet-like from another. This is breakin' an' enterin', plain an' simple, love. It'll be dangerous as fuck. But if we get lucky, we'll find Liv Gelman first."

Cat says, "In."

Tom Fairweather takes over one of the tactical monitoring rooms at the New York field office. He has twenty-five agents, men and women, at his disposal. All the top brass of the field office are there, along with Stella Ansara and Dez.

A projector shows a crystal-clear satellite photo of the Panthera

Works auto plant in Upstate New York. Fairweather never sounds more like a schoolteacher than when he's handling a briefing.

"Panthera. One point two million square feet. Surrounded by high wire fences and concertina wire. Thirty-five buildings on campus. This one"—he holds a remote and one very large building suddenly is brightly limned—"is the likely site. Our civilian adviser tracked two of the assassination targets here. The surviving target identified this as the site of a homicide, twenty-four years ago. Which is what my English lit professor would have called 'the inciting incident.'"

A couple of people chuckle.

"This building is six hundred yards wide by six hundred yards deep, and five stories tall. We do not know how deep it is underground, because our primary suspect in the hiring of the assassins has the quarter-century-old blueprints. We couldn't very well ask for them without balloons going up."

Dez had the same thought. He spent the evening trying to hack into the computers of Frankfurt Landesbank's New York headquarters, finally giving up when he realized the blueprints of all older land acquisitions are still stored as paper copies in giant filing rooms.

Fairweather says, "This incursion runs the gamut from boring as heck to live gunfire exchanged. There also could be booby traps, because we know that's how this Russian PMG, the Leningrad Konsortsium, rolls. We could find no one. We could find the brains behind a murder-for-hire operation known as the Thiago group. We could find the remnants of the Russian mercenary team that attacked The Liberty. Or, we could breathe in asbestos and run into rats with rabies."

Someone says, "Or we could step in front of a bus leaving the field office."

Fairweather says, "Or that. Right. So if the likelihood of violence runs from none to full-on military engagement, I would like us assuming the worst, and hoping for the best, and ready for anything. Questions? Anyone?"

Dez raises his hand.

Fairweather says to the other agents in the room, "This is Mr. Desmond Limerick, our civilian adviser. He is going to be in situ."

A senior FBI agent sits bolt upright. "He's going to be there? During the incursion? A civilian?"

Fairweather says softly, "That's right. Mr. Limerick?"

"Two thoughts. When I was at Panthera Works, I encountered a frequency dead zone. No radio signals, no Bluetooth, even the sat-phone features of me mobile didn't work. Dunno why?"

"That's one point two million square feet of nothing but iron," someone says, gesturing to the screen.

"True. Could've been that."

Fairweather says, "Good information to have. Thank you. Your other thought, sir?"

"The CEO of a German bank might be at Panthera, as well."

Stella looks up quickly. "Diedrich? Why?"

"Because Jonas Diedrich of Frankfurt Landesbank was supposed to've flown to Germany yesterday. But I did some pokin' 'round, and when in Germany, he has his own company car. A Rolls-Royce Phantom, mind ye. An' said car is outfitted with a transceiver, so Diedrich can tool about on German toll roads. Yeah? Only, I hacked the transceiver, and Diedrich's fancy car hasn't moved in a couple of weeks. I don't think he's in New York, an' I don't think he's in Germany. He's someplace." Dez points to the projection on the wall. "An' it might be there."

Several of the FBI agents of the Hostage Rescue Team turn to look at him. Then turn to Fairweather. There's a muttering of appreciation around the room. Stella quietly smiles.

Fairweather nods. "Well, then there's that. Thank you, Mr. Limerick. Any further thoughts? Questions? No? Okay, good. Here's how we are going to get in. . . ."

CHAPTER 65

Cat Valdivia wears a black sweater and a black leather biker jacket, which she's had retrofitted with many small, interior pockets. Black leggings and black, ultra-light sneakers. Black, wrist-length gloves. He hair's in a low pony. She has the many, many tools of her trade in the pockets of her jacket. She looks slim and sleek.

She's added a heavy black coat and gloves and a scarf and a stocking cap over all that, which she'll ditch when she and Dez get inside.

Dez is in all black, too, but then he always is. He also dons the same winter outerwear. He also has the shoulder-strapped bag for his professional hunting slingshot, and he's got a pocketful of inch-in-diameter ball bearings.

They rented another Jeep and drove through the night to get to Panthera Works. Cat parked a good mile away and they've hiked in, coming from the Lake Ontario side, opposite the road and the vast parking lots.

Dez leads as they approach the plant. He's brought binoculars, and stops to check the site, the roofs, the windows. He spots nothing. He looks for infrared sensors or weight sensors out here, outside the imposing fence, but there are none.

When they get to the fence, Cat first tests it for voltage. None.

She brought small but powerful wire cutters. Dez's hands and wrists are stronger than hers, so she passes it over and Dez snips a long, vertical slit in the fence. He holds it open as she skitters deftly through, then he wedges through himself.

He pauses, going for the binoculars again, glassing the roofs and windows.

He checks his phone. They're within the radio frequency dead zone again.

He checks his watch and shows its face to Cat. She nods. They have nearly an hour before the FBI Hostage Rescue Team and Stella Ansara arrive.

Dez peeks at Cat a few times. She is neither nervous nor excited. Deadpan. All business.

Dez draws the folded printout of the satellite image. He unfurls it and, crouching, they study it together. The building they want is south and east of them. Dez gestures, suggesting a route: left, left, then right.

They get moving.

They sneak up on the massive manufacturing building, the one they found Mark Ivanson and Wade Selkirk staring at. The one that matches Ivanson's description of the site of the death hunt, twenty-four years prior.

Now that they're inside the grounds, Cat leads and Dez follows.

She gets to the building. From within her jacket of many wonders, she produces a micro-camera on a thin, flexible antenna, and attaches it to a monitor no larger than a deck of playing cards. She crouches by a door and slides the stalk under it. Dez peers over her shoulder as she plays the antenna back and forth, the fish-eye lens raking the darkened room within. Light comes from the window over their heads, but it's overcast, and that light is meager. No interior lights are showing. She retracts her camera, disassembles it. She checks the door for a charge and finds none. She draws lockpicks. Her hands flash with deftness and dexterity, and the door opens silently at her bidding.

Dez isn't used to working with anyone as good at doors as he is. He quite enjoys watching her work.

They get inside, get the door shut silently. They doff their winter gear and hide it behind a barrel. This room had been used for storage, and features long, long rows of rusty, dusty iron shelving. The ceiling is thirty feet over their heads.

Dez draws his bespoke mobile and scouts the EM spectrum. He gets her attention and shows her his screen. He whispers, "No radio frequencies going out, but there are active radio frequencies within. This isn't the random signal scattering of two-score metal buildings. This is a frequency blocker."

She whispers, "Like the Russians had at The Liberty."

"Like Liv provided for the Russians at The Liberty, aye."

They arranged for Dez to send burst-transmission signals to the Hostage Rescue Team, every fifteen minutes. Should they not receive his signals, then the radio jamming effect would still be here.

She gestures to the display on his phone. "Can you use this as a direction finder?"

"Aye. Will lead us right to 'em."

He rises and begins moving, Cat at his side.

CHAPTER 66

When the ill-fated auto company built the Panthera Works plant in Upstate New York, they designed the Primary Chassis Construction Building Number One—PC1—to include state-of-the-art conference rooms for executives. State-of-the-art by 1970s standards, anyway.

The building's massive generators have been updated to work once again. The conference room, abandoned for half a century, is in use again. The dust swept, the cobwebs removed, the rats poisoned. Thirteen people are in attendance. Today's meeting includes the partners of the Thiago group, plus three armed security personnel. Plus Liv Gelman.

Also Russian colonel Maksim Baranov of the Leningrad Konsortsium paramilitary contractor, who organized the terrorist assault on The Liberty, and his two top aides.

And finally, Jonas Diedrich and two bodyguards, former German KSK special forces, or Kommando Spezialkräfte, soldiers.

Liv works for the Thiago group but does not know the names of the principal partners. Nobody, as far as she knows, does. She thinks of them as the Chinese Gentleman, the French Gentleman, and the Texan.

All three are very rich and all three appear to be in their sixties. But Jonas Diedrich's lux camel overcoat and bespoke suit and French-made shoes—Liv recognizes the handiwork of an exclusive cobbler on Rue de Rivoli, Paris—set him apart. Liv knows that there's rich, then there's *rich*. Diedrich is among the latter. It's Liv's lifelong goal to be counted there as well.

The Thiago group partners sit together at one table, like a tribunal of judges. They're looking a little peaked. Things have not gone as they planned, although many, many things went spectacularly right. The three partners are aware that that's not how their clients perceive things.

Diedrich stands, hands thrust into his trouser pockets, an air of overall superiority radiating off him. "You were contracted to kill six people. To do so simultaneously. To do so in a way that would preclude a traditional criminal investigation. For this, ah, shall we use the colloquialism, 'hat trick,' I paid your organization the princely sum of fifty million dollars. And yet, you have failed."

The Chinese Gentleman says, "The work is not complete, sir. Five of your targets are dead, and we continue our efforts to locate and eliminate the sixth."

"Who is in federal custody!" Diedrich bellows, pacing, now gesturing with one hand, his Patek Philippe glinting. "Talking! Singing, perhaps! Writing down his little confessional like a good Catholic schoolboy! *Forgive me, Justice Department, for I have sinned!*"

Liv sits cross-legged atop another small table, smiling, watching the show. Her lustrous hair drapes her head and shoulders, and she's wearing cobalt-blue leather today. She looks radiant and oddly serene.

Colonel Maksim Baranov and his two soldiers stand apart from everyone else, a tight cluster of crossed arms and guttural sotto voce asides and very, very Slavic scowls. "I am no happier," the colonel growls. "I paid five million of your dollars for the return of the *Kocatka* and her captain and crew, yes? Where is my facking warship!"

The French Gentleman says, "Efforts are underway, even as we speak, to liberate it from the American and Turkish forces that hold it, Colonel. I assure you—"

Diedrich snorts derisively. "Perhaps we have both been assured a bit too much, Colonel Baranov? Perhaps the Thiago group's vaunted reputation is unwarranted."

The Russians grumble.

The Texan says, "Now see here!" and Liv giggles. *Now see here.* Dialogue heard in every 1950s film ever made, a useless expression, devoid of any meaning. The quintessence of bluster.

Every male eye in the place turns to the sound of her musical laughter.

Diedrich peers down his patrician nose at her, sitting on the desk as she is. "I have amused you, madam. Splendid. My day is not without some small victories, yes?"

Liv raises her hand, asking permission to speak.

The Chinese Gentleman, the French Gentleman, and the Texan glance at one another. The Texan says, "You got something to add, Gelman?"

"I have," she says, smiling. She turns to Colonel Baranov first, then to Diedrich.

"I have failed to apprise the partners of the Thiago group of the latest information, I fear."

The Chinese Gentleman says, "What information?"

Liv addresses the clients, not the partners. "That the *Kocatka* has been freed. And Mark Ivanson is dead. And the evidence of what he may or may not have done twenty-four years ago, in this very building, goes to the grave with him."

CHAPTER 67

Cat leans close to Dez and whispers, "Ivanson's dead?"

Dez shifts position to whisper in her ear. The two of them are lying on their stomachs in a ventilation shaft, twenty feet over the PC1 conference room, listening to the meeting. "He was safe when Stella and me left him in New Rochelle. Stella's handpicked lads was flying him to a witness protection program black site in mid-America. He should be safe as houses. C'mon."

Dez begins shuffling back a few feet farther down the ventilation shaft. Cat follows. He's hoping this will further mask their conversation, and they can still hear the discussion below, albeit less clearly. Both of them are chalked with decades of dust.

Cat says, "Witness protection. That should be as ironclad as you can get, right?"

"Well . . . that's a story for another day. Think this is another bluff, like sayin' your parents was in danger."

"I still owe her for that one. Scared the hell out of me."

"I know."

"The bitch says she's killed your witness. But he told his story to the FBI, right? Doesn't that make his death useless?"

"I'm no barrister, love. No idea about the evidentiary rules of your fair land. But in principle, I'd say you're right. If so, what's Liv playin' at?"

"Lying to get out of there without the three old dudes—who gotta be her bosses, right?—from them handing her over to Diedrich and the Russian. She's the one didn't complete either contract. Her life should be forfeit. Which, I vote yes."

"If anyone could steal a Russian warship from the hands of the American and Turkish navies, it'd be Liv. But when the hell would she have had the time? She's been in New York through all this, near as I can tell. She didn't even lead the team to snatch you in Positano."

"Then she's bluffing to save her skin."

"Lord knows I lost enough money to Liv over poker hands, back in the day." His ancient Ancre 15 Rubis watch isn't luminescent, so Dez draws his phone and checks the time. "The FBI should be here in ten minutes. You an' me, we took out the hidden cameras, trip wires, an' mics leading from the main entrance to that room down there. Building's as open as a confessional on a Saturday morning."

"Not the first time I've waited in the dark for law enforcement. First time I ever wished they'd hurry." Cat begins inching closer to the discussion below.

Liv waits as all the men in the room chatter meaninglessly for a bit. She likes that they're shouting over one another to force her to speak, so she sits, cross-legged, calm, her Cheshire cat smile in place.

"Please, please!" The French Gentleman gets everyone to shut up. He turns to her. "Olivia. Explain kindly."

She uncrosses her legs and hops down. She has hidden a laptop and a frequency jammer, identical to the one used at The Liberty, behind the table. She retrieves them both and opens the laptop on the table so it's facing the dozen men—counting the partner's three guards, Diedrich's two guards, and Baranov's two soldiers.

"The colonel will recognize the frequency jammer. It allows my signals to penetrate this building, but no others. Yes?"

The colonel nods.

Liv activates the laptop via the remote. The image flickers, then settles on the face of a well-known news presenter from the BBC World Service. The image is frozen. She unfreezes it.

"*. . . in Geneva. Also today, the American Department of State is crying foul, as a Russian warship, which had been in the joint custody of the American and Turkish navies, went missing overnight. Ayesha Naqvi has more.*"

The image shifts to a woman reporter, standing on a dock. The chyron across her middle reads THE AEGEAN SEA.

Liv pauses the taped broadcast. "From the time stamp, you can see this aired less than forty-five minutes ago." She touches the remote control.

"*A Russian warship known as the* Killer Whale, *or* Kocatka *in Russian, was boarded nearly one month ago by a combination of U.S. and Turkish forces, and taken into custody on allegations of war crimes near the shores of Crimea and Ukraine. Both sides had denied holding the ship. But this morning, a paramilitary contractor known as the Leningrad Konsortsium announced to the world that their vessel has been liberated. Now both the Americans, and the Turks, are admitting that the vessel, once in their possession, has been retaken by hostile forces. We believe——*"

Liv pauses it.

Colonel Baranov is beside himself, his eyes wide, the first hint of a smile now forming behind his beard. "My God! This was not our men! We didn't do this!"

Liv laughs. "Of course not. I did. I stole the *Kocatka*. It was not the most difficult thing I've ever stolen, but it was by far the largest. The damn thing displaces eight thousand tons of water! I could've pulled a muscle."

Her smile is impish.

The Russians chatter to one another, excitement pushing aside their earlier anger.

The French Gentleman says, "Miss Gelman? May we ask, how?"

"Yes, of course, but first I need to show Herr Diedrich something."

With the remote, she changes to a different image. This one shows a woman of Middle Eastern origins, standing in a conference room packed with people. She's at a lectern, using a portfolio and notes. The image is high-res black-and-white; security footage.

"You'll note the designation in the lower right-hand corner, gentlemen? This feed came from the FBI Headquarters in Quantico, Virginia."

Liv starts the tape.

"I've just received word that a person of interest in the assassinations at The Liberty is dead. His name is Ivanson, comma, Marcus John, age forty-seven, of New York City. Ivanson was shot from long distance by a sniper at 6:16 A.M. today and was pronounced dead at the scene. Before dying, he was unable to clarify for us the situation regarding The Liberty assassinations."

Liv pauses it.

In the ventilation shaft, Dez whispers in Cat's ear, "It's a deepfake."

"You sure?"

"Am. Recognize the voice on the tape. That's Stella Ansara. She's been in New York or New Jersey since this thing began. She's not been in Virginia and she'll be landing here in one of five helos in"—he checks his mobile—"two minutes."

Cat nods. "If this one's a deepfake . . . ?"

"The BBC broadcast likely is, too. She's buyin' her way out of this trap."

Cat says, "Guts of a cat burglar. And when *I* say that . . ."

Below them, Liv makes a dramatic bow toward Jonas Diedrich. *"Mein Herr."*

Diedrich is stunned, unmoving, his jaw slack.

The Texan, among the Thiago triad, rises to his feet. "Gelman? You did this? For real?"

"Of course. These fine gentlemen paid for the best, did they not?" She makes a stage magician's gesture of legerdemain. *"C'est moi."*

The Chinese Gentleman also rises, turning to the Russians and the German. "Then there is the matter of our payment."

Baranov turns to his two soldiers. They consult, in Russian, and he turns back, nodding. "If this is a trick . . ."

"Then our lives would be forfeit, yes," the Chinese Gentleman says with equanimity.

"Then it is agreed. I will release the five million."

"Thank you. And Herr Diedrich?"

Diedrich studies the triad for a moment, then turns his hawk's glare on Liv. Who smiles prettily. "A hefty price."

The Frenchman says, "Return on investment. You're about to control an international bank worth an estimated hundred and fourteen billion dollars."

"Yes." Diedrich smiles and nods. "Fifty million. As agreed."

Liv, still holding her remote, says, "There is one teeny-tiny hurdle, which perhaps needs addressing first."

Every eye turns her way. She activates the laptop.

A low-lying camera shows five Pave Hawk helicopters, vectoring in from the south, landing on the derelict street directly outside the PC1 building. Each bears the FBI logo on its flanks. One helo is down, and men in full battle regalia, sporting Heckler & Koch MP5s, begin deploying in a protective pattern to guard the incoming birds.

"This is live, gentlemen. We've guests," Liv says. "Not unexpected guests, as luck would have it."

The Russians bellow in Russian. The Thiago triad are on their feet, turning to their three guards. The three guards remain unmoving.

Liv raises her voice over the tumult. "Gentlemen! Gentlemen? Herr Diedrich? Colonel Baranov? The FBI forces will be upon us in seconds. Fortunately, I have prepared a contingency. There is a specific door through which they shall enter and, if I may, I'm rather damn good with doors. I can keep them out. And I can get all of us out via the sub-sub-basement."

A beat, then Diedrich bellows, "Then do it, girl!"

Liv smiles. "I shall. But first, a gesture of good faith from our Russian friends?"

The triad start yelling at her. Liv ignores them.

Maksim Baranov nods to her to continue.

She gestures to the Thiago partners at their table. "Colonel? If you could kill these three gentlemen, please?"

The triad explodes in outrageous shouts. The Texan turns to the three guards. "Shoot down that bitch! Now!"

The three guards do not move.

"I'm afraid these fine young cannibals work for me, now," Liv says. "We made a prior arrangement for their early, and lucrative, retirement. *N'est-ce pas?*"

The Thiago guards keep their guns in their holsters.

Colonel Baranov smiles, nods, and gestures to his soldiers.

Who draw their handguns and mow down the principal partners of the Thiago group.

In the ventilation shaft, Dez starts backing out again. "I know her
endgame. Jay-sus but that's smart! C'mon! We have to get to the
FBI first!"

CHAPTER 68

Liv steps aside and gestures to her laptop. "Thank you, Colonel. Expediently handled. Now, if you and Herr Diedrich could take care of your financial transfers, I shall get all of us out of here."

Diedrich stands tall, shoulders back, staring at her. "So you, and you alone, are Thiago now, madam?"

"Not alone, no. Think of me as the spokesmodel." She laughs, and gestures to the laptop as the hostess of any good TV game show learns to gesture toward the appropriate items. "Would you be ever so good, sir?"

A pause, then Diedrich crosses to the computer. He sees that it now is set to a private and secure website for a bank in the Cayman Islands. He bends at the waist and inputs his own banking codes.

The transfer begins.

Finished, he steps aside so Colonel Baranov can do the same.

Liv checks the balances. Fifty-five million dollars. "Splendid! Gentlemen, if you could follow me?"

She leads Diedrich, his guards, and the Russians toward an exit.

Dez and Liv brush dust off their clothes and out of their hair as they race to the northern side of the massive complex. The place is monstrously large, dark and cavernous, and their footfalls echo crazily off all the inert, rusty iron machinery.

They get to the spot where, twenty-four years ago, Jonas Diedrich led six rich, young, and morally corrupt men into a hunt.

"Stop stop stop!" Dez says, stutter-stepping to an abrupt, arms-flailing halt.

Cat stops, too, but much more gracefully.

Dez drops to his hands and knees and lowers his head to within a few inches from the dusty floor. Ahead of them is a field of parquetry, thirty feet wide and long; black-and-white ceramic tiles leading down the lightly canted floor to the vertical main door, a good twenty-five feet high.

"What?"

"Big door like that?" he says, peering from a very low angle. "Ye'd use it for massive trucks, scissor lifts, front loaders. Yeah? Why in the world would ye put ceramic tile here? Would be pulverized to dust in a day."

Cat says, "Trap?"

"Aye. Land mines is me guess. We've no comms, so we can't warn the FBI that they're walkin' into a trap without opening this door. An' we can't get to the door controls without crossing these tiles."

"You can't," Cat says. She turns to some iron scaffolding leading up to the ceiling. She snugs her leather gloves tighter, then deftly climbs up about fifteen feet. She turns sideways, leaps, and lands on her feet on an iron girder that runs the length of the room.

"Couldn't do that on the best day in me life!" Dez hollers up to her.

She quick-walks the length of the girder, her arms held out to her sides for balance. She gets to the far wall, where the main door is, then grabs a vertical iron water pipe, tugging on it to make sure it's securely bracketed to the cement wall despite decades of neglect. It is, and she spiders deftly down toward the floor.

She stops when her sneakers are five inches from the tiles. She hugs the water pipe with her thighs and arms. She can reach the door controls from here.

"The door controls could be booby-trapped, love."

Freeing one arm, she reaches into one of the hidden pockets of her biker jacket and produces a screwdriver, and begins disassembling the faceplate of the door controls. "Not my first *corrida de toros*, big guy."

"Good thinking. We—"

A spray of gunfire sends up sparks, hitting metal a dozen inches from Dez's head.

He turns and sprints into the dark.

The two guards—who work for Liv, even when everyone thought they worked for the Thiago partners—approach from two different angles. Both hold automatic rifles.

Neither of them has spotted Cat, hanging on to a water pipe, perched inches above a likely and camouflaged minefield.

Not yet, they haven't.

Outside, all five Pave Hawks are down and the exterior of Panthera's Primary Chassis Construction Building Number One is secure.

Stella Ansara and Tom Fairweather are the last to step out of their helo, Stella with her gun drawn, Fairweather with his stowed, and with a look of calm concentration on his hangdog face. It's the look of a man doing the math for a financial audit: detail conscious, exacting, but slightly bored. As if he done this very thing a hundred times. Which he has.

He speaks softly yet somehow his voice carries over the whoosh of the props. "Yang. Collins. Let's get this door open, please."

His breach experts move into position.

CHAPTER 69

Dez drops to one knee behind something that—a half century earlier—might have been a giant's version of a lathe. He doffs the small backpack and draws the slingshot with its forearm brace. He switches the ball bearings to the left-hand pocket of his black windbreaker.

Liv Gelman sent her guards to cover her flank. She apparently still takes nothing for granted. Her gatekeeping skills have not withered over the years.

The trick now is to keep these lads' eyes off Cat.

From one knee, Dez nocks a ball bearing in the rubber sling, aims upward at about an eleven o'clock angle, and releases.

The ball bearing disappears into the dark in a third of a second.

But he—and the two gunmen—can hear it pinging madly, bouncing from one iron bit of arcana to another in the vast confines of the murky manufacturing facility.

★ ★ ★

Cat sees the two gunmen turn away from her position, machine guns in their hands, searching for the echoic sounds of what, Cat realizes, must be one of Dez's ball bearings.

She hugs the water pipe with one arm and both legs, flakes of rust raining down to the floor, her sneakers inches from tiles that may or may not hide mines. She reaches out with the screwdriver for the faceplate of the door controls.

She hears something from outside. The sound of metal on metal. The FBI's here.

The faceplate is loose now. She just needs the additional reach of the screwdriver to touch the hinged plate. She shoves it open.

She spots a grenade, notched into the controls, the pin removed, the door controls themselves holding the arm down.

She glances up. One of the gunmen disappears from her sight.

The other stands, facing forty-five degrees from her, scanning the room.

In the sub-sub-basement of the PC1 building, Liv leads the Russians, Jonas Diedrich, and his two KSK bodyguards through a darkened, concrete-and-metal labyrinth, the ceiling lined with sputtering fluorescent tubes. The route is twisty and convoluted. They have four flashlights between them.

At one point, Colonel Baranov whispers, "*Bozhe moi!* I know this place!"

It's the same sub-sub-basement he toured a week before the hostage situation at The Liberty.

"Yes," Liv lies easily. "An exact replica."

Diedrich doesn't know what she means by that. Exact replica of what? But he has other concerns on his mind and doesn't ask.

Dez finds an iron washer the size of a silver dollar. He notches it into his slingshot and fires it up and away. It makes a different, tinnier sort of pinging sound than his ball bearings. He hopes Liv's gunmen are following the trail of audio breadcrumbs, away from Cat and the main door to this place.

He pauses, down on one knee, eyes well-adjusted to the dark, listening.

He hears the scuffle of shoe leather on cement. To his left.

He nocks a ball bearing, draws back on the sling.

He inhales, holds it.

He rises and swings out from cover, spots his man.

Who spots him first and who brings up his Heckler & Koch 433 and fires.

Dez ducks back in time as bullets ping off the metal around him. He turns, sprinting into the dark.

The second gunman is turning on his heels, Cat at the edge of his peripheral vision, when they both hear the two-second burp of a HK433, firing from somewhere within this vast, dark room.

The guy turns away from her, his gun braced against his hip, advancing cautiously toward the sound of gunfire.

Cat returns her screwdriver to the hidden pocket of her jacket. She adjusts her grip on the water pipe, reaches out as far as she can. Her fingertip slides off the metal egg shape of the grenade.

She hears a grinding sound from outside. The FBI, attempting to gain entry.

She strains, thighs gripping the pipe, holding her up off the tiled floor. She can almost reach the grenade.

The grinding sound increases.

The second gunman hears it, turns.

Spots a movement in the dark.

He raises his HK.

Cat stretches her arm, grips the grenade, removes it from the door control housing and, without a second thought, hurls it under-hand, bocce ball style.

The gunman peers into the dark, makes out her figure, and brings his gun to bear.

The grenade bounces across the tiles, once, twice, three times, before it hits one of the mines that Dez predicted.

Part of the floor erupts in a geyser of dirt, cement, and ceramic bits. The grenade itself is launched into the air, heading toward the gunman, when it finally detonates.

The explosion puts him on his ass. He fires straight into the air.

Liv ducks her head into the crevasse of her brace arm and the pipe, eyes squeezed shut, as debris rains down on her. Her ears are ring-ing, and she has barely kept her arm-and-thigh grip on the rusty old pipe. She feels herself slip downward two inches.

She dares to reach out again, blind, fingers groping for the con-trols of the electric door.

The first gunman stands now at the exact spot where he saw Dez, squinting to see in the dark, Heckler & Koch leading, slow-sweeping the space before him.

He hears an explosion; feels the floor vibrate under his boots.

He turns, gun leading, moving toward the noise.

Dez ducks out from behind a massive scissor lift, slingshot at arm's length, and lets slip a ball bearing.

It flies through the air.

Then through the man's eye socket.

As the man falls, Dez dashes to his side, slides the slingshot into his belt, bends to grab up the HK433 en passant, and races toward Cat and the front entrance.

The second gunman shakes off the shock of the multiple explosions. He tries to make sense of what happened.

Liv Gelman had mines planted under tiles at the main entrance to the building, fearing an incursion by law enforcement. The mines must have been triggered, but by what?

He remembers seeing a woman, all in black, clutching a vertical pipe near the door.

He rises to his feet, watching the fallout of soot and asbestos and dust and cement and tile still raining down from the cavernous ceiling of the room. He racks the slide on his automatic rifle, steps closer to where he saw the woman.

He gets clear of the debris field, gun aimed, as the sound of the big metal door rising finally reaches his ringing ears, and a second before Special Agents Stella Ansara and Tom Fairweather, standing at the egress, half empty both their Glocks into his chest.

"Mein Gott!" Jonas Diedrich exclaims as the walls in the sub-sub-basement shake and as dust sifts down from the pipes that snake across the ceiling of their byzantine route. "What was that?"

"Trouble that's best left in our wakes, gentlemen," Liv Gelman says. She points the way. "We're well outside the footprint of the PC1 building now. Two more lefts, down that longish corridor, and we'll find stairs leading to the surface and to vehicles. Quickly!"

The Russians, Diedrich, and his bodyguards race down the echo-laden corridor.

None of them notice that Liv has stopped running. She spies the half-hidden handle of the door of a service shaft. A door whose hinges she has generously oiled, several days earlier.

She ducks into the service shaft, spots the ladder leading upward, adjusts the cross-body strap of the bag containing her laptop computer, clips the flashlight to her belt, and begins climbing to the surface.

Stella Ansara says, "I'd suggest you freeze but you're pretty well frozen."

The dark-haired woman, clinging to a water pipe just inside the door, says, "Mines. Under the tiles. Don't know where or how many."

The special agents glance down. Tom Fairweather says, "Funny place for tiles."

Dez Limerick sprints into sight. "Hold fire! She's on our side. There are mines—"

"Your friend told us," Fairweather says. He nods to two of his burliest FBI agents, who reach through the egress without stepping through, grab Cat, and haul her outside and to safety.

Stella and Dez are maybe thirty meters apart. She raises her voice. "Are you all right?"

"Am, aye. Liv Gelman's here, an' on the move. We spotted the Russians an' Diedrich. An' three older gents who might or might not be the late, unlamented heads of the Thiago group. Liv had 'em killed an' looks to be taking over."

Cat stretches her aching muscles. "The other gunman?"

Dez shrugs. "No threat."

Standing outside the threshold, Cat, Stella, and Tom Fairweather begin looking about, taking in the enormity of the PC1 building. Fairweather says, "Good thing I've got a lot of guys. We—"

"Freeze!"

Guns rise and agents go to combat crouches as, thirty feet behind them, a door to another building is thrown open and out step Jonas Diedrich, his guards, and the Russians, in the shadow of the five FBI Pave Hawks.

It was so dark and cold in the tunnels, everyone in Diedrich's party bursts out into the open before pausing to see if it's safe. Only then to find themselves staring at the openings of more gun barrels than they can count. The armed members of the party drop their weapons quickly. As orders are barked at them, everyone falls to their knees, fingers laced behind their heads.

Diedrich glances around as he finally notices that Olivia Gelman is not with them. He has no idea exactly when, nor where, she disappeared.

As he's pushed down onto his chest and his wrists cuffed behind his back, his eyes steal to the helicopters looming overhead. He thinks: *Well, she did promise we'd find vehicles. . . .*

CHAPTER 70

Dez and Catalina Valdivia make love in a hotel room in Midtown Manhattan. After which, they hit the hotel bar. No brekkers on the menu, but postcoitus, they order a cheese tray and bowls of nuts and chips and olives, and a bottle of a really nice, straw-yellow Fiano di Avellino that comes from a vineyard not ten kilometers from Cat's place on the Amalfi Coast. They celebrate in style.

It's been two days since the chaos at the Panthera Works auto plant. The media has gone bonkers, covering the arrest of German banker Jonas Diedrich on charges of murder and conspiracy to commit murder. The International Criminal Court doubled down on the seismic shockwaves within the banking industry by releasing the results of an investigation, showing that Frankfurt Landesbank AG has been selling forbidden Iranian oil on the black market. The list of bank indictments, single-spaced, takes a page and a half of the press release.

Hours later, the FBI announced that they've rounded up the

last remnants of the Russian paramilitary group that stormed The Liberty, including the group's leader, Colonel Maksim Baranov.

Tom Fairweather's twenty-five-member Hostage Rescue Team unit scoured the Primary Chassis Construction Building Number One at the Panthera plant. They found no sign of Olivia Gelman or her laptop. Later, close to eighty law enforcement personnel fine-toothed the vast building, and then the rest of the rotting auto plant.

Liv Gelman is in the wind.

At the plant, Dez introduced Cat as "me friend Jane Smith," and left it at that. Reluctantly, the Feds agreed not to pursue it. Cat's anonymity remains locked in place.

But just yesterday, Stella Ansara came by for coffee and croissants, and to thank Dez one last time.

She came with three bits of news.

First, blushing, she says Harlow is back from Florida and they have plans to get coffee.

Also: Ray Harker has died. Not of his wounds; he died of polonium-210 radiation poisoning.

"Liv's signature," Dez says. "Leave nothing to chance."

"Maybe. Here's the last bullet point: Your friend Gelman has decapitated the Thiago group. The FBI raided the homes of the French and Chinese men, and the guy from Texas. It will take months for a full forensic audit of the information, but from what we can tell now, these three were the brains behind the entire murder-for-hire empire."

"Which would suggest that Thiago is no more?"

"Looks like."

Hours after Stella Ansara shook his hand, thanked him again, and made her exit, Dez and Cat enjoy their leisurely meal in the hotel bar. There's an open-air balcony with a lovely view of the brightly lit Lexington Avenue but they sit inside. They chat about everything and nothing whatsoever.

Dez says, "This wine's amazing!"

"I know. Tastes like home. So what's next for you?"

"Dunno. Could catch up with Kansas Jack and the Blacktop. Quite enjoyed gigging with them lot. Wouldn't mind being a tourist in New York for a bit. Take in some music, maybe a show. You?"

She sips the white wine, tasting hazelnuts and orange blossom. She nibbles on an olive. Dez gives her the time and the space.

"I have jobs lined up," she says at length.

"'Jobs' being a colloquialism for . . ."

"Yes, D: heists."

"There may be better ways for a lass with your skill sets to make a living."

"Different ways," she says. "Not necessarily better. And one of them is lined up for next week in Montreal. Which means . . ."

Dez smiles and reaches out, touching his glass to hers. *"Farewell and adieu to you fine Spanish ladies,"* he sings the sea chanty softly. *"Farewell and adieu you ladies of Spain . . ."*

She laughs, clapping, pleased that he's not making a thing of her exit. She narrows her eyes in mock annoyance. "And here I remember someone once telling me my Spanish accent isn't *Spain* enough."

She reaches into her purse, finds a business card with no writing on it, and a pen. She writes out a URL, then slides it under his plate.

"Desmond Aloysius Limerick." She smiles and shakes her head. "Someday, you'll be in trouble and you'll need me. And you'll call for help, because if you don't, I will kick your lily-white ass."

Dez laughs. "Yes, ma'am."

She leans in toward him. "I'm a mutant. My mutant power is: I'll always know when you need me."

Dez kisses her. "The same goes for you."

—— 382 ——

Catalina Valdivia pays for the room and for the food and wine with a black Amex card. Then she gathers her things, kisses him once again, and heads for the door.

Dez decides it's time to switch to a cognac. He orders, then draws his mobile and types. He sets the phone, face down, on the table.

Liv Gelman slides into Cat's seat.

She's wearing a gold lamé top that bares one shoulder, a skirt, and tall heels. She sets a velvet clutch on the table. She looks incandescent.

"Hallo, Liv. Wotcher."

Her smile radiates. "You're not surprised to see me."

"Spotted ye. You always was one for dramatic entrances and exits."

"Look who's talking."

Somehow, the waiter got the word and brings two cognacs to the table. Liv swirls, sniffs, and sips.

"Ahh. For a boy from the wrong side of the tracks, Desmond, you've remarkable taste. Superb."

"Not bad, innit. So you're running Thiago these days, are ye?"

Liv laughs; she has a hearty, head-thrown-back kind of laugh. Other patrons turn and smile. "Gods, no! That would entail a great deal of paperwork. Ugh." She mock shudders.

Dez sips his drink. "For the longest while, I wondered why you lured me into The Liberty. Thought you just wanted to play chess against your 'oul mate and another gatekeeper."

"Well, it was fun, wasn't it?"

Dez shakes his head. "No, it wasn't. And I was never there just for you to joust with. Finally figured that part out, thick bastard that I am. If the Russians had discovered that there was no sub-sub-basement, they'd have paid not one red cent to Thiago. Like as not, they'd've killed you, and the triad what ran the Thiago group. So you needed a spanner in the works to bollux their attack. So they'd never discover that you lied to 'em about an exit."

Her grin lights up the room. She swirls her cognac. Dez is right, and can tell by the glint in her eyes.

"An' you needed me to save at least one of the six assassination targets. Kill all six, and the trio runnin' Thiago would've gotten paid before you was in position to rip them off. You needed the hostage situation at the convention center, and the hexagonal hits, to *almost* work. That was the only way to keep the money unpaid till the bitter end."

"Oh, I'm stealing *hexagonal hits*. I quite like that. And it wasn't bitter for me, Desmond! I've just stolen fifty-five million dollars, American. Fifty. Five. Million."

Her eyes flutter and her breath catches a little. "I might very well be the greatest thief in history."

"Eleven civilians died at the conference center. Five men died at the hands of you and Harker. You even poisoned Harker and killed him."

"Tell me you're not mourning his loss!"

Dez shrugs. "The trainin' we got? Gatekeeping?"

"Beginnings and gates," Liv intones, softly. "Transitions and time. Duality and doors. Passages and endings."

"The training was designed to do better than this. To do more than this. And ye know it."

Liv laughs. "Oh, I will steal more. Just you wait!"

Dez smiles, sips.

"No clever retort, handsome boy?"

Dez says, "I've made a bit of a decision, love. It goes like this: You did rip off them Russian paramilitary types for a cool five million, and they's arseholes, so ye should get to keep that. But the fifty million from Jonas Diedrich? That should go to the families of the people you helped kill at The Liberty."

Liv says, "I promise to make a mental note to consider that proposal."

"No worries. I already redistributed your money."

Liv pauses, studying his eyes. Her smile grows. "You're bluffing!"

Dez sips.

"Desmond! Please. The bank I use in the Caymans is utterly, breathtakingly, scintillatingly crooked! It's a mob bank! No government on Earth can hack it. I couldn't hack it. And if I couldn't, you certainly couldn't."

Dez says, "True, that."

He waits.

Liv waits.

Dez says, "But Peng Shanshan of Hong Kong could."

Liv starts to reply, but it dies stillborn. She studies his eyes.

Dez turns over his mobile the way a poker player turns over a hole card. She glances at his screen.

"Spot?"

"That gel hates terrorists. Hates 'em. When she found you was helpin' the Russians? She went right mad, her."

Liv reaches into her clutch. She draws a cell phone and begins typing.

Her eyes shoot wide, turning to Dez.

Who sips his cognac.

She types some more, studies the information flowing from her bank in the Cayman Islands.

"Ye've established a trust in honor of the families who lost loved ones at The Liberty. A touching tribute. Brava," he says. "An' here's the rest of the deal. The other five million ye get to keep. And all of the data Spot mined from your account in the Caymans? The history of your account? If ye ever go after Catalina Valdivia, or her friends, or her family, or her work, or anyone in her zip code, or anyone sharing her zodiac sign, or anyone whose name ends in an 'A,' Spot and me will share all that information with every law enforcement agency on God's green. D'you follow, love? Cat is Chernobyl. And you're to stay well clear. Aye?"

Liv stares at her phone. Her eyes go from the numbers, to Dez, to the numbers, to Dez.

She stands and walks on stilettos to the bar's balcony. She passes a table and deftly snags a champagne flute without the diners noticing, drains it at a go, deftly leaves it at another table.

On the balcony, she stands at the balustrade, staring out at Lexington.

Dez sits and sips.

It takes Liv maybe a minute to process everything. A minute plus. She walks back to his table, her face serene. She stands over Dez.

"You had one last play, and you played it for all it was worth. Masterful. Masterful."

She shakes her head and sighs.

"You seem t'be handling this well."

"The money isn't important. Well, that's a lie. It's very, very important. Just not as important as the competition. To be the world's greatest gatekeeper."

"An' from where I'm sittin' it looks to be a draw. Yeah?"

Liv smiles. It's a genuine, if sad, smile. "Oh God, I did so love our little match. I've not competed against anyone who plays at my level since I began."

Liv drains her cognac. She rises and, leaning over the table, one hand on the back of Dez's chair. She stares at his eyes from only a few inches away. "Do you know why I despise football, *mon cœur*?"

"Because ye can't stand any sport that can end in a tie."

"*Exactement.*" She leans in and kisses him softly. "Guns are aimed at random diners, darling. Don't leave for a good ten minutes, and stay off your phone, kindly."

Liv Gelman stands straight.

"And Desmond? We will play again. I absolutely guarantee it."

Her fingertips glide gingerly, maybe even lovingly, over his shoulder as she makes her exit.

Dez finishes his cognac, then signals for the check.

ABOUT THE AUTHOR

James Byrne has worked for more than twenty years as a journalist and in politics. He's the author of *The Gatekeeper* and *Deadlock,* the previous Dez Limerick thrillers. A native of the Pacific Northwest, he lives in Portland, Oregon.